"You not see I leave early th Always I do encore!"

"Well, I noticed about the encore," Morgan said.

"There is loose part in stage. I must dance around this part. I not dance good like this! I feel floor give under my foot and I think 'Boom! I fall on face in front of all these American peoples.' I twist ankle or maybe worse."

"Mr. Nijinsky, I assure you if anything's wrong with the stage, it's the fault of the workmen. An accident."

"Accident? You think this? Hah. I think no." He sighed. "Now I wish to leave quick."

"Now?" Morgan was stunned. "You mean, sneak away? Creep out the back door?"

"Sneak, yes!"

"I can drive you to the station," Morgan said recklessly. "Heck, I can drive you all the way to the city!"

"You have motorcar?"

"How soon will you be ready?"

"I need ten minutes only."

"I'll wait outside." Morgan finished off his champagne and left the room. He noticed that Nijinsky had not touched his again after the first sip.

A FRIEND OF MR. NIJINSKY

CARO SOLES

FOREWORD

I have always been intrigued by the Ballets Russes. What interested me most about the troupe's visit to the United States in 1916 was imagining the impression they must have made on the society of the day, especially the impact of the idolized Nijinsky, whom everyone from kings to presidents had worked so hard to bring out of war-torn Europe. But this book is not about Nijinsky, but about the reflected glory of the dancer on young Morgan Vanheusen, who has many doors open to him because of his unlikely and serendipitous friendship with the man. This book is Morgan's story.

When I read a novel featuring historical characters, I always want to know who is real, who complete fiction. I have tried to base the part of the story that concerns the ballet on fact as much as possible, right down to the dates of the actual performances and the quotes from the New York Times. However, I have taken some liberties to make the story work, such as giving Nijinsky a facility with English that he did not possess and sending his wife off to the Hamptons for a large part of the book to give more opportunity for my characters to interact without her hovering presence. When possible, I have used real people for minor roles–dancers, Russian attachés and the like– but the Vanheusen family is purely fictitious, as is the ballet *Le Prince du Lac* during which the equally fictitious Galina makes her debut.

I have also taken a few liberties with time, so that although the quotes from newspapers opening each chapter (other than those from the fictitious New York Bugle) are real and actually appear as written in 1916, they were not necessarily in the spring editions. For this reason, I decided not to use precise dates for any of them, except the first, sometimes omitting dates altogether.

ONE

"Nijinski, Dancer, Arrives!"

—*New York Times*, April 6, 1916

Morgan loitered behind the high hedge while he rubbed the last trace of grease off his hands from the engine of the Peugeot Bébé he had been inspecting in the courtyard. In the interest of peace, his secret life had to remain invisible, but he couldn't resist checking under the hood of that beauty. He wondered who owned her.

His sister's laughter floated in the air from the other side the meticulously clipped greenery, joined almost immediately by the horsey snorts of Nigel, one of her constant suitors.

Morgan adjusted his waistcoat with a sharp tug and strolled around the end of the sculptured hedge. Gloria and a few of her debutante friends stood close together as if exchanging secrets. They appeared to ignore the young men who hovered around them, yet they were subtly aware of their erstwhile suitors, playing to their audience with every tilt of the head, every laughing sideways glance. Their long summer dresses skimmed the grass, the latest fashion allowing an alluring glimpse of dainty ankle.

Muriel was with them, her lustrous dark hair curling enticingly from under her wide-brimmed hat. She always seemed a little apart, even when in a group. Muriel. Even her name was music. He felt a faint quickening of his heart as he moved closer.

"Did you know there was a riot when he danced in Paris?" Gloria's voice shook with excitement.

"Actually, there was more than one," Muriel said, drawing one glove through her hands with a worldly air. "My Aunt Carrie was there. She said it was…quite depraved."

"I'm surprised your father invited him here, Gloria," said one of the young men indignantly.

"It was Mother," Gloria said. "She's the chairlady of the Committee to Raise Money for War Orphans, and the wife of someone from the Russian embassy is on the committee, too, so she asked her husband, who asked Count Nikolai Golejewski who is the attaché there or some such, and he knows Mr. Nijinsky, so…" She caught her breath and smiled.

"I think it's Colonel Golejewski, isn't it?" Muriel said. "He's a military attaché, after all."

Gloria shrugged. "Anyway, so now we are going to actually see the great Nijinsky dance before anyone else in New York."

"They say he's quite… provocative," Daisy said, and she blushed. At fourteen, Daisy was the baby of the Vanheusen family, and worked hard to keep up with the others.

Gloria laughed again and laid a hand to her throat, just like photographs of Isadora Duncan. The ribbons in her hat waved for a moment in the breeze. Morgan caught them and gave them a playful tug.

"Giddy girls," he said. "What are you gossiping about now?" His words were for Gloria, but his eyes strayed to Muriel, who ignored him.

"We're talking about Mr. Nijinsky, of course," Daisy said, "and about how brave Mother is to invite him here to dance. I mean because of the…talk…"

"It's not even Easter yet," one young man said. Toby his name was, Morgan remembered, glancing at him.

"That is irrelevant," Nigel said, dismissing his moon-faced young rival.

Morgan smiled.

"Mrs. Vanderbilt has also invited him," Muriel said.

"Really?" Gloria said, surprised. "Why didn't you tell me before?"

"I don't tell you everything." Muriel favored them all with a slow smile and then turned and glided away over the perfect grass to another group.

"Morgan, I don't know why you're so keen on her," said Gloria, shaking her head at her brother. "And is that engine grease I spy on your wrist?"

"Don't be ridiculous," Morgan snapped, shoving his hand in his pocket.

Gloria smiled knowingly and touched his arm, drawing him away from the others. "Morgan, I want you to introduce me to Mr. Nijinsky."

"Of course. We're all going to meet him later, after he dances."

"No, no, silly, I mean, *really* meet him. Just us. Invite him for tea somewhere and take me along. You can be chaperon. It's not such a big favor."

"It's out of the question." Morgan loved his sister, but this was asking too much. He looked out over the heads of the girls at the elegantly dressed ladies and gentlemen crowding the manicured lawns and terraces of the Vanheusen country house. Sunlight sparkled on the ornamental pool and on the beads of water caught in the newly sprayed roses and lilies brought from the conservatory. The air was fragrant with hyacinths and lilacs.

"Morgan." Gloria tilted her head and played with the locket at her neck. "Would you like to be my escort at the Flower Fête next week? I wasn't going to go, but if you'd like to dance with Muriel…"

Morgan felt an unwelcome flush rising steadily on his cheeks. Damn the woman. Why did Muriel have this power over him? "It wouldn't do any good, anyway," he said glumly.

"You never know," Gloria went on. "Or perhaps I'll just have a little talk with Father about how you were spending your time this afternoon." She stared pointedly at the hand still thrust in his pocket.

"You little minx!" Morgan exclaimed. He tried to laugh it off, but the threat, if carried out, would have real and very unpleasant consequences. "Blackmail is most unladylike!"

"Come on, Morgan. Just one little hour with you and Mr. Nijinsky?"

"Don't you think everyone here wants that?"

"Keep your voice down, brother dear. Just promise me you'll ask."

"All right, all right."

"Oh, thank you! But this is just *entre nous*, isn't it?"

"*I'm* certainly not going to advertise it. He probably won't be able to come to tea anyway. According to the papers, he's been besieged by invitations from all the best people."

"Well, then, if he doesn't come, I may have to have that little chat with Father." Gloria plucked a rose from the nearest urn, reached up, and fit it among the silk flowers in her hat. As she walked away, she glanced over her shoulder and winked at her brother.

Morgan bit his lip and turned away, anger twisting in his stomach. How could she? His own little sister!

April was daringly early for a garden party at the summer home of Mr. and Mrs. Vanheusen, almost as excitingly daring as the guest of honor, but after a few hours of uncertainty that morning, the weather was co-operating magnificently. There was an air of eager anticipation in the smartly dressed gathering. Heads were constantly looking towards the stage erected in front of the main terrace, and Gloria was not the only one repeating the rumors and speculation about Mr. Nijinsky. What would he be like, this man who caused scandal in a place like Paris? Who was a friend of princes and knew all the artists and writers everyone talked about. Who had managed to get out of war-torn Europe with his family with the help of several governments and the King of Spain.

The small orchestra broke into a blast of trumpets, and everyone moved to fill the remaining chairs. A hush fell over the assembled guests. For a moment, the sun slid behind an errant cloud. The music paused. Drums hummed and buzzed, quickening the pulse of the crowd. Sudden chords crashed over them, and the sun came out. Nijinsky was on stage.

Morgan knew very little about dance. Although he often accompanied his family to their box at the Met, he preferred attending musicals and Ziegfeld's Follies with his friends. Yet even he knew that what he was seeing was exceptional. The figure on the stage moved with animal grace, his oriental costume sparkling in the sudden sunlight. He seemed from another world, hypnotic, god-like. Every movement was poetry, and his effortless leaps and sudden pirouettes breathtaking.

Silence had fallen over the crowd. This was totally new to them. Even those who had seen the Ballets Russes earlier, without Nijinsky, were not prepared for this elemental rawness. The glittering dancer held them in the palm of his hand, drawing their eyes, their hearts, their souls along with him as he spun and leapt in a magic all his own. It was as if he were part of the music, lifted by the surging melodies, pushed along by the power of the brass. Even when still, sensuality radiated from him, causing an unexpected shortness of breath among the women and an unfamiliar unease with the men. But for Morgan, it was the sheer physicality of the dance that took his breath away. The dancer paused, sinking almost to the ground, then leapt with a sudden spiral in the music and disappeared. The crowd gasped. They sat staring at the empty stage, not yet sure of what they had seen. Finally, applause burst out, and they turned to each other, eyes sparkling, cheeks bright with unusual color.

"How wonderful!"

"Incredible!"

"A bit barbaric, though, don't you think?"

Morgan said nothing. He was stunned that mere dancing could affect him like that. He saw Gloria and her friends clapping madly, their white-gloved hands a blur of motion. As Nijinsky reappeared at last on the stage, Gloria tore the rose from her hat and flung it to him. Barely breaking his stride, he swooped down and caught the flower, cradled it in his hands, and walked to the edge of the stage. He bowed. Simply. Without any of the ostentation Morgan had seen with other performers. He turned right, then left. He bowed one last time, and then left the stage.

He did not return, in spite of the applause.

TWO

"MALE DANCER OVER WHOM DUCHESSES RAVED, CREATOR OF 'THE FAUN', JUST A PLAIN MORTAL."
—Nicola Greeley-Smith, *Fort Wayne Journal Gazette*, April 1916

"Well, you'd think he'd give an encore, surely," exclaimed one pearl-bedecked dowager to her companion, turning away from the stage.

"He was lovely, though, wasn't he?" Her companion sighed.

"That's not the word I would·choose, Susan."

Morgan finally made his way through the slowly dispersing crowd and took two glasses of champagne from a passing waiter. His father had told him to look after their honored guest, and now he was glad this job had fallen to him. Quickly, he rounded the hedge and jogged up the steps to the glassed-in conservatory. From here, he walked down the hall to the music room, which had been given to the dancer as a dressing room. He paused, suddenly unsure how he was going to approach this amazing man. At last, he knocked.

"*Entrez.*"

For the first time, Morgan wondered if the man even spoke English. He opened the door and went in.

Nijinsky, a bottle of Vichy water in his hand, sat on a bench beside a dressing table that had been carried down from one of the guest bedrooms. The dancer had removed the stiff headdress and jewel-encrusted tunic. His bare muscled chest was drenched in sweat. His valet hovered in the background.

"That was magnificent," Morgan said.

"You journalist?"

"No, no. I'm Morgan Vanheusen. I've brought you some champagne." He passed the glass to the dancer who smiled and took a sip, before setting the glass on the table.

"Please to excuse. When we arrive Tuesday, many journalists come to boat before we get even to harbor. They ask so many questions, about my partners, about the war, even about Rasputin. How to know about Rasputin? He is not dancer."

Nijinsky shrugged and rubbed a towel over his head and chest. He was small and dark, with high cheekbones and strange slanted eyes. The muscles in his thighs were so overdeveloped as to be almost obscene. Morgan looked away.

"You won't be bothered by reporters here," he assured the dancer.

"*Ochen horoshowe*. Is very good."

"We are honored that you agreed to come here to dance," Morgan went on, feeling called upon to be some kind of spokesperson for his family.

"I dance for orphans," Nijinsky said. "I know what is like, war. In Europe, in train, we see many things. Sad things. Frightening things. And Count Golejewski ask me, as favor. So I dance." He took a long drink of the Vichy water. "The Metropolitan Opera House not want I dance anywhere but there. This is different, I say. Special..." He plucked at the air with one hand.

"Case?"

"*Da*. Special case. So I come. But even here are enemies."

"Enemies?"

"You have list for me? So I find out who is here?"

"Ah...I suppose so, but—"

"You not see I leave early the stage? You not see I not do encore? Always I do encore!"

"Well, I noticed about the encore."

"There is loose part in stage. I must dance around this part. I not dance good like this! I feel floor give under my foot and I think 'Boom! I fall on face in front of all these American peoples.' I twist ankle or maybe worse, so Metropolitan Opera people not have to pay me. I not know who do this. So I need list."

"Mr. Nijinsky, I assure you if anything's wrong with the stage, it's the fault of the workmen. An accident. They're not used to this kind of work, putting up stages for dance. And it was done very quickly. We only heard yesterday that you would come for certain."

"Accident? You think this? Hah. I think no." He sighed. "Maybe soon this *brouhaha* is over about my money. I want dance."

"I'm sure you do." Morgan had paid little attention to all the fuss about the money Nijinsky was demanding from Diaghilev of the Ballets Russes before dancing at the Met. All he knew was that it was an enormous amount. Something around $30,000? Now he felt a little uncomfortable, not knowing more. He cleared his throat nervously. "You know, my sister Gloria is dying to meet you, Mr. Nijinsky, and I promised I'd ask you—"

"No, no, please. I cannot meet peoples now. Not after that... near—*catastrophe*."

"It doesn't have to be now," Morgan assured him quickly, rubbing his sweaty palms together.

"Yes, later is good. Now I wish to leave quick. This is possible, yes?"

"*Leave*?" Morgan was stunned. Everyone expected the dancer to come out and mingle with the guests. That's why they had come. That was why they had parted with a lot of money for his mother's charity. His parents....

"I know, is very bad, no? But I cannot do *la politesse* now someone out there try to hurt me."

"Mr. Nijinsky—"

"And I see Sergei Pavlovitch is here."

"Who?"

"Diaghilev. He is here with Massine. I cannot bear this. I am so angry with him, so...I wish to crawl away."

"You mean, sneak away? Creep out the back door?" Morgan felt a sudden kinship with the Russian. He had often felt the urge to 'crawl away' from this great house so often full of guests, where he was expected to perform his son-of-the-house' role under his father's disapproving eye. Filling in for Harry, he thought, and even after two years, his heart lurched.

"Sneak, yes! Is my wife who speak English, you see. Me, I not speak good."

"You're doing just fine. Yes, we can sneak away. I can drive you to the station. Heck, I can drive you all the way to the city, but the train is actually faster."

"You have motorcar? I love motorcar! I wish to buy for family!"

"How soon will you be ready?"

"Ten minutes. I need ten minutes only."

"I'll wait outside." Morgan finished off his champagne and left the room. He noticed that Nijinsky had not touched his again after the first sip.

Outside, he paused for a moment, thinking over what the Russian had said, then headed for the terrace. The garden party was in full swing. Waiters circulated with trays of champagne, and people crowded under the brightly striped tent to help themselves to the sumptuous spread. Morgan strolled along by the stage and reached up, running his hand over the wooden flooring. Sure enough, there were two loose boards halfway down, near the edge. Careless, but surely not sabotage. Not here in his own summer home where his mother's beautiful flowers filled the air with sweetness and his father's expensive cigars spread contentment among the men. He hurried back to the music room just in time to meet Nijinsky coming out.

Standing up, the man seemed barely taller than Gloria. He was dressed conservatively, Morgan noted, his hair brushed carefully and parted just off-center. Apart from that vague air of foreignness, due perhaps to the cut of his obviously expensive suit, he could have been any friend of his father's from the financial district. Except maybe for those strangely slanted eyes...

"Your valet will see to your things?"

Nijinsky nodded. "We go now, yes?"

"I think through the kitchen would be best," Morgan suggested. He knew that someone would be coming any minute to check on the honored guest, so the sooner they got out of there, the better.

Morgan led the dancer through the swinging door into the servants' area of the house. The hall opened into the cavernous kitchen humming with activity as cooks and kitchen maids, waiters and house maids bustled about, preparing and serving the mounds of pastries and jellied molds, small cakes and sugared fruit for the guests. Masses of dirty dishes were being washed and stacked away. Trays full of used glasses waited their turn.

Everyone looked startled at Morgan's sudden appearance with the guest of honor. As Morgan rushed past, smiling at them and apologizing for taking this route, they stood aside. The two new kitchen maids dropped a curtsy and giggled.

"Anything I can help you with, sir?" asked Edgar, his father's chauffeur, jumping up and opening the door to the courtyard.

"No, thanks, Edgar. I'm going to take our guest out for a spin in my motor car."

"I see, sir." Edgar bowed as Nijinsky passed him, and then softly closed the door. "The young master will get himself in trouble with that foreign fellow, you mark my words," he said, but everyone had gone back to work and paid no attention.

The coach house door slid back smoothly on its well-oiled track as Morgan pushed it, revealing four motorcars and two carriages.

"*Formidable*," murmured Nijinsky admiringly, running his hand over the sleek green bonnet of the Pierce-Arrow.

"That's my father's favorite," Morgan said. "See how the head-lights are sunken into the mudguards? Only the Pierce-Arrow has that shape. And that snub-nosed one over there is an old electric car. My sister Gloria likes to fool around with it. But if you like something sporty, look at this beauty. My granddad brought it back for me from England just before the war. It's a Vauxhall Prince Henry and it can reach speeds up to eighty-five miles an hour since I modi-fied the engine. Not on these roads, of course," he hastened to add.

Nijinsky looked relieved. "I see one in London last time I go," he said. "Is first time I am in one."

"It's a four-cylinder engine with seventy-five horsepower and a four-speed gearbox."

"Is nice red color."

Morgan smiled, realizing his euphoric descriptions of the inner workings of his beloved vehicle were lost on the Russian dancer. "Let's go," he said as he swung up into the driver's seat and started the engine. "I love driving!"

Nijinsky hopped up on the running board and jumped in beside him. As they drove out through the courtyard and under the brick archway, Morgan felt his spirits lift. The wheels crunched over the smooth gravel of the driveway. The sun glanced off the silver engine cover and sparkled on the shiny red body work. As he coasted through the gates and switched gears, the engine coughed a few times but then settled down into a steady hum. It was amazingly quiet compared to his father's motor.

They drove for a time in silence, Morgan lost in the enjoyment driving always brought him, his companion wrapped in his own thoughts. From time to time, Morgan glanced at the dancer, but the dark slanted eyes were not taking in the scenery they passed. The road followed the coast for a while, the sea a constant presence of sparkling blue, sliding in and out of view among the trees like a shy girl at her first dance. They passed numerous summer homes, many far grander than the Vanheusens': fantastic fairy tale structures set way back from the road, raising their towers and cupolas and extravagant crenellated peaks in the midst of carefully tended parkland. Morgan always enjoyed this part of the drive, and today was quiet and free of dust since they passed only a few delivery wagons, the horses rolling a cautious eye in their direction.

When Nijinsky finally spoke, it came as a surprise. "Thank you for help me escape," he said.

"A pleasure. To tell you the truth, I'm glad to escape, too." Morgan smiled conspiratorially. There would be consequences, he knew, but for now, at least, he felt at peace.

"Is good, no? In Paris I crawl…er…sneak away from Sergei. I chase tarts sometimes, sometimes just walk."

"Chase tarts?" Morgan laughed. "Really? I can take you to Madame Hahn's if you like. It's a fine bordello. My uncle Paul introduced me there when I was eighteen."

"We go, Monsieur Vanheusen. Yes!"

Morgan had heard the rumors about Nijinsky, the half-understood whispers and innuendos. Maybe some of them were true. Maybe not. Nijinsky was a man of the world, and the world Morgan knew must seem quite provincial to him. "It's a deal," he said, reaching over to shake the man's hand. "And please call me Morgan."

"Morgan, yes. Americans so friendly. I am Vaslav."

Nijinsky suddenly stood up, holding onto the frame of the windshield. "Is wonderful, no? Such speed! Such freedom!"

"Vaslav! Sit down!" Morgan laughed and pulled at the man's overcoat.

"Is like boat I sail on to America. We have storm. I go up and watch waves roll about! It makes boat dance!"

"I should call you High Jinks!" Morgan said. "It suits you better."

"Is American name, this Jinks?"

"Well, it could be a nickname, for just between us."

"Is good." The dancer sat down again, his face alive, no longer dark with thoughts. "Is name for friend."

"Okay, Jinks it is," Morgan said. The name felt better on his tongue than the real one. At least, the dancer looked happier now. Maybe he had forgotten the accident with the floorboards and the stage. Relieved, Morgan pushed the incident out of his own mind and concentrated on his driving.

By the time they arrived at the Hotel Claridge on the southeast corner of Broadway and 44th, it was getting dark. They made an appointment to meet the next afternoon, and the Russian stepped out of the car.

"Thank you, Morgan," Nijinsky said, shaking his hand fervently. "You save me this day."

"Well, maybe that's putting it a bit strong," Morgan said, suddenly uneasy.

"We meet tomorrow. We chase tarts, yes?"

"Why not?" Morgan waved and watched his diminutive new friend walk away. As he turned north, he glanced back and saw Nijinsky head away from the Claridge and cross the street, disappearing quickly into the crowd.

"What the—" Morgan jerked the wheel as horns blared. A horse snorted and veered away. Morgan shrugged. He wasn't Nijinsky's nursemaid. Nevertheless, he had a sinking feeling that this spur-of-the-minute escapade would have long-lasting repercussions.

Jinks. Change the spelling and it had another meaning.

THREE

"ALLIES' DIPLOMATS AVOID RITZ-CARLTON
They Are Careful Not to Visit House Where Enemies' Envoys
Have Apartments."

—*New York Times*

The doorman of the Ritz-Carlton Hotel at 46th and Madison snapped to attention as Diaghilev and his entourage swept up the steps and into the foyer. Inside, they paused, discussing where they should go for a drink. The vaulted lobby soared above their heads, the marble pillars encrusted with gilt leaves near the ceiling far above. Chandeliers dripping with crystal showered them with muted light. The reception desk of walnut adorned with brass stretched along one side of the room. Heavily carpeted stairs swept up in a great curve to the mezzanine. A fountain splashed in the center of the lobby, spring flowers clustered around its base.

Diaghilev removed his hat and smoothed his thick black hair. The streak of white at his forehead made him look even more arresting. "My dear sir, you have been most helpful," he assured the nervous bald man carrying his carpetbag. "The train ride could not have been more comfortable."

"Thank you, Mr. Diaghilev. I'm sorry about the error in the number of tickets you required."

"It is nothing. Nothing." Diaghilev waved his hand, reducing the mishap to ashes scattered on the air. "All the time these little misunderstandings arise in the organizing of events. *Toujours*. But you, you take care of it like a true professional. Am I not right, Léonide?" He turned to the young man at his side who nodded and smiled. The others in the group followed suit, all assuring the American that everything had gone perfectly.

Reassured, the little man nodded back and dropped the carpet-bag at Diaghilev's feet. He shook hands and backed away, murmuring his thanks.

"It is you who should be thanked," Diaghilev shouted after him. "You wish to join us?"

"No, thank you. Maybe…some other time?" The little man bumped into a pillar, then turned and almost ran out of the hotel.

"Good," said Diaghilev. "That one, he is incompetent fool. Now, where shall we go? The dining salon? The food is good here."

The reporter who had been following Diaghilev since his arrival at Grand Central Station suddenly pushed forward and pointed. "Look! Isn't that Mr. Nijinsky?"

"Isn't he staying at the Claridge?" murmured one of the group.

"Vaslav!" Diaghilev rushed towards the dancer, who was just about to slip by on the other side of a pillar. "You come to see me. You come to apologize for not dancing an encore and slipping away like naughty boy!" He reached to grasp the dancer by the shoulders, meaning to kiss him on both cheeks as was his custom, but Nijinsky backed away.

"Sergei Pavlovitch, I am no longer boy," he said, his eyes flashing with anger.

"Then why do you run away like one?" Diaghilev towered over the diminutive dancer, his dark bulk menacing.

Nijinsky stepped backwards towards the stairs and moved up the first three steps. Now he stood just above Diaghilev, looking down on him with cool composure, but the big man knew from experience that Nijinsky's nervous picking at his thumbnail meant he was anything but calm. How well I know you, little one, he thought to himself. You do not play these games well.

"Why do I wish to be at gathering where you are, Sergei, ready to spread your lies about me?"

"My dear Vaslav—"

"No! I am not dear to you! I hate you, Sergei! You not even keep your word to me! Me you treat like cheap…." He jerked his hand in the air, unable to think of an English word the Americans there would understand.

"Vaslav, do not do this. You know how much you mean to me."

"*Nyet!*" Nijinsky burst into Russian, both hands now gesturing with a life of their own. "You lied to me, Sergei! You brought me over here for what? To mock me and lie to me some more? To throw this...this pretty dancing boy in my face and pass him off as a choreographer?"

Massine jerked into life. "But sir, it is not—"

"Be quiet, Léonide!" roared Diaghilev, completely forgetting where he was. Massine subsided, his usually pale face flushed.

"You will listen to me, Sergei!" shouted Nijinsky, beside himself with fury. "You will stop all performances of *Faune*! All! It is my ballet and I know what you are doing with it! You have made it a simpering bland farce!"

"Vaslav—"

"That is final, Sergei. If you perform this bastardized version of my ballet even one more time, I'll never dance for you again!"

"Mr. Nijinsky—" The journalist pushed forward, trying to get the Russians to at least switch into English, but he was shouted down.

"Vaslav, my lawyers are even now working this out with your lawyers at the Metropolitan Opera. I talked with Mr. Gatti-Casazza and Mr. Kahn a few hours ago on the telephone. Everything is progressing well."

Nijinsky was breathing hard, his hands clenched. The skin around both thumbs was bleeding. "Sergei Pavlovitch, the money is a different matter, a legal matter arranged long ago, which you do not honor. This matter of *Faune* is separate. Remove it from the program until I can rehearse the company in the way it should be. That is all I am saying."

"Vaslav—"

Nijinsky finally looked him in the eye, and Diaghilev felt the look like a shudder of remembered pain. He forced himself not to look away, not to let the hurt show. "I made you what you are today," he said quietly.

"I danced with Pavlova when I was seventeen! I was a star before you took—" Nijinsky stopped himself with a visible effort. "I have nothing more to say. Good evening." He bowed briefly. As he went down the three steps and ran headlong across the floor, the crowd parted before him.

"Mr. Nijinsky, could I have a few words with you?" The reporter rushed after him, but the dancer didn't stop or even turn his head.

For the first time, Diaghilev became aware of the other guests in the lobby, standing and looking at his group in amazement. One does not carry on a quarrel at the top of one's voice in the Ritz-Carlton Hotel. Bah. From the corner of his eye, he spotted the hotel manager making his way towards him.

The Russian bowed, sweeping his hat to the floor.

"Forgive us," he said, his rich deep voice easily filling the big space, "but artists are very tempestuous at times. We forget ourselves, you understand. You will all be thinking the Ritz-Carlton is now the war headquarters of the Ballets Russes as well as for the German and Austro-Hungarian ambassadors! Please accept my apologies."

The manager stopped, nodded at him, and backed away, a relieved expression on his face.

Diaghilev turned to the reporter. "Mr. Cass, why do you not come to my suite?" he suggested. "We will order supper there for everyone and drink Russian tea and vodka, and I will explain all this to you." The reporter agreed eagerly, as expected, and the Russian smiled. There is always a way to make good publicity out of an apparent disaster, he thought. "Come, let us get into one of these magnificent American elevators and go to my suite!"

Léonide Massine picked up the carpetbag and followed him.

The elevator boy, resplendent in his maroon and gold uniform with the tight-fitting trousers, smiled broadly at Diaghilev as the doors slid open.

"Good evening, sir," he chirped, ignoring the others.

"It is indeed," replied Diaghilev complacently. As the gilded cage rose to his floor, he touched the inside of Massine's wrist and felt the boy's pulse beat under his finger tips.

The hotel had given Diaghilev a large corner suite. Tall French doors opened onto a terrace high above the tumultuous traffic of New York. A heavy green damask cloth covered a round table near the windows, and a steamer trunk stood open near a mahogany secretary spilling papers and sketches, notebooks, and files out of the crowded drawers.

"My office," Diaghilev said, motioning towards it with a laugh.

"Everywhere I go, it comes with me. Along with my samovar and Josef, of course. Without him, I am truly lost."

The valet nodded without any change in his dour expression, helped his master out of his overcoat, then took the coats and hats of the visitors.

The samovar was, in fact, more of a prop than anything else. Diaghilev had lived in Europe for so long, he was less Russian than most of his dancers. Nevertheless, he always served Russian tea to his guests, along with a plentiful supply of vodka. By now, it was an established tradition.

Diaghilev sat back on the plush-covered chair and looked around at the assembled group. Massine sipped tea through a sugar cube, his dark intelligent eyes watchful; later on, Diaghilev knew, the boy would entertain him with insightful impressions of the company in exquisite and amusing detail. Andy Cass, the American journalist, had the kind of young, eager face that he had come to associate with the breed. But there was something different about this one. Diaghilev couldn't quite put his finger on it, but there was something… Beside Cass, Marvin Seidman, the lawyer for the Ballets, tasted the vodka, nodded his satisfaction, and took another drink. The man looked old as time, but his reputation proved that his mind was as agile as ever. Seidman was talking to the young artist, Pierre Delaville. Diaghilev had had high hopes for him, but he was proving rather a disappointment, although he certainly looked the part with his long chestnut curls and Werther-like look of tragedy in his deep eyes. However, it seemed to be mostly superficial. Oh well, he would drop the young man soon. Beside the young *artiste manqué*, Baron Von Meyer sat back at ease, lighting one of his ever-present French menthol cigarettes, a habit he had picked up from Marcel Proust. He was one of the stalwart backers of the Ballets Russes, a man who knew everyone and was invited everywhere. He and Count Golejewski had set up the Vanheusen benefit with Nijinsky, since Diaghilev knew Vaslav wouldn't perform there if Diaghilev's name was attached to it in any way. That woman who had trapped him into marriage was going to ruin him.

He waved away the baron's proffered silver cigarette case and selected one of his own Russian cigarettes. They were becoming harder to get, he'd noticed. Perhaps he should try one of those

Murad Turkish things he saw advertised everywhere. He could feel
the vodka sooth its way inside, smoothing out the nervous knots
and focusing his thoughts.

"My dear Mr. Cass," he said, his voice easily dominating the
others, "you must think me extremely rude." He proceeded to make
the necessary introductions.

"I appreciate getting this chance to talk to you, Mr. Diaghilev."
The young man was getting out his notebook, leaning forward
with an intense interest. "I've been trying to get an interview for
ages."

"Well, now you have it." Diaghilev settled back and studied
Cass through the curling smoke of his cigarette.

"About Mr. Nijinsky, could you ––"

"Ah yes, Mr. Nijinsky." Diaghilev paused and refilled his glass.
"You must understand that artists tend to be somewhat…tempera-
mental, by their very nature. It is what sets them apart, what gives
them the fire they burn on stage. And off, as you have seen."

He smiled. "Vaslav is a great dancer. Of that.there is no doubt.
But in many ways, he is but a child. How could it be otherwise? He
has devoted his life to the dance."

"Yes, I understand, but—"

"No, Mr. Cass, you do not. I am trying to explain what you
thought you saw downstairs so that it makes sense to you. So that
you do not leap to conclusions that are false. I have guided Vaslav's
career from the first, as you may know. But since he left the company in 1914, he has made many decisions that are, how you say…
well, not for the best. Now he is back, but he is trying to make up
his monetary losses from me, looking to me, as he always has, to
take care of things. Vaslav is, as you have seen, very highly strung.
He does not understand business, and lately, if I may be blunt, he
has been led astray by his wife. She may mean well, but she has
little understanding of the business world, either. After all, she is a
woman, no?"

"So you mean he's trying to recoup money from you that he's
lost due to… poor management."

"My dear Mr. Cass, that may be putting it too harshly. I would
never want to portray Vaslav in such a light. Never! Would you like
more vodka?"

"No, thanks. So would you say that all the problems began when Mr. Nijinsky got married?"

Diaghilev laughed. "Me, I would never say such a thing! Romola Nijinska is a charming lady and I'm sure she has her husband's best interests at heart. Why would she not? But she is an actress and inexperienced in business. She is, how do you say, a babe in the woods, no? Now, if that is all..."

"Just one more question, sir. Why is Mr. Nijinsky so angry with you?"

"You see? It is as I thought. You do not understand what you saw. Vaslav, he has the temper tantrums, like a child. This is what I was trying to explain to you. If he does not get just what he wants..." Diaghilev snapped his fingers in the air. "One time in London, I remember, he ripped up some costumes, he was so angry about a change we have to make in the program at the last moment. He would not get changed, but screamed and threw things about the dressing room, terrorizing everyone backstage. I had to come and give him a severe talking to, as if to a young child. I gave him the right costume and said, 'Put it on now, Vasli,' and I went out and listened outside the door. I heard him shout something, then silence. But when he heard his music cue, he came onstage and danced like a dream."

Diaghilev paused, his face growing pensive. "I do not wish to tell you these things," he said at last, "but I see it is necessary to make you understand that little scene in the lobby, to put things... in perspective, if you will."

Andy Cass was busily scribbling in his notebook, darting glances at Diaghilev from time to time as he wrote. Now he cleared his throat. "Do you have one final word for my readers?"

"Mr. Cass, you may tell your readers that they will see Mr. Nijinsky on the stage of the Metropolitan Opera house as soon as I can arrange it."

"Any idea when that will be?"

"I am not a fortune teller who looks into the future, Mr. Cass. Soon. That much I know." He stood up and reached across to shake the young man's hand.

"It has been a pleasure, sir," Andy said fervently.

"Indeed," Diaghilev replied with a smile. "I always enjoy talking to young men of the press, especially ones who know what is, as they say, off the record and what is for public consumption." His monocle twinkled in the light.

Only half the lights in the dusty chandelier were working, casting a sickly yellow haze over the crowded space. The ceiling was so high that the chain the chandelier was suspended from was lost in shadows, giving the place the feel of a stage set. In fact, bits and pieces of garishly painted flats were visible here and there, and some of the furniture was painted in the same gaudy colors. Dust was everywhere.

Andy stood near the door, peering into the gloom. At first, he could see no one in the jumble around him. Then a candelabra caught his eye. As he watched, the wavering flames moved across a small purple table, pushed by a broad hand. The stooped man sitting next to the table was watching him intently out of deeply sunken eyes. Wax spilled over his fingers as he stopped the forward motion of the candles. He didn't appear to notice.

"You have news?" The voice sounded old and frail.

"I talked to Diaghilev."

"And? And?"

Andy came closer and sank into a dusty chair. He felt very tired. He had been following his story since early morning, trying unsuccessfully to get onto the grounds where Nijinsky was going to dance, trailing the Diaghilev party all the way back in the train. He had had little to eat all this time. He smoothed his forehead with his fingers, trying to push the ache away from behind his eyes. Why was he here? Why did he let himself be caught up in the twisted ugly fantasies of this man? Across the scarred table, the old man leaned forward, his glittering eyes looking deeply into Andy's. Andy sighed. There was no way to cut the cord that bound them together. It was too thick, went back too far.

He told the man what he had been able to find out. "I know it's not much, George," he said wearily. "From what I could pick up, Nijinsky will definitely not be dancing with the company any time soon, and the word around town is the Ballets Russes will be finished without him."

George shook his head. His long, grey-streaked hair flew out around his face. "You think so? You have talked to Diaghilev and still do not see? The man is a sorcerer! His words are like silk and you do not feel the pinprick of the needle as he sews up your soul with them! He speaks with the accents of the court and has the bearing of an aristocrat, but he moves in the gutter and preys on the young. He is evil!"

"George, please, don't get overexcited. It's not worth it."

"He steals my life over and over, and you say it's not worth it?" The old man burst into a coughing fit, waving his arms to keep Andy away. "All right. I'm all right now. And yes, I do understand what you say, but I do not want to hear it."

"Can I get you something?" Andy asked, looking around vaguely in hope of seeing some signs of a pantry. He never could fathom how George lived.

The old man shook his head again and began to tug at something under the table. "No, no, I have here what I need." He finally pulled out a large wooden box inlaid with mother-of-pearl and laid it on his knees. "Everything I need," he murmured, opening the box. The lid swung up and away from him, shielding whatever was inside from Andy's view. George raised a hand and made pushing motions in the air. "Go now. I know what I must do. I talk to Rudy now. He will help."

Andy got to his feet. "George—"

"Come back when you have more news."

Reluctantly, Andy moved back along the narrow path through the boxes and chairs and stools, the tables and divans and footstools, many of which could never be used again. When had the old man begun to loose touch like this? Why had Andy not noticed? Or was it fear that silenced him, fear that recognizing George's growing odd behavior would somehow make it more sinister? Raise it from eccentricity to something malevolent with a power all its own?

Andy paused at the door and looked back. The candles had been extinguished and he could barely make out the figure of the old man, whom he had loved for so long, bent over something in the wooden box on his knees.

FOUR

"Foreign Entries Few in 500 Mile Race, but Make Up in Quality What They Lack in Quantity"
—Dick Farrington, *Syracuse Herald*

As Morgan drove back home after letting the Russian dancer off at his hotel, he wondered what he would do with himself this evening. All his friends thought he was in the country, so he had not been included in any invitations to dine or have cocktails and then on to a lobster house, as they often did of an evening. There was always Madame Hahn's, but his mind had wandered back to the news he had read just this morning about the 500-mile race in Indianapolis. His racing cronies would know the latest on that, and for once, he wouldn't have to think up a story as to where he had been in case he ran into his father.

Traffic thinned out considerably the farther north he went on Fifth Avenue. The pace of life seemed less frenzied here. There was time to admire the imposing scale of the big houses, the barbaric mix of architectural styles, the tumble of turrets and cupolas and gothic finials in copper and stone. Morgan's family home was one of the few set back from the avenue behind a wrought iron railing, the driveway curving around under a porte-cochère. They had moved here from the large brownstone built by his grandfather about nine years before in the Washington Square area, and he was still enjoying the feeling of space and brightness of their newly fashionable neighborhood. His father never tired of pointing out that Mrs. Astor lived just up the road.

Young Cooper looked startled when he opened the front door. "We didn't think anyone in the family would be back tonight, sir," he stammered, touching his collar as if to make sure it was straight.

"Don't worry, Coop, I won't be dining at home," Morgan assured him. "And I'll let myself in when I return."

He caressed the bronze breasts of the Huntress Diana where she stood rooted to the top of the newel post, a liberty he rarely had the chance to take when the whole family was in residence. He grinned and leapt up the steps two at a time, ignoring the menacing paintings of mighty elk, moose, and lowering sylvan hunting scenes from his father's art collection that climbed the walls beside him. He noted that his mother had finally prevailed, and the large and bloody scene of carnage portrayed in the 'Hounds and Fox' painting had been replaced with 'The Monarch of the Glen,' a majestic stag surveying his domain. Much as his father did after Sunday dinner, Morgan thought with a grin.

The house was eerily quiet without his sisters. Most of the staff had gone to the country to help out, leaving a strange void in the air, as if some important piece of machinery had been removed. In the unusual silence, he began to worry about what his father would have to say about his spur of the moment agreement to spirit away their guest of honor. It wouldn't be pleasant. Still, he had only done what the 'God of the Dance' had asked. What was the harm in that?

An hour later, his father forgotten, Morgan swung into the Greenwich Village lane where a row of converted stables, rechristened Blitzer Motorworks, housed the racing cars owned by Buzz Remington and several other enthusiasts of motorcar racing. A motley collection of racing enthusiasts, owners, and mechanics gathered here at all hours to discuss their passion, usually upstairs in the makeshift bar run by one of the mechanics and his wife and buxom daughter. Morgan didn't come here as often as he used to. The place stirred old passions, old dreams. Tonight, however, he would make an exception.

As he made his way up the dark wooden stairway, the smells of oil and grease mingled with an underlay of the now-vanished horses. He swung the door open. The heavy pall of cigar smoke almost made him cough, but he welcomed it, feeling a lifting of his spirits as he stepped inside the familiar space. The place was decorated with posters advertising big-name races like the American Grand Prix, the Vanderbilt Cup, the Elgin National Trophy,

Brighton Beach, the Indianapolis 500 Mile Race, and, of course, the Metropolitan Trophy Race that opened the eastern season here in May. Colorful photographs of cars hung on one wall: Remington's Bearcat, Bragg's Peugeot, and a new one he didn't recognize among them. It looked very small, pointed in the back like a child's toy. In pride of place behind the bar were pictures of the drivers who had dropped in, however briefly: the millionaire Caleb Bragg, "Terrible Teddy" Tetzlaff, Barney Oldfield, Louis Chevrolet, De Palma, even Dario Resta. A few years ago, Morgan had hoped to be there someday, but now that dream was dead, along with his brother Harry. He tried not to think about it much.

He waved to a familiar group of men clustered around the old table by the window, some in well-cut suits and stiff collars, others in caps and soft shirts open at the neck. Two men he didn't recognize wore old-fashioned dusters over their clothes, obviously just in from working on their cars. A quick scan of the room showed Morgan that Remington was not here, but he spotted his old school friend Langley Blackwell-Thomas at the bar.

Almost at the same moment, Langley spotted him. "What are you doing in town, old sport?" he drawled in the mid-Atlantic accent he had adopted ever since his English relatives had arrived for one extended visit.

Morgan sighed as he sank down on the high stool and told Langley a quick and amusing version of his escape from the country with Nijinsky. "I will live to rue the day, of course," he finished, paying for his drink.

"No doubt, but in the meantime, follow me and meet Dick Farrington, auto racing reporter from Syracuse. He's in town to see the trials of Chuffy Harris's new motors, and, more important to me, he has the low-down on the 500 Mile Race."

"What about the Metropolitan Trophy? That's coming up earlier and right here in Sheepshead Bay Speedway."

"Ask him yourself." Langley picked up a tray of drinks and walked over to the smoky wooden booth in one corner of the dark bar.

Three men were sitting there, heads ringed in smoke from pipes and cigars. Langley introduced the tall, toothy young man as Farrington. Beside him was the round, beaming Chuffy Harris, and opposite him was Lars, the mechanic whom Morgan used to pump for arcane information.

"You're too young to be an owner, surely," said the reporter, shaking Morgan's hand. "So are you a driver or a railbird?"

"He just drove the great Nijinsky back from their summer house today," Langley said, grinning. "Does that count?"

"You don't say!" Chuffy Harris leaned forward, eyes bright. "What's he like, then?"

"A bit…eccentric," Morgan said, "but he loves cars. He got quite excited when I cranked her up on a straightaway stretch. Says he's going to buy one soon."

"Well, that's not a bit eccentric."

Farrington was studying Morgan's face intently. "You look familiar," he finally said, leaning his elbows on the table. "Didn't you used to test drive for Hochman a few years ago when he was developing his KarlzKar? Yes, I'm sure of it! You were a real speed demon!"

"I was a college student having a good time," Morgan said deprecatingly.

"You broke a few records, as I recall."

"Broke a few bones, too, while I was at it, That damn Karlz 600T had an airplane engine in it, and it was a bear to handle."

"I was there. You were handling it fine. Who are you driving for now?"

"These days I'm just a railbird."

"That's criminal! You're a great driver."

"He raced against Mr. Remington a month ago at the Raleigh Roadway." Langley said. "Remember, Morgan?"

"Langley, don't be a jackass. That was just a friendly match, and I was racing my own stripped-down coupe against one of his modified Maxwells, so it wasn't much of a contest."

"It was damn close, nonetheless, old sport," Langley said loyally, sliding into the seat beside him. "Just think what you could have done with a real machine!"

Morgan kicked him under the table.

"What have you got now?" Farrington asked, leaning forward across the table.

Morgan told about him his beloved Vauxhall Prince Henry and

the adjustments he had made to the engine, thanks in part to Lars.

"I've always said the problem is one of weight," Lars said. "Wouldn't you agree, Mr. Farrington?"

Farrington nodded. "Your machine is a great model for general driving, but you need a light body to break more than seventy-five MPH, in my opinion."

"I know. I've tried to strip it down as much as I can, but…" He shrugged.

"He hit eighty-five in that run against Remington," Langley said.

"Then my hat's off to you. You've still got that magic!" Farrington raised his glass and threw back his head to finish the golden liquid remaining.

"So who do you think is going to win the 500 Mile?" Langley asked, throwing a peanut into his mouth. His question sounded casual, but Morgan knew the answer was of the utmost interest to him. Knowing the odds was Langley's bread and butter, a major source of funds now that his family had lost nearly everything, thanks to his father's naïve trust in an investment scheme.

"All the drivers and cars aren't registered yet," Farrington said, picking up another drink that had magically materialized in front of him. "Not many Europeans in yet, but so far, my money's on Ralph De Palma. Of course, there's always Oldfield, who seems to be pulling himself together lately, and who knows what the next few weeks will bring? Don't lay any bets yet."

"And the Metropolitan Cup right here in our fair city?" another man asked. "Any news on who's driving what and for whom?"

"Ask Chuffy. I hear he has a few surprises up his sleeve."

Chuffy Harris laughed and knocked the ashes out of his pipe. "And that's where's they're staying, boys," he said, standing up. "Time to be off, my friends." He beamed at them all. "Mr. Vanheusen, the next time you see your friend Mr. Nijinsky, ask him when he's going to dance, could you? The ladies in my house are most anxious to see him perform. Here's my card."

Morgan handed the man his own card and slipped Harris's into his vest pocket. "Nice to meet you, sir."

Harris waved and started towards the door, calling over his shoulder, "Come along, come along. Time waits for no man."

The other two followed, Farrington collecting his hat and walking stick from the bartender on the way. They made an odd threesome: the tall reporter; the short-legged, wiry Lars, who walked with a pronounced limp; and the rotund little Harris, who bounced along like a happy baby.

"First you bring up Nijinsky, then you bring everything back to betting," Morgan muttered, finishing off his beer.

"It's not as if you haven't been known to take a flyer or two on the races, old thing," Langley said, unconcerned. "You can't talk machinery all the time."

"Not with you around, certainly," Morgan said, pushing some money across the table to add to what was already there. "Sometimes I wonder why you come here."

"Makes a change from the Jockey Club, although I must admit the food is much better there."

Morgan laughed. "Jackass."

"Hungry?" Langley asked, taking out his pocket watch as if to reassure himself that it was, indeed, time to eat again.

Morgan was surprised to find out that he was, and the two thumped down the old staircase and climbed into Morgan's car.

An evening on the town with friends usually started with cocktails and then moved on to some lobster palace like Diamond Jim's or Rector's. But tonight, even the shapely seductive chorines of La Bohème, the new cabaret on 42nd Street, couldn't hold Morgan's attention, and he left early amid the jeers and catcalls of the friends he had met there.

Milk carts and delivery wagons filled the early morning streets, going about their business of being the invisible purveyors of food to the big houses and restaurants and stores. Morgan was just glad to get home. As he went though the back hall from the courtyard door, he was yawning.

Stepping into the main hall, he stopped, suddenly alert. The house felt different. He crossed to the staircase. And that's when he smelled it: cigar smoke.

"How dare you?" His father's voice came out of the shadows behind him.

"Sir?" Morgan turned around, a cold hardness sinking to the pit of his stomach.

"How dare you take it upon yourself to ruin an event that your mother and sister have worked on so hard? Have you any idea what you've done?"

"Mr. Nijinsky asked me to take him back to the city, sir."

"And are you his servant? Have you fallen under his thrall? Have you no will of your own anymore?"

"Of course not, sir, but I thought—"

"That's exactly what you did not do!" thundered his father, clutching the lapels of his smoking jacket and rolling forward onto his toes. "You do not think about others! You left us with over two hundred guests who had come to meet the great Nijinsky...and no Nijinsky! What in the name of all that's holy were you thinking?"

Morgan felt himself sway with fatigue. The wine he had consumed was not helping. "Could we talk about this tomorrow, sir?"

"We'll bloody well talk about this now! I came back early to find out what the Sam Hill was going on. Your Uncle Paul even wondered if that man had...had... Tell me what happened!"

Morgan sagged against the banister. "He asked me to take him back to his hotel. He said there were people at the party he didn't want to meet. He said there was something wrong with the stage and that someone was out to sabotage him."

"Utter nonsense!"

"Maybe so, but that's how he felt and what he said. He refused to come out. What else could I do?"

"For one thing, you could have let us know." His father shook his head. "This is what comes of trying to deal with eccentric foreigners." He pulled a cigar out of his pocket and offered it to Morgan. "When I left, your sister was in tears and your mother had that glazed hostess look she gets when dealing with emergencies. I just hope this doesn't affect the rest of Gloria's season."

He walked towards the library and Morgan followed, relieved to see they were nearing the reconciliation stage of the blow-up. The last thing he wanted was a cigar, but it was de rigueur at this stage, so he took a seat opposite his father and began to prepare it for smoking.

"You know, Chesleigh would never have done such a thoughtless thing," his father said.

Morgan felt himself stiffen, but clamped his mouth shut. Comparisons with his older brother now that Harry was gone were all too frequent and never to his advantage. He lit his cigar, drew on it, and watched the smoke curl upwards while his father waxed eloquent about that paragon, his older brother.

"Then why wasn't Chesleigh here?" he burst out suddenly. "Why didn't he come to meet and look after our guest?"

"Chesleigh has responsibilities! He's in charge of our major rail coach factory, and you know that!"

"I just mean that since he's so responsible, it would have made sense to have him here. He isn't that far away."

"This was one thing I thought you could manage," his father said icily. "Just one little thing we asked you to do: look after the Russian. Not a big thing, but important, so that we could look after everything and everyone else. But did you do it? No. You have to follow your impulses. Again."

"I'm sorry!" Morgan shouted, butting his cigar savagely in the huge crystal ashtray. "I'm sorry I can't live up to Chesleigh's impossibly high standards!" He was on his feet now, facing his father across the table. "I'll apologize to Mother when she gets back," he went on, "and to Gloria, if I need to do that, too."

"You'd damn well better, young man, if you know what's good for you! Now get out of my sight!"

Morgan turned and almost ran out of the room.

FIVE

"O Mr. Nijinsky, Where have you binsky?"
—Musical Courier, 1916

For his first few days in New York, Nijinsky loved nothing better than to ramble up and down Broadway, taking it all in, dazzled by the electric signs hoisted high on buildings, flashing news of the wonders to be had by sampling their products. Now he joined the crowd gawking at the huge colorful display towering above one of the hotels, representing horses galloping around a track. They appeared to be really moving, even stirring up puffs of dust with their flashing hooves, while above them in letters four feet high were the words 'Leaders of the World.' He had no idea what that meant, but the whole scene intrigued him. No matter how long he stayed in this city, he knew it would be constantly fascinating. But today he had no time to linger, to look in windows or wander into any of the shops.

At the corner of Broadway and 39th, he reached the Metropolitan Opera House. Several men tipped their hats to him as he turned in at the stage door. He couldn't remember their names, but they didn't look like reporters. He bowed, raised his hat in return, and hurried upstairs to the rehearsal hall. He could hear Cecchetti's voice above the piano, the beat of his staff against the floor. That sound used to be as familiar to him as the beat of his own heart. Hearing it again made him smile.

By the time he had changed into his black close-fitting dance trousers, white stockings, and white shirt, the others had arrived and were standing around in groups talking amongst themselves. Picking up the water can from a chair, he sprinkled the area of the dance floor they would be using and began his warm-up exercises.

When he was ready, he bowed to Cecchetti, who sat watching in his chair. The others fell into place around him.

"Vaslav Fomitch, you may be celebrated big star for everyone else, but in rehearsal, you are like pupil, *entendu*?"

"Yes, maestro."

"Alors, commençons! Un, deux, trois."

Nijinsky sprang into action, his body remembering the strict set of exercises Cecchetti insisted on each day as if he had not been absent for two years. Cecchetti watched closely, leaning forward in his chair, thumping out the beat with his stick. The exercises at the barre were done with the same precision, students and teacher both reaching for impossible perfection, until the hour was over and they took a break.

When they reassembled half an hour later, they started to rehearse a scene from *Petrushka*, the ballet Nijinsky had choreographed several years earlier. The strident music of Stravinsky took him back to the painful days when he was first teaching them the steps for this ground-breaking production, the frustration as he tried to communicate the jerky spastic motions of his vision to a group of dancers trained to a system of smooth and classical movement. It was different now, but as he danced, his whole being was still attuned to that perfect vision in his mind. He could sense the presence of each member of the company, each soloist, as they moved around him.

Suddenly, he stopped and looked at Cecchetti.

"Vaslav Fomitch, it is your ballet. Take the rehearsal."

Nijinsky turned to face the male dancer behind him. "It is not right, Ivan," he said. "You move too slowly here. You should be more...more...like this."

Ivan watched him sullenly. "That's what I did," he said.

"Not exactly. Watch." Again Nijinsky leapt and spun, jerked his arms, paused, then slumped to the ground. He got to his feet and looked expectantly at Ivan.

"I have danced the role of the Moor for two years. I dance all the New York season. Now all of a sudden, you arrive and I am not good enough?"

Nijinsky gazed at him, baffled. Wouldn't anyone want to improve? "I show you again?" he asked.

"No. I've got it."

"*Alors, répétez!*" cried Cecchetti, breaking the tension and taking back control with a thump of his stave on the floor. The music started again and they all jerked to life.

After the rehearsal, Nijinsky joined Ivan, who was cooling down at the barre.

"You understand what I was trying to explain?"

"I think it's you who don't understand some things, Vaslav Fomitch Nijinsky. Do you have any idea what you're doing to Monsieur de Diaghilev, the man who rescued you from war-torn Europe?"

Nijinsky paused, staring at this dancer he had known for years who now sounded like a stranger. What was he talking about? "This isn't about Sergei," he said.

"Oh yes, it is!" Ivan's nostrils flared. "Why do you persist in this… this stupidity? You've become like the role you created, Narcisse, the young man who dreams only of himself. You rehearse everyone so hard in *Petrushka* and you refuse to dance on stage. Don't you ever think about the bad publicity the company is getting because of you?"

"It's not because of Vaslav that audiences started to fall off, Ivan." Pavel wiped the sweat from his neck and face with a small towel as he leaned casually against the barre.

Nijinsky hadn't been aware of Pavel standing there. He felt the animosity shiver in the air around Ivan, but he didn't understand it. Even after all his time with the company in Paris and on tour, he never understood the petty jealousies and backstage politics. Nevertheless, he knew there was more to this than his own insistence on being paid.

"We know where you stand, Pavel," Ivan snarled. "You worship Nijinsky. You care nothing for the rest of us."

"I care for art," Pavel shouted.

Ivan turned abruptly on his heel and walked away.

"Should I thank you?" Nijinsky asked, glancing after Ivan.

"For what? Making an enemy even more implacable? He didn't want you here in America, you know. Massine was dancing most of your roles, but Ivan had managed to snare a few. He was hoping for more."

"Does he not want to improve?"

"Vaslav, you are a great dancer, but you are naive." Pavel shook his head at Nijinsky's uncomprehending expression. "Look, Massine is a competent dancer, but he's young and he was trained primarily as an actor. You, Vaslav, are Ivan's only real rival."

"Bolm?" Nijinsky said.

"Bolm is a *danseur noble*. He doesn't do the same kind of roles as you and Ivan. You know that."

"I see."Nijinsky shivered. "I thought I had come home after two years of exile," he said quietly.

"You have," Pavel agreed. "But home isn't always a refuge from envy, hatred, and jealousy."

Forty minutes later, Nijinsky walked into the grand salon of the lobby of the Claridge Hotel where he had arranged to meet his new American friend, giving himself a chance to escape for awhile the dark swirl of suspicion and jealousy back at the theater. Sunlight poured into the room through the glass skylight high above and a small chamber group played cakewalks and tangos and sprightly ragtime. People sat about at round marble-topped tables, the bright hats of the ladies nodding as they talked, their gloved hands holding thin teacups and tiny sandwiches.

"Mr. Nijinsky!" A reporter rushed up to him, followed by a man with a camera.

Morgan was suddenly by his side. "Not now, gentlemen, please." He spoke with surprising authority for a young man, but the reporters still argued for a few minutes before giving in.

"Phew! Is it always like that?" Morgan asked.

"They know I live here in hotel. They wait always. Already they take pictures of me and Romola and Kyra. Enough!"

"That's what I say." Morgan laughed as he led Nijinsky through the room to a table near the orchestra. A young lady sat there, her strawberry-blond hair a shining light in the already bright room.

Nijinsky stiffened.

"I'm sorry I didn't warn you I was bringing my sister, Gloria," Morgan whispered. "She's dying to meet you, and since she didn't get a chance in the country... Just a half an hour, I promise."

Even new friends betray me, Nijinsky thought, glancing around the room, looking for an escape. He had been looking forward to a little relaxation, a light repast, and then a ride in the red motorcar while Morgan showed him another side of New York. And now? He swallowed, bowed, and sat down abruptly.

"Good afternoon, Mr. Nijinsky. I am so pleased you agreed to meet me, even though I know it is most…unorthodox." She smiled and looked at her brother mischievously.

"But I did not," Nijinsky said.

Her smile faltered. "Well now, how odd. Would you like some tea? The profiteroles are quite marvelous here."

Nijinsky noticed her striped skirt was fashionably short, showing a good flash of slender ankle. Morgan cleared his throat nervously and made quite a show of choosing just the right sweetmeat from the tiered tray.

"Morgan told me how you two made your daring escape from our garden party," Gloria went on. "We were all left quite desolate, feeling abandoned like a bride at the altar."

"I fear it necessary." Nijinsky glanced around the room again, feeling a slight prickle under his skin as if eyes were watching him. He saw nothing out of the ordinary. Resignedly, he settled down to drink the tea, weak and tasteless by Russian standards, and listen to the girl prattle on. She talked quickly, all in a rush, her words running together. She also had a slight lisp.

After a while, he learned to decode her rapid speech and made a few comments of his own. He looked at her more closely, noting the way she moved, the way she gestured with her gloved hands. She was pretty in a way that was quite different from the women he was used to. Taller, for one thing, and with a certain freedom in her speech that he found novel.

"You are *très charmante, mademoiselle*," he said at last, bowing slightly.

"Oh, Mr. Nijinsky, you make me blush! You must have met many beautiful women. Princesses and that sort of thing."

"I expect being a princess does not make one automatically beautiful," Morgan observed.

Nijinsky nodded. "Is true. Many are ugly and boring." He pulled out his gold watch and snapped it open. A faint melody played.

"What a beautiful watch!" Gloria exclaimed, leaning closer.

"Is gift from Czar Nicholas. I dance for him at summer palace. See? Here is imperial eagle."

"Oh my," breathed Gloria. "You must have some wonderful things."

"Things not all." He spread his hands on the table. "The body more important. How you move. How you control. This you need for art of dance."

"Still…" Gloria was looking at the watch, following it with her eyes as Nijinsky slipped it back in his waistcoat pocket. "I certainly wouldn't mind being given a present by a king."

"I not say I mind," Nijinsky said, and smiled.

She smiled back, obviously delighted to have coaxed a smile from him at last.

"Gloria loves presents from anyone," Morgan said, laughing. "Well, sis, I'm afraid it's time to take you home."

"I can go by myself," she said, "in a motorcab."

"No." Morgan's voice was firm. "I brought you here. I'll take you home."

"Is good," Nijinsky agreed. "I have sister also. She is dear to me."

"Is she a dancer, too?" Gloria asked, checking the contents of her reticule.

"Yes. She is with husband in Europe." And I miss her, he thought.

He rose to his feet as they did, and bowed over Gloria's hand.

"It was a real pleasure meeting you," she said.

"I'll be back in about twenty minutes," Morgan whispered as his sister moved away. "Then we'll go to Sadie Hahn's. I promise." He winked and followed Gloria.

Nijinsky sat down again and watched them leave, the feathers in the girl's hat stirring as she walked. The orchestra was playing a syncopated number he had heard before. He pulled a piece of hotel stationary someone had left behind and began to doodle.

It was the waiter coming to see if he wanted anything else that made him notice the time.

"Vichy water is all." He looked around and realized the orchestra was packing up. He pulled out his watch again. More than half an hour had passed. Where was Morgan?

As he sat there alone waiting, he felt eyes on him. Not the usual sort of look when people recognized him and pointed him out to their companions. No, this was something else. Someone was watching him. Staring. Eyes drilling into him, trying to see what was inside, trying to take away his privacy. He felt his skin prickle. His fingers dug convulsively into the skin around his thumbs.

When the waiter brought his Vichy water, he signed the bill and took a long drink. The fresh coolness did nothing to soothe his sense of being spied on. And with this thought came memories of the police in Hungary questioning him about his system of dance notation, sure he was a spy.

Abruptly, he got to his feet and left the salon. He crossed the lobby and hurried into the bar, sitting down in a booth where he could keep a watch on the door. He waved away an approaching waiter, showing him his glass of Vichy water. The waiter bowed and backed away.

Another ten minutes crawled by.

Suddenly, Nijinsky felt his heart stutter with dread. One of the men who had been in the salon came in and sat down at the bar. He was an old man wearing a long full coat of good material but shabby and with something of a theatrical flair to it. Odd for such a place. Their eyes met in the mirror behind the bartender's head. Nijinsky jumped to his feet, sending the water glass skidding across the table, and rushed out the back entrance and through the dim narrow hallway. He heard shouting. In panic, he pushed on the iron door at the end of the passage and dashed out into the dim alley beyond.

The door clanged shut behind him.

SIX

"NIJINSKI AT ODDS WITH BALLET RUSSE"

—*New York Times*

"I told you it wouldn't work." Rudy threw himself into the sagging armchair by the dirty window. The radiator hissed. It was too hot in the room, but the window was painted shut. He loosened his tie, undid the top button of his shirt. "What happened?"

"I went to his hotel rooms, like we planned."

"*You* planned, not me, Galina," Rudy corrected.

"I even got into the parlor of his suite."

"So your feminine wiles worked that far?"

"Yes, but no farther. I begged, I pleaded, but the great man refused to see me."

"I told you. Think about it. Why would he change his mind about dancing *Le Spectre* just because you come along, sniveling that you need to dance that role with him right now to help your sagging career?"

Galina seemed to run out of steam and collapsed into a high-backed chair. What she had tried to do did sound childish the way Rudy said it. There was silence in the overheated room except for the hiss of the radiator and the impatient tapping of Galina's toe against the threadbare rug. Finally, she threw back her head and sighed. "You've got to sell it."

"It's too soon. I told you."

"Please. Can't you find another buyer?"

"Why not ask Diaghilev for a raise?"

"Are you crazy? I've only been with the company since January. I can't ask for a raise yet, not until I dance one big role. And don't tell me to use my 'feminine wiles' on Diaghilev! Even *I* noticed Massine sporting a new sapphire ring lately."

"They say it's from Tiffany's."

"For God's sake, Rudy, I need the money *now*!"

"You could go on strike like the subway workers." Rudy grinned, giving his thin face a mischievous little boy look.

"Oh, you idiot!" Galina exclaimed. "As if he'd care! I'm no God of the Dance." Her stomach suddenly cramped and she bent over protectively, waiting out the pain.

"What's the matter now?"

"Nothing."

"If you get sick, you can't dance at all."

"I'm not sick! It's just from all this constant worrying over money. Just sell the damn thing!"

"It's too dangerous."

"Then give it back to me and I'll take it to Levine!"

"And get a fraction of what it's worth? No. We'll wait." Rudy pushed himself smoothly out of the chair. "You'll have to figure something else out for now." He started across the dingy room, scooping up his suit jacket with one hand.

"Wait! You can't just walk away like that!"

"My dear *Galina*," he said, pausing and turning towards her with exaggerated courtesy. "You got yourself into this mess, you can get yourself out."

She reached for him, but he dodged out of her grasp. "How could you say that to me?" she shouted. "How could you?"

"It's true, isn't it?"

"Rudy! Please!"

"Look, I've tried. I've done way more than my part, in case you've forgotten."

"How could I? You're always reminding me!"

"That's gratitude for you! I crossed the line for you many times already, but nothing is ever enough, is it?" He opened the door and swung the jacket over one shoulder. "*Dasvidanya*."

"Thank you very much!" She threw a cushion at his retreating back. It fell short and hit the floor, scattering feathers from a split seam. "Damn it all!!" She stamped her foot as the door swung shut behind him.

She felt tears, hot and painful in her throat, prickling just behind her eyes. She swallowed. Damn Nijinsky! If he had only performed on schedule, she would have a raise to look forward to by now. She knew it! She was good, and dancing with him, everyone would see it. Diaghilev would be forced to notice her!

She began to brush her hair, short brisk strokes crackling with energy. The whole world was against her, but she would fight back! She'd get the money somehow. She paused and looked down at the jumble of dirty glasses, hairpins, teacups, and a bottle of cheap wine. And the sketch she had slid into her purse from the table in Nijinsky's hotel suite while the valet was out of the room. A pencil sketch by Nijinsky should fetch a good price. She smiled with satisfaction and began to put up her hair. At least there was one thing she had salvaged from that embarrassing scene. One thing Rudy didn't know about.

The window was so grimy, it was hard to tell how light it was outside. Galina filled one of the wine glasses and drank, thinking carefully about where she would go first. Only as a last resort would she visit Levine's gloomy den. On the other hand, the devil you know is often preferable to the devil you don't, she reminded herself. Levine was certainly a known devil. She felt the tremor of fear when she thought about him and the power he held over her life.

Setting the wineglass down firmly, she put on her wide-brimmed navy-blue hat with the bird's wing of feathers sweeping back to the left. She scowled at her pert image in the dusty mirror as she pushed the hatpins carefully into place. The hat went well with her new navy-blue and white checked coat, which had cost a breathtaking fifteen dollars at Ralph and Company. She shouldn't have spent her last few dollars on it, but a girl has to look sharp. Not that it was doing her much good lately. For a few weeks, she had thought she might have something going with Adolph Bolm, who she suspected might have something to say about the running of the company. But then his fiancée had arrived from Europe with the Nijinskys. It was almost as if that man was destined to be her nemesis, rather than her deliverer, as she had hoped.

She picked up the sketch and carefully slipped it between the pages of the diary Rudy had given her on her birthday. Making a sour face, she dropped the book into her handbag and took one last look in the mirror. Not bad. Let's hope the old geezer still had an eye for a pretty young woman.

As she emerged from the alley, the wind caught at her skirts and whipped the feathers in her hat against her face so forcefully that the wings threatened to take flight and carry the whole hat away like some great new bird with odd plumage. She clamped one hand on the top of her head and bent into the wind, watching her feet in the worn boots hurry over the cracks and blowing garbage.

Ordinarily, she enjoyed her walk to the subway, taking a keen interest in those around her. There was every sort of person here in this mostly immigrant neighborhood: runny-nosed scrawny children, shrill overworked women whose lives were lived for others, men whose gait was always uncertain with gin. She sometimes thought that people here were born tired. There were others, of course; people like herself who were only passing through, who walked with a hopeful spring to their step and smiled and nodded when she went by, almost as if they recognized her as one of the special ones, someone who was going somewhere. Moving up in the world.

I will join them at Sherry's, she often told herself. I will give interviews and drink champagne backstage with Diaghilev and Nijinsky and the others. I will be someone.

But today, she kept her head down, too concerned with her own thoughts to notice her surroundings. Her mind whirled with anxiety, and if she had looked in a window, she would have seen the same pinched look of fear in her eyes that she often observed in others ever since moving to this neighborhood in January. Today, for the first time, she questioned her future. If she couldn't raise the money, there was nowhere for her to go. Nowhere.

Above her, the El rattled and shook its way along, heading north, as she was. When she reached Canal Street, she joined the crowds that spewed forth from the El, hardly noticing that it was now drizzling with rain. Once more, she hurried along with her head down, almost as if ashamed to even acknowledge to herself where she was going. Every now and then, she paused to catch her breath, to wait for a stabbing cramp to fade. Catching her skirts with both hands, she scuttled across the street, careful to avoid the steaming piles of horse manure left by the jostling carts. The smells that assailed her were strong, mingling animal and spices and onions and garlic with the stink of unwashed men and women. Exotic odors of cooking drifted over the street, reminding her that she hadn't eaten since early morning. Rudy had helped himself to the last of her bread and cheese.

With a quick glance over her shoulder, she darted into a narrow lane between two buildings. Someone not knowing the street might well have missed it. She could feel eyes on her as she made her way along the dim passageway to the barred door that led to Sol Levine's place of business. As she opened the door, tiny bells tinkled, sending cold fingers of dread dancing up and down her spine.

Dust hung in the motionless air. She breathed in careful shallow pants, trying to keep her expression neutral, determined not to register the fear and revulsion the sour smells stirred in her. The room was dark, long, and narrow with only one window, which was so grimy she could see the outside only as shadows, shifting constantly, seemingly without purpose. This half-seen world frightened her almost as much as the airless dead feeling of the piles of cast-off things tumbled behind the high wire grill. Before she even touched the bell on the high wooden counter in front of the wicket, she saw him, incongruous in his neat cleanliness and cheerful youth. The grandson.

"So, the pretty lady comes back to see Sam! You cannot stay away, you love to see me so much, is that it?"

She smiled weakly, knowing she would have to withstand a barrage of what Sam considered sparkling wit before she could broach any question of business. She cocked her head in a listening attitude and leaned forward slightly, as if delighted with his prattle.

Sam always wore a hat that was a little too big for him and his longish hair escaped from underneath its stiff brim in ringlets of reddish gold. His deep-set eyes were pale brown with a glint of red in them, and although his mouth was always curved in a smile, those strange eyes glinted with a watchful reserve. She had no idea how old he was. His face was round and almost unlined, but once they began to discuss business, it was as if the youthful mask slid off to be replaced by the face of his grandfather, a cunning ancient who had come from Poland with all his family twenty years earlier.

Sometimes she thought it might be easier to deal with the grand-father. At least then, the whole humiliating transaction would be quick and impersonal. She would not be expected to laugh at jokes she didn't understand or pretend to respond to Sam's flirtatious cruelty.

"You break my heart, you know that?" Sam said, shaking his head sadly and throwing out his arms. The dark coat he wore was loose and shapeless, but the white shirt sparkled and there was a diamond pin in his black tie. "Do you care how I feel? How my soul yearns for a pretty dancer in my life?"

"Mr. Levine—"

"Sure, sure. All you want is business. They say I have ice water in my veins, you know that? I say they should meet *you!*"

His voice was loud in the cluttered room and Galina drew back, battered by his words. She smiled, her whole face feeling strained.

"So, what have you got for me today?" The transition was so sudden, Galina was left was a silly smile on her face as she leaned confidentially across the high countertop.

She pulled herself back and stiffly opened her bag. "I have some-thing very special," she began. "Something that is rare, valuable because he is in the news now all the time, a name everyone is talk-ing about." She pulled out the diary with the drawing inside.

"Yeah, so?"

"Look. It's a drawing by Mr. Nijinsky. He did it just this morning."

"Nijinsky? He's not an artist. Why should I care what he draws?" But he moved the sketch towards him with one finger, almost as if not wishing to have too much contact with it. His golden eyes stared at it without expression.

"He's so famous now," Galina went on, trying to push him into interest with her words, even though she knew he had already made up his mind. "Many people would pay lots of money to have a drawing by him. Look at how they invite him everywhere. They write about him all the time in the newspapers."

Sam shrugged and pushed the sketch back across the counter. "So sell it to one of those rich people. Me, I'm not interested."

"But look—"

"If you would look at it yourself, you might notice it is not signed. Now me, I trust you with my life if necessary, but the rich ones who buy these things, how do they know the great Nijinsky himself draws this, hmmm? You tell me that."

"But I saw him," she said, the lie slipping out easily. "He did draw it."

"And I believe you. But you see my problem here?" He shrugged again and turned away, suddenly bored with her. He paused. "Of course, if you happen to have any more of those icons once belonging to your dead grandmother, then I'm interested."

"But I don't have anything else with me..."

Sam Levine was already disappearing through the dark red curtains that blocked off the private quarters from the shop. Over his shoulder, he said, "You come back when you have it with. Then we talk."

Galina felt the anger course through her small frame. Anger at herself for not realizing the sketch wasn't signed; anger at Sam for embarrassing her and making her lie; anger at the whole desperate situation that had forced her to come to this place. She pushed the sketch back between the pages of her diary and crammed the book into her purse. For a moment, she struggled with the heavy door before it swung suddenly open, releasing her into the alley.

Back on Canal Street, she dragged herself through the crowds, as exhausted as if she'd been on stage for an entire evening. At least then, she'd have the exhilaration that came when the curtain fell. This time, there was only bone-chilling fatigue. She was near the subway station, but if she bought a ticket, she would then be totally penniless. What would she eat? While Nijinsky and his friends were dining at Sherry's, where would she be?

Putting her head down, she pushed on.

For a while, the streets she passed seemed leached of color, the clamor and shouting mute, as if she were passing through a scene in a moving picture. She plodded along doggedly, heading for her room by instinct, like a hurt animal seeking its den. She wasn't aware that someone was calling her name until a boy jumped in front of her and waved his cap under her nose.

"Lady, you deaf?"

She jumped back, alarmed. "What? What is it?"

"That old geezer's been shouting himself hoarse over there. Can't you hear?" He pointed across the street.

She caught hold of her hat in a sudden gust of wind and peered across the noisy chaos of traffic. An old man in a huge black coat with a red sash was waving and calling her name. She stared, disoriented, the man's image oddly familiar yet grotesque, unreal. She looked at the old face creased in smiles.

"George?" A sudden warmth flowed through her. "George!" She pulled off her hat and waved back to him as she plunged into the thick of traffic. Horses reared. A motorcar honked loudly. Galina paid no attention, rushing across the noisy road into a warm and welcoming past.

George had given her her first real break on stage with his Russian Dance Theater. He seemed to really appreciate her talent, often coming backstage with flowers before the curtain went up, always back afterwards with compliments and smiles. He had believed in her when no one else would. It was the time spent with his company that got her the audition with the Ballets Russes. She wondered if they knew about the dancing bears.

"Ah, Galina, you are a delight for these old eyes!" George exclaimed in Russian as she arrived out of breath in front of him. "You were coming to see me, *da*? I do love these surprises!"

Galina felt the tears spill over as she looked at him. How had he become so old? And this bizarre coat! She recognized it as one of the costumes from the *Peasant* ballet. She started to tell him how often she had thought of him, how many times she had meant to drop into the theater. But wasn't it closed now? The rush of words tangled in her throat and she coughed.

"Are you all right, Galiusha?" His smile faded into uncertainty as he bent to peer into her tear-filled eyes.

"I'm just so glad to see you," she stammered, cramming the hat back on her head in embarrassment. "It's been so long, I mean… It's so good to see a friendly face." She almost burst into tears again.

The old man bent over her solicitously, his rheumy eyes trying to probe the source of her pain. "But the tears. Why is this?" he murmured, his gloved hand patting her arm.

"This hat pin," she mumbled. "I stabbed myself. Can you believe such clumsiness?" She continued to struggle with her hat as he made tutting noises and began to herd her around the corner and down a side street.

"My dear, you must come in for tea and some honey cake. I'm sure there's some left. Maybe even some raisin torte," he went on to himself. "Vera brought me some just the other day. Or was it last week? Of course, you know what they say: If you've eaten it Tuesday, don't look for it Wednesday. No matter. There's something, I'm sure. And tea. Always tea. Here, Galina. Just in here and up these stairs, remember?" He pulled open a side door just down a narrow alley and ushered Galina inside and up the narrow stairs she remembered so well. "My office," he said grandly, opening another door at the top of the stairs.

"Your office." This was not what she remembered. She looked around at the dust and confusion, the old theater posters, the tipsy piles of ropes and boxes of paper, the bits of costumes hanging on hooks along one wall, even three papier mache pillars leaning in a corner. It was as if the old man had tried to cram the whole backstage into this one long room.

George hung up his coat and hat on the huge oak coat rack and then took hers and hung it up, too.

"Quite a commotion at the moment, everything all sixes and sevens, no? But it's early days yet. Always a commotion before the start of a new season. Early days yet. This way, Galochka. Through here."

He opened another door and she followed, speechless. She felt like the confusion she saw around her. "A new season? But I thought…"

"Here we are. It's a bit better in here, you see. Now sit right down here. Just let me…" He grabbed an armload of dusty costumes and flung them in a heap in one corner of the small room.

Galina sank into the tattered recesses of the old wing chair and looked about her wordlessly. Some of the posters she recognized, others were before her time. Leaning against the wall next to the crowded table was a sketch of a girl in a peasant-style dress, her hair in braids, flowers and ribbons flowing down her back.

George was pottering about making tea, boiling the water over a gas ring, gathering sugar cubes and spoons and glasses, all the while murmuring and muttering. Now and then, he would throw a question to her over his shoulder, but she had no idea of what he had said and compromised by making noncommittal noises in reply.

At last, the tea was ready, and he poured her a glass and handed it to her gallantly on a tarnished silver tray. She smiled and thanked him and sipped for a while, finding her own tumult fading as she looked at the familiar face of her old benefactor.

"Your hat is most becoming," he said suddenly, as if noticing it for the first time.

"Why thank you." She smiled, warmed by the compliment. "You always notice the details."

"Aha! It's the details that make a good production better!" He waved his arm in the air with a flourish and beamed at her. "Always the details. So you come to talk about the new production." It was a statement, not a question.

She raised her head, her peace shattered. "Uh, why don't you tell me about it," she suggested, after a moment's hesitation.

"You see that sketch?" He pointed to the peasant girl. "In the fall, we open with a new ballet. And there is a place for you, Galina. If you say the word, the main part is yours."

"But, I thought—"

"No, no! No need to thank me. I know a good dancer when I see one. Now you come back to George and this foolishness with Diaghilev is over, is that not so? A flash in the pan, that one. I always say so."

"George, I can't leave just yet." She looked around for inspiration, looked back at the old man's eager face. "Maybe after I dance with Nijinsky—"

"Bah. That one is all talk about money. With me, you are star. With him, what are you? Window dressing!"

She felt the ready tears threaten again and bent her head over her glass of tea.

"Have a piece of spice cake. Very good. Vera bake it for me. You remember her? She is getting too old to dance now, but she cooks. Oh, such wonderful things she cooks, now she doesn't have to think about her figure any more!"

Galina blinked, trying to remember the woman he was talking about. She felt as if she had slipped into a deep pool and was slowly sinking. Stolidly she chewed her way through a piece of stale cake, like sand in her mouth. Only then did she feel free to extricate herself from the strange dream-like scene.

"Thank you so much for the tea," she said, opening her purse to get out her gloves. She saw the diary, the paper with Nijinsky's sketch sticking out of it. "I wanted to give you something before I go," she said suddenly, pulling it out. She handed it to him with a wide smile. "Nijinsky drew it this morning while I was with him. Isn't it lovely?"

"Nijinsky… Very interesting." The old man peered at the sketch closely, adjusting his glasses. "Thank you, my dear, but I must pay for it."

"No, no." She backed away towards the door, smiling and shaking her head.

"But I insist. This is very valuable." He was digging around in a carved box on the table as he spoke.

"But it's not signed," she said.

"That's not important. I know who did it. Here, and thank you, my dear, for adding to my collection of dance sketches."

He thrust the bills into her hand, looking into her face as he did so. She looked away, stuffing the money into her purse quickly. George began to talk about his new season again as he helped her on with her coat, then escorted her to the door.

Once outside, she breathed in a great gulp of air. As soon as she was around the corner, she looked at the money in her purse. Twenty dollars! A fortune! George, you have saved my life, she thought. She didn't notice the tears rolling down her cheeks.

SEVEN

"Present-Day Men Worship Style Rather than Beauty of Women, Says Mme. Chenu, of Paris."
— *The Washington Post*, April 1916

Girls are flighty, Morgan thought. They waste time – their time, your time. He was annoyed with himself for letting Gloria talk him into a side trip, keeping Nijinsky waiting back at his hotel. As if picking up her new hat was that important. And then insisting on buying gloves to match. It was always like that with women. Just one thing, which led to another, and another. Even his mother was guilty of involving him in long afternoons of errands that started out with two things and ended up wasting his entire day in perfumed salons, drinking tea he didn't want and eating sweetmeats he didn't need.

As Morgan hurried up the steps of the Claridge Hotel, he pulled out his watch and checked it. Nijinsky had every right to be annoyed. He might even have left. And he, Morgan, wouldn't blame him. But the dancer had said he had a sister, so perhaps he would understand.

"Is the Russian gentleman still here?" he asked, pausing at the entrance to the grand salon where he had left Nijinsky.

"I will find out for you, sir," the maitre d' replied. He snapped his fingers and a boy in the hotel uniform rushed over. "Find the Russian gentleman, boy. Mr. Nijinsky. You know who he is?"

"Oh yes, sir." The youngster nodded so vigorously that his flat round hat wobbled dangerously on his head and then dashed off to search through the large room and the bar, darting smoothly around the potted palms and glittering tables.

Morgan wasn't surprised when the boy returned crestfallen. He tipped him anyway and set off upstairs to Nijinsky's apartments.

"Master not here," Yuri said, ushering him inside and closing the door. "He not with you? He say he be with you."

"He was. We were going out, but I had to take my sister home first. That took longer than I expected. You know women."

Yuri made an explosive noise with his thick lips. "Womans all same. Every country. But where he is?"

The tall valet was wringing his hands, his moist dark eyes searching for clues in Morgan's face. The close scrutiny made the young man uncomfortable.

"I'm sure it's nothing to worry about," Morgan said, turning to go. "He just got tired of waiting. We can go another day."

Yuri slid his thin body between Morgan and the door. "You not understand, sir. Maybe bad thing happen. Robbery, accident. Maybe some bad people steal him!"

"Steal? Oh, you mean *kidnap*? But why?"

"Ohhhhh, in America you not know how things go. Bad things sometimes."

"Yuri, everyone wants to see him dance. Why would they kidnap him? Or hurt him?" On the other hand, Nijinsky must be a very wealthy man. His fees for dancing were extraordinarily high.

"You not know. Not everyone love the master."

"I'm sure he's just out doing a little sightseeing," Morgan soothed, but the man's obvious fear was contagious, bringing back memories of gossip and rumors of how bitter the struggle between the Metropolitan Opera House and the Ballets Russes was over Nijinsky's refusal to dance. Memories surfaced about the dreaded Black Hand and their threats against the famous singer Caruso's life. But that was long ago.

Morgan shook his head as if to rid himself of this foreign melodrama. Then smiling, he laid a hand on Yuri's arm and gently persuaded him to move away from the door. "He'll be fine," he told the valet, "but I'll check to make sure there was no accident. Will that make you feel better?"

Yuri nodded, his anxious eyes tearing up with gratitude.

Outside in the sunlight, the dark web of fear spun by Yuri dissipated somewhat as Morgan hailed a cab and traveled home through the bright, bustling streets. The Russian was excitable, overly dramatic. There was nothing wrong. Still, he had promised he would telephone the hospitals, and he would.

As he came into the house, the voices of his sister and mother raised above a more masculine rumble startled him. He glanced at Boothby as he handed him his hat and gloves.

The butler raised an eyebrow slightly. "Miss Gloria," he said, "was caught driving a motorcar alone in the streets. It has caused some…consternation."

"Boothby, you are a master of understatement. What's Uncle Paul doing here? Is he the one who did the catching?"

"Indeed, sir."

"Bad luck for her."

He was just about to take the stairs two at a time to his own rooms when he heard his name shouted by Gloria. Damn, what was she getting him into now? He wheeled around and strode across the marble entry into the conservatory. Gloria, red-faced, with her hair tumbling down on one side, was still wearing the dress she had worn to meet Nijinsky. Please, God, let her not have mentioned that!

"Ask him!" Gloria cried, seeing Morgan. "Just ask him if I know how to operate the vehicle well or not!"

Uncle Paul looked even more pale than usual, looming over the women like a bad dream. "Tell me you're not to blame for this atrocity?" he said, turning to Morgan.

"Atrocity?" Morgan said innocently. "It's hardly an atrocity if a young lady learns how to drive, surely?"

"In the country, dear," his mother said, "it's not remarkable. But in the city? She could have been killed! What were you thinking of?"

"I wasn't even here!"

"But you're the one who asked that the electric car be brought into the city, as I understand it," Uncle Paul said.

Damn the man for his interference, Morgan thought. He felt his face getting warm. "Yes, but I never said—"

"I fail to understand what all the commotion is about," Gloria interrupted, throwing back her head, which only managed to dislodge more of her strawberry-blond curls. "I was just going to visit my friend Elsie who doesn't even live that far away."

"But the traffic is wild!" her mother said, clasping her hands. "It's dangerous!"

Morgan felt the words cut through him. Harry, he thought. Killed in a traffic accident. My fault, just like this.

"The Scottish Women's Corps are risking death every day to drive ambulances in France!" Gloria exclaimed. "I read about them in the *Times*."

"That's irrelevant," said Uncle Paul.

"They are not New York debutantes," her mother added.

"It all comes from women not wearing corsets." Aunt Hattie emerged from behind a rubber plant. Morgan hadn't realized she was there. "In my day—"

"We're not talking about corsets, dear," his mother said, lowering her voice, "but automobiles."

"The devil's invention," Hattie said crisply, shaking out her lace hankie and dabbing at her lips. "I told William no good would ever come from the things. And I was right."

"Oh, for heaven's sake," fumed Uncle Paul. "William went down with the Titanic four years ago. Pull yourself together!"

"Cruel beast!" Hattie stared at Uncle Paul, her hankie clutched to her chest.

"Paul, really," chided Morgan's mother gently. "Have a heart."

"I do apologize, madam." Uncle Paul bowed his head stiffly in Hattie's direction. "However, that does not let *you* off scott-free, young lady. I shall tell Augustus to take a firmer hand with you."

He turned to Morgan. "I need a word," he went on, laying a hand on Morgan's arm and leading him out of the room. "What a lot of caterwauling. That sister of yours needs a husband."

Morgan grinned. "I couldn't agree more," he said. "They're lining up already. Not sure who's in the lead so far."

"Aren't you supposed to be with Mr. Nijinsky this afternoon?"

"How did you know that?" Morgan asked, taken aback.

"Someone mentioned it. When I told your father, he was not best pleased, but we agreed you should keep up the connection in case there's a way to make up for the fiasco at the benefit at some time in the future."

Morgan bit his lip. Why didn't Uncle Paul get married, beget his own sons, and leave him alone? He took a deep breath. "I went to the Claridge about twenty-five minutes ago, but he had already left. I even went upstairs to his suite. His valet was quite convinced something had happened to him." He shook his head. "Excitable people, the Russians."

Uncle Paul put down his gloves on the center table, staring thoughtfully at the huge flower arrangement that filled most of the space. "Perhaps he has his reasons to be worried," he said.

"But surely that Black Hand business—"

"There are other things to fear besides the Black Hand, and they are every bit as dangerous. I think you should go and search for him. I'll contact hospitals in case he has had an accident. He is a stranger to our city, remember."

"Yes, but he's used to European capitals," Morgan protested. "Surely he can handle New York."

Uncle Paul was heading for the alcove where the telephone was kept in a specially built cabinet beside a bench. "Do you have any idea where he may have gone?"

Morgan stared at his uncle, completely mystified at this sudden concern for their foreign visitor. What was the man not telling him? Morgan knew his uncle had ties with the police department, something to do with the League of Decency. Could he be aware of things he couldn't tell Morgan? Perhaps he had been too cavalier about leaving Nijinsky in the first place. But how could he have known the man would suddenly disappear? I wasn't gone that long, he thought. Why didn't he wait? Unless…

He grabbed his hat and gloves. "I have an idea," he said. "If I'm right, I'll let you know."

As he hurried out, Uncle Paul was already at the telephone, asking Central to connect him to Mercy Hospital.

Morgan hailed a motorized cab. There wasn't any need to tell the man the address of Sadie Hahn's; all the cabbies in New York knew the fashionable sporting-house. Although it wasn't far, it took longer than usual to get there through the chaos caused by a horse bolting and overturning a wagon loaded with barrels, which rolled about, blocking motorcars and frightening other horses and pedestrians.

At last, the familiar steps of the old brownstone came into view. A mulatto girl answered the door and ushered Morgan inside.

She looked so young and innocent in her schoolgirl's white eyelet embroidered party dress and the large blue hair ribbon at the nape of her neck. Her voice held the sun of New Orleans in its cadence, and the exotic beauty of her face took his breath away. As she ushered him into the front parlor, he felt at once the immediate falling away of tension as the languor of the place exerted its spell. In this house, everything was arranged for the enjoyment and entertainment of gentlemen. Nothing was expected of him except to pay his bill and respect those within. He sank into the atmosphere with relief, his main reason for coming here forgotten as he sipped his favorite cocktail.

The front parlor was called the Madrid Room. A portrait of Sadie wearing a mantilla hung over the fireplace, the mantel draped with a Spanish shawl. Several ornate fans hung on one wall. An older man with a handlebar mustache was singing 'Ireland Must Be Heaven, for My Mother Came from There,' accompanied on the piano by the young Negro boy who often entertained at Sadie's. Sadie herself sat in an ornate throne-like chair, sipping sherry and smoking a cigarette in a long holder. When she saw Morgan, she came over at once.

"You'd think the Irish were the only ones to have mothers, now wouldn't you?" she said with a laugh. "It's good to see you again, young man. I see you've met Sapphire. Isn't she lovely?"

"An exotic flower in a hothouse of lovelies," he said, bowing over her hand. "And you, the loveliest of them all," he finished. Funny, he thought, he was never flowery with language until he came here. This place with its overripe atmosphere and closed-off languorous air seemed to demand this sort of thing.

"Flatterer," she crooned. "You'd think you were Irish yourself, what with all the blarney," She laughed.

"Only the unvarnished truth," he replied, looking at her heart-shaped face. He had no idea how old Sadie was. She looked young, although there was something in her eyes that belied the svelte hourglass youthfulness of her figure. She probably wore a corset, he thought. Aunt Hattie would approve of that, at least.

There were many rumors about Sadie. Some said that she came from a rich family in Philadelphia and had run off at seventeen with a married man who deserted her in Paris. Others said that she had been a dancer. The thought reminded him of why he had come here.

"Would you happen to have had a Russian gentleman come in within the last hour or so?" he asked, trying to concentrate as Sapphire leaned up against him, her warmth, her subtle perfume teasing him, making his mind lose focus.

"Ah yes, Mr. Nijinsky. Sapphire here did not recognize him and was not going to let him in, but he mentioned your name. Or she thought it might be your name; you know he is not easy to understand when he gets excited." She smiled indulgently. "I, of course, recognized him right away. I saw him dance in Paris with Pavlova years ago." She sighed, looking off into space for a moment as if seeing it all again. "I hope to see him dance again soon," she added. "Can you persuade him?"

"Me? I think you or Sapphire would have more success with that."

"Perhaps. He's in the Turkish Parlor. And the next time one of your friends whom we don't know wishes to visit, would you let me know in advance, kind sir? It could have been quite embarrassing."

"Of course. I apologize. I expected to be with him, so I didn't think of it."

"No need to explain. You'll have to excuse me now. I'm going upstairs to dress for dinner. Would you and your friend care to join me later in the private dining room?"

Morgan rose to his feet and beamed. He had never had an invitation from her before and knew that he had Nijinsky to thank for this one. "I don't know if Jinks has any plans, but I'll ask." He bowed and watched her drift out of the room.

Morgan headed for the Turkish Parlor, a smaller room that he knew was behind the heavy maroon portières on the other side of the entrance hall. Just as he was reaching to part them, he heard raised voices: Nijinsky and another man arguing in a foreign language. Surprised, he hesitated. Who could Jinks possibly know here? As he drew the curtains aside, he saw Nijinsky throw a brass elephant at a young man with a mop of curly dark hair. The man leapt aside nimbly, then turned and rushed out a small doorway Morgan had never noticed before.

"Vaslav!" Morgan rushed over to retrieve the elephant, which luckily had landed on the thick Turkey carpet, doing no harm to any of the carvings placed about the room. He put it back on the brass table. "Are you all right? Should I call the bouncer?"

"Is private." Nijinsky stared ahead for a moment, obviously trying to regain his composure.

Morgan sensed someone behind him and smelled the now-familiar perfume he associated with Sapphire.

The girl seemed to sense what to do. She picked up an empty glass from the brass table and sniffed it. "Cognac?" she asked, her voice caressing the word.

Morgan shook his head. "Look, Vaslav, I apologize for springing my sister on you like that. It was presumptuous of me."

Nijinsky looked at him blankly.

"Gloria can be very persuasive, but I should not have let her disturb you. I apologize." When there was no response from the Russian, Morgan shrugged. "Well, shall we join the others in the Madrid Room? Sadie has invited us to dinner, by the way. Can you stay?"

"I stay." The Russian turned and looked at him for the first time. "That man not honor."

"Honorable?" Morgan suggested.

"*Da.* Not honorable. Me, I have honor."

"I never doubted it," Morgan said, guiding him through the door and across the hall. What on earth was the man babbling about? "Sapphire here will look after you until I get back. I have to make a telephone call."

Once Nijinsky was safely installed in the parlor, Morgan went to the small telephone cabinet under the great staircase and called Uncle Paul.

"I found him. Everything's all right."

"Where are you?" Uncle Paul asked, his voice tense.

"At Sadie's. We're invited to dinner."

"Good. Morgan, I want you to keep a close eye on Mr. Nijinsky, understand?"

"Why? What do you mean?"

"I want our distinguished visitor to be safe. Do you want to go through this again? Worrying that something has happened to him? No? Then keep tabs on him and report to me."

"To you? Why—"

"Listen to me. If you do this, we'll know where to look next time he does a disappearing act. Someone should know."

Why, Morgan wondered. What should someone know? It felt like spying, but he had long ago realized it was useless to argue with Uncle Paul. He was already on the outs with his father; he couldn't afford to alienate another member of the family. Reluctantly, he agreed, but it made him uncomfortable. If I do this, he wondered, am I honorable? And why would Uncle Paul possibly need to know where Nijinsky is?

EIGHT

"HOW MANY CARS CAN THIS COUNTRY ABSORB?;
Reeves Predicts 5,000,000 Motor Vehicles in Service in the United
States—1,000,000 New Ones a Year."
                                        —*New York Times*, April 1916

Great-Aunt Edwina was the only member of the family who lived in an apartment. She had moved into the Dakota on West 72nd Street when it opened in 1890 and she fully intended to die there, as she was fond of telling anyone who visited. In spite of her acid-tipped tongue, she knew a great many people, although she often said she had more love for animals than humankind. After spending a few tense times with his family lately, Morgan was beginning to share this opinion.

"Nobody mentioned his name, Gaddie," he said, unconsciously using his childhood name for Edwina, "but I knew they were thinking about Harry when they jumped on me about teaching Gloria to drive. I know they blame me for his death."

"My dear young man, they do nothing of the sort," Edwina said. "What utter balderdash! Harry was killed by a runaway horse. Have some dandelion wine. It does wonders for the outlook."

Morgan lifted the glass to his lips automatically and took a sip. He shivered slightly and looked at the cloudy greenish-yellow liquid in the glass. He had always been able to talk to his great-aunt about anything. And no matter what he told her, she never judged him. She watched him intently now, canted to one side in her Morris chair, her twisted back pushing her forward, her dark eyes bright like tiny searchlights never leaving his face. Usually there were several dogs sharing the space with her, most of them as misshapen as she was. She wanted only the abandoned dogs, she said. The perfect ones would find good homes on their own. Right now, she had a toothless King Charles spaniel lolling at her side and a beagle with only three legs curled at her feet. A black and tan dachshund with no toes peered out from behind her back, its dark eyes as inquisitive as hers.

"I know you were very close to your brother Harry," she said now, refilling her glass with the cloudy liquid. "You did everything together and it's natural that you miss him, but his death was an accident. You had nothing to do with it."

"But if I hadn't decided to race that Karlz car for Hochman that day—"

" 'If' is the biggest word in the English language," she said, pushing the dachshund out of the way so she could shift her position. "That happened two years ago, Morgan. I know, this time around Easter brings it all back for you, doesn't it?"

Morgan nodded. He and Harry had been going home for the Easter holidays. They had agreed to motor to New York together in Morgan's car, but at the last moment, Morgan decided to leave later after driving one last test run for Hochman's latest modified car. He had dreams of qualifying for the Metropolitan Cup Trophy a few weeks away in that car.

"I always suspected that was the reason you stopped racing," Edwina said.

Morgan shrugged. "It's just a hobby, Aunt Eddie." He smiled at her. "I enjoy following it as a sport, but right now, I need to find something more respectable to do with myself."

"Aha! A career. Well, you know what you don't want to do." She grinned impishly.

Morgan groaned. "Yes, indeed I do. My effort at reading law was a dismal failure."

"Of course, it was. You were trying to take Harry's place, follow in his footsteps, and that never works out."

"Father thought it was a good idea."

"Yes, and sometimes your father is a blithering idiot. Now help me out of this cursed chair. Martha! Bring me my turban."

Edwina's maid, who was not much younger than Edwina herself, came limping in, plumed turban and walking stick in hand, as if she had been waiting behind the door for this summons.

Without a word, Edwina plunked the hat on her stiff white curls and thrust two long jeweled hatpins into it. Morgan winced.

"Drive me to the Roof Garden, Morgan," she said, taking the walking stick form Martha. "I'm meeting some of the girls there for tea. Not that I ever touch the wretched beverage."

With Edwina clutching Morgan's arm, they swayed out to the elevator and descended in regal silence to the porte-cochère and Morgan's motorcar.

"And where are you going now?" she asked, bending her neck to look at him sideways.

"Another stop on my road to possible employment."

"Good luck, dear boy." She fitted a cigarette into her porcelain holder, lit it, and settled herself for the drive. "It's never a good thing to let go of a dream."

Morgan was sitting in a leather armchair in the Colbert Club, sipping Old Fashioneds with Bunter Picket later that day when he received a telephone call. Bunter puffed out his already-full cheeks, an annoying habit that was only one among the many that Morgan had put up with for the last hour as he tried to find out if Bunter would have a place for him in his real estate empire. It was galling to come here like this since Bunter had been only three years ahead of him in school, but there was at least a slim possibility that these old school ties might give him an in. And getting a position on his own was worth any groveling necessary if it meant he could please his father.

Both young men knew why Morgan was there, but so far, topics of conversation had ranged from the war and the troubles of the Romanovs to the right way to savor oysters. The wily Bunter was not going to be the first to bring up the real subject.

"You had better take that call," Bunter said.

Pompous jackass, Morgan thought as he made his way to the telephone booth. Whatever happened to that funny young man he remembered at school? Like the Billy Bunter character in the Greyfriars stories they all read in the school library, Bunter had been allowed very little pocket money and was perpetually figuring out clever ways to get more food or to wheedle a loan out of someone so he could buy candy. Morgan figured he was probably laying the groundwork for his business skills later on. His pilfering exploits had been notorious, but his sense of humor and generosity with his friends always got him by. Now, however, he had lost some weight and much of his sense of humor and had apparently turned into his recently deceased skinflint of a father.

Morgan made his way to the telephone booth and sat down on the padded chair as the club's steward closed the door to give him some privacy.

The voice on the line surprised him. "Chuffy Harris here, Vanheusen. Sorry for tracking you down like this. Your friend Langley is to blame, I'm afraid. I do apologize."

"Nothing to apologize for, I assure you," Morgan said. His heart sped up a little.

"I wanted to know if you'd be interested in driving for me next week. It's just an exhibition event to test how my cars will work out on the new wooden track I just built. You'd be driving my modified Maxwell. Dickie Farrington said you used to test Hochman's specials, so I figured you can handle it. What do you say?"

Morgan moistened his lips, cleared his throat. "That was two years ago, Mr. Harris."

"My regular driver's in the hospital with a collapsed lung, so he's out of commission. I've asked around, and you seem to be a reliable choice."

"Thank you, sir, but as I said, I'm not driving anymore."

"You'll be doing me a favor, believe me. A big favor. And it's just till I can find a replacement for Jimmy."

Morgan hesitated, tempted by memories.

"These are the best German engines money can buy, Vanheusen," Harris went on, as if sensing Morgan's secret longing. "They're better, easier to control than Hochman's modified airplane engines, and that's a fact. And it's just a few times, okay? Help me out here. I need to see how she stacks up with a group of good drivers at the helm."

"I don't know, sir," Morgan hedged.

"Can we at least meet today? I can give you all the specs, and you can talk to one of my mechanics. We're at the Checkered Flag. Can you come now?"

"I can be there in twenty minutes."

"And I can tell you how to get to my country place," Chuffy said happily, as if was all a *fait accompli*. "Oh, and by the way, I've promised to take the ladies to the ballet as soon as that Nijinsky fellow decides to dance. I hear you're a friend of his. Is there any way you can introduce us to him? The ladies would be over the moon about it if you could."

"Ah, well, I can ask him." Morgan frowned. "I'll have to let you know."

"Very good, very good."

"I'm afraid I can't guarantee anything, sir," Morgan went on, remembering the crowds of people at Sherry's waiting to talk to Nijinsky, the mounds of flowers at his hotel, the telegrams and letters piled everywhere, the constantly ringing telephone.

But Harris had already hung up.

"Right," said Morgan to the dead line.

"You look a little out of sorts," Bunter said, looking him up and down when he returned to his chair. "Who was on the line?"

"Chuffy Harris."

"Made his money in something rather unsavory, didn't he?"

"No idea. Look, Bunter, I'm sorry to leave so suddenly, but he's invited me to drive one his new cars in some demonstration or other, and we have to discuss things."

"Everyone else on his long list of drivers more out of sorts than you?" Bunter asked, with a sly smile.

Morgan smiled back. Nothing could ruffle him now. "Apparently."

"So now he's counting on the amateur to save the day. Can't stay for tea first?"

"Not if I'm going to save the day," Morgan said.

As he made his way jauntily out of the club, he wondered if giving in to temptation would qualify as saving the day. Or would it do just the opposite for him? At the moment, he didn't care.

NINE

"NIJINSKI WILL DANCE
Signs Articles of Peace with Managers of the Ballets Russes"
—*New York Times*, April 9, 1916

News that the Russian star had agreed to dance at the Metropolitan Opera House was greeted with delight at breakfast tables all over Manhattan on Sunday morning. In a grimy café a world away from the Claridge Hotel where the man of the hour nervously paced, George Kassevetsky pored over the *Times* article, moving his finger along each line. The news filled him with consternation. He read the short article twice to make sure he had understood every treacherous English word. "'Army of lawyers'," he muttered. "All so crooked, they could hide behind a corkscrew, just like Diaghilev."

"You should ask that Nijinsky fellow to dance in your theater," the young waiter suggested, putting a saucer of sugar cubes on the table. "That would bring in the crowds."

"Don't put crazy ideas in his head," cried Misha, George's stage manager. "He has enough of his own already." He looked at his old friend in alarm, watching for the telltale flush of anger. But instead, George just nodded his head slowly, as if agreeing.

"Misha, I am not mad, but there is something to the suggestion…something…" George murmured.

Misha shook his head and poured vodka into his tea.

George spread the newspaper out and began to look for information on the program Nijinsky would be dancing. He found the ad and began reading: "Diaghileff's Ballets Russes, Wednesday matinée. First appearance of Nijinsky: *Petrouchka, Scheherezade, Le Spectre de la Rose*."

"Pretty safe choices," Misha remarked.

"And a new ballet, *Le Prince du Lac*. Look! My Galina will dance with Nijinsky! At last, she gets her dream."

"And you're happy? I thought you wanted her to come back?"

George's hooded dark eyes gazed into Misha's face. "That's my dream, old friend, not hers. I know that…most days." He smiled sadly and dropped another sugar cube into his glass of tea. "Besides, after she dances with that fellow, *then* she comes back to me!"

By Monday afternoon, most of the good seats for Wednesday's mat-inée performance at the Met had sold out. By Tuesday, there was nothing left, and scalpers were doing a brisk business. Those who were lucky enough to have boxes at the Met, like the Vanheusens, were besieged by friends who usually didn't care for ballet, every-one curious to see the notorious dance star.

Nijinsky himself was experiencing frightening emotional swings. At first, he had been elated, seeing this settlement that was mostly on his terms as a victory, a symbolic cutting of the cord between him and Diaghilev. But as time went on, he began to worry. It had been two years since he had danced in public, and part of this time had been spent interned by the Hungarians as a Russian spy, cooped up in a small house with no one to talk to from the outside world. He had kept in shape, although there was barely enough space in those narrow rooms to practice the leaps and pirouettes for which he was so famous. He had practiced every day on the ship coming across the Atlantic, had rehearsed faithfully with the company in spite of the chilly atmosphere, so different from the old days when he was Diaghilev's darling. He heard the rumors of what that man was saying about him: that he had let himself go, had grown fat and lazy. Without the strong guidance he was used to, he rode his fear and insecurity alone, plunging from dazzling joy to dark despair. One thought gradu-ally emerged from the swirl. The American people should know how he felt about them, how much he appreciated their help in getting him here and how he would give them his best, in spite of what they might have heard. Diaghilev had taught him much, including the importance of publicity.

Nijinsky decided to give an interview about this to one of the legion of journalists who had besieged him on hearing the news he would be dancing.

He chose a reporter from the *New York Bugle,* a smaller paper perhaps, but their reporter had written his note in Russian and said he, too, had been born in Poland. They could speak in Russian, and that was important. He knew his command of other languages was tenuous at best. Without either his wife or Sergei to interpret his words, he needed to know he would be understood.

The reporter was waiting in Nijinsky's dressing room after the dress rehearsal. He jumped to his feet, looking very American with his red hair springing up on either side of the part in his unruly curls, his casual jacket, a soft-collared shirt, and his tie a little askew.

"I'm Andy Cass. I am honored, sir. Thank you so much for choosing me for this interview."

Nijinsky grunted and shook his hand. "I need everyone to know that these delays were not my doing. I need everyone to know that I appreciate that the American government did so much for me and my family, helping to rescue me from imprisonment, hunger, and fear. All I want is to dance. I am glad that this is now possible."

The young man was scribbling furiously in his notebook as Nijinsky accepted a fresh shirt from his dresser and slipped it on. "Tell them the version of *Faune* they will see now is the true version, the one I directed, not what has been performed since January. I had no idea what had been done to some of my ballets in my absence. This was done without my knowledge. You understand? You have that down?"

"Yes, yes."

"So I want to tell everyone this has not been just about money, though of course an artist of my standing ought to be paid an appropriate amount. It is about artistic integrity. I have nothing against Léonide Massine, you understand," Nijinsky went on, flushing with the effort of getting everything out and appearing fair in the process. "It is just that the changes were made without my consent, and it is *my* ballet." He heard his voice getting shrill and paused to take a deep breath.

"I have heard that the girl dancing the new ballet with you is American. Isn't this unusual?"

Nijinsky took a moment to answer, startled by the sudden shift in subject. "She is Galina …Petrovna. I don't know where she is from, but she speaks Russian like everybody else in the company. She is an understudy, and the principal she is replacing sprained her ankle last week. She had a fall on some stairs, I understand. Very bad luck for her."

"But good for Galina," Andy said, with a engaging grin. "Speaking of luck, our readers love to hear about backstage life. For instance, do you have any little rituals you perform each time before you go on stage? Any good luck charms? I have heard many dancers are very superstitious."

"I have my silver flask given to me many years ago by Prince Pavel Dmitrevitch Lvov. I keep it near me always when I am to perform." He held the flask up for Andy to see: the carved silver with gold tracings, the diamonds tracing his initials on the side.

"It's beautiful."

"And who is this, Vasli?" came a voice from the door. "A secret admirer?"

"Sergei," said Nijinsky, clearly startled. "Why are you here?"

The big impresario surged into the room, followed tentatively by a slender young man with large dark velvet eyes.

Andy jumped to his feet. "Andy Cass, sir, from the *New York Bugle*," he said in English.

"Yes. I remember you." Diaghilev smiled, then turned back to Nijinsky, one heavy eyebrow raised.

"You talk to the press, so can I," Nijinsky countered, looking like a sulky child beside the towering impresario.

The young man with Diaghilev stepped forward and shook Andy's hand. "I am Léonide Massine," he said.

"He's a choreographer," Diaghilev added, staring at Nijinsky with piercing eyes.

"Didn't you dance some of Mr. Nijinsky's roles before he arrived?" Andy asked, looking at the slight, dark-eyed man more closely.

Massine dipped his head in acknowledgement and touched Diaghilev's sleeve. "We must go, Sergei," he urged in his soft voice. "We have appointment, remember?"

The impresario glared one last time at his star dancer, bowed curtly to Andy, and withdrew.

"So that's the one who changed the choreography," Andy

murmured, switching back to Russian.

"He says they made him do it." Nijinsky slumped down in his chair and seemed to have lost interest in the interview.

"I'd better go now," Andy said, getting to his feet again. "I have more than enough for an article. It will be in tomorrow's paper, right before the matinée."

Nijinsky jumped up and reached for an envelope on his dressing table. "Tickets for the performance," he said. "I always have a few to give to friends. I have few friends here, so I give to you."

"Thank you! I really appreciate this."

Nijinsky smiled, his face suddenly playful, faun-like, the transformation startling. "I appreciate a good interview."

Wednesday afternoon, and the Metropolitan Opera was filled with balletomanes and society people, curious to see the dancer whose story they had been following in the papers for weeks. Some saw him as the one who would save the Ballets Russes, whose season had become lackluster and disappointing. Others were only interested in seeing the latest big name, so they could talk about the experience with their friends. And some were drawn by the slightly salacious reputation attached to the name of the Russian star.

In the opera house, the great staircase was crowded with well-dressed patrons, and the murmur of their voices filled the glittering hall. Far up in the gods, poor Russian immigrants mingled with dance students, cramming the steep aisles and shouting to each other, waving their programs like fans to move the sluggish air. Below, the boxes fanned out in a golden semicircle, slowly filling with the families and friends of the wealthy patrons, and even though this was a matinée, jewels and formal dresses were the norm there.

In the Vanheusen box, Gloria settled herself on her velvet chair, craning forward to see if she could spot any of her friends.

"Don't peer so, darling, it's unattractive," her mother said, dropping her shawl over the back of the chair gracefully and raising her lorgnette.

"Is Papa coming?"

"Not this time. He says he can't take time away from his work."

Gloria smiled. From the tone of the response, she suspected her mother thought her father was nowhere near his great oak-paneled office this afternoon. She glanced at Morgan. He shrugged.

"Uncle Paul will be here," her mother went on, "though why, I cannot imagine, considering how he goes on against poor Mr. Nijinsky."

"Probably wants to makes sure he is wearing a League of Decency-approved tutu," Morgan whispered.

"Men don't wear tutus, silly," Gloria whispered back.

"Look, there's Molly Hewet-Astor in a positively bilious green hat," her mother said.

"She's wearing rather a lot of jewelry for a matinée," Gloria murmured, and then she spotted her friend Muriel a few boxes along on the next tier up. Not recognizing any of the other people in the box, Gloria's curiosity blossomed. At that moment, Aunt Hattie arrived with her companion, making such a commotion that Gloria was able to slip away unnoticed.

As the brocaded door of the Vanheusen box whispered shut behind her, Gloria felt a great bubble of lightness rise inside, a ridiculous sense of freedom that bore little relation to reality. In truth, most of the people she passed knew her face, if not her name, either from her recent coming-out photographs in the society pages of the paper or from one of the numerous parties and balls she had been attending during the season. Or perhaps they recognized her face because she loved coming to the theater, the excitement, the emotions rising from the stage making her heart swell with joy or sorrow. And secretly, she loved another chance to wear her new gowns, although to admit it would smack of vanity.

She paused to get her bearings, watching the surge of people still coming up the stairway as she thought about how lucky she was to even be here after the incident with the electric car. If Uncle Paul had had his way, she would be at home now doing needlework. She shivered. She hated needlework.

"Did someone walk over your grave?" A young man with springy red curls was holding a program out to her. "Yours, I think?"

Gloria drew herself up to her full five feet, three and a half inches. "I beg your pardon?"

"Forgive me, that was very forward of me. It's just that you shivered, and where I come from, we have this expression…" He stopped. "My apologies. You dropped your program." He again held it out to her.

Gloria looked at him, one hand on the single string of pearls at her throat. She was sure she had left her program back in their box, but the man had such lovely bright eyes, the color of amontillado in a glass. And he was someone new! She was bored with all the young men in her circle. She extended her gloved hand for the program. "Thank you. I have heard that expression before." From my Irish nursemaid, she thought. "But I was just thinking of something unpleasant."

"You are far too lovely to think of unpleasant things," the young man said with a bow.

"You are a flatterer, sir." She fanned herself with the program. She should turn away now with another word of thanks, but she couldn't bring herself to do so.

"I'm not very good at it, am I?" He smiled disarmingly. "Andy Cass, at your service." He bowed. "I'm a journalist, so I'm here working, doing a piece on Mr. Nijinsky."

"How fascinating. I'm Gloria Vanheusen." She held out her hand and they shook. "I'm so excited to be here to see Mr. Nijinsky dance in a real ballet. We held a benefit where he danced at our summer place, and that was simply amazing. But here on stage with the full company...oh, that will be something special! Which paper do you write for, Mr. Cass?"

"The *Bugle*. We're small, but growing all the time. Usually I don't get a chance to write about theater, but since I speak Russian, this was a natural for me."

"What do you usually write about?" she asked.

He looked a little uncomfortable. "City politics, crime, nothing very nice."

"Oh, you must lead such an interesting life!"

The crowds had thinned and the lights over the rows of boxes were dimming, signaling that the curtain would be going up soon.

"I've enjoyed talking to you, Miss Vanheusen," he said, as if suddenly aware of the change in the atmosphere. "I don't suppose..."

"I've enjoyed talking to you, too. If you like walking in the park, perhaps we will meet again. I favor Central Park by the reservoir in the morning, around eleven or so. It's so beautiful there, is it not?"

"One of my favorite places," he said. "I often take a stroll there myself." He bowed and she turned away, her face burning. She had to stop herself from running back to the box. All thoughts of Muriel's mysterious friends had completely vanished.

TEN

"NIJINSKY PUTS LIFE IN THE BALLET RUSSE.
He Shows Grace and Finish at His Debut in *'Le Spectre de la Rose'"*

—*New York Times*, April 13, 1916

Nijinsky paced around his lavish dressing room, now and then stopping to stretch, leap, twirl. In spite of the luxury and size of the place, there wasn't enough room to really let loose in a way that would release the tension quivering all through his body. Romola had come back for his debut, as loving and supportive as ever, but he had finally persuaded her to go to her seat in the house. She was not enough. He needed what he used to have backstage, what he used to feel before a performance: the support, the love, the waves of admiration. He had thought he could step back into that, into all of it. He hadn't realized how much had come from Sergei alone, how things had changed in three long, strange years. Although most of the company treated him with the utmost respect, it was not universal. His encounter with Ivan an hour ago in the drafty backstage area as he was making his way to his dressing room came back to him as a vivid illustration.

"I am glad you have come to your senses at last," Ivan growled, blocking his way. "I just hope it's not too late to save the company from ruin."

"Let me pass."

"Have you any idea how close we are to the brink? And then you finally arrive and haggle like a fishwife in the marketplace."

"Is it my fault I couldn't get here faster?" Nijinsky exploded. "I was a prisoner! There is a war on over there!"

"That is no excuse for what you did once you got here," Ivan shouted. By now, others were arriving, including Yuri, his tall form inching closer and closer. "This is Galina's debut, too, remember," Ivan hissed, and stepped back. Nijinsky walked by, his head high, but he was sure he heard the sound of spitting once he was past.

He shook his head to clear it of the sour memory. The music of *Le Spectre de la Rose* rushed in, filled his mind, thrummed in his body. He longed to be on stage, to lose himself out there in the lights, the hum of expectation, the rustle of the unseen perfumed crowd in the darkness beyond his world, the stage: that faceless, breathing mass that made him come alive in ways nothing else did. And yet he was afraid of it now.

He looked around wildly at the many bouquets of flowers that filled the dressing room, at the hundreds of telegrams of good wishes. But it was all foreign somehow, all from a world he no longer knew. America saying they loved him, without even knowing him. Right now, he wanted love from someone who did know him. He yanked a handful of flowers from one of the bouquets and flung it against the wall.

Silently, Yuri moved to pick everything up, rearrange the flowers, wipe the water from the striped wallpaper.

"All will be well, maestro," he soothed.

Nijinsky gnawed at his thumbnail in silence.

"He is a very busy person tonight," Yuri went on, watching his master carefully.

"It is very rude," Nijinsky exploded, jumping to his feet and beginning to pace again. "It is an insult!"

"No, no. Never an insult for you from Diaghilev." Yuri made a soothing noise low in his throat, almost like a purr. "It's because of the letter sent to Lopokovna a while ago. She opened it and a strange white powder flew out into her face. She thought someone was trying to poison her."

Nijinsky turned around and stared at his valet. "It was meant for me," he said, his voice low.

"No, no, there is no mistake. It was definitely for her, and it was harmless."

"So that's why we had to change the order of the program," Nijinsky said. But he wasn't convinced the letter incident was as harmless as Yuri insisted, and the uncertainty only added to his stress.

He turned back to the mirror and checked his heavy stylized makeup, then added powder and outlined his eyebrows again. "He still could have found the time to drop by." But the fire had gone out of him, and now he sounded like a sulky child. He adjusted the petals on his flowered cap. At least, Massine had not danced this role. It was his alone.

"Are they ready backstage?" He twisted around to look anxiously up at Yuri's broad, dark face. "The men, are they ready to catch me?"

"Yes, maestro. Just as you rehearsed. I checked myself that they were in place."

Everyone who had been in the company in Paris knew about this: how important it was to have strong men, their arms linked, ready to catch Nijinsky in the wings. When he came flying through the window of the set for *Le Spectre de la Rose*, the force of his leap was so powerful that it was impossible for him to stop himself. There was always someone in place as well to massage his heart. That, too, had been arranged, Yuri assured the star. A doctor, called in by Diaghilev. But Nijinsky remembered the days when one of those men used to be Diaghilev's valet, the days when he didn't have to think of these details himself. He felt calmer now as he put the finishing touches to his makeup, trying to banish all thoughts that had nothing to do with the dance. He was the Rose, a young girl's dream. He touched the flask that Prince Lvov had given him years ago. A symbol of love, the Prince had said, and now his good luck piece.

Seeing the gesture, Yuri leaned forward. "It will be in place backstage as usual."

Nijinsky nodded and got to his feet as the five-minute knock sounded at his dressing room door. "*Allons-y*," he said and thought of Paris, suddenly feeling the warm breath of another on his skin.

The drafty backstage was filled with dancers crowding around to see Nijinsky perform in public for the first time in two years. Some of them had never seen him, having joined the company after he had left, and although they had been in rehearsals with him, had all been pulled up several notches higher by his exacting presence, there was nothing like the magic of a first appearance, especially one that had been so long in coming. They parted before him respectfully, murmuring their good wishes, and although he barely heard or saw them, he felt their presence like balm on the soul, soothing away the salt of his run-in with Ivan.

Lopokovna was on stage, dancing languidly, dreamily, a vulnerable inexperienced young girl. The high-backed moss-green chair she would fall asleep in was waiting, the needlepoint stand nearby, the gilded harp in place. A swath of white filmy curtain fluttered from the high window frame through which he would make his entrance and exit.

Lopokovna sank into the chair, her eyes closing in sleep. Nijinsky took a deep breath and stepped into the spotlight that now hit the window. He lifted onto his toes, his arms curved above his head. The crowd burst into applause. He was home. Nerves drained away as he sprang through the window and began the delicate dance of seduction as the girl's dream-lover, heady as perfume, insubstantial as a flower, strong as desire. After the first burst of applause, the entire theater fell silent, all eyes following the flickering, leaping creature they had waited so long to see. As he made his incredible flying exit through the window at the end, they gasped, then burst into wild applause.

Nijinsky lay panting for air in the arms of the burly men who had caught him as he came hurtling into the wings. Another man knelt beside him, massaging his heart.

"Can you go on, sir?" the American stage manager asked, looking anxious. He had never witnessed this strange ritual before, and his face was pale in the dim light.

Nijinsky nodded, still not trusting himself to speak. The men helped him to his feet. Out front, the applause swelled as he walked on stage to join Lopokovna. Rose petals fell around him. They bowed together, then she urged him forward. Everyone rose to their feet, clapping and shouting. He stood in the middle of the stage and bowed once more. Simply. First straight ahead, then to each side. He stood a moment longer, then walked off stage and went to his dressing room.

"It was not my best," he said at once.

"It was wonderful, maestro," Yuri assured him.

Nijinsky frowned, thinking of several tiny details that had not been quite perfect. It was never quite perfect. One day, perhaps…

Massine rushed in, his face flushed. "I have seen genius!" he exclaimed.

"Just as we expected!" Diaghilev boomed, coming in behind him.

"Wonderful, darling Vashti! Amazing!" Romola threw her arms around him, careful not to get greasepaint on her dress. But Nijinsky only smiled and nodded, murmuring his thanks as he began to take off the heavy makeup, his mind already in the world of the next ballet he was to appear in.

His performance in *Petroushka* was equally appreciated, and after that, everyone backstage but him was drinking champagne and laughing, praising him, toasting his success, not even waiting for the last *pas de deux* he would dance in *Le Prince du Lac*, the new ballet that closed the program. He frowned as their excited voices drifted into his dressing room from the hall, He was sure they hadn't noticed the slight wobble at the beginning of *Spectre* when he went almost on pointe. They hadn't noticed any of the tiny details that now nagged at him to improve on next time. Even Sergei had not noticed. He leaned closer to the mirror as he checked his makeup for the final role this afternoon.

Galina, in makeup and costume for her brief shining moment with the star, was watching it all from the wings. The *corps de ballet* was on stage now, swirling around in the court dance that opened the new ballet. She would go on next, with the world's greatest male dancer as her partner. Galina Petrovna had arrived. By the time Nijinsky appeared beside her in the stunning gold and turquoise costume of the unknown prince, she was almost hyperventilating.

"Deep breaths, deep breaths," he murmured in Russian.

Her mouth was dry, her throat scratchy like sand. "Water," she said. "Anything." Someone handed her a silver flask and she drank greedily, finally forcing herself to stop. Too much would be worse than nothing at all.

She tightened the cloth bands that made the chiffon into clouds around her arm. The corps rushed past them. The lighting changed. The flute warbled the opening bars, and Nijinsky nodded to her. She glided on stage, a young girl waiting for the unknown prince from the neighboring kingdom to answer her invitation to the ball.

She didn't have long to linger in the courtyard before she turned and saw him: the one she thought was the prince, bathed in a blue light, his turquoise costume shimmering like the surface of his secret watery domain beneath the lake glimpsed in the background.Galina knew the part of the uninvited Prince of the Lake had been choreographed for Nijinsky, but the short ballet had never been performed before. Their *pas de deux* was only six minutes, but it gave full reign to Nijinsky's power to project an odd otherworldly seduction as he slid and leapt about the stage, luring her on further, farther into his world from which escape was impossible. She knew Nijinsky had never been really satisfied with how she danced the role, and she flung herself into it now with more intensity than she had ever danced before in her life; his physicality seemed to draw it out of her, just as his fascinating character drew the princess to her doom.

Nijinsky was pleasantly surprised by her passion, although her technique was still shaky. Luckily, the part was relatively simple and the girl's considerable acting skills could carry it well enough. Halfway through the piece, Nijinsky swept her up in his arms and they leapt across the stage together. The Prince had almost vanquished her, but at the last moment, she turned, hesitating, floating back towards center stage. He leapt after her and took her in his arms again. She shivered, almost stumbled. Gently, he swung her into the next position, but she clung to him, shaking now more violently.

Pulled out of the dream, Nijinsky held her more firmly. "Not yet," he murmured, but her eyelids flickered strangely and she slid to the ground, a full thirty seconds too early. He bent over her, arranging her arms in the right position on the floor, then leapt away, improvising as he went, taking the spotlight with him, away from the inert girl in the middle in the stage. Some female trouble? he wondered, part of his mind reorganizing the steps. The orchestra crashed on and the spotlight continued to follow, though the man operating it must be confused. With a final perfect series of *jetés*, Nijinsky paused, did a pirouette, then stooped down, gathered the girl in his powerful arms and carried her triumphantly off stage, followed by deafening applause as the corps rushed past him to continue with the closing scene.

"What happened?" asked Adolph Bolm, in costume as the real invited prince, waiting to do the final *pas de deux* with the girl's sister. "What's the matter with her?"

Nijinsky shrugged, patting the sweat from his face with the towel handed to him by a stagehand. "I think she fainted."

"Christ! Just what we need," muttered Bolm. "Never mind. She'll snap out of it. They always do." Hearing his cue, he moved into position.

"That silly girl has ruined my new ballet!" shouted Diaghilev, rushing in to join the crowd. "She's fired!"

The doctor, who had stayed backstage after his stint with Nijinsky, was kneeling beside Galina, taking her pulse. "She's dead," he said quietly.

"She just fainted," said Nijinsky, staring at the pale girl at his feet.

"Nonsense, you fool! She can't be dead. You heard what Vaslav said."

"Nevertheless, the girl has no pulse."

On stage, the dance went on. Bolm and his partner finished their *pas de deux*, and the corps surrounded them in a ring of ribbons as the curtain came down.

"Get her out of here," shouted Diaghilev. "Clear the space for the curtain calls. Listen to them! I haven't heard music like that since Paris!"

"What'll we tell them?" asked one of the dancers.

"She fainted in my arms," Nijinsky repeated.

"There, you see? Nerves. They'll understand that, especially after the letter excitement of a few hours ago."

Somehow, Diaghilev saying this seemed to make it so, and they all took their curtain calls as usual. The impresario explained about the nerves of the neophyte dancer, and the audience clapped and clapped until at last, the curtain came down for good. The doctor was waiting for them in the wings. There was no sign of Galina's body.

"Maestro, I had to call the police."

"You *what*?"

"This is not Russia, Mr. Diaghilev. It is not even Paris. I tell you, it was not a natural death. I *had* to call the police."

Diaghilev's face was very red as he glared at the cowering doctor. Then he reached over and gathered Nijinsky to his side. "Come," he said, "we go to Sherry's. Now!" With his other arm, he grabbed Lopokovna and shepherded both dancers through the backstage area towards the star dressing rooms. "Get dressed quickly and come out the stage door. I will have motorcars waiting. We do not want to be here when the police arrive. That doctor is a crazy mad person. She died of some nervous ailment. A heart attack. We go and celebrate the success of our Vaslav. Nothing will spoil that. We do not speak of this other thing, you understand?"

"But Sergei—"

"Hush, Vasli. Go. I'll wait in the car. I'll send someone to tell Romola to meet us at Sherry's." And he swept out the stage door with Massine in tow.

Adolph Bolm stood watching after him for a moment. "Nerves," he said, shaking his head. "Even Sergei will not convince the police she died of nerves."

Nijinsky shrugged. "Maybe it's true," he said, heading for his dressing room, the music of the *Le Prince du Lac* still faintly singing in his mind.

ELEVEN

"Young Dancer Faints in Nijinsky's Arms."

—New York Bugle

"That poor girl, swooning away like that right on stage," Mrs. Vanheusen remarked, smoothing on her gloves as the party started down the great staircase at the Met. "How embarrassing for her."

"Far too highly strung, those people," Uncle Paul said. "Look how that Nijinsky bolted after dancing at our garden party. No manners, these Russians."

"If you want my opinion, it's because of the corsets," Aunt Hattie said.

Gloria stifled a laugh. "But I thought it was good to wear corsets, according to you, Aunt Hattie." Her mother shot her a warning look.

"Well, yes, indeed it is, unless you lace too tightly, my dear. That is nothing but vanity. We just witnessed what that can accomplish, didn't we, Georgina? Public humiliation."

"Georgina?" Morgan said, looking around.

"You may be right, dear," Mrs. Vanheusen agreed soothingly. It was not a good sign when her sister's imaginary friend, Georgina, showed up outside the house. Perhaps she should take Hattie home quickly.

"Nijinsky was heavenly to watch as the Rose, wasn't he?" Gloria enthused. "And as the Prince of the Lake luring her away to her death under water—just perfection! Worth waiting for, wouldn't you agree?"

"A little too girlie, that Rose thing," Uncle Paul remarked, with a faint shudder. "And that costume! Like something Gloria would think up."

"That was the point," Mrs. Vanheusen murmured.

"But that *Patricia* was not at all genteel. The music." Hattie shuddered. "And the colors! So primitive."

"*Petroushka*, dear," said Mrs. Vanheusen. "We saw it in February when you were ill, with Mr. Massine dancing the Nijinsky part. Quite different, wouldn't you say, Gloria?"

"He moved more like a puppet. This way was more emotional, I thought. I liked it better."

"Terrible music," muttered Aunt Hattie. "I'll thank you to warn me next time they do that program and I'll stay home with Georgina."

By this time, they were standing outside with the well-dressed crowd, everyone heading for places like Sherry's or the Ritz, hailing cabs lined up at the curb, or signaled to their own drivers double-parked in front of the theater. Uncle Paul snagged a cab and waved them over.

"Are you coming, Morgan?" Gloria asked, leaning out of the window.

"I'm meeting friends."

Gloria grinned. "Vroom, vroom," she whispered. "I know where you're going."

"That's what you think." He laughed as she retreated into the cab, to be replaced by Aunt Hattie's anxious face.

"Georgina!" she called. "Wait! We can't leave Georgina!"

Uncle Paul pulled her back inside, none too gently. "She's gone home," he said firmly.

Morgan heard Hattie burst into wailing tears as the cab drove away.

Detective Sean 'Danny Boy' Sullivan stood on the stage of the Metropolitan Opera, hands on hips, glaring at the nervous policemen grouped around him.

"Gone?" he shouted. "What do you mean 'gone'?"

"Skedaddled?" suggested Constable Hopper, his round, scrubbed face beaming with hope that he had guessed the correct answer.

"Sir, we didn't get the call in time," Sergeant Riley stepped in quickly, seeing his boss's face turning a dangerous red. "I'm thinkin' mebbe the toffs waited till the high mucky-mucks took off, like, sir, before givin' us the call. The girl was dead. She wouldn't be any deader is what I'm thinkin'."

"Swell. Thanks so very much for enlightening us all with the brilliance of what you're 'thinkin',' sergeant, and it's lucky for us you're here now, isn't it?" He rocked back on his heels, his blue eyes blazing. Secretly, however, his sergeant's conclusion was more or less what he had decided himself, but he preferred to keep the troops on their toes and fear worked well for him.

There were six of New York's finest assembled around Sullivan, all more used to dealing with petty criminals and lowlifes than people who attended the theater or foreign dancers. Most of them felt 'all to sea,' as one of them put it, but in a way it was exciting, too. Something new. Something to talk about in their neighborhood bars after work. It was a pity Mr. Nijinsky and the Astors and such had already left.

"We locked the doors once we got here," the sergeant went on, "except for lettin' Lady Divers and that swell from the Russian embassy leave. I mean they couldn't have done anything, now, could they, sir?"

"You nincompoop!" shouted Sullivan. "That's not the point."

The sergeant took off his hat and scratched his head. "It's not, sir?"

Sullivan sighed and rocked forward on his toes. "We've got to look like we're impartial, see? We can't give anyone special treatment."

"But sir, we always—"

"Members of the press may be here," hissed Sullivan. "You want to make the wrong kind of headlines, you do it on your own time. Now we need to question everyone before releasing them, in the slim hope that someone might actually have noticed something."

"Sir, the ones we talked to already didn't even know anything had happened. They thought it was part of the act, like."

"Lord save us. A girl dies right in front of them and they think— Gianelli, take Peters and Hopper and talk to the few ladies and gents in the salon. Riley, you're with me. The rest of you, help the others guard the doors."

There was a scuffling of feet as they thumped off to do their jobs.

Sullivan got the stage manager to bring a table and three chairs, and then invited him to sit down. He opened his notebook, then looked at the man for a long, cool moment. The stage manager was an American, tall and rail-thin, dressed with the casual informality favored by theater people: his shirt open at the throat, his sleeves rolled up, his velvet waistcoat hanging open. Although the man had seemed at ease to begin with, he soon began to fidget under Sullivan's scrutiny.

"Your name is Donald Wynters, correct?" the policeman began.

"Yes, sir. I'm employed by Mr. Gatti-Casazza of the Met to oversee all the productions here."

"And you were here tonight?"

"Yes, sir. Right over there." He pointed off stage right.

"Who else was about when it happened or right before?"

"Well, it was pretty crowded. It's a short ballet, but uses a lot of dancers. The whole *corps de ballet*, for example, and Mr. Bolm and Miss Lopokovna, the other two soloists, were waiting to go on, so it was crowded."

"Anyone else?"

"Their props man and another guy who came to give Galina something."

"What? What did he give her?"

"It looked like a locket. She put it on and kissed him, and then… I don't know. I was busy."

"What's the name of this man?"

Wynters shook his head. "I've seen him around, but frankly, I don't know all their names. I think he's a set painter, if that helps."

"Is there anything else you can think of?"

"Well, someone gave her a drink of water from a flask, I think."

"And where is the flask?"

"I don't know. I didn't pay much attention."

"Is the doctor still here?"

"I don't think so, sir."

"Oh, Lordy."

"He gave me his card, though." Wynters handed over a card

with a Russian name and an address in a fashionable part of town.

"Any of the main dancers still here?"

"Ivan, sir. He's the only principal who seems to want to talk to you."

"Good! Now we're getting somewhere! Send him in, please."

Wynters smiled and stood up. "Good luck," he said and went off to find the dancer.

Sullivan was just thinking that this was an odd parting remark when a dark young man wearing an extravagant red cravat bounded across the stage towards him.

"At last, you here!" he cried, reaching across the table and taking Sullivan's hand in both of his. "I wait for you. I talk, tell what others not say because they fear Sergei."

"Hold on there. Please sit down and tell me your name."

"Ivan Alexsandrovich Novikoff."

Sullivan started to write, then passed his notebook to Ivan. "Now tell me what happened."

"What happen? I tell you. Nijinsky murder only woman I ever love! My Galina!"

"Nijinsky! Now wait a minute here—"

"No one listen to me! I tell you, is true."

"Were you there?"

"I tell you, I see all! All! I come to watch her dance with Vaslav."

"Who?"

"Nijinsky. I see her take drink from silver flask. I see her die in his arms! Only woman I ever love!"

"Let me get this straight. You saw Nijinsky give her a drink from a silver flask?"

"Well… I only see flask. Nijinsky on other side of her."

"Sir, I'm afraid we can't look into this kind of accusation. No one actually saw him give her anything."

"But is flask of Nijinsky!" shouted Ivan, leaping to his feet and leaning over the table in his intensity to be understood. "All know silver bottle belong to Nijinsky! He has it with him always. No one would dare use it."

"My dear sir, the young lady most likely died of a heart attack brought on by all the excitement of her first major performance. I'm afraid this drink from a flask means nothing."

Ivan dropped back onto his chair and burst into tears. "No! No! Is not true!"

"Jesus, Mary, and Joseph," muttered Sullivan, handing over his handkerchief. "Pull yourself together, young man."

In another part of the city, another man was in tears about Galina's death. George Kassevetsky sat on the floor in his cluttered office, his knees to his chest, his arms wrapped around his head.

"Is my fault! All my fault! I should have tried harder to get her to come back to me!" he sobbed in Russian.

"No, no, George." Andy knelt in front of the crouched figure, patting his heaving shoulders. "You know she wanted this more than anything. And to die on stage—in her idol's arms, no less— what a way to go! She will be remembered now."

"You are cruel boy, Andrushka."

"George, listen to me. Her heart failed. I was there. I saw it."

"Me, too, I am there. Upstairs in second balcony. I run down, but no one was allowed backstage. Diaghilev's orders. That…that… sorcerer!"

"George, I talked to the doctor."

"Pshaw! Doctors. What do they know?"

"There was no foul play, just really bad luck and bad health. She must have had a heart problem for ages, but no one knew."

"Oh, my little Galina! Look how no one mourns for you but old George. My lovely little flower, always promising to come back to me after one more dance, one more role, and now… Oh Lord, kill me now! My life is worthless after this."

"For God's sake, George, your life is far from over! You have others to think about, remember. Your theater to think about."

"But without Galina, what is the use? I am old and tired. Oh little one, my flower. I am so sorry! Forgive me! Forgive!" He flung himself full length onto the floor in front of Andy and began to wail in earnest.

Alarmed, Andy got up, dusted himself off, and looked around. He went to the rosewood chest inlaid with mother-of-pearl, took out a blue vial, and tipped some of its contents into a glass. He added water and knelt down beside George. Supporting his shoulders, he held the glass to the old man's lips. George drank down the cloudy liquid. His watery eyes found Andy's for a moment and gazed into them.

Andy felt like a traitor. He got up and put a record on the Victrola. The strains of *Les Sylphides* filled the room, dancing with the dust motes in the air.

George leaned back against the wall, his eyes closed. Andy just hoped the old man wouldn't remember that this was the role Nijinsky would dance on Friday at the Met.

TWELVE

"NIJINSKY EXCELS AT THE MET"

—*New York Times*

At Sherry's after the performance, Nijinsky withdrew behind a mask of silence, barely aware of Caruso's exuberant greeting, the mayor stopping at their table, all the congratulations and bravos and toasts drunk in his honor. He sipped his Vichy water and nibbled at his food, letting Romola and Diaghilev speak for him. When the early evening editions came out, people took turns reading the words of praise about his performance. Although the *New York Times* thought his dancing as the Rose a bit on the feminine side and his costume far too girlish, the dancing itself was extravagantly praised. The *Musical Courier* had no doubt he was "the greatest of all male dancers." "Nijinsky is not of this earth," proclaimed the *Globe*.

It was amazing to him that no one seemed to have noticed the girl's stumbling, her slide into unconsciousness, seeing only a lack of technique, a not-expected nervousness in a young and inexperienced understudy thrust too soon into the spotlight. He was the toast of Manhattan, but he felt as if he was acting a part. But Massine was the actor, not him. He glanced across the table and met Massine's dark velvet eyes studying him. He noticed the large sapphire ring on Massine's slender hand and looked away.

The sight of Lopokovna in a group of admirers across the restaurant reminded him of the letter she had received, the frightening cloud of powder released into her face. And he saw Galina take his silver flask from some young man's hand and drink from it. My flask, he thought. That was meant for me. Both were meant for me, and no one even noticed.

He leaned forward to catch Diaghilev's eye. "The poison was meant for me," he said in Russian.

The big man turned towards him and smiled soothingly. "No, no, Vasli. There was no poison today." He leaned closer, his wine-flavored breath caressingly warm on Nijinsky's face. "I have always taken care of you," he said, and for a blissful moment, Nijinsky relaxed into that warm voice. Then Diaghilev turned away again. The dancer felt a sudden fury boil inside him and poked Romola.

"We go now," he said, standing abruptly.

Back at the hotel, his anger focused into one point: Someone had tried to kill him and no one seemed to care. He shut himself in the bedroom and screamed and threw things, shouting unintelligible words when Romola tried to reason with him. At last, exhausted, he flung himself into bed and refused to get up again. Hours went by, and he still hid under the covers, unresponsive to his wife's pleas, while the maid cowered in her tiny cubicle and Yuri hovered uncertainly.

He couldn't explain even to himself why he felt this pressure, this fear. His debut had been a wild success. That should have meant something, and in one way, it did. He barely knew Galina, knew only that her fainting had nearly spoiled the new ballet, had detracted from his role, although the audience barely noticed.

"I will never dance that ballet again!" he screamed through the door in one last coherent sentence before resorting to pure sound to express his pain.

On the other side of the door, his wife shook her head, knowing he couldn't dance that ballet again here anyway. There was no one left who knew the role of the young girl. Reluctantly, she admitted to herself that this time she might need help from Diaghilev.

Detective Sullivan took in the large elaborately furnished room that formed part of the Nijinsky's suite at the Claridge Hotel, the two chandeliers, and the group of men and one woman grouped around a pale, exhausted-looking Nijinsky seated behind an oak table. He had not been expecting this. It was almost, he imagined, what having an audience with the pope might be like. Well, maybe the cardinal of New York. He recognized the bulk of the Russian impresario

Maestro Diaghilev, the foxy face of the manager of the Metropolitan Opera House, and the well-known lawyer who had taken part in Nijinsky's legal dispute earlier in the month. He also remembered the warning phone call he had received from the mayor's office.

He bowed. "Thank you for seeing me, Mr. Nijinsky. I have only a few questions to—"

The woman raised her hand. "My husband has a typed statement of what he remembers about the incident," Romola Nijinska said. "There are two copies: one in Russian, one in English, which I have translated." She rose to her feet and handed the English version to Sullivan.

Abruptly, Nijinsky began to read the statement in Russian, the foreign words flowing seemingly without a break until he was finished. According to the version Sullivan had, it didn't amount to much. He thought the girl had fainted from all the excitement, so he carried her offstage and left her in the care of a doctor. Then he went to his dressing room, changed his clothes, and left for Sherry's on 44th Street.

"Sir, are you telling me you did not know the girl was dead before you left the theater?"

Romola cried out, put her hand over her mouth, then whispered into Nijinsky's ear. On the dancer's other side, Diaghilev was also whispering something.

"He knows nothing about this," the impresario said, his voice booming in the large room. "Mr. Nijinsky has told you all he knows of the matter."

"And I appreciate your co-operation, sir. Can you tell me anything about the dancer Ivan Novikoff? What is his connection to the girl?"

Nijinsky looked up, obviously surprised by the question. "I come here only one week," he said. "The girl, I do not know. Ivan is in Paris when I am with company there. Is good dancer, not great, but good."

At least, I've got you talking, Sullivan thought, but the man had a point, The star dancer had not been here long. "Could you tell me someone who knows both the girl and Ivan?"

"Anyone in the company now except Mr. Nijinsky would know them," Diaghilev said, "but all I can say is that Ivan falls in love with girls all the time. Yesterday, it is Katia. Today, it is Galina. Tomorrow, who knows?"

A blond young man stepped forward and bowed his head. "I am Pavel Yevtchenko, *monsieur*. I know Galina a little. We talk. She not love Ivan back. He has the heart broke… is very very sad about this. He think maybe she change one day and love him. I think not." He stepped back.

"Thank you. That's a help." Sullivan was about to turn the page on his notebook when Diaghilev stepped forward.

"We have answered your questions. Now the maestro needs to rest. He will dance tomorrow, and this is very tiring, you understand."

"Yes, yes, of course." It galled Sullivan to have to back away, but he didn't want another call from the mayor's office, either. Slipping his notebook into his inside breast pocket, he bowed and left.

"Jesus, Mary, and Joseph," he muttered to Reilly as they hurried down the stairs. "I felt as if I practically had to back out of the ruddy room!"

His sergeant chuckled. "All part of the job, sir. Nice change, I would think."

"I don't know, Roge. Give me a good honest crim any time. Know where you are with a crim, now don'cha?"

"Mebbe so, sir. Mebbe so." But he wasn't convinced. He liked hanging about in luxurious corridors as opposed to smelly back alleys. Gave him something interesting to talk about with the missus. But he decided it was wise to keep this to himself. After all this time, he didn't even know if Sullivan had a missus.

For the majority of New Yorkers, life went on undisturbed by the death of a girl who had lived among them all of her short life. The majority of them were completely unaware of what had happened since none of the major papers had even picked up the story, it being difficult to get any information from the Ballets Russes.

But Andy had been there, had waited by the stage door until the girls from the *corps de ballet* came out and he had talked and charmed his way into their confidence.

"Galina, she was in heaven with this part," one of them gushed, "and then the devil struck her down."

"I saw her American man give her that kiss of death."

"The letter to Lopokovna with the witch powder? That was a sign, a warning."

"I saw Galina drink from a crystal goblet and then it vanished. Poof. Just like that."

"I saw a flash of light and a stranger was there, handing her Nijinsky's silver flask, and then he was gone and she turned really pale, as if she'd seen a ghost."

"Some say she made Irina fall down the stairs and get injured so she could take over the part. She paid the price."

"I saw her die," another said. "I saw her soul leave her body."

"No, you didn't," objected the young man who had his arms around her from behind. "She died in the taxi on the way to the hospital."

"I saw it, I tell you! Her spirit rose right up into the catwalk above the stage, a writhing puff of smoke like the willis in *Giselle*."

Andy had forgotten how superstitious dancers could be. He wondered what the police were making of all this. He turned to another one of the men. "Did you see anything before it happened?" he asked.

The man shrugged. "I was watching Nijinsky," he said. "I was thinking how I would like to dance with him."

Andy thanked them and walked disconsolately out into the street. He had just started to make an impression on his editor with his first interview with Nijinsky. This story had looked like the chance of a lifetime, but he couldn't get anything tangible to follow up on. His one ace was that he had known Galina before she was Galina, when she was just plain Gail McKinnah, whose Irish mother took in laundry and lived two doors down the street from his family. He remembered his own mother trying to help when the McKinnah son got into some trouble with the law. He remembered the anguish when the second son died of whooping cough. The McKinnah children spent a lot of time with the Russian family next door, where Gail must have picked up the language, as children do. But what counted was that years later, he remembered Gail turning up as Galina and joining the Kassevetsky Russian Dance Troupe. He sighed. Poor George.

Andy figured it was a minor miracle that Nijinsky had chosen him for the interview, was it only yesterday? But there was no chance he could get in to talk to the man again. Not now. Once again, he felt the story of his life slipping away. What he ended up writing was more of a puff piece about a young girl achieving her dream, only to die in the arms of her idol, and about a man who was devastated but vowed to go on with the dance.

"Talk about fairy tales," Andy muttered to himself later that day after seeing what the editor had done to his story: where he had placed it, how little attention would be paid to it. "Story of my life," he muttered. He took out his watch. Time to head to the reservoir at Central Park. Would Gloria be there? The way his luck was going, he doubted it.

"Gloria Isabelle Vanheusen, I'm surprised at you!" Muriel threw her head back and laughed, the feather on her hat trembling with her mirth. "To look at you, you'd think butter wouldn't melt in your mouth."

"This from the person who actually knows one of the bloomer girls," Gloria countered.

"How did you convince your mother to let you take the motorcar?"

"She wasn't home. Fritz won't tell her. He promised."

"You've got the male staff wrapped around your little finger, haven't you?"

"Just Fritz," Gloria said, "and maybe Boothby on a good day." She steered the electric car carefully into a vacant spot near the path into the park and turned off the engine. "Morgan usually pays some boy to look after the motor for him when we go out together," she went on. As she looked around, several ragged urchins appeared as if summoned by her words.

"We'll look after it for you, miss," one of them piped up, holding out his grubby hand.

"Wait," said Muriel. "We'll give you a penny now and one more when we come back, if the car is safe."

The boys grinned widely. "Sure, miss. We'll shine it up for youse, too, won't we, mates?"Gloria handed one of the boys a penny and hurried into the park. The odor rising from them was unpleasant. "Why can't they take more baths?" she murmured.

"My maid went to a suffragette meeting last night," Muriel said as they strolled along. "I'm thinking of going with her next time."

Gloria stopped. "You're going somewhere with your maid?"

"This isn't about Alice. It's about women. All women. Wouldn't you like to be taken seriously? Be allowed to discuss politics with the men after dinner? Get to vote like your brother? Women in California can, you know."

Muriel had talked like this before, and it always disturbed Gloria. In theory, she agreed, but politics bored her and the idea of discussing anything with the men made her feel sick. They always smoked cigars after dinner when the ladies had retired, but saying this would probably make her sound stupid to Muriel.

"It's dangerous going to those meetings," she said instead.

"And what you're doing?" Muriel snapped open her parasol.

"What I'm doing may get me into hot water with my mother and father – if they find out. I don't risk going to jail and getting my name in the papers. Besides, maybe he won't come."

Muriel patted her arm. "He'll come," she said. "And I think you're brave to do this. Maybe your next step will take you even further. Maybe even to a meeting with Alice and me."

Gloria shook her head. She didn't want to think any further than this moment right here in the park, with the nannies walking babies in perambulators, boys running with hoops, and three girls sitting in a circle playing a clapping game. She used to play this with her sister, Daisy. That seemed so long ago now.

"You must think me very shallow," she said hesitantly. "It's just that all that scares me. Mother is strongly against it. All I hear at home is about the brazen hussies—"

"Is that the one?" Muriel interrupted, nodding her head slightly towards the water.

Gloria caught her hat as a gust of wind swirled around them. She jammed a hat pin more firmly in place. "Yes," she said. She felt her stomach flutter pleasantly as she looked at the bright red curls, the jaunty assured walk, the careless clothes. So different from the young men in her circle, none of whom would have picked up on her subtle invitation or would have ever worn that checked suit, which looked as if Andy had slept in it. "Sloppy and loud," her mother would say, but she thought it looked cheery.

"Miss Vanheusen," Andy exclaimed, stuffing a notebook into his pocket and extending his hand as he came up to her. "Such a pleasure to see you again."

"Indeed, Mr. Cass. And so unexpected." She felt her cheeks blush as their hands touched. "This is my friend, Muriel Standish." She paused for a moment, on the brink of mentioning what they had been discussing, then afraid he might think Muriel more interesting than she.

"Serendipity is such a wonderful thing when it occurs, is it not, Mr. Cass?" Muriel said with a sly smile. "I hear you're a lover of the ballet. What do you think of the sensational Mr. Nijinsky?"

"I think he is indeed a sensational dancer, Miss Standish," Andy replied. "I just did an interview with him yesterday."

"And how is he bearing up after the unfortunate incident during his debut?"

"It's more than an unfortunate incident when a young girl dies," Andy said, his light brown eyes flashing.

"One wouldn't think so, reading the papers," Muriel said, turning away. "Excuse me for a moment, will you? I see a friend I wish to speak to." She moved away, soon disappearing as she sank down on a bench, presumably to talk to her friend.

"Please excuse her," Gloria said, upset about being left after Muriel stirred up this strange unsettled atmosphere. All she had wanted was some light pleasant chat to get to know the man a little. "She isn't usually so sharp-tongued."

"She was not to know that I knew the girl," he said.

He offered Gloria his arm, and they began strolling under the arch and along the central walkway, heading east.

"You knew her?" Gloria faltered. "I'm very sorry."

"It was a long time ago, Miss Vanheusen. Please don't distress yourself. It's just that I agree with your friend. It *is* sad that Galina's death caused so little attention."

"It's like a cruel fairy tale written by Hans Christian Anderson," Gloria said. "She gets to dance with the prince, but then she has to die."

"Exactly," Andy said, his voice soft.

Gloria wanted to hold her breath, to stop time, to keep this moment close and seal it up in memory so she could revisit it any time she wished. This perfect moment when two near-strangers understood each other completely, shared the exact same feeling at the same time. She had never felt this way before.

"Are you all right?" Andy paused, looking at her with concern.

"Just a little out of breath," she said.

"I apologize. I tend to walk quickly. Shall we return along this footpath?"

Gloria smiled and nodded, tilting her head in such a way that he would not be able to see her face under the broad brim of her hat. Would not be aware how wide her smile had become.

THIRTEEN

"SPEED RECORDS WILL BE BROKEN.
Chuffy Harris says his speed demons push to new records."
                                                    —*New York Racing News*

Driving out of town to Chuffy Harris's place on Thursday took longer than Morgan expected. The streets in town were crowded with shop girls and clerks with slicked-back hair and shiny suits all pouring out of offices and stores to breathe some fresh air and find somewhere to eat. Once traffic thinned out, he opened up the engine and sped along, leaving a trail of dust in his wake.

It felt good to be out in the country, away from the clatter and screech of the elevated trains and the constant crowds of the city, but Morgan was still a bit nervous about getting in a motorcar trial run again. It had been two years since he had driven anything with that much power. Add to that the fact that he wasn't used to the track Chuffy had constructed behind his sprawling country house, one part of his brain kept telling him he was a fool for agreeing to do this. The other side, however, exulted at the chance to get back to something that gave him so much pleasure, something he was really good at, or had been. And *I'm doing him a favor,* he reminded himself. *Just this once.*

Where was the place? It should be coming into sight by now. He slowed down and checked his watch, then pulled over, looked around, and realized he was lost. He had been so caught up in his thoughts, he must have taken a wrong turn somewhere along the way in the tangle of similar-looking country roads. With a curse, he swung the motorcar around and headed back the way he had come, keeping an eye open for the right turn.

He had never visited the Harris place. His father, like Bunter Picket, considered the man a parvenu with no taste or social standing. But the racing world, including Morgan, was not interested in anything but what motorcars Chuffy had and the purses they might win for the betting crowd, not to mention the drivers.

Morgan found the turnoff, but as he slowed down at the open wooden gates, he was surprised to see horses in the field: fine Arabians, by the look of them. Perhaps a few of 'the ladies' Chuffy kept mentioning were learning how to ride. Or perhaps horses, like a big house and staff, were considered a necessary adjunct for the newly arrived man of the world.

He drove around the long sweep of driveway and parked beside a varied group of long shiny cars and sporty little two-seaters. Quite a few people seemed to be here for this private affair. A young man-servant in a ridiculous dark-red uniform escorted him through the house to the back garden where a munificent spread had been laid out on white tablecloths that were waving in the breeze. A crowd, mostly men, wandered about with plates in hand, talking and drinking. Some sat in a group further away; among them, Morgan recognized a few reporters, including Dick Farrington. This must be a more important event than Chuffy Harris had let on. Still further, half hidden by a dense hedge, was the track Harris had had built so his drivers could gain experience on wooden surfaces. Morgan swallowed. He had never driven on a wooden track before; Hochman did his testing on dirt tracks.

While he was digesting this, Harris swooped down on him and pumped his arm enthusiastically.

"This is the man I was telling you about," Harris said, pulling Morgan over to the nearest group. "He's a friend of Mr. Nijinsky."

"An acquaintance only," Morgan said quickly.

"Wish my wife was here," said one man, nodding and smiling. "All she talks about is this man. What is it about him that's got all the ladies in such a state?"

"Not this lady," said a young woman, waving her cigarette in a long tortoise-shell holder. "I interviewed him for my paper, and believe me, I have no idea why ladies are swooning about so. He has enormous feet and thick ankles, and no social graces that I could see. Why, the man is a Cossack who can barely put a sentence together."

There was a pause while everyone stared at the woman. She smiled a slow, lazy smile and took a puff at her cigarette. "It's all true," she whispered and turned away.

Chuffy laughed nervously. "I guess she's entitled to her opinion," he said, "but I'd rather form my own assessment of the man when I meet him." He winked at Morgan. "Excuse us, ladies and gents."

"I apologize for being a little late, sir," Morgan said as they walked towards the outbuildings where the track was. "I took a wrong turn."

"Won't need to worry about that on the track," Harris said with a grin. "But I guess you won't have time for a practice run. Not that it matters," he went on, not giving Morgan time to protest. "This isn't a race against the other drivers. It's a test for the car. It just arrived this morning, so nobody really knows what it can do."

"I see."

"Nervous?"

"Yes. As I explained to you earlier, I haven't driven for two years. I may have lost the knack."

Harris shook his head. "One never loses the knack, only the nerve. Have you lost that?"

"I guess we'll find out," Morgan replied coolly.

One of Harris's specials was coming off the track when they arrived, driven by a man Morgan recognized, a professional driver from Philly. Behind him came another car driven by millionaire Carlo Benedetti, whom Morgan had met at various debutante functions in the city. They exchanged nods, and Morgan turned away with a silent oath. His secret life could get very public, very soon. Why hadn't he thought of this?

"Good luck, Morgan," Harris said, clapping him on the back. "Burn up the track, just not the car."

Morgan smiled and watched Harris bounce over to talk to the mechanics. He began to run over in his mind the checklist of things Hochman used to go over with him before each run. I wish he was here now, Morgan thought. But Hochman was out of the racing business these days, having turned in another direction: building planes, which he shipped over to England for the war.

Morgan stepped into his coverall, shoved his goggles up on his head, and waited while two mechanics pushed his baby-blue Special to the ramp. Unlike the stripped-down open cars he had driven for Hochman and a few others, this one was more like a Delage, with a small cockpit the pilot climbed into and then slid his legs out of sight inside. Morgan thought it looked ugly and unbalanced—the front too long compared to the stubby round back. And where was the spare tire? On the other hand, it should corner better than some.

He climbed in and looked about, getting the feel of the machine: instruments, clutch, gas, brakes. It didn't need a crank to start, he noticed, but it was a distinct disadvantage not to get a chance to warm up. Still, it was a test, not a race, he reminded himself.

And then he looked over at the car next to him and stiffened. Kit Caulder.

"Hey, Vanheusen! I heard you were all washed up after your brother frightened the horses."

Morgan's fingers tightened on the wheel. Steady, steady, he told himself. You know he always does this, tries to knock you off-balance just before a race. And this isn't a race, he reminded himself again. He turned away, focused on the dash, checking his instruments. He hadn't seen Caulder in two years and would have been happier never to see him again.

"What's the matter? Don't want to shoot the breeze with a pal before I plow you into the dirt?"

Before Morgan had a chance to answer, Harris walked over to the edge of the grass and put his hands on his hips. "Just get out there and pull out all the stops," he said, his loud voice carrying easily to the four drivers and the mechanics and pumpers standing a few feet away. "Don't pay any attention to our visitors. I count on you to feel her out, let me know what you think, and why. Good points, bad points; you know the drill. Now, gents, to the starting line. Remember, qualifying speed is ninety miles an hour at Sheepshead Bay. We're pretty sure these cars can all do that. The question is, how much more can they do, eh?" He winked, bounced up on this toes, rocked back on his heels. "So when the flag goes down, twenty laps around for the first run. We'll see how that goes. Gentlemen, start your engines."

A combined roar split the April sunshine as all four motorcars burst into life. The sound focused Morgan as nothing else could, and he followed Beneddetti onto the track, taking his place beside the wiry Italian. To his right, Kit pulled up to the starting line, revving his engine and grinning like the imp of Satan he was. Just before the flag went down, he called, "Eat my dust, has-been!"

Morgan felt the insult like a hot stiletto under the skin. Never mind that the man might be right; never mind that this was not a race; never mind that this was just a favor he was doing for Harris, a one-time thing. He was damned if Kit Caulder would win!

The flag came down. The dull roar accelerated into an earsplitting screech as the machines took off around the track. Morgan nearly ran into Benedetti, the powerful engine of his car responding faster than he had anticipated. Recovering, he slowed down for a moment, letting himself get the feel of the machine, drive with his brain, as Hochman always told him.

First turn, he swung a little wide, compensated, slipped back on track. Kit was in the lead now, followed closely by Benedetti. The pro from Philly was biding his time, probably doing his job and not worrying about his ranking, Morgan thought, as they rumbled into the fourth lap.

Caulder whizzed by in a blur and waved at him.

Morgan poured on more power, checked his speedometer. Eighty-five. Ninety. Ninety-five. He swung a little wide on the turn again and cursed. Keep to the inside, he told himself. Into the stretch, he revved up, hitting a hundred and ten as his machine shuddered and bucked. He had passed Benedetti, who seemed to be having some kind of engine trouble, and was closing in on Caulder.

By lap fourteen, the pro from Philly was out with a broken axel, Benedetti had dropped back, and Morgan was neck-and-neck with Caulder, going into the far turn. Morgan glanced over and saw Caulder's mouth moving, but the roar of the engines made it impossible to know what he was saying. The next instant, Caulder swung closer, trying to cut him off. Morgan set his jaw and held firm. Caulder pulled ahead, then slowed slightly, his machine almost scraping the blue special. Morgan turned the steering wheel, trying not to overreact, moving closer to the inside edge. But Caulder moved with him. Morgan pulled on the brakes, turned the wheel, but he was travelling too fast. His machine spun out of control, lifted into the air.

Bastard!

The car hit the ground on the inside oval, tilted to one side and almost flipped. Morgan held it steady, plowing into the grassy bank piled with sand bags and spun around, facing the track. The engine stalled.

Morgan swore. He was still jammed into the special. Voices were shouting, coming nearer and nearer. He clasped the steering wheel tighter in his sweating hands. It steadied him.

A group of men in coveralls rushed towards him, running across the track, leaping over the plowed-up ground. One carried a fire extinguisher; another had a leather case over his shoulder, like a doctor's bag.

"Are you all right?" shouted the man with the bag.

"I'm fine," Morgan shouted back. "The track needs a steeper bank on that side." He pushed up his goggles and twisted around to watch the lone car still on the track slow to a stop near them.

"Bad luck, sir," said the second man. "You almost had him there."

Morgan blinked and set his jaw as he clasped the proffered hand to help him out.

"Hey, Vanheusen! I said I'd bury you, didn't I?" Caulder stood on the rise of ground Morgan's car had just plowed up, laughing.

"I'm not dead yet," Morgan shouted back. In fact, he felt curiously elated. I'm back, he thought, and you'll regret what you just tried to do!

FOURTEEN

"WHO WAS GALINA PETROVNA?"
—Andrew Cass, *New York Bugle*

"*The young dancer who fainted on stage during a performance at the Ballets Russes on Wednesday, only to expire shortly afterwards, was identified in the program as Galina Petrovna. She was in reality a young American girl named Gail McKennah, who grew up in New York in a poor area favored by Russian and Polish immigrants. Under the name Galina Petrovna, Miss McKennah danced for several seasons with the Kassevetsky Russian Dance Troupe and joined the Ballets Russes in February of this year, where she was an understudy for several roles and danced as a second soloist in two ballets.*

'*We are much saddened by this tragedy,' said Sergei Diaghilev, impresario of the company. 'We had no idea she had a weak heart.'*

When contacted by this reporter, George Kassevetsky was distraught. 'She was returning to my company in the fall,' he said. 'She had a brilliant future ahead of her.'

The dancer is said to have had a brother and two sisters, none of whom could be reached for comment."

"Did you see this, sir?" The sergeant pushed the newspaper article across the desk towards his boss. "Seems like this Andrew Cass character knows more about the lady than we do."

Which isn't that much, Sullivan thought, glancing over the article. "Bring him in," he said, lighting his pipe. "But go gentle. He hasn't done anything wrong, remember. Yet." he added darkly. He didn't have a very high opinion of the fourth estate. "We need an address. Where did she live? See if you can find out."

A few hours later, having learned little from Cass apart from an address, Sullivan, his sergeant, and a beat cop were climbing the stairs to Galina's room behind her arthritic landlord, whose legs were wrapped in malodorous rags.

"Galina, she gots one room right at top," the man said, pausing to catch his breath. He pointed up the final narrow flight, apparently having no intention of climbing any more stairs.

"Did she live alone?" Sullivan asked, as the old man struggled to take one key off the ring he carried on a chain attached to his belt.

"Is for one only, but I not blind, me. I know a man up there sometimes." He shrugged. "Pretty girl, all alone. What can you do?"

"Is it the same man or different ones?"

"Ah no, no. Galina, she not like that. Is same one, Of this, I am sure. Or maybe two," he added thoughtfully.

Sullivan held out his hand for the key. "You've been real helpful," he said. Behind him, the beat cop shuffled on the narrow stairs. He was the one who had led them to the building and told Sullivan where to find the landlord: at a café around the corner filled with old men drinking very strong coffee. Sullivan wasn't sure exactly what they were, but he didn't think they were Russian.

"We'll take it from here," he said to the landlord as he started up the last flight of stairs.

The walls were so close together, his broad shoulders almost touched them. At the top was a tiny landing with two doors, one to the roof and the other to Galina's long narrow attic room. The air in her room was stale, the light dim, and the slanting walls felt as if they were closing in on him. He forced open the one dirty window.

"What a pigsty," remarked his sergeant.

"And you would know," Sullivan countered, righting a chair that had fallen over by a round table. It looked as if there had been a fight here of some sort. A cushion was split open, feathers drifting out as he picked it up. Some pictures were hanging askew on the wall, as if they'd been hit by a soft object. The pillow, perhaps? He found a few articles of men's clothing in the clothespress. They were cheaply made and well-worn, nothing that could lead them to a tailor or reveal where they had been bought. He spread out the shirt. Could this belong to that reporter, Andrew Cass? Is this where he got his inside information about the girl?

On the table was a pile of newspaper clippings about the Ballets

Russes and Nijinsky. A photograph of Galina in some costume, smiling at the camera as if she were on stage, lay on top. There was a photographer's name on the back, which Sullivan copied down in his notebook. He slipped the photo into his breast pocket.

"Perhaps she was keepin' a scrapbook," the sergeant suggested, looking at the clippings.

"There's no sign of one, is there?" Sullivan snapped. His sergeant's face fell. "Search the place," Sullivan continued. He doubted that they would find anything useful, but it was what they did. Search, examine, deduce. And he had a feeling, like a cool breath down his spine, that this was not a simple case of heart attack, as they had been told.

Perhaps her only secret was the identity of her gentleman friend. Perhaps he was the oddly acting Nijinsky. Just because the man was married meant nothing. The dancer had a peculiar reputation, and he was Russian and apparently an idol of the girl for a long time. On the other hand, the clothes they had found were not the fine European style worn by the star of the Ballets Russes. Or maybe the mystery man was Ivan, who loved her so much. But Pavel Yevtchenko had said she did not return his feelings, and unrequited love could turn dangerous. But was that true? Or was there a reason for this Pavel character to lie? A rival, perhaps?

"Bring all the men's clothing you can find to the police station," he told the beat cop. At least, they could find out the size of the mystery man. That might cut down the list.

He took one last look around, glanced at the few pictures on the walls: cheap reproductions, a few postcards, pictures cut out of magazines someone had probably thrown away. And one garish religious one with lots of fake gold, painted on wood. It was a Russian thing, he remembered. He had seen them in Russian homes and Russian churches, but couldn't recall their name. He scratched his chin, trying to remember the term, then clapped his hat on his head and thumped down the stairs. If the dead woman had any secrets, she was better at keeping them then he was at ferreting them out.

"Where to now, boss?"

The detective chewed his lower lip. It wasn't even a case; they both knew that. He didn't have any excuse to keep nosing around.

But something was bothering him. No one except the histrionic Ivan seemed to care about the girl. No one had come forward to claim her body. None of her fellow-dancers even knew where she lived. And the speed with which they had acted to get her out of the theater, to distance themselves from her death! Even the doctor had backed down about the time of her death so that now it wasn't clear whether her heart had given out in the theater or on the way to the hospital.

"We're going to the morgue," Sullivan said.

The sergeant sighed.

Detective Sullivan's wife, Margie, had prepared a strong-smelling paste made up of mint, lemon juice, and cloves for her husband to use on his visits to the odoriferous places around town that he was forced to visit in the course of his work. Sullivan pulled the small enameled box from his vest pocket and rubbed some ointment under his nose as he and the sergeant arrived at the building that housed the morgue.

"Doc Webber might have some news for us," Sullivan said, trotting down the stone steps, the vaulted ceiling making his footsteps echo. In truth, the medical examiner was his last hope of making this into a case worthy of investigation. If the good doctor had found nothing out of the ordinary, Sullivan would have to move on.

Dr. Webber came from London, where he had worked in Guys Hospital and for a time even had a practice on Harley Street. Then fire had destroyed his house, his wife, and his two children. Dr. Webber was destroyed, too. As far as Sullivan could discover, the man had never recovered from the loss. He took to the bottle and made one mistake too many with his patients, although that part was a little vague. The doc had then closed down his office, booked passage to New York on the Titanic, and nearly drowned. That experience seemed to have wakened him. He applied for the post of medical examiner when it became vacant and had been performing his duties competently ever since.

"I have found my place at last among the dead," he had told Sullivan the first time they met. "It is where I belong. And where I will be the next time disaster comes calling. I missed the first two visits, but now I am ready."

"Can I just stay out here, do you think?" the sergeant now asked, pausing outside the swinging doors of the morgue.

"Use some of this." Sullivan handed him the enameled box and pushed the double doors open. "You home, Doc?" he called.

"At your service, sir." Dr. Webber emerged from the shadows, tall but stooped like an old man although he didn't appear to be much older than Sullivan himself. Behind him, a Bunsen burner flamed under a beaker half-filled with a pale brown liquid. On another table, a row of bottles gleamed in the flaring light of a gas ring. The doctor's experiments were becoming legendary, particularly after the time he had nearly blown himself up, yet another escape from death that Sullivan thought made him eerily close to immortal. Further back, several draped bodies lay still in death on metal tables. The smell was nearly overwhelming, a mixture of putrefaction and the strange chemicals the doctor was experimenting with.

"Have you got anything for me about the Russian dancer?"

The doctor pushed a long lock of blond hair out of his pale blue eyes. "She was beautiful, with that pale ivory skin and coal-black hair that is typical of the Black Irish and some Russians. But her bone structure was more Irish, I would say."

"I know what she looked like." Sullivan ground his teeth in frustration; it was always this way with Doc Webber. Perhaps it's because he doesn't see enough people from above ground, he had thought in one of his more charitable moods. Today, he wasn't feeling so charitable.

"Ah, yes. Quite." The doctor felt the pockets of his lab coat, pulled out a small flask, and took a pull. He straightened his shoulders. "I don't understand how they could have missed this at the hospital," he said. "I should think they see this quite frequently."

"See what?"

"Laudanum. She had imbibed laudanum recently. Her pupils were contracted into pinpoints."

"But don't women often take laudanum? There was a small amount in her room."

"For toothache, yes. I've prescribed it myself many times. And for nerves as well, but in small doses."

"Then she just overdosed herself."

"My dear inspector, as I understand it, she was about to realize a lifelong dream: to dance with the world's greatest male dancer. Why would she risk this?"

"Was she in pain, perhaps? Did she have anything wrong with her at all?"

"She was not well-nourished, but I see a lot of that. Her feet were a mess, but again, that's not unusual for dancers." He checked his notes, written in a rumpled notebook he pulled from his pocket. "But her heart wasn't as good as it should be."

"So they were right about that."

"It was probably just a guess on their part," said Dr. Webber witheringly. "Without an autopsy, it's a guess on my part, too, but in my case, an educated guess." He shrugged. "I don't think her heart was bad enough to kill her in the ordinary course of events, but helped along by drugs, quite possibly. How much laudanum did you find in her room?"

"A small dropper bottle about the size of my thumb. It was almost empty, too."

Dr. Webber shook his blond mane. "That amount wouldn't be enough. This was a large dose, probably twice that, though probably not enough to hurt a more robust person," he added thoughtfully.

Sullivan scratched his head. "The reports from witnesses were confusing, but they all agreed she drank something before she went on. Most seem to agree it was from a flask, and the only flask back there, according to the stage manager, was Nijinsky's. He always has it there within reach, should he want it."

"He wouldn't have laudanum in it," Webber said. "From what I hear, he doesn't drink much alcohol, if any. And laudanum slows one down to a crawl, quite the opposite of what one would wish before going on stage to dance, I should think. It's probably just mineral water in his flask, with maybe a little sugar for energy, something like that."

"But someone could put some of that stuff in it," the sergeant broke in, his excitement letting him forget for a moment the overpowering smells of the place. "Some rival, perhaps, sir. Another lady dancer. Poison is a woman's weapon, you always says."

"Where is the flask?" Webber asked. "I can test it easily and find out what was in it and how much."

Sullivan shook his head. "Nijinsky insisted on taking it with him. It was a gift from some prince or something. My people didn't know what to do. They let him take it."

"Pity."

"So I guess we'll never know," Sullivan said sadly, slouching against the table.

"About the flask, no. But cheer up. Laudanum was the least of her worries."

"What do you mean?"

"Once I got all the greasepaint off, I noticed her skin had a slightly yellowish tinge. I got curious. I tested a bit of her hair and found traces of arsenic. In her fingernail clippings, too"

"So you don't need an autopsy to know this?"

"No. I'm willing to write up my findings right now in the death register. Not that it'll do much good if no one pays any attention."

"They won't. I've been warned off already. I told you that."

"So why are you putting your career in jeopardy for this one, if I may ask?"

"I'm not. I want to know is all. And it irritates the bejesus out of me that a girl gets killed—an American girl, mind you—and everyone just sweeps it under the rug. No one has even claimed her body."

"Now there, you're wrong," Dr. Webber said. "Mr. George Kassevetsky of the Kassevetsky Russian Dance Troupe has claimed her body and is paying for her funeral."

"Now ain't that grand," murmured Sullivan. "And who may he be when he's home?"

Dr. Webber shrugged elegant shoulders. "I have no idea."

FIFTEEN

"NIJINSKY DANCES AGAIN
His Grace and Great Agility Shown in 'Les Sylphides'."
                                              —*New York Times*

Morgan slouched in the back of his family's box at the Met, sti-fling a yawn. He had had little sleep after yesterday's wild ride at Chuffy Harris's, the bittersweet experience reawakening his passion for the speedway, sweeping him up to heights of exulta-tion only to have Kit Caulder's poisonous tactics bring him crash-ing down again. Harris had congratulated him on his handling of the special on the 'tricky turn', had actually invited him back, but Morgan had hesitated—because of Kit. All night long, the race played and replayed in his head: the excitement of the track, the wind rushing by, stinging his skin; his body vibrating with the shimmying of the motorcar as he pushed it to higher speeds; the horror at seeing what Kit was trying to do; the sick feeling as he realized the depth of the man's loathing.

Two years had apparently not diminished Kit's hatred. A local farm boy with a talent for machinery, Kit had been a pumper when Morgan arrived at Hochman's dirt track to test-drive one of the specials. It was hate at first sight apparently, and although Kit had always been civil when others were around, his vitriol spilled out when they were alone, especially after Morgan was promoted to driver the following year and they were often pitted against each other. Kit had done sneaky things before, though cleverly so Hochman wouldn't suspect. But never had he been so blatant in his desire to demolish all competition, and Morgan had no idea why.

After such a night dealing with demons, he would ordinarily

have stayed home, but tonight he had hopes of meeting Muriel at intermission. Unfortunately, things had not gone well.

"And the dance goes on," Muriel said, twisting her gloves in her hands, "and no one even tells us what really happened to that poor girl."

"What girl?" Morgan asked, confused.

"You see? You have forgotten already."

"The dancer? She died of a weak heart. I read it in the paper," Morgan said, smiling at her.

"Hidden near the back, in among ads for corsets and theater tickets!"

"Muriel, I don't understand—"

"And that's the problem, don't you see? Morgan, if she had been an aristocrat like Mr. Diaghilev, or even just famous like Pavlova, it would have been in the headlines! And the only reason people are talking about the plight of the Ladies' Garment Workers is because thousands of them are threatening to go on strike."

"Ladies'…? But that won't affect you, Muriel. You have your dresses made at Harry Angelo's, like Gloria, don't you?"

"Morgan! That's just what I'm talking about, isn't it?"

"What is?" asked Morgan, even more confused.

But Muriel was walking away, heading back to her box, her back straight, the white ostrich feathers in her dark hair quivering.

Morgan watched her stalk off. He wondered why he continued to yearn for a woman who so clearly disdained him.

He leaned forward now, tapping Gloria on the shoulder. "Are you sure Muriel said she likes me?" he whispered, desperate for some crumb of encouragement.

"She said she likes you well enough," Gloria answered behind her fan. She, too, had been behaving oddly before the performance began, flitting in and out with feeble excuses about looking for this friend or that, but now her eyes were glued to the stage, watching Mr. Nijinsky's every movement. It was amazing how the dancer could command every eye when on stage, even the men's.

Morgan craned his neck so he could catch a glimpse of Muriel. She looked pensive, he thought. Was she regretting her harsh words? He would leave during the curtain calls and wait for her outside her family's box. Perhaps she could be persuaded to join them for a late after-theater dinner. Satisfied with this plan, he sat back and began to watch the ballet, making mental notes of things he thought Muriel might be interested in discussing.

But Muriel turned out to have other plans, and Morgan watched in wretched fury as she descended the great staircase of the Metropolitan on the arm of Marcel Vanier, a young man from the French embassy, who was probably consumed with interest in the Women's – or was it Ladies'?– Garment Workers Union.

This contretemps with Muriel had come on top of another tongue-lashing from his father, who somehow had heard about his test run at Chuffy Harris's. Morgan wondered briefly if he would have said anything if Morgan had not allowed himself to be outmaneuvered and ultimately run off the track. As it was, his father had quite a bit to say, mostly along the lines of putting away childish things and not worrying his mother, even though she didn't know anything about the test run. It was, apparently, time for him to get serious and make up his mind about what he was going to do with his life. "I thought you had this nonsense out of your system," his father had said.

Ordinarily, Morgan thought as his father droned on, I would be traveling in Europe now, as Chesleigh and Harry and most of my older friends did, 'acquiring polish', as Mother would put it, by soaking up culture and the European way of life. But their wretched war had spoiled things, leaving him at loose ends, floating around New York, getting underfoot and far too close to his father. The current fad of 'See America First' did not appeal to him. Besides, the parties were fun and the girls beautiful, although he knew most of them and the only one he really wanted spurned him. Between his father and Kit Caulder, his exultation at racing again had plummeted into the slough of despond. I'm just marking time, he thought. Waiting. But for what?

So now when his old schoolmate Rolly Danvers clapped him on the back and suggested Morgan join his party for a night on the town, he readily agreed.

"You know Jeb Nickles, I think," Rolly said, waving a careless hand at the stocky young man with the pince-nez standing beside him by the railing.

Morgan recognized the man, the way one recognized someone

who is often part of the scenery but never center stage. He was an attaché at the British consulate, and had been in New York so long that he considered himself an honorary Yank. Now he smiled and waggled the fingers of one hand in Morgan's direction.

"And these are my new friends, Prince Dmitry Romanoff and Count Fyodor Ostroffsky," Rolly went on. "They came to see the great Nijinsky."

"All the way from Russia, Your Highness?" Morgan asked as they shook hands.

The Russian prince wore a medal of some kind of order around his neck on a red and gold ribbon. The count wore a diamond and sapphire cross. Perhaps another order? Morgan noticed others turning to look at them as they made their way down the great staircase and into the lobby. The Russians were strikingly good-looking: the count slender and fair, the prince dark and tall, and they both moved with surprising grace.

"*Très amusant, mon cher*," the dapper count remarked, his blue eyes dancing. "We know Vaslav in St. Petersburg when he is *petit ami* of our dear friend, Prince Pavel Lvov. We all know him then, did we not, Dmitry? We miss him so when Diaghilev take him away from us."

"Morgan's a friend of Nijinsky, too, aren't you, Morgan?" Rolly went on, holding the door open for them.

"Rolly, for heaven's sake!" Morgan hissed, pulling his friend aside. "Where did you meet these two?"

"We all met up at Beasels last night," Rolly said. "We played cards till five in the morning. I could hardly see the damn things by the end of it."

"Was grand night!" the prince said, joining them. "But tonight, our friend Mr. Nickles promise new entertainments, no?"

Jeb nodded and smiled enigmatically.

"You in, Morgan?" Rolly asked.

"Why not?"

The Russians insisted on flagging down a horse-drawn cab outside the Met, in spite of the driver explaining he was about to go home. "Carriage give us *la nostalgie* for home," the count exclaimed. "Like *troika* with one less horse."

As they moved off into the night, Morgan saw Jeb lean over

to speak to the driver, slipping him some coins. A few minutes later, they swung onto a side street and stopped in front of a small restaurant.

"They know me here," he said. "We can pick up some champagne."

"Oysters!" shouted Rolly.

"Chicken," suggested Morgan, suddenly hungry.

"We have rolling picnic!" exclaimed the count, jumping down and leaning back to pull the prince after him by the hand.

As they all swept into the tiny restaurant, a blushing young waiter rushed over, hands clasped in front, bowing, smiling. "We are about to close?" he said, but he raised his voice at the end of the sentence, as if not entirely sure.

"Need champagne, oysters, fowl." The count perched on the edge of a table and took a cigarette out of a gold case. "Go. Go." He waved the waiter away impatiently.

"It's all right," Jeb assured the young man, who was barely out of short pants. "Tell Remy it's all right."

The young man fled, disappearing behind a curtain at the back.

There were only two couples still in the restaurant, both trying hard not to stare at the bejeweled foreigners and their well-dressed friends. Morgan shifted uncomfortably. He was about to suggest they wait outside when the waiter returned, followed by an older man wreathed in anxious smiles, who smoothed back his thin black hair nervously as he bowed.

"It is an honor, sirs, but unfortunately, you have caught us unprepared. We have—"

"You have champagne?" the count interrupted. "Oysters?"

"Yes, Excellency, but—"

"Is good." He tossed a gold coin on the table beside him and turned away.

Stunned, Morgan followed them, noticing that Jeb stayed behind to speak to the man. It must be good training for a diplomat, spending time with these people, he thought wryly as he climbed into the carriage.

Soon the young man struggled out with a basket and with much difficulty maneuvered it onto the floor of the carriage.

"You. Get in," the prince said suddenly, pointing at the boy.

"Sir, I can't." He glanced back desperately at the older man who merely shrugged.

"We need server."

"Go. Go!" The owner grabbed the apron off the young man's waist and pushed him into the carriage.

The prince smiled and leaned back, idly stroking the boy's arm. "Your name is?"

"Louis, sir." He began to take out the glasses from the basket as the carriage moved off. Jeb opened a bottle and poured, the prince insisting that Louis keep having sips from his glass. Rolly found the tray of oysters, nestled on a bed of ice. Two quails lay near the bottom, sliced neatly in two. Morgan was impressed at what the poor man had been able to rustle up at a moment's notice.

Soon the party was in high spirits. Louis sat cross-legged on the floor of the carriage, pouring champagne and handing around plates of chicken and rolled ox tongue on stale toast points, though he was getting more and more sloppy as his wine sampling continued. Soon he gave up altogether, his head resting on the prince's thigh and his eyes closing in spite of the rollicking drinking songs Rolly was belting out at the top of his voice. By the time they crossed 14th Street, Morgan had joined in, standing up with one hand on his heart, the other clutching the carriage lamp for balance.

"Americans, you drink, you get happy," the prince said. "Russians, we drink, we get lachrymose and weep in each others' arms."

Morgan sat down abruptly as the carriage swung around a corner. He threw back his head and stared up at the stars and at the black lace tracery of tree branches on each side of the street. It's not Fifth Avenue, he thought, and smiled with relief.

About ten minutes later, the carriage stopped. Morgan looked around, confused by the sudden lack of motion. The Russians seemed not at all affected by all the champagne they had imbibed, jumping to the ground and looking around the narrow street alertly.

"Where we go?" asked the prince.

"My question exactly," Morgan said, stepping over the sleeping Louis and climbing down uncertainly. He suspected they must be in Greenwich Village, judging by the twisting streets they had just come through, but he couldn't tell exactly. "Is this a slumming tour, Jeb?"

"We're going to the Libera Club," Jeb said, crossing the street and trotting down a flight of area steps.

"Not cards?" said the count.

"Definitely not cards," Jeb called back over his shoulder.

"What about Louis?" Morgan called after the retreating backs of his new friends.

The prince shrugged. The count kept walking. Jeb had disappeared, and Rolly was endeavoring to roll one of the champagne bottles along the middle of the street.

"Oh dear," said Morgan uncertainly, swaying a little.

"At times, one understands the French Revolution, sir," the driver said unexpectedly.

Morgan stared at him. The man was dressed in the usual sort of unofficial livery worn by hack drivers, but his face was young under the top hat, his eyes bright, gleaming with intelligence.

"Are you going to wait?" Morgan asked, uncertain what had been arranged. He felt around for his billfold. "I'll pay you."

"It's not necessary, sir. I'm going to take the young man home now. It's better he not be here when your friends come out. Good night, sir."

Morgan watched him go, Louis still slouched out of sight on the floor of the carriage. Then he grabbed Rolly by the arm and followed the others down the steps and inside the club.

The door was opened by a Negro dressed extravagantly in a velvet suit with an orchid pinned to his lapel and a colorful silk ascot around his neck.

"You are with the prince's party?" he asked.

Morgan handed over his hat and realized his gloves were missing. "Yes," he said, straightening his shoulders.

There was a churchy smell about the place, Morgan thought, and then realized it was incense. Popish. He tried not to giggle. Uncle Paul would not approve. He wouldn't approve of the half-naked sylph-like creatures gliding about serving tables either, he thought, as he headed towards the rowdy bunch gathered around the Russians in the corner. He slid onto a velvet chair and looked around more closely.

To one side was a small stage where a slim young man wearing a turquoise jacket pinched in at the waist, his hair gleaming with brilliantine and combed into spit curls across his forehead, was thanking three tall dancers who had apparently just performed. The room was long and narrow, with booths lining one side, the dim lighting broken into stained glass colors by Tiffany lamps here and there. On the other side of the room, at a table on a raised platform sat a group of girls, laughing and whispering together, glancing at the other patrons coquettishly from behind their lace fans. Lights winked from the beaded fringes and embroidery on their elaborate dresses and sparkled on the ornaments in their hair. Morgan smiled at the blond girl. She smiled back and laughed, showing dimples on her rouged cheeks.

"Not bad," whispered Jeb, and winked. He sat wreathed in smoke from yet another French cigarette, looking relaxed, a lazy contentment in his eyes.

Perhaps there was something else in his cigarettes. "Where do you get those things these days," Morgan asked, curious.

"There are always ways." Jeb smiled and leaned against the padded high back of the bench. "You knew Rolly in school?"

Morgan nodded.

"How well do you know him?"

Morgan shrugged, irritated by the question, by the subtle probing.

"He is always open to new experiences, isn't he?" Jeb murmured. "You, too, perhaps."

"Welcome to Libera." The master of ceremonies was at their table, clicking his heels together and bowing. A faint smell of powder and tobacco floated around him, a confusing mix.

As Jeb was apparently known here, he introduced the company. "And this is Mr. Vanheusen," he finished, indicating Morgan.

The man stiffened, drawing himself up to his full height. "Sir, you are not welcome here," he said at once and motioned to the tall Negro still hovering in the hall. "I am surprised you show your face after what you have done."

"Me? What have I done?" asked Morgan indignantly. "I just got here, but if this is how you treat customers, I will be glad to leave." He started to get to his feet.

Jeb reached over and pushed him back. "Let me explain. This is Mr. *Morgan* Vanheusen."

"He's a friend of Mr. Nijinsky," Rolly said, and hiccupped.

The man bowed with a flourish worthy of the prince himself. "My humble apologies, sir. I should have realized."

"Realized what?" Morgan looked at Jeb, waiting for an explanation as the MC walked away. "And what has this to do with Mr. Nijinsky?"

"Not a thing." Jeb leaned closer. "Your uncle," he whispered, "is not popular in certain circles."

"Wait." Morgan was trying to think of a good defense of his uncle, but couldn't marshal his thoughts, especially as he was unsure what the transgression might be in their eyes. Champagne arrived at that moment, a gift from the club for the embarrassment, and Morgan settled back to enjoy himself, dismissing his uncle from his mind. That blond beauty was still watching him, flirting from behind her fan.

"And for a different taste treat..." The MC motioned towards the stage where six scantily clad young men carried on a huge door-sized platter covered with food in the shape of a person and laid it on velvet-draped trestles.

As they moved closer, Morgan saw there was a person under all the food, and patrons were lazily running fingers and hands through the confections to touch the sweet-covered skin underneath. The prince thrust his whole hand into the whipped cream, blueberries, and chocolate syrup, sliding up to the wrist near the inner thigh of the proffered body.

Morgan shivered with forbidden delight. Nothing at Sadie Hahn's had prepared him for this. Beside him, the prince licked his fingers, chocolate dripping down his chin. Morgan touched the long, seaweed-like hair glinting with sugar and laughed nervously. He slid one finger over the chin and down to the throat. And felt... an Adam's apple. He glanced farther down the table to see one of the men with his whole hand thrust between the legs of the figure.

"Jesus," muttered Morgan, sobering up. "It's a man?"

"There is beauty everywhere, is there not, *mon cher?*" asked the count. He extended one long slender finger covered with whipped cream and thrust into a maraschino cherry towards Morgan's mouth.

The room grew still. Everyone was watching, including the

master of ceremonies. I am not my Uncle Paul, Morgan thought. He leaned forward and plucked the cherry from the tip of the count's finger with his lips and ate it.

"One never knows," remarked Jeb. "Perhaps you will win the bidding on the delectable dessert."

Morgan reached for more champagne.

SIXTEEN

"...And I learned about women from her."
—Rudyard Kipling, "The Ladies"

The cab was redolent of the smell of cologne and good cigars. Morgan leaned back and closed his eyes, both hands braced against the leather seat as he waited for the world to stop spinning.

"Are you all right, sir?" The old cabbie peered around to look at him anxiously. One side of his face flamed a deep plum color from a birth scar.

"Too much champagne," Morgan said, opening his eyes and straightening up. "Take me to Sadie Hahn's. Do you know where it is?"

"Certainly, sir." The cab turned a corner and headed east into the deepening night.

The strange, exhilarating, conflicting tensions at the Libera Club had left him frustrated and confused. He drummed his fingers against the leather upholstery. You know where you stand at Sadie Hahn's, he thought. He winced as he felt again the brandy-scented breath of the tall blond with the dimples warm and moist against his neck, felt the length of her against him, felt a hardness where there should have been only soft, yielding flesh.

And he felt again the hot surge of desire.

He needed Sadie's. He didn't want to play games, to make conversation. He didn't want anything to drink. He needed a girl, and at Sadie's, she would be real.

His head had cleared a little by the time he arrived and stumbled up the steps and inside the familiar house. Someone spoke to him, but he ignored the soft voice, heading down the hall to where he saw Sapphire leaning seductively against the banister, a smile of welcome on her dusky face.

"You look like a man who knows what he wants," she said.

He reached up to brush a strand of long black hair away from her face. "I want chocolate," he said, his voice husky.

"Perhaps chocolate's not on the menu tonight," she teased.

He slid an arm around her slim waist and pulled her against him roughly. "Oh, Sapphire," he breathed. A tremor passed through him. "Don't toy with me."

The girl pushed him away and laughed. "Oh my, but you *are* impatient tonight." She took his hand and led him up the stairs. As they went, she began to undo the tiny pearl buttons on her lace camisole with her other hand. One by one, they fell open, displaying more and more of her smooth, warm, café-au-lait skin. Morgan moaned softly and pulled her along faster, heading to the high-ceilinged room at the end of the hall.

Someone was playing ragtime in the Red Room when Morgan came downstairs again, the joyful, syncopated tune drawing him in. He stood at the door and stared, amazed. Nijinsky was dancing with the Negro boy, Sherman, while one of the girls played the piano. Everyone was standing up watching, some trying to imitate the Russian's athletic steps. The ones who tried were soon out of breath.

"Is new dance," Nijinsky said, seeing Morgan. "Come! You try, Morgan! We dance!" He dropped the boy's arm abruptly and reached for Morgan.

"Not me, Jinks," Morgan said. "I've had all the exercise I need for awhile. All I want now is a drink."

The girl had stopped playing, and the Negro boy had taken her place. He was much better at it.

"Come. Dance," said Nijinsky, drawing Morgan closer and swaying into the rhythm.

Morgan pulled away. "No, no, Jinks. I'm exhausted. I think I'll go to the Green Room, if it's free." He glanced at Sadie.

"You've been celebrating for a while, I see," she said, leading the way down the hall. Sadie opened a door into one of the small intimate rooms reserved for regulars who just wanted to drink and talk. "Shall I get you your usual libation?"

"Yes, please." Morgan sank down into one of the welcoming wing chairs.

"I'll send someone along soon." She shut the door behind her.

Nijinsky had followed. He sat down in the chair opposite Morgan, looking concerned. "You have bad time?"

"The night started out with woman troubles, but everything's fine now."

"Ah. Womans always trouble."

"I met some old friends of yours tonight," Morgan went on, slipping a stud into his pocket. "Prince Dmitry Romanoff and Count Fyodor Ostroffsky."

Nijinsky's dark eyes looked startled. He shook his head. "Not friends," he said quickly. "Only friends with each other."

"They were at the ballet. As was I," Morgan added, suddenly remembering his manners. "Bravo. Wonderful performance."

The dancer nodded absently. "Worries about poison almost spoil everything," he said.

"Poison?" Morgan took his cocktail from the wisp of a girl who glided in. He gave her a quick smile as she sank to his feet on the ottoman, then looked back at Nijinsky. "What poison?"

"They after me."

"Who?"

The dancer looked around then shrugged. "Enemies. If I know, I tell policemans. I only know someone try kill me."

"Jinks, the girl who died—"

"She drank poison in my flask. Was for me."

"She had a heart attack."

"Also, someone try to make me fall at your house."

"At my house! But that was an accident!"

The dancer shook his head. He, too, had a glass, this time not just water, Morgan noticed. "Look, that was carelessness on the part of the workmen. They were reprimanded severely."

"And," Nijinsky continued, holding up two fingers, "letter backstage go to wrong dancer. Powder inside."

"Not poison," Morgan quickly pointed out.

"Is warning," Nijinsky said darkly. His black slanting eyes burned into Morgan's.

Morgan sighed and took another drink. The dancer he now

considered a friend was making him nervous. He wished he had never seen the Libera Club, had never held that pretty youth in his arms and felt that surge of longing. He was used to things being black and white, right and wrong, male and female. He wanted that certainty back.

"Look, Jinks, you come from a war-torn place and I understand you're worried about safety issues, but you're in America now. Everyone is safe here."

"Everyone?" Nijinsky raised one eyebrow. For a second, his face looked very attractive, like a fawn, alluring, mysterious. Morgan took another sip of his drink.

"I say goodbye," the dancer said abruptly, getting to his feet. "Taxicar here now. I go."

"I'll see you to the door."

They walked together through the perfumed hallways to the front door where the taxi was waiting patiently. Morgan went back to the Green Room. Almost at once, he noticed Nijinsky's gloves on the footstool. He rushed back through the hall and out into the damp night. The rain had stopped, but the air was filled with the smell of damp earth and lilacs.

And the sounds of grunting.

He paused, then walked towards the thumps and muffled voices. Distinctly Russian words. After an evening spent with Rolly's new friends, he would recognize the sound of the language anywhere.

"Jinks!"

The thud of running feet. A car engine roared into life and accelerated into the night.

"Jinks!" Morgan rushed around the corner and found his friend doubled over, smeared with blood and dirt. He wasn't moving.

"Help! Help!" Morgan yelled as he knelt beside the man, looking for signs of life. "We need help here!" He had no idea how to take someone's pulse but he put his face close to Nijinsky's and detected a faint puff of breath from his lips. Thank God the man was still breathing.

"Wake up," he urged, but the pale dancer didn't respond.

Behind him, he heard footsteps on the path. "What's wrong?"

"Some men attacked Nijinsky. They must have been lying in wait."

"No! Is he all right?"

"I think so."

"It happens sometimes here. They steal money, jewelry, watches."

"I interrupted them, I guess. He forgot his gloves." Morgan looked at the rake-thin young man who had come to his aid. He had seen him before but he couldn't remember the circumstances. The man wasn't well-dressed, wasn't wearing an evening coat. Morgan looked again at the dancer.

"I think he's all right, just winded," the young man said. "He's coming around now. Why don't you telephone a friend to come pick you up?"

"I'll call a cab," Morgan said, turning towards the house.

"No. Please. Many of the drivers are Russian. They'd recognize him. He couldn't bear the gossip. Please."

"How do you know so much about him?"

"A good friend of mine is a dancer with the company," the young man said. "The side door is closer." He pointed.

Nijinsky opened his eyes and looked around, confused. Seeing the young man, a flood of Russian exploded from his lips. Morgan left quickly, heading for the door the man had pointed out.

He had never come in this way. The hall was dimly lit. A bronze statue of a naked Mercury glowed in a pool of light next to a winding flight of stairs. Beside the statue sat an ornate telephone, a slipper chair covered in lavender velvet beside it.

Morgan tried to contact five of his friends, but all of them were out. There was a lot going on in the city, he reminded himself. They had probably been out at some after the theater late-dinner event and had taken the ladies home before setting off for more manly pursuits.

The ladies.

He thought of Muriel and shook his head. Then he thought of his sister. Gloria knew how to drive the electric car.

His hand poised over the receiver, he paused. Gloria wouldn't answer the telephone; Boothby would. And Boothby would be suspicions. Maybe Maggie would answer. Maggie, who was sweet on Fred, the boy who worked for the Drexlers, three houses down the street. Now, if he could reach the boy, he could take a message to Maggie to wake up Gloria to come and get them. The plan was risky and complicated. He didn't like it.

He was about to go back outside to explain that he would have to telephone a cab when the young man appeared. "I told him you were calling a friend. He is very upset about being seen like this. He thinks he was attacked because of who he is."

Morgan sighed, picked up the phone again, and asked Central to be connected to the Drexler residence. Although it was highly irregular to be calling a servant to the telephone, especially this time of night, he managed to convince their butler that it was not a prank and that he needed the boy's assistance. Luckily, Fred was a bright lad and he appeared to follow the complicated instructions easily.

"Mr. Nijinsky is waiting on a bench beside the lilacs," the young man said. "I must go now."

"Thanks for helping," Morgan said. He hesitated, not sure whether the young man would be insulted if he offered him money. Then it was too late.

He hurried back to Jinks. The Russian was huddled in the shadows. His teeth were chattering with nerves and his hands trembled. "You see? I tell you, I tell policemans, I tell everyone they chase me. No one believe."

"Jinks, I'm sorry, but this sort of thing happens in a big city. It's robbery. They want money and things."

"They take nothing."

"Because I surprised them. Really, it's not personal."

"You think not?" Nijinsky looked at him, his dark eyes large with fear. Blood trickled from his temple and his cheek was stained with grass. Suddenly, Morgan remembered the muffled voices. He was sure they were speaking Russian. But if he told Jinks, the man might get even more hysterical.

"*Mon ami,* I no go home like this," Nijinsky said, his voice almost breaking.

"No, of course not. You'll come home with me, and we'll get you cleaned up and your clothes dried. There's no need to alarm your wife. You can call her from our house, if you like."

He nodded. "*Spaciba.*"

It occurred to Morgan as he sat waiting that the sensible thing would be to go inside Sadie's to clean up, but he was afraid of unleashing more hysterics if he suggested it. So he sat quietly and waited, worrying now about Gloria all alone in a motorcar in the middle of the night. At least, they weren't far away, and there was very little traffic in this neighborhood.

At last, they heard the hum and rumble of the electric motorcar. Jumping up, Morgan ran to the gate and waved at Gloria.

"You took long enough," he muttered, his relief so strong that his knees were weak. "Did you bring blankets, by any chance?"

Gloria jumped down and turned to pull a red plaid steamer rug from the back seat. Her cheeks were flushed, her eyes bright. Droplets of rain sparkled on the dark old-fashioned man's cloak she had thrown on over her hastily donned dress.

Nijinsky climbed into the back seat, and Gloria tucked the blanket around him. She handed him a ceramic pig filled with hot water for his feet.

"Thank you, mademoiselle," he said with a bow of his head. "*Vous pensez à tout.*"

"*C'est mon plaisir,*" she replied.

Morgan breathed a sigh of relief. "I'll drive," he said.

"No." Gloria jumped into the driver's seat before her brother could get there. "If I'm a good enough driver to come and fetch you, I'm good enough to take you home."

Morgan shrugged. He was too tired to argue.

SEVENTEEN

"WOMEN'S GARMENT WORKERS WALK OFF THE JOB"
—*New York Bugle*, late edition

Andy Cass felt out of place walking behind the funeral coach pulled by the team of black-plumed horses. Visible through the glass window of the coach, the casket was draped with flowers, splashy tokens from people Galina hardly knew, people who, during her short life, had mostly ignored her: Diaghilev and the Ballets Russes, Nijinsky, the Metropolitan Opera House. George's more modest bouquets filled the spaces in between. Andy wondered how the old man was paying for all this.

George had insisted Andy be there, even though he had lost touch with Galina long ago. He knew George needed him, so he came, filled with dread that no one else would show up. He was wrong. Many of George's old friends were there, tottering along in their rumpled dark suits, wearing mourning bands on the sleeve. Dancers from the Kassevetsky Troupe Andy hadn't seen in years showed up in dark veils, holding small bouquets, some of the men in Russian blouses and high boots with tassels on the side. Some of the women, Andy guessed, were the usual crowd from the Russian Orthodox Church who went to all the funerals, a kind of macabre rite celebrating their own survival. Only a few showed up from the Ballets Russes: several girls from the *corps de ballet* and first soloist Adolph Bolm accompanied by Pavel Lermontov and a weeping Ivan Novikoff. Even though Andy knew the company had a performance that afternoon, he was irritated that no one official had been sent to represent them, unless Adolph Bolm was their representative as the highest-ranking dancer available. He walked with a cane, his ankle still bothering him from a recent fall during rehearsals, Andy noticed. He wouldn't be dancing for another week at least.

As they passed slowly through the crowded, sun-filled streets, people stopped and bowed their heads in respect, some crossing themselves, some muttering a prayer. Some merely stared at the unusual procession swaying along behind the gilded double bars of the Russian cross carried by the altar boy, followed by the high-hatted Orthodox priests, their long black beards flowing over the colorful vestments, the stylized icon carried before them. Even the mourners looked foreign, some wearing embroidered scarves over their heads. Andy walked on, keeping an eye on George who tottered just ahead of him between two old friends. Motorcars and horse-drawn wagons swerved around them, giving them as wide a berth as possible. A wind sprang up, fluttering the long black ribbons on the top hats of the men from the funeral parlor.

The horses snorted as they came to an intersection crowded with men and women milling around, filling the whole area. They were shouting, seething with anger as they surrounded a speaker who had climbed up on a wooden box in one corner and was haranguing the crowd. They carried signs, and now and then a ragged slogan would erupt, only to die down as the speaker raised his voice to be heard. 'The Women's Garment Workers Union,' their signs said. 'On strike! We're 60,000 strong!'

But even this crowd parted to let the funeral procession through. Andy breathed a sigh of relief. He remembered the riots in Union Square two years before, the violence so sudden and unpredictable. He had ended up in the hospital that day. Now he felt his gut relax again only when the procession turned into the small cemetery under the rusted iron archway a few blocks later.

As people gathered around the newly dug grave, Andy was surprised to recognize Detective Sullivan and Dr. Webber, the coroner, standing a little back from the others. Why were they here? His reporter's instinct urged him forward, but George's pallor stopped him. The man might need a strong young arm to lean on to get him through this. Galina had been like a daughter to him, after his own had died.

There was another man lurking about, too. Drawn by curiosity? The story of Galina the dancer hadn't lasted long enough in the papers to get the notoriety needed for that, surely. He looked familiar, but as Andy stared, trying to place the face, the man seemed to sense his interest and withdrew into the shadow of a mausoleum. But he didn't leave. He's here for her funeral, Andy thought. And he's been crying. A lover, perhaps? He thought of asking George, but it would be rude to interrupt at this point, when Galina's body was being laid to rest.

But apparently others were not so thoughtful. Suddenly, Pavel Lermentov let out a cry and sprinted across the cemetery, leaping over graves and shouting in Russian something that Andy couldn't catch.

Andy moved over close to Adolph Bolm and whispered in Russian, "What is going on?"

"He thought he saw his lover, who disappeared a few days ago. He was frantic, thinking that something terrible had happened to him. Pavel is…highly strung." He smiled at Andy, his eyes saying, We are, of course, not that way. "This is in confidence," he added, as if suddenly remembering Andy's status as a reporter.

"Yes, of course. Do you know his name?"

"Rudy…something."

"And he speaks Russian?"

"So do you," remarked Bolm. He was looking at the young girl opposite him, one of the Kassevetsky dancers. "Do you happen to know who that girl is?" he asked.

"Sadly, no." Andy shook his head.

"No matter." Bolm sighed, the sigh of a married man whose wife had recently joined him.

The service droned on. Two gravediggers stepped forward, ready to lower the casket into the grave. George burst into tears. The priest chanted something, stepped forward, and reached out his hand to scatter ashes from the censer. The chant and response continued as the casket descended slowly. Women's voices broke into a wail. Andy wondered if George had hired professional mourners, their voices rose and fell so rhythmically. The casket disappeared from view.

"*Nyet!*" Ivan leapt forward and flung himself into the grave on top of the casket, his wailing sobs startling the women into silence. For a moment, nothing was heard except for Ivan's anguished cries and the cawing of crows in the distance. Then the women took up their wailing again with redoubled effort, as if they were now in competition with the spurned and abandoned lover.

"*Zhopa na palochke*," muttered Bolm.

For a moment, Andy wished he was able to write this up for the *Bugle*. Then he caught sight of George's stricken face.

He rushed forward and knelt by the grave. "Get out of there, you fool!" he hissed.

"I loved her so!" Ivan sobbed in Russian. "She took a bullet for Nijinsky."

"You're desecrating her memory!" Andy reached down and began to pull on the man's arm. But Ivan was strong, a dancer with toned muscles, and Andy nearly ended up in the grave with him.

"Listen to me," he snapped. "This is what people are going to remember: you making a mockery of her funeral, not Galina. Is that what you want?"

The sobbing stopped. Ivan wiped his tear-stained face, pulled himself out of the grave, and rushed off in the opposite direction from that taken by Pavel, leaving Bolm as the only male dancer from the Ballets Russes.

The service continued. Andy wondered if the priest was editing the prayers to wind things down quickly before something else bizarre could happen. A line of cabs was waiting when everyone finally turned away and headed out of the cemetery.

Andy walked up to the detective.

"What a circus," remarked the policeman.

Andy ignored the comment. "You're still interested in Galina's death?"

"Officially, no," the policeman replied, checking his watch.

"But you still have questions."

"Off the record?"

Andy nodded.

"It seemed she had a little help with her heart attack," Sullivan said. "Dr. Webber noticed she had had a dose of laudanum before she died. All we know for certain is that she drank from Mr. Nijinsky's flask."

She took a bullet for Nijinsky, Andy thought.

"There's not a vestige of proof," Sullivan added hastily. "Just a few loose ends, like a hint of arsenic poisoning that had been happening for a while. It could have been accidental, of course. Ratbane, wallpaper paste, that sort of thing. Anyways, the case is officially closed," he added, digging out his pipe.

"Of course," Andy said, resigned. Another intriguing story he would not be allowed to write.

"If anything changes, I'll let you know," Sullivan said unexpectedly.

"Thank you, sir." Perhaps he would get a story after all.

Andy started walking along the path that led to the western entrance of the cemetery, closer to where he lived. He thought back to his meeting with Gloria in Central Park. Such a happy place, and she was such a happy person. He couldn't imaging her weeping like the woman he was passing now, her face red and twisted in pain. At the thought of Gloria being that unhappy, he winced. They had met only three times, once at the Met and twice in the park, but already she held a place in his heart that he had guarded up till now. But he had no chance at all with her. He knew that. Maybe she did, too. Or maybe he had never been more than a mere adventure to her.

Here and there, old women dressed in black tended to the graves of their loved ones. Two men were digging a new grave in the distance. A young woman, her face slick with tears, sat with a baby on a bench nearby, rocking the child.

As he turned a corner, he saw the dancer Pavel talking to the man who had been standing in the shadows at Galina's funeral. At sight of Andy, the man started. He would have run if Pavel had not grabbed his arm.

"I've seen you somewhere before," Andy said pleasantly as he walked up to the two men. "You knew Galina?"

"Why you persecute us?" cried Pavel. "Why?"

"You've got it wrong, sir. I'm not doing a story. I was here because I knew Galina when she was a little girl. And I know George Kassevetsky. I owe him a lot."

"Many people owe George a lot," the young man said suddenly, in unaccented English. "You, me, half of Little Russia. But in my case, he has ruined me! Galina! Oh, my Galina!" He turned away. Pavel grabbed his hand and kissed it, whispered something in Russian that Andy couldn't hear.

When he turned back to Andy, his face was wet with tears. "Rudy think he is responsible."

"How could that be?" Andy asked in Russian.

"He was backstage that day. He came to see me, and he saw Galina, too. Gave her a good-luck charm. Then he gave her Vaslav's flask to drink from because she was thirsty and there was nothing else handy. But that's all! He did nothing wrong!"

"Does Mr. Nijinsky take any stimulants before he dances?"

"Stimulants? Vaslav? No! Never! Only mineral water, maybe some honey. Everyone knows that. The flask is more like a token for him, a good-luck thing." He was still holding Rudy's hand in both of his. When he saw Andy noticing, he dropped it quickly and blushed. "We go now, yes?" he added in English. "Rudy has to go to work and we go first to tea room. For tea," he added. He shook Andy's hand. His friend was already walking away.

"Wait!" Andy called after them. "What's your full name?" But they didn't stop, didn't even turn around.

Rudy who? he wondered. And what was his relationship to Galina? Whatever it was, Sullivan might be interested. He might be able to fill in some blanks in this case that wasn't a case, this story that wasn't a story. And it was always useful to do the police a favor, assuming they didn't already know about Rudy.

He headed downtown, the cemetery soon far behind him.

EIGHTEEN

"DAINTY FASHIONS DECREED BY PARIS FOR SPRING SEASON UNITE NOVELTY WITH SIMPLICITY INCIDENT TO WAR"

—*New York Bugle*

Gloria sat at her mother's elegant kneehole desk in the morning room, addressing envelopes for the invitations to the reception they were planning for the following Thursday. Every few minutes, her mother would bustle in to check the growing pile, discarding the ones that weren't absolutely perfect and making Gloria redo them. The one for Colonel Nikolai Golejewski she ended up doing three times before it met her mother's stringent standards.

"I don't understand why we're inviting him anyway," Gloria complained. "We don't even know him."

"I do. He's on my War Orphans' Relief Committee. He was the one who persuaded Mr. Nijinsky to dance at our garden party fundraiser, remember?"

Gloria made a face. "I don't see how he would want to come to another of our functions after that fiasco," she muttered.

"It doesn't matter if he comes," her mother said sternly. "What matters is that we invite him."

Gloria sighed and selected a new envelope. She had spent an exhausting morning with her mother, the cook, and Boothby, going over menus, seeing to the tuning of the piano, instructing the maids about hanging the summer drapes, checking that the gilt chairs were all in good condition to be brought into the salon for the evening. Some of these things would have been done already except that the gala event in the country house had thrown off her mother's usually precise 'everything ready by Easter' schedule.

"Those four should have new braid," her mother had pointed out, barely pausing to look more closely at the offending chairs.

Gloria knew she wouldn't have noticed the slight fraying along the front. As her mother kept pointing out, she had a lot to learn.

"When I was barely older than you, I suddenly had a large household to run and no training whatsoever. I only knew I didn't want to have my house run by ignorant servants, so I learned the hard way. I don't want you to have to go through that."

Gloria sighed. This seemed the hard way to her. But at least her mistakes had no consequences. She knew the servants weren't making fun of her below stairs, not laughing at her behind her back, comparing her incompetence to Mrs. So-and-So whose house was so well run, all stories her mother still told with as much fire as if they had happened only yesterday. When Daisy complained that she was missing all the fun at boarding school, Gloria wrote to her about all the boring things she had to do, that it wasn't all going to debutante balls and parties.

Trips to Harry Angelo's for fittings for the dresses that had been picked out for the spring season were much more fun. There was little that Gloria had to learn about fashion. Even the high-waisted styles that were the coming thing for warmer days suited her. She loved the feel of silk against her skin, the sheen of taffeta and velvet, the floating charm of organza. She loved the shorter skirts with their bold showing of slim ankles. Even the walking back and forth pretending she had a book on her head, as she had been taught in dancing school, didn't bother her.

But what was taking the most time for this party and causing the real headaches was the guest list. Originally, this was supposed to be a small at-home in keeping with the Lenten season, but somehow, without Gloria or her mother realizing it, the event had blossomed. Great-Aunt Edwina had met some charming Russian aristocrats at a musical evening at the Astors, and discovering that they were both single, had invited them. "One is a Romanoff," she had burbled when she had rushed over to tell them. "A real Romanoff! Imagine if he should take to our Gloria!"

Uncle Paul had invited a German millionaire who had made his money in explosives and whom Paul was representing in some civil suit. This angered Gloria's father, who thought they should keep away from people involved in the war, but everyone agreed they couldn't embarrass Uncle Paul by not sending an official invitation now. And then there was the usual tired list of eligible young men who came to all the social events. None of them interested Gloria, but they had to be invited anyway because of their social position, or their father's business relationship with her father, or some faint hope that she might change her mind about one of them. She sighed and addressed another envelope.

"It's not centered properly," her mother said, pausing to look over her shoulder. "Do it again."

Gloria was beginning to hate the event she had been looking forward to just a few days earlier.

"Only a few more and then they can go to the post," her mother said, handing her a few more names to add to the list. "We'll need help now that the numbers are higher. Mrs. Beattie says her two nieces can come and help out in the kitchen, and Boothby is looking after borrowing a footman and three maids from our neighbors. We have more than enough crockery and silver and crystal, thank goodness, so we don't have to send anyone out to the country to fetch anything."

Her mother paused and tapped her foot as she went over things in her head. Her cheeks glowed. Her whole being radiated energy. She was in her element.

"Flowers?" Gloria asked tentatively.

"Done. They'll be delivered the day before and kept in the conservatory." Her mother paused again and looked at Gloria closely. "Straighten your shoulders, dear," she said. "You'll get a hump on her back like poor dear Great-Aunt Edwina. Not that it seems to slow her down," she added absently.

"She did snag us a Romanoff," Gloria said, and instantly wished she could take back the words.

Her mother scowled at her. "You should appreciate what we do for you," she said, "not criticize or make fun of our efforts. You must marry well. It's your duty, and it's ours to help bring that about."

"Yes, mama." Gloria hung her head.

There was silence in the room for a moment. Then she felt her mother's hand smoothing her hair gently. She heard a sigh and then her mother left the room.

Gloria wondered what the Romanoff looked like. She had seen a few pictures of Czar Nicholas, and he was handsome. On the other hand, Grand Duke Whatshisname looked like an imbecile.

She was just finishing the last invitation when she heard sniveling at the door. Maggie hovered there, a handkerchief in her hand, her eyes red from crying.

"Good heavens, Maggie, what's the matter?"

"Oh, miss! They've gone and fired Fred!" Maggie ran into the room and burst into tears.

"The Drexlers? Why, for goodness sake?"

"For our little adventure, miss. With Mr. Nijinsky. Remember?"

"What? But that's...that's ridiculous!"

"They say he's not allowed to receive calls on the telephone, miss. And they say he's not supposed to leave the house at night without telling anyone, neither. So they fired him without references. He doesn't know what he's going to do, miss!"

"Oh, Maggie, I'm so sorry. Morgan will talk to them. He'll explain it's all his fault. It'll be fine."

"I don't think so, miss."

"I'll call Mrs. Drexler right now," she said, getting up and heading for the telephone.

But as she sat down in front of the instrument, she began to have second thoughts. Morgan had told them it was a prank. But Fred had been told the address of that house of ill repute; he had given it to her. What if he told the Drexlers the truth? What if he already had told them? In horror, she drew back from the telephone table and stood up. Maggie was right. This wasn't just a simple misunderstanding that could be fixed with a few words of explanation.

"Morgan will know what to do," she said to Maggie, who was watching her from the door to the servants' quarters. "I think we'd better wait until he comes home. Come upstairs and pin up that skirt for me, the one that drags at the back, would you?"

"Of course, miss."

Gloria ran up the curving stairway, pleased that she had thought of something to occupy Maggie for a while at least. There was no telling when Morgan would be home. These days, he seemed to be out more and more, perhaps in an effort to avoid their father and his uncomfortable questions.

Gloria slipped on the deep-blue moire skirt and balanced on a footstool while Maggie pinned up the hem. The girl was talented with a needle for simple projects, but everything more complicated went to their dressmaker.

They were almost finished when she heard a scream from upstairs. Maggie stabbed a pin into her finger and cried out, thrusting her finger in her mouth as she sat back on her heels.

"Aunt Hattie!" Gloria jumped off the stool and rushed through the door and up the stairs to the third floor where Hattie lived with her companion, Miss Green. She flung open the door, then paused, one hand to her mouth. Hattie was on the floor in her white lace nightgown, surrounded by shards of colored glass glinting like jewels in the sun streaming in the window. A Tiffany lamp lay on its side in one corner, its beautiful glass shade shattered. Hattie's usually elegant pile of gleaming brown hair was disheveled, hanging down her back in disarray as if she had pulled it that way herself in her mindless fear. Tears ran down her cheeks, and the palms of her hands were streaked with blood.

"What happened?" asked Gloria, trying to keep her voice down so as not to frighten Hattie even more.

"I've been trying to get her dressed, as we usually do, but she's not herself today."

"Why didn't you call for help?"

"Lately, she's been so good, so... normal." Miss Green's narrow face squinched, her watery grey eyes brimming over with tears. "I kept at her, thinking she just needed to stick to a strict regime as the doctor said and she'd come around. You remember him saying that, don't you, miss?"

"Yes, yes. So what happened?"

"She began her crazy talk, playing with the sunbeams and trying to catch the colors from the lamp that was on the window sill. She said she wanted to make a picture, so I said certainly, but after she got dressed. She got more and more agitated, miss. Finally, she threw the lamp on the floor and began to try to make her picture out of the glass shards. I couldn't stop her!" Miss Green covered her face with her hands and began to weep in earnest.

Hattie cried out to the invisible Georgina to help her paint the picture with the pretty colors as she ran her hands through the broken glass. She screamed again as her blood mingled with the stained glass on the pale Aubusson carpet.

"Willy! Oh, William! Why did you leave me!" she cried.

Gloria ran to the door and rang the bell to summon help. Almost at once, it seemed, the room was full of people.

"Gloria, go!" her mother said firmly. "Make yourself useful elsewhere."

Banished from the third floor, Gloria smoothed her hair nervously in front of the morning room mirror. Her hands were shaking. She walked to the desk, picked up the invitations and took them to the front hall. As she laid them on the table to be picked up for the post, she noticed a smear of blood on the corner of the top one. She slipped it into the middle of the pile, out of sight.

Faintly, the sobs of Aunt Hattie floated down the stairwell. Then a door slammed, and all was quiet.

NINETEEN

"Seems as if your Russian friend is the target of some very bad luck," Mr. Vanheusen said, looking up from the newspaper at the breakfast table on Monday.

Startled, Morgan glanced involuntarily at Gloria, whose hand, holding a piece of toast, stopped midway to her mouth. Obviously, they were both thinking the same thing, seeing the same image: the star of the Ballets Russes standing in their kitchen, disheveled, his clothes streaked with dust and dirt.

"Quite the hero it seems," his father went on, oblivious, "saving his wife and carrying his baby daughter to safety down the fire escape like that."

Gloria began to eat her toast.

Morgan took a deep breath. "When did this happen?"

"Yesterday, it says here."

"Poor man!" exclaimed his mother. "What a dreadful experience."

"Some people are dogged by misadventure."

"How is Aunt Hattie?" Gloria asked, looking at her aunt's vacant chair next to her mother.

"Not well, I'm afraid. The doctor has given her a sleeping draft and another for her nerves. She'll be all the better for a good rest. Too much stimulation of late, I suspect."

"I suspect we've all had a bit too much stimulation lately," Mr. Vanheusen said, glancing at Morgan. "And what are you doing today, young man?" He folded the paper and tossed his serviette on the table.

"I was thinking of calling on Mr. Rinner," Morgan said. "At the club the other night, he said there may be an opening there for someone with my education."

"But Rinner's in stocks and bonds. Since when are you interested in that?"

And since when do you care what I'm interested in? Morgan thought rebelliously.

"Now, Gus, he's showing some initiative and that's admirable, don't you think?" His mother smoothed down her dress as she rose and pecked his father on the cheek. "Have a good day, dear. I'm off to deal with my correspondence. Will you be home for dinner?"

His father paused, nodded, and left for his meeting.

"You don't need to go into Mr Rinner's business if you don't like it, dear," his mother said, "but I'm glad you're taking some positive steps, even if it's not in the right direction." As she left the room, a trail of lavender lingered in the air.

"I thought we were done for there, for a moment," Gloria murmured and stifled a laugh.

"So did I. Can you imagine the mileage Uncle Paul would get out of it if we'd been caught, with you driving through the streets at midnight to pick up the notorious Nijinsky after a brawl?"

"Outside a house of ill repute," Gloria added. "I'd be sent to a nunnery for sure."

"I doubt it. Father's an Orangeman, remember?"

Gloria clapped a hand over her mouth, but her laughter filled the room. "Wasn't Maggie's young man wonderful that night? And Maggie pitched right in, cleaning up Mr. Nijinsky's clothes and making hot toddies. It's a wonder Boothby didn't wake up."

"Luckily for us, the walls are thick below stairs and he's a heavy sleeper." Morgan poured the last of the coffee.

"Speaking of Maggie," Gloria began. She paused, then launched into the unexpected repercussions of their adventure. "Poor Fred! You have to do something, Morgan."

"All right, I'll see if I can get him another job. But there's no way I can explain the whole thing to the Drexlers, Gloria. You must realize that. I can't get his old job back for him. Are you going to the ballet tomorrow, by the way?"

"I think so. Don't you think it's beginning to look as if Mr. Nijinsky was right about someone being after him?"

"The fire could just be a coincidence, I suppose," Morgan said. "The paper said it was a candle that fell over, setting the curtains on fire."

"Why would there be a candle in a modern hotel suite that uses electricity? Besides, the maid would have doused them if candles were used for a meal or some such occasion."

"Accidents happen," Morgan persisted. He didn't want to admit the possibility of sabotage. It was too frightening, too European. Not something that could happen here in New York. It was as if the Russian dancer had trailed the European turmoil with him, letting it loose in the streets of Morgan's own city. Violence against himself; and perhaps against anyone else who got in the way? The cowardly thought shocked Morgan.

Gloria rang the bell, summoning the maid to clear the dishes. "I have an elocution lesson in a few minutes," she said. "Are you really going to see Mr. Rinner?"

Morgan stood up. "Maybe later. Right now, I'm going to call on Mr. Nijinsky."

The fifth floor of the Claridge Hotel was alive with activity as lines of chambermaids and young men in the hotel uniform carried the last of the Nijinskys' possessions from their old suite to the new one down the hall. Madame Nijinsky's voice could be heard giving orders, keeping the lines moving, making sure everything was going to the right place. It had taken a little persuading to get the elevator operator to take him up to that floor, but luckily, the man had recognized Morgan as a frequent visitor.

"It was a madhouse up here earlier," he said as the gilded cage rose majestically upwards. "Mr. Nijinsky got his family out before we knew anything was wrong. Then his valet came down and shouted at us, and no one knew what he was saying, he was so upset. It was nothing really serious, they tell me. By the time I got up here, the fire was out, and Mr. Nijinsky was sitting on the floor in the empty suite the manager gave them, carving a little wooden animal for Kyra, the little girl. She looks so much like him, don't you think?"

"Maybe she'll be a dancer, too," Morgan said, not wanting to say he had never seen Jinks's daughter. "Which way?"

"Number 512, sir. Right at the end where no one will disturb them."

The faint smell of smoke lingered on the air, growing fainter as he neared the new suite. Yuri stood at the open door, his dark face lined with fatigue.

"Is everyone all right?" Morgan asked, handing the man his hat.

"The master, he want Madame to go visit again the friends," Yuri said. "He is afraid for all. But Madame, she not want to go. She fierce to stay."

"Who are you betting on?"

Yuri shrugged. "Is good you come, take him away."

Morgan hadn't planned on that, but on second thought, it was probably the best way to get his friend's mind off the fire. "Tell him I'm here," Morgan said. "I'll wait. I don't want to intrude."

Yuri disappeared. Morgan stepped aside to let the line of movers carrying three wardrobe trunks pass by. At last, the hall was empty except for two maids who now began to sweep the long runner, making all traces of the recent furious activity disappear.

Nijinsky appeared beside him quite suddenly. "My friend, you see my life in danger. Now my family in danger. They must go."

"Good morning," Morgan said with a smile.

"Not good. Not good for me."

"Let's get out of here. You need some fresh air."

"Vashti!"

Nijinsky turned at his wife's voice and sighed. "My wife, she put all in order. Not need me. Tell her I go out." He took the hat Yuri held out to him. Morgan took his and winked at Yuri, who looked startled.

Outside, Nijinsky walked fast, muttering to himself in Russian, now and then shouting something at Morgan. The street was noisy with the usual honking of horns, clatter of wagons, and whinnying of horses, everyone jostling for the right of way.

Turning down a side street, Morgan spotted a café and headed inside, pulling Nijinsky with him. Several men looked up as they entered, nodded, and then went back to their conversations. Caruso's latest aria played on a large gramophone that held pride of place on the highly polished wooden counter.

Nijinsky tilted his head to listen for a moment. "Enrico have bad time, too, he tell me. Some years past, people after him. But now all is good."

"You know Caruso, sir?" The portly waiter beamed down at Nijinsky.

"Yes, Enrico very nice man. We have dinner at Sherry last week."

"Oh, sir! It's an honor to have friend of Caruso here. There is no payment for you. *Niente.* Anything you want: café, chocolate, antipasto, is yours free."

"That's not necessary, sir," Morgan said, worried that Nijinsky might not take kindly to the Italian tenor being recognized when the world's greatest male dancer was not.

"Yes, yes. What would you like, sir? Espresso? Cappuccino? Chocolate?"

"Chocolate good," said the Russian, nodding in time to the music.

It occurred to Morgan that his friend might not have understood the situation. He ordered espresso. Nijinsky watched a lithe young man jump up and turn the record over when it came to an end. 'Ave Maria' filled the small café.

"I must discover who is after me," Nijinsky said, looking at Morgan, his slanted dark eyes unsettling in their intensity.

"Jinks, I know things look bad on the surface, but really, last night was an accident-"

"And outside Madame Hahn is accident? Galina is accident? Someone want me not dance. To fail. Maybe to die."

Morgan reached for his espresso, which thankfully arrived at that moment. In one way, this made sense. But surely if Galina's death were not an accident, the police would have investigated, wouldn't they? Then suddenly, he remembered his friend Rolly's scrapes with the law: how the young man had been handed back to his parents on more than one occasion with nothing on the books, no charges ever brought against him, his father's money paying fines and making restitution to whomever had been harmed. The law is an ass, Dickens said. But in Morgan's limited experience, the law was for sale. And maybe someone was paying this time to keep the Ballets Russes out of court.

"Jinks, what do you know about Galina?"

Nijinsky looked up. "Technique not great, but she feel music inside, move well enough on stage. Diaghilev hire her, not me."

"She was hired here in New York?"

"I think yes. She speak Russian, but not good. Not…like Sergei, you understand?"

"You mean not upper class?"

"Yes. More like what I speak when I come to St. Petersburg and everyone make fun. Me, from Poland, you know. But I learn. And I learn French some in Paris, with Diaghilev." He stopped abruptly.

"So she's an American girl who picked up Russian here somehow, maybe from people in her old neighborhood. But why would someone want to kill her?"

"Me, they want to kill! Me!"

"But let's think about this. Maybe it's her all along. What did she do to upset someone that much?"

"Nothing! Just young girl."

"With a gentleman friend?"

"How I know this?"

"I thought you might have noticed a man hanging around her dressing room."

"I not hang around her dressing room for man!"

"What? No, no, of course not." Morgan stopped, momentarily sidetracked. "Do you know where she lived?"

Nijinsky made an exasperated noise. "How I know this? I am here only some weeks. I not know this woman before. The others I know…most. Not Galina Petrovna. And not Léonide Massine," he added.

"You think he—"

"No, no."

"Okay. Originally, Galina was not going to dance this role with you, was she?"

"No. Irina hurt leg. No dance."

"How did she hurt her leg?"

Nijinsky shrugged. "Before I am here, this happen. You think Galina…?" He shook his head wonderingly.

"I don't think anything. I just know that ambition can make us do strange things, even out-of-character things sometimes." Or love, he added to himself. "If we want to find out if she was really the target and not you, we have to go to her rooms, talk to her neighbors, and see if we can find out more about her. What do you say?"

"I say *I* am target. If nothing there, I am right, so we go look. Then you know."

"How will we find her address?"

"We go to Met. I find out."

"Just like Sherlock Holmes and Watson," Morgan said happily as they reached for their hats.

"Who?"

"Nothing. Let's go. The game's afoot!" And it promised to be much more interesting than calling on Mr. Adolphus Rinner.

TWENTY

*"AMERICANIZATION MOVEMENT TO DEAL WITH
IMMIGRANTS*
*Eastern Europeans flood through our ports and form foreign islands
in the midst of our cities."*

—*New York Bugle*, late edition

Nijinsky kept the taxi waiting while he went to find out Galina's address. It took longer than Morgan expected, but at last, the Russian came back, waving a piece of paper triumphantly.

"Wynters gets for me," he said, climbing into the taxi. "He tell me not go alone. I tell him you go, too. Is not alone."

Morgan looked at the address scribbled on the paper, trying to place the area of the city, but the name rang no bells. He leaned forward, thrusting the paper at the cabbie. "Do you know where this is?" he asked.

"Lower East Side, I think. You don't want to go there, sir." The driver twisted around in his seat to look earnestly at his passengers. "That's a pretty tough neighborhood. All immigrants… Russian, Poles, you name it."

"*I* am Russian," Nijinsky said, puffing up his chest.

"Sir, you live at the Claridge Hotel. If I may be so bold, there's a difference."

"We go."

"You heard him," Morgan said. "We go."

"Don't say I didn't warn you."

As the cab made its way through the chaotic streets, Nijinsky seemed to withdrew, staring ahead of him as if not really seeing anything. Morgan wondered what he was thinking about, if he was thinking about anything, or if he was hearing music in his head, seeing a stage, perhaps himself in the spotlight, dancing with the dying Galina. Morgan settled back to enjoy the little adventure. It wasn't racing motorcars, but it was bound to be more interesting than stocks and bonds.

They were heading southeast, cutting through narrow streets that gradually became little more than alleys. The crowds increased, the people looking more and more foreign: women in aprons with embroidered shawls over their heads, babies wrapped in the folds; men in long coats and scuffed worn shoes, their faces thin and full of care. Young boys wearing heavy aprons too big for their small frames loaded wagons. Girls sat in doorways, minding younger children, mending drab clothes as they chattered together. The shrill cries of barkers hawking their wares from makeshift barrows lining the street grated on his ears. The smell of backed-up sewage made him wrinkle his nose in disgust. Where were they?

At last, the cab pulled over and turned off the engine. "I can't get any closer, sir," he said. "As far as I can tell, this address is in behind number 227 there." He pointed to the tenement in front of them.

"Behind?" Morgan asked, leaning forward and staring at the dilapidated building.

"Yes, sir. In these parts, years ago, they needed more places to live, see, so they built more tenements in behind the ones they already had, see? There used to be gardens back there, but now it's just more buildings. You have to get to them through an alley. Should be one around here somewheres."

"An alley?" Morgan was beginning to have second thoughts, but Nijinsky suddenly pulled open the cab door and jumped out.

"*Allons-y,*" he said.

"I thought he was Russian," the cabbie said, looking at the dancer suspiciously.

"He's spent a lot of time in Paris." Morgan paid him and followed Nijinsky along the street, looking for an alley. Almost at once, they were surrounded by ragged urchins holding out their skinny arms, asking for money. Some waved plaster trinkets for sale, but most just whined and importuned, their voices a stream of never-ending pleas, their eyes large with hunger and desperation. This was a childish idea, Morgan thought, slipping his gold watch fob out of sight and pushing his way after the Russian, who seemed immune to the beggars.

"No here." Nijinsky stopped and stared at the house numbers. An old man dressed in black was coming slowly down the steps of the nearest house. He stopped when he saw Nijinsky.

"*Gospadin* Vaslav Nijinsky?" His voice was thin and rose at the end as if he couldn't believe what he was saying.

The dancer smiled and began talking to him in rapid Russian. The man kept bowing and smiling and touching the dancer as if he needed to reassure himself that the legend was standing in front of him.

At length, Nijinsky turned to Morgan to explain. "He see me dance in St. Petersburg since ten, twelve years. He say this house back on other side." He gestured wildly, trying to explain. The old man joined in with his own gestures. Morgan watched for a moment, trying to figure it out.

"You're saying the driver let us out on the wrong street?"

They both nodded.

"We go to the corner, turn right, and then there's an alley. Is that it?"

"I show, I show." The old man was nodding his head enthusiastically. He began trotting along the uneven street, looking back to make sure they were following.

It wasn't far, but if it hadn't been for the old man, they might have missed it, the alley was so narrow and dark. Morgan stood peering into the dimness, wondering how he had managed to end up in a place like this with the eccentric Russian. When he turned around, Nijinsky was close behind him. The old man had disappeared.

"We go, no?"

Morgan breathed in the sour smells, the mold and decay and filth of buildings no one cared about. The despair of the inhabitants leaked from every crevice. Were these rotting buildings owned by someone like Bunter Picket? Maybe by Picket himself? For a moment, he felt a sort of panic as he plunged into this netherworld. Pull yourself together, he muttered to himself, and tried not to see the child defecating so close he nearly stepped on him.

When he emerged at the end of the tunnel, he saw number 274 ahead. Above, he could barely see the sky, and the towering tenements behind them facing the street gave the place a claustro-phobic atmosphere made worse by the rank neglect…except for one window ledge crowded with flower pots. What courage to try to grow things here, he thought.

Nijinsky seemed to be unaffected by their surroundings and was concentrating completely on their search. He marched up the crumbling steps and opened the door into a dark hall. "Man say she live at top of house," he said, starting up the stairs.

"But how do we get in?" Morgan asked, following.

Nijinsky didn't answer.

There were five floors and they trudged up all of them. The last staircase was so narrow, Morgan wondered if it led to the roof only, but at the top, a door was open into a long narrow room. Someone was inside.

"Rudy!" exclaimed Nijinsky. "Why you here?"

"I have a right to be here!" the young man exclaimed. His face had a ravaged look, as if he'd been crying for a long time. "More right than you. I just came to get my things."

"You live with Galina?"

"No. I'm leaving now."

"Pavel know you here?"

"Oh, God! Look, I don't need any lectures from you. Please let me pass!"

Nijinsky stared at him. "Why you do this to Pavel?"

"I'm not doing anything!" He suddenly burst into a storm of Russian.

"Wait!" cried Morgan. "You're the one who helped me out at Madame Hahn's!"

The young man pushed past him and thumped down the stairs.

"Who is he, Jinks? I wanted to thank him."

"Is Rudy. I know him because he is *petit ami* of friend Pavel Lermontov, a dancer with the company. He is there a lot to see Pavel, and he know Galina, too. I don't know how well until now."

Morgan looked around the room. If Rudy had been living here, there was no sign of it now. Perhaps he had moved most of his things out earlier. In either case, Morgan didn't understand why Nijinsky would care. The place was narrow and dark, with nothing to sleep on but a lumpy-looking divan covered with a rumpled shawl. The room was untidy, as if someone had been looking for something. Rudy, perhaps? Or the police?

"What are we looking for?" he asked.

Nijinsky shrugged. He was looking around the room with a baffled look. He pulled open a few drawers, shook his head. Rifled through a packet of letters, read a few. He glanced in the pile of clippings on the table, then looked more closely.

Morgan moved beside him. "All of the clippings are about you," he said.

"Not all." Nijinsky sifted through the pile, pointing out others about art exhibits and auctions.

"She was interested in art?" Morgan said, surprised. Perhaps she had fed her starved soul with visits to museums. She would certainly need something to look forward to besides the theater. He glanced at a few photographs sticking out of a book: one taken at Coney Island, one of Galina in costume, one with a young man standing on the roof of a building. He dropped them in his pocket to examine later and looked around at the walls. There was nothing to suggest a love of art here, except a few pictures cut from magazines and a card, the kind you write on one side with a picture on the other.

He reached up and pulled the postcard off the wall, then flipped it over.

"It's in Russian," he said.

Nijinsky took the card and read it. "From Aunt Olga. She say she glad to see Galina again after long time. She say come see again. She use French, too. Very elegant style, like…like Sergei write."

"So she's educated, you mean."

"*Très culturée*. Is same writing like letters." He pointed to the dresser where he had left the packet. "She say there she glad Galina come back to see her. After years, she glad."

"Is there an address on the letters?" Morgan interrupted. "Perhaps we should visit her."

Nijinsky shuffled through the small pile of thick creamy paper and extricated a letter, which he showed to Morgan. There was an address written in beautiful copperplate script on the top under an embossed crest.

"Is Ostroffsky crest," Nijinsky said, staring at it.

"She's related to the count? In this neighborhood?"

"Perhaps."

"Let's pay the lady a visit," said Morgan. "Maybe she can tell us something."

He felt a physical sense of relief as they emerged into daylight again at the end of the alley. Following directions from several men Nijinsky talked to in a mixture of languages, they made their way through the teaming noisy streets into a side street where the houses were smaller and better kept. There was a strip of grass outside each door, guarded by a freshly painted iron railing. Only a series of doorbells outside the main door gave the lie to the first impression that these were single-family dwellings.

"Down here," Morgan said, opening the gate and making his way down the area steps to the door to the basement apartment. He turned the bell in the middle of the door several times, listening to the series of rings echo inside. He was just thinking there was no one home when the door was opened by an erect elderly lady, greying hair piled on top of her head, held in place by jeweled combs.

Morgan bowed. Nijinsky took off his hat, opened his mouth, and stared.

Startled, Morgan smiled nervously. "We are looking for Madame Olga Ostroffsky," he began. He glanced at Nijinsky, who was still staring intently at the woman. "We apologize for calling so early in the day," he went on, fishing a calling card out of his pocket, "but we would like to talk to her about Galina Petrovna."

"Ah, *la pauvre* Galina." The old woman opened the door wide. "I am Madame Ostroffsky. Please…" She gestured for them to enter.

Nijinsky, still mute, handed over his calling card as well, and they followed the stately woman into the house, down a narrow corridor and into another world.

Morgan almost caught his breath. After the squalor of Galina's surroundings, this place looked absolutely opulent. Sunlight glinted on polished crystals hanging from Tiffany lamp shades, on gilt from a series of Russian icons hanging on the walls, on a large brass samovar standing on a table against one wall. There were several framed portraits of ballet dancers on one wall as well as an oil portrait of a solemn young man in a uniform with a red sash across his chest. Her husband, perhaps? He looked Russian. Morgan noticed that Madame Ostroffsky seemed to steer her way by touch between the occasional tables, the lamps, and the brass statue of a hunter with his dog, over to a worn chair near the window. He wondered how well she could see.

"Please be seated," she said, smiling at them with a quizzical expression. "Your friend is very quiet. Is something wrong?" Her smile wavered.

Nijinsky stepped forward now and took the woman's hand. "Madame Olga Pinyakovkska, it is an honor," he said and kissed her hand. The old lady smiled in delight, her face instantly transformed into that of a young, vibrant girl. "You recognized me! After all these years!"

"I train in Imperial Ballet Theater, Madame. I dance in Maryinsky Theater. You are legend." He burst into Russian.

Morgan looked more closely at the portraits and saw the resemblance at once. She was a dancer. Had been a dancer—and a famous one, judging by Jinks's reaction. That must be the connection to Galina.

"Monsieur, we are leaving your friend behind, I fear." Madame Ostroffsky smiled at Morgan. "He does not speak Russian?"

Morgan laughed. "I'm afraid not, madam. I am just an American. I did study French in college, but it didn't stick, I'm afraid."

"No matter. We speak English. And thank you, Mr. Nijinsky. I can't tell you how wonderful it feels to be recognized after all these years, and by someone like you. It is an especial honor. Galina talked about you all the time. Poor girl."

"Did you know her well, madam?" Morgan asked, hoping to steer things back to the reason for their visit.

"Indeed I did. It's a long story. Shall we have tea?"

Morgan stifled a gesture of annoyance and looked at Jinks. If this involved complicated maneuvers with the samovar, they might be here all day.

"My maid is out, I'm afraid, but she prepared everything before she left." The old lady moved gracefully across to the gently smoking samovar, poured a little tea from the small teapot on top into a glass with a silver handle, added water from the spigot and passed it to Nijinsky, who handed it to Morgan. She chattered on. "It seems Annya forgot to put out any biscuits. I'm so sorry."

"No, no. Thank you is enough. Is for me…*la nostalgie*, yes?"

"Yes. You must be homesick, away for so long from Russia."

"But not as long as you, madam," Morgan said, smoothly getting things back on track. Now that he was used to the room and to her, he was noticing things: the way her dress, though expensive, was very worn along the seams; the way several tiny buttons were missing and a section of seed pearls was also gone from the back. And the style was like something his mother used to wear years ago. He wondered if she really had a maid at all or was she living in a fantasy world?

"I taught Galina to dance," she said. "I found her one day on the street, dancing for money to the music of a hurdy-gurdy man. She moved so gracefully, so naturally, with an intuitive understanding of the music. I talked to her for a while, and then invited her to my home. She longed to dance, really dance. Even though she knew nothing about ballet except what she had glimpsed at street festivals, she knew that was what she wanted to do."

"She was lucky to have met you," Morgan said.

"I was the lucky one. I loved teaching her. She was such an apt pupil."

"Apt? What is?" Nijinsky asked.

She explained in Russian and then went on to talk in English about Galina's rapid progress in dance. "Later on, I taught others for money after my husband passed on, but no one was as good or showed such promise. When the time came for her to audition for a real company, I was the one who suggested she change her name. She wasn't Russian, you know, and it's very difficult to be taken seriously in the dance world if you're not."

They both nodded and she went on.

"So she became Galina Petrovna. She spoke a kind of street Russian she had picked up, and I tried to help her accent, but she was a much better dance student than she was at languages."

"I never noticed her accent not real," Nijinsky said.

"Oh, she was fluent enough in the argot she had picked up from her neighbors. She just didn't want to bother learning the finer points."

"Where she dance?" Nijinsky asked.

"First, there were appearances at church fairs and street festivals. But as she got better, she auditioned for the Kassevetsky company and got in. She made rapid progress there and was soon second soloist, then first. I was so proud. But then I lost touch. Very sad."

"Do you know why?"

She shook her head and slowly began to tell them her story about how her own fortunes had rapidly waned. Her husband died, leaving debts she had known nothing about. She began renting out parts of her beloved house, until at last she ended up in the basement, living where her staff used to live and work. "Annya stayed with me, fiercely loyal even now when she has to work in a garment factory to help out with food and heat." She put her hands over her face for a moment. Nijinsky made a move as if to comfort her, then pulled himself back.

Morgan looked away, as if trying to find help somewhere in the room. He wasn't used to displays of open emotion.

"Please forgive me. When I think of my dear Yevgeny who lost everything because he loved me so much he wanted to marry me, I get quite overcome. I miss him so."

"Your husband, he is related to Count Fyodor Mikelovitch Ostroffsky?" Nijinsky said.

"A distant relative, but yes. When Yevgeny married me, it was a scandal." She laughed. "But he didn't care. He said we would start a new life and forget them all. And we did, traveling with mountains of luggage to the New World. Everyone was so surprised, they didn't think to stop us. His mother used to send money. Yegeny said it was his money anyway, but it stopped when she died."

"You must be lonely," Morgan said awkwardly.

"Galina filled a gap in my life. Yevgeny and I never had any children, and I poured everything into her. When she stopped visiting, I was very lonely, I admit. I even went to find her a few times, but that place she lived in..." She grimaced. "I know this isn't a wonderful neighborhood anymore, but compared to that..." She shivered. "But please, don't feel sorry for me. I am content now with my remaining treasures and my memories.

"Did you notice the icons, Mr. Nijinsky? We brought them with us in a false bottom of a trunk. Yevgeny was so afraid they would be stolen. They're heirlooms that have been in his family for many years."

Nijinsky got up and inspected the icons lining one wall.

Morgan walked over and looked, too.

"I've never seen anything quite like them," Morgan said truthfully.

Nijinsky said nothing.

Morgan thought Madame Ostroffsky looked disappointed at their lack of praise for her treasures. Jinks could say something, surely, he thought. But his friend was making his farewell speech now, and Morgan picked up his cue. He retrieved their hats from the hall, bowed over the old woman's hand, and followed Nijinsky out.

"Well," said Morgan. "Why the sudden rush? I think she was a little upset."

"Those icons, I not know what to say."

"Neither did I," Morgan agreed.

"No, no, you not understand. Icons, art: I know these things. Prince Lvov, Sergei: They teach me much. I study art with Chagall under Baxt in St. Petersburg one time. I know icons. These ones, they are...not true...not real."

"You mean fake?"

Nijinsky nodded vigorously. "Fake. Yes. But she not know."

"I don't think she can see very well," Morgan said.

"Someone take the real ones. Maybe maid Annya. We talk to Annya when she not at work, yes?"

Morgan paused, ignoring the shouting crush of all the people pushing around him. "But she works in a garment factory. They're on strike."

"Strike? Hit?"

"No, they've gone off the job, trying to get better pay and working conditions, I suppose. Anyway, she won't be at work today. They closed the factories. So where did she go?"

"If one job stop, she get other job, no? Need money for house, old lady, food. Maybe not far away." He turned to an old woman sweeping her front steps and talked in Russian for a while. The old lady called a young girl and the three conferred for a moment longer.

Nijinsky turned back to him "She say Annya is saint. She work in kitchen at restaurant three blocks away. We go. Talk."

"And Madame Ostroffsky doesn't know?"

"Madame Olga not go out no more. She know nothing."

"Some saint," muttered Morgan, shouldering his way along the crowded street.

They found Annya two blocks away in an alley behind the restaurant, dumping refuse into an overflowing bin. She flinched when Nijinsky called her name.

"You're Annya, who works for Madame Olga Ostroffsky?" Morgan asked, hoping she spoke English even half as well as her mistress.

Her thin, pale face grew even more drained of color. "Something is wrong? Madame is sick?" She dropped the heavy metal bin, which clanged against the chipped bricks of the alley.

"No, she's fine," Morgan reassured her. "We're curious as to what happened to her icons, though. Mr. Nijinsky here recognized them as fakes right away."

Annya sank back against the building, one hand going to her mouth. "You tell her?"

"No, but you're going to tell her what you did. And make it right."

"Me? What *I* did? Oh no! Is not me! Is that ingrate, Galina!" She spat on the ground.

Morgan and Nijinsky looked at each other. "Galina? And you never said anything?"

"It would break Madame's heart, sir. Please don't tell her. Is all she has: her memories, her little treasures."

"But she has no more," Nijinsky said.

"She loved Galina so much. She like daughter to her, you know? When Galina not come back for long time, she was so sad. She stay in bed for days, not want to get up. It took a long time to get her to do anything. Then Galina come back. Poof! Madame happy again. But Galina, she is not...I don't know how to say it...not quite the same."

"In what way?"

"She is not the sweet girl any more. But Madame do not see this. She is so happy. And Galina bring her world of ballet again, bring news of you, sir." She bobbed her head at Nijinsky. "All she wants now is to dance this new role with you. She talk all the time and she start to do some other dance things she had stopped doing before, like dance at parties for gentlemen."

"You think she needed money?"

"Need? I don't know need. Want, yes. And then she start talking about cleaning the icons, about her friend who cleans old painting. She talks about getting the icons back the way they used to be. As if we could ever do that! But Madame, she is in dreamland. She say yes. Take! The moment the first one come back, I know something not right, but I am no expert. And what can I do? Madame, she cannot see well enough. She see only brighter colors, so she is happy. She think they are like new, like they were two hundred years ago in her dear husband's home."

Annya was crying now, wiping her face angrily with her stained apron. "Why she do this to us?"

Morgan shook his head. "I don't know, Annya, but we're going to find out."

TWENTY-ONE

"REICHSTAG BACKS SUBMARINE WAR.
Adopts Committee Resolution Indorsing
Campaign Of the German U-Boats."

—*New York Times,* 1916

George Kassevetsky piled an armload of sketches on top of a chair in his office and swept the rest of the things off his desk into a wooden tea crate. "All goes," he said. "All goes. Is the past."

He grabbed a broom and began to sweep, stirring up clouds of dust that made him cough, forcing him to pause and look around bewildered as if he didn't understand what had happened.

"George, just sit down, will you? We'll have tea, talk, figure things out." Misha sat on the only comfortable chair in the room, his feet up on an old trunk.

George began to sweep again, more vigorously this time. Every now and then, he would stop and take a swipe at the cobwebs that hung thick in the corners. "No time, Misha. I know what has to be done." The Russian words rolled from his deep voice, filling the room with an energy he hadn't shown in months. "I've set things in motion already."

"George, you have no money."

"Rubbish. Kassevetsky has patrons. Kassevetsky has backers."

Misha sat up and leaned forward, his face creased with concern. "You *used* to have patrons and backers. They're gone, George. All gone, like the money you *used* to have."

"I have money."

"I know you had to pawn some props and costumes to pay for Galina's funeral. How can you stage a production now?"

"We have plenty more " George whirled on him angrily, his face red. He shook the broom at his old friend. "You spy on me! You betray me, like so many others!"

"No, no. I'm your friend, as ever. I don't spy, but I'm the company manager, George. I have to keep on top of the money situation."

"You don't know everything," George said darkly. "You think you do, but no, you do not." He threw the broom down and flung out the door and down the rattling spiral stairway to the stage below. A large canvas was spread out, nearly covering the whole space. Pails of paint stood along the edges, and a young man was splashing it about, skillfully outlining trees and a lake and the spires of a castle in the distance. His feet were bound in rags, and as he moved about, he left no marks on the canvas.

"Oh my God! What have you done?" Misha exclaimed as he stood behind George, his hands framing his round face.

"We are coming back," George said. "Like the phoenix, Kassevetsky will rise again with a new production. I hire dancers. We clean the theater. I hire Rudy here to paint new backdrop in style of Ballets Russes."

"And how do you pay for all this?" Misha whispered fiercely. "We haven't even paid the rent for this space in the last three months."

"We do it for Galina," George went on, crossing his arms.

"Wake up, my friend, before it is too late and we are all out on the street!" Misha shouted.

Rudy stopped working and turned around, startled. A lock of dark hair hung over his tired eyes. The deep circles underneath hinted that he hadn't slept well for a long time.

"Paint! Paint!" shouted George, waving his arms.

"For Galina," muttered Rudy, shuffling over the canvas.

"Anybody here?" The loud American voice startled them all.

George peered into the gloom of the small theater, trying to see the intruder. "Out! Out! Private place here!"

"I'm Detective Danny Sullivan," the man said, coming towards them down the center aisle. "I'm looking for George Kassevetsky."

"Why?" asked Misha, stepping forward protectively.

"Just a few routine questions, sir. My sergeant and I just have a few questions regarding the death of Galina Petrovna. Could I ask who you are, sir?"

"I'm Misha Markevitch, the manager of the Kassevetsky Dance Troupe."

"And you are Mr. Kassevetsky?" Sullivan turned towards George, a friendly smile on his broad freckled face.

"I am." George glowered at him suspiciously. In his experience, the police were rarely on good terms with theater people. Unless your name is Nijinsky, he added to himself. He scowled.

"And this young man?"

"He work for me," George said, dismissing Rudy's presence with a wave of his hand.

"Did you know Galina Petrovna, young man?"

Rudy stared at the two policemen, dropped his long-handled brush, turned and fled.

"After him, sergeant!" shouted Sullivan.

The sergeant leapt up on the stage and galloped after Rudy, his boots tracking wet paint across the canvas and into the wings.

"No! No!" George started after them, then stopped and turned on Sullivan. "You ruin his work! Hours of work you ruin! You pay, you...you barbarian!"

Sullivan held his hands out to the Russian in a gesture of conciliation. "My apologies, sir. My sergeant acts without thought sometimes."

"Rudy, he just work for me. Many times, he work for me. And Galina, too," he added. As he said her name, the fight seemed to go out of him. He sank down to the floor and began to sob.

"Look what you do!" exclaimed Misha angrily. "He is old man only. He know nothing of this. He hire the girl to dance for a few seasons is all."

"No, not all," George said, raising his head. "She come back to me. She dance next season for me."

Misha shook his head in exasperation.

"And you paid for her funeral," Sullivan said softly.

"Is true, she come back," George went on, looking up at the policeman earnestly. "Her dream, you see, is to dance with Vaslav Fromich Nijinsky. After that, she come home to me. She is like daughter."

"George," Misha said, his voice tired.

Off stage, the crashing noises and shouts were getting fainter.

Then they stopped. Someone screamed.

With surprising agility, Sullivan leapt up the steps onto the stage and sprinted in the direction of the noise.

"I did it!" Rudy's voice came back to them in a high wail. "Arrest me now! I'm guilty!"

"What is that fool talking about?" Misha asked George in Russian. "What does he mean?"

"*I* am the guilty one!" George moaned, covering his face with his hands. "It is all Kassevetsky's fault!"

"Long whiskers cannot take the place of brains," muttered Misha.

TWENTY-TWO

"GRANADOS MAY BE SAFE.
Hope That Composer and His Wife
Are on a Hospital Ship."

—*New York Times*

"Is that for me?" Morgan asked, his eyes on the small package in Boothby's hands.

"This is for Miss Gloria, sir," Boothby said, pausing.

"I'll take it to her." Morgan reached for the slim parcel. "I was just going to talk to her anyway."

"As you wish, sir."

Morgan got the impression Boothby was not pleased to be deprived of this job, but he could never be sure how Boothby felt about anything. He took the package and headed to the music room where Gloria had just finished her piano lesson.

"Have you turned into Paderewski yet?" he asked, flinging himself into an armchair.

"I'm still waiting," she said. "It may take a few more lessons."

"Will you be ready in time to perform at the great reception Mother's planning for next week?"

"Don't remind me. What will you be doing for your part of the entertainment?"

Morgan shivered dramatically. "I'm planning on coming down with a really bad cold," he said. "By the way, this arrived for you." He threw the package across to her.

She caught it awkwardly and flushed.

"Secret admirer?"

"Don't be silly." Her slender fingers teased the paper away from the package.

Morgan sat up straighter. Her cheeks were flaming, her eyes very bright. He watched as she took a book out of the package, looked at the title, and smiled. "Who is it from?"

"Oh, just a book I wanted and Muriel said she'd send it over."

"Muriel? What's the book?"

"It's the latest by Booth Tarkington." She swept the wrapping paper into a ball and got to her feet. "I have to go."

"Where?" Morgan jumped up and cut off her retreat. With a sudden quick gesture, he grabbed the book from her hands and flipped it open to the title page. "Who's Andy?"

"Give that back! It's not yours."

"You said it was Muriel's. Why does it have this man's name in it? Someone Muriel knows?"

"Stop!" Tears welled up in her wide grey eyes. "Why are you doing this?"

"If this is Muriel's and it's from some man named Andy, I need to know about it. And if it isn't Muriel's and you know this Andy, I need to know about it even more."

"You're jealous!"

Morgan moved closer, forcing her to back up. "Tell me, Gloria. This is serious. I do need to know."

"No, you don't." Her face had gone pale.

"It's not Muriel's, is it?"

"You're bullying me." Tears threatened to spill down her cheeks now, but Morgan's anger made him push harder.

"Is it Andy Stuyvesant?"

She laughed. "You think I would be interested in that fop?"

Morgan smiled. "No, but he's the only Andy I can think of."

"You don't know him," she said. "He's a writer."

"What? How did you meet this cad?"

"Promise you won't tell Mother and Father! And Andy's not a cad!"

"A man sneaking around a young girl in secret without meeting her family? Of course, he's a cad!"

"Listen to me, Morgan! I helped you when you needed me, when no one else could. I never said anything about that midnight adventure. Now I want you to keep quiet about this."

"It's not the same at all!" Morgan exploded.

"It is so!" Tears rolled down her cheeks freely at last.

"For heaven's sakes, Glory, stop blubbering." He fished a handkerchief out of his pocket and handed it to her.

She sank back on the divan and blew her nose. Morgan sat beside her. After a moment, he patted her hand awkwardly.

"Tell me about him. Where did you meet?"

"The Metropolitan Opera House." She sniffed. "Don't tell."

"All right, all right. At least, that's a respectable place to meet someone."

"More respectable than a house of ill repute," she muttered.

"What is so wonderful about this paragon?"

"He's so full of enthusiasm. We talk about everything, not just who is wearing what dresses and going to what parties. He writes for the newspaper. He even knows Mr. Nijinsky."

Not that that's much of a recommendation, Morgan thought ruefully. "How have you been meeting him? Where?"

"Muriel's been helping me."

"Muriel!"

"Yes, Muriel. We go to the park and walk. I've met him there about three times, and I said I'd be there today. You've made me late! And now Muriel may be gone!"

"Oh, don't start blubbering again. I'll take you."

She looked at him suspiciously. "Don't interrogate him, Morgan."

"We'll see," Morgan growled. "We'll take the Maxwell. I haven't driven it for a while."

"Don't be ostentatious."

"Too grand for your beau? Should I dress down?"

Gloria gave him a playful push. Her eyes were shining.

By the time they got to Central Park, Gloria was beside herself with worry that Andy would have given up on her and left.

"He knows I can't always make it," she said as they hurried along the path, "so he only waits a little while."

"You have hidden depth, sis," Morgan muttered, hurrying to keep up with her.

She stopped suddenly. Morgan almost bumped into her. "You stay here."

"Not on your life, my girl." Morgan glowered at the young man coming towards them.

Andy was barely as tall as Gloria, with a broad face and flaming red curls that he had tried to tame with pomade. His suit coat was open, the sleeves shiny with wear. The wide smile faltered as he saw Morgan's stern expression.

"This is my brother, Morgan," Gloria said quickly.

"Andy Cass," the young man said, extending his hand.

The two men shook hands, taking each other's measure in silence.

"I'm with the New York *Bugle*," Andy said at last.

"That yellow rag," Morgan said without thinking.

"Sir, it is not a rag. We write hard news, not gossip. Have you read the paper?"

Morgan admitted he hadn't. "But I will," he added.

"I'm glad to finally get the chance to meet someone from Gloria's family," Andy said. "I've felt a little uneasy, meeting like this, but we didn't mean to be underhanded in any way. It just seemed—"

"Less complicated," Gloria said quickly.

"Why don't you come to our little soirée this Thursday?" Morgan suggested. He felt Gloria's shocked reaction, but ignored her. "Come around eight thirty. Gloria can give you the details."

"Morgan!" she whispered angrily, turning away from Andy.

"We can say Andy's a friend of mine," Morgan went on smoothly. "Everything will be fine. Right, Andy?"

"Thank you, yes. I'd like that."

Gloria pinched her brother. He stepped away. "I'll be right over there on that bench. We'll leave in half an hour."

As he walked away, he felt quite proud of himself. But why was Gloria upset now? Wasn't this what she wanted? Andy to be included in her life? He shook his head. Women.

Gloria talked a blue streak on the way home, bubbling over with Andy's ideas about everything: from the subway strike and taxing jitneys, to the housing crisis and the new lofts being planned north of 14th street, to the latest scandal at Tammany Hall. Morgan hadn't suspected Gloria even knew what Tammany Hall was. He wasn't sure he was pleased with this new side to his sister.

"But you shouldn't have invited him to our soirée, Morgan. Sometimes you just don't think before you do things."

"For heaven's sake, Gloria, I thought you'd be pleased!"

"To have him interrogated by Father? Even if he's introduced as your friend, Father will want to know all about him, about his father, and his grandfather. You know what he's like. And what will Andy wear? Did you ever think of that?"

"If you want to go on seeing him, even as a friend, you'll have to work these things out. Didn't you think of that when you started all this subterfuge?"

Gloria sighed. "You're right. I guess we're both cut from the same cloth."

"I guess so." Morgan pulled the car through the archway into the porte-cochère of their house and helped her down. "It'll all work out for the best."

"You think so?" she said.

Boothby came out the door, a worried expression on his face. "Sir, there is a message for you from Mr. Nijinsky. It was difficult to figure out exactly what he was saying on the telephone, but the gist seems to be he is at the police station at Center Street and he would like you to meet him there as soon as possible."

"The police station?" Gloria said.

"Go inside, Gloria. Thanks, Boothby. I'll take a taxi cab."

"Wait a minute." Gloria turned around to face him. "Weren't you supposed to see Uncle Cedric this afternoon? About joining his firm?"

"I can still do that. Stop worrying about my life, Gloria, and start thinking about yours!"

"Oh! You…you ingrate!" She whirled about and swept into the house, head held high. How did she know he had forgotten all about Uncle Cedric and his musty office?

Morgan had never been in a police station. Even his wildest university hijinks, like taking the dean's motorcar apart and reassembling it in the middle of the dining hall, had not involved any powers outside the university. The station was an imposing building, heavy with its own importance. The entrance was crowded with all manner of miscreants, huddled in corners, hooked together with handcuffs, shuffling along in a long row towards cells he assumed must be in the basement somewhere. The smell was a sickening mix of sweat, unwashed bodies, urine, and carbolic acid. Misery hung in the air.

When he finally got to the high counter, a uniformed officer ushered him through to the small interview rooms that lined the inner hall. Inside one, Nijinsky was trying to calm down a blond man who seemed on the verge of tears. A tall skinny man in an ill-fitting serge suit stood off to one side, looking embarrassed.

"I came as quickly as I could," Morgan said, taking off his hat. "What happened?"

"They take Rudy to jail!" exclaimed the blond man.

"We get him out, no?" Nijinsky said. "How we do this?"

Morgan looked at the man he took to be a detective.

"O'Conner, sir. Look, they don't seem to understand. He's been charged with murder."

"Murder? Is there bail? Does he need a lawyer?"

"Not to post bail, he doesn't, but these people are difficult to talk to." He lowered his voice. "Just between us, sir, I think the blond one is a little…hysterical about this, if you get my drift?"

"That's not surprising," Morgan said, drawing away physically, as much from the implied intimacy as from the innuendo. "And how do we pay the bail?"

O'Conner drew back as well. "It's set very high, sir. We're waiting for the paperwork to come down now." He went to the door. "I'll send someone in with it when it's ready."

Morgan walked over to Nijinsky. "It seems we only have to wait, Jinks. The bail money they want is a lot, but the paperwork will come down eventually and then we'll know how much.."

"I pay," Nijinsky said. "Pavel is good friend from old days."

"It said in the papers when you first arrived that you have an army of lawyers working for you. Could they help?"

"This private matter."

They probably specialize in contract law anyway, Morgan thought. He selected a chair from the three lined up against the wall, moved it closer to the table, careful not to get too close to the anguished Pavel, and sat down. His first instinct had been to contact Uncle Paul, who was a criminal lawyer, after all, but then for the first time in a long while, he remembered his promise to his uncle to report back to him about what Nijinsky was doing. The League of Decency, he thought. Who were these people who had closed down a play on Broadway, who had protested about books being published, who had banned readings and closed down drinking establishments in some poor neighborhoods? He remembered the reaction to his last name in the Club Libera. He had never paid much attention to the Committee of Fourteen, or the League, since nothing they did really touched his life. Until now. But what would he say when Uncle Paul showed up some day soon and demanded a report about his friend?

A uniformed policeman put his head around the corner. "Excuse me, Mr. Vanheusen, but Detective Sullivan would like a word?"

Down the dingy hall, Sullivan lingered in an alcove. He cleared his throat and scratched his ear. "I'm sorry, sir, but I thought you oughter know about this person's background. A young American gentleman like yerself, sir, might want to put a bit of distance between you and him, once you know. Forewarned is forearmed, my da used to say. Not to put too fine a point on it, sir, but this person, who is now charged with the murder of a young woman, already has a record of petty theft and—" He lowered his voice even more. "—prostitution. He is not a person of good repute."

"Well, sir, I'm grateful for your fatherly concern, but since you are not my father, it is no business of yours whom I choose to associate myself with. So unless you're telling me this so I will know to hire him one of the best lawyers in town, I have nothing more to say to you." Morgan paused and took a quick breath. "I came here to help my friend, Mr. Nijinsky. I should think it would be in everyone's best interest to move this along quickly so he can get out of here."

With that, he stormed back to the interview room where the Russians were still waiting, Nijinsky pacing back and forth, Pavel hunched over the table, his head in his hands. Morgan leaned against the wall and put his hands in his pockets, where he touched the fly-specked photographs he had taken from Galina's room yesterday and forgotten. He pulled them out to look at them more closely. One was clearly of Madame Olga on stage. It was a postcard with garlands of roses around the edge like a frame. The next one showed Galina and a handsome young man around her age, the two standing awkwardly in their Sunday best beside a carrousel. The last one was also taken at a fair: Galina and a much older man smiling into the camera, their heads thrust through cardboard cutouts of a man and woman in bathing costumes; *Coney Island, 1914* was written along the bottom.

Morgan moved closer to the light and studied the photo carefully. "Holy Jehosaphat," he murmured, stunned. The man was Uncle Paul!

Nijinsky reached for the pictures. "This man Rudy," he said, pointing to the handsome young man by the carrousel. "Brother of Galina."

Morgan nodded absently. He sank down on a chair, still thinking of Uncle Paul. "The hypocrite," he said. "The goddamned stinking hypocrite! And I was going to call on him for help!"

TWENTY-THREE

"The boy stood on the burning deck
Whence all but he had fled"
—"Casabianca" by Felicia Dorothea Hemans

Margaret Vanheusen stood still for the first time that day and looked down the wide vista stretching from the front reception room all the way to the conservatory. With the doors open like this, the space was almost equal to the ballroom she had always wanted, had repeatedly asked for when this house was being built. Not that there would be any dancing tonight, of course. Easter was still a few days away and no balls could be held during Lent. Tonight was a way around that unspoken agreement, although now that the guest list had expanded so much, she hoped the *bon ton* would not see this as bending the rules to the breaking point. How had things gotten so out of hand?

Daisy bounced to her side, her hair ribbon undone and hanging down her back, tangled with her untidy curls. "Everything looks wonderful!" she gushed, reaching out to touch the cherry blossoms spilling from the huge chinoiserie vase by the window.

"What are you going to sing tonight?" her mother asked, one hand smoothing her younger daughter's long ringlets.

"'Orpheus with His Lute', I think. Is that all right?" Her sweet, heart-shaped face, suddenly looking every bit the face of an awkward fourteen-year-old, turned anxiously to her mother. "I thought 'Annie Laurie' was too... Well, not sophisticated enough." She blushed and pushed a lock of hair carelessly out of her eyes.

"A perfect choice, dear." Her mother gathered her into a quick hug and released her just as suddenly. "No, no!" She sprang towards the two footmen who had just come in, their arms full of flower arrangements. "They go on the table in the center room. Let me show you." Her dress rustled as she moved, the long skirts swirling about her, showing a touch of slim ankle.

Daisy watched, admiring the sureness and poise of her mother's every move. I want to be just like that, she thought. I want to know, absolutely *know*, what's the right thing. All the time. She turned away and tried to emulate that poise as she walked towards the front hall. Everywhere was filled with the scent of flowers, and underneath that, the sugary spice smell of just-delivered sweetmeats piled on a table in one corner, waiting to be arranged on silver trays. "What are these doing here?" she wondered. Someone would be in trouble! She peeked into one box and her mouth watered at the sight of the delicacies she rarely had a chance to sample at home and never at school: marzipan in wonderful shapes and colors, tiny pastry bowls of fruit swimming in brandy, Turkish delight, and candied orange peel à la Josephine. Her fingers hovered over the powdered sugar dusting the bottom of the box like snow. But a noise behind her made her pull back.

"Caught in the act!" Morgan exclaimed, poking her in the ribs on both sides.

She shrieked and pulled away. "Stop that! I was just looking."

"So that's why there's powdered sugar on one finger? Hmmm."

"Killjoy!"

Morgan opened the top box again and took out two pieces of Turkish delight. "Here," he said, handing her one. "Might as well be hanged for a sheep as for a lamb. Now get on upstairs and try to do something with your looks, if possible. Ring for Maggie!" he called after her as she ran lightly up the carved oak staircase. "You'll need all the help you can get!"

"Look who's talking!" she shouted, her head appearing briefly over the banister on the second floor. She stuck out her tongue and disappeared in a peal of laughter.

Outside, the day was slowly dying. Pale sunshine pushed back the mist that had shrouded everything earlier on, leaving behind a world sprinkled with muted diamonds. Gloria stood at the window, her forehead pressed against the cool glass, feeling the beating of her heart. She enjoyed at-home parties more than the big balls held during the full season. Sometimes she felt trapped at those affairs: everyone watching, the women commenting behind their fans, whispering in corners, trying to read her mind, her feelings. How full was her dance card? Why had she danced three times with Avery when it was Nigel she had favored the previous week? Nigel, whose eager eyes followed her everywhere. Nigel, so thoughtful it was nauseating. Nigel who was coming tonight. But Andy was coming, too. She smiled, pleased on one level but apprehensive as well. She still wasn't convinced that Morgan's reasons for inviting Andy were as simple as he had claimed. But perhaps Morgan was right and she really did tend to overcomplicate everything. Perhaps Andy wouldn't come.

She turned as Maggie came into the room, softly closing the door behind her. "I want to thank you for getting Fred hired for this evening, miss," she said. "It's a lifesaver for him. I was so worried, with him practically living on the streets."

"It's only one night. I'm afraid I couldn't get Father to—"

"That's all right, miss. You tried. And it's better than nothing." She went over to the bed where Gloria's dress, hose, and underthings were laid out.

"I can start, Maggie. I imagine you need to help Daisy."

"She's so excited, miss. And she looks so pretty in her new dress. But her hair is a regular rat's nest. I'll just pop in and see how she's getting on."

Daisy will need her own maid soon, Gloria thought. In a few years, she'll be dressing for parties, putting up her hair, dancing with all the eligible young men. Singing to bigger groups than tonight's gathering.

She sat down at her dressing table and frowned at her reflection. Why did she have to be the only one in the family cursed with freckles? Around her, she could feel the house gathering itself together, humming with heightened activity. Through the open door, she heard her father's voice calling to his valet. The slam of a door. Her sister laughing. Running footsteps. She smiled, reached back and carelessly spun her hair around one hand, slipped it into a twist on top of her head, and stabbed it into place with hair pins. Maggie would fix it later, but this would do for now. She picked up a pot of cream and leaned forward, studying her face in the mirror. She dabbed a scoop of cream onto her finger and carefully smoothed it over the offending freckles. Nigel said he loved her freckles, but she knew there was nothing sophisticated about them. She had no intention of looking like a dairymaid to the Russian prince.

Outside the big house on Fifth Avenue, daylight slowly faded and shadows inched across the wide street, creeping over the low brick walls surmounted by iron railings that cut the property off from the street and from its neighbors. As if on some hidden signal, sleek shiny motorcars began to turn up the curved driveway through the heavy porte-cochère, the gravel crunching under the narrow tires. As the lights came on along the avenue, the visitors trooped through the brightly lit front door of the Vanheusens', while their drivers followed the narrow path to the tradesmen's entrance at the side of the house, each one looking forward to an entertaining evening downstairs in the vast fragrant kitchens of the big house.

Margaret Vanheusen stood beside her husband in the first reception room, arresting in her shimmering dinner gown, her crown of chestnut curls piled high on her head. She was wearing the rope of pearls inherited from her grandmother. "So good to see you," she murmured, as Boothby announced each arrival. "Go right in and help yourself. We're quite informal here this evening."

As the guests continued to arrive, her earlier jitters subsided, but one part of her mind still kept track of the details of the evening, keeping an eye on her maids and the new helpers hired for the event, all the while chattering on animatedly with her friends.

"His Highness Prince Dmitry Grigorivitch Romanoff and His Excellency Count Fyodor Mikelovitch Ostroffsky," Boothby announced, a little louder than usual.

"He must have been practicing," Augustus whispered, the sound barely carrying to Margaret's ear.

She didn't dare look at him, smiling instead at the two foreign noblemen. "Welcome to our home, Your Highness," she said, extending her hand and looking into the dark mocking eyes of the prince.

He bowed over her hand, raising it to his lips.

Don't, she thought. Please don't.

The count took his place. "Your Excellency," she murmured as he bowed with a little flourish that looked almost theatrical. Do they always do this, she thought, or are they putting on a show for the proletariat?

"We thank you for invitation." The blond count was barely taller than she was, and his blue eyes sparkled with a kind of frantic joy that she found unsettling. "We rarely have occasion to take part in such homely events." He gave her another dazzling smile and moved away with the grace of a dancer, nodding pleasantly to the ladies as he went.

"Lord help us." Augustus stifled a laugh.

Margaret glanced around, looking for Gloria's strawberry-blond head in the crowd. "I'm never going to speak to Aunt Edwina again," she murmured.

Morgan watched Muriel talking to Daisy. How like her to make an effort to put the youngest one there at ease before all else. His chest felt tight with the emotions that swept over him as he watched.

"Careful, old man," Langley murmured. "Can't make it too obvious or you'll never get anywhere with the fair sex."

"Shouldn't you be courting Amy?" Morgan asked, drawing away from his old friend.

"I'm letting her miss me," Langley said. "You watch. After a while, she'll search me out. I'll bet money on it."

"You'll bet money on anything."

"True enough." Langley popped a Turkish delight in his mouth and chewed with enjoyment. "So what are you contributing to the entertainment?"

"I suggested you and I and Rolly reprise our rendition of 'Three Little Maids from School', but for some strange reason, Mother nixed the idea."

"What a pity. We do it so well."

"Keep an eye on Rolly for me, will you? I don't want him to make a spectacle of himself and ruin Mother's party."

"Why don't I just lure him into the library and knock him out with the latest tome by Dickens? So much easier."

The crowd began to move, everyone having noticed at the same time that Boothby was sliding open the doors to the back reception room where chairs had been set up and the square grand piano stood waiting. Morgan noticed Carlo Benedetti in the group around Gloria. *The last time I saw him, he was climbing out of his Peugeot Special at Chuffy Harris's,* Morgan thought with a start.

"Showtime," whispered Langley.

"Morgan, a word." Uncle Paul was at his side, sliding his arm under Morgan's, guiding him against the crowd towards the library.

Morgan resisted the instinct to pull away. "Don't you think we should be there for Daisy?" he murmured, but Uncle Paul paid no attention.

As they crossed the hall, he could hear his father welcoming everybody, then Daisy's clear true soprano, gathering strength as she went on.

Uncle Paul went over to the library table and poured a splash of scotch into a Waterford glass. He passed it to Morgan and poured one for himself, a little bigger this time, Morgan noted.

"I've been waiting for you to contact me about our mutual friend's nefarious activities," Uncle Paul said as he sank down into a high-backed wing chair and stared at Morgan over the top of his glass. His long legs were stretched out in front of him, his elbows propped up on the arms of the chair.

Like a spider, Morgan thought, waiting to catch some unwary creature in his trap. "I'm sorry, sir. I don't quite follow." Morgan added water to his drink and leaned against the table in an effort at nonchalance.

"I'm glad you had the sense not to invite him here tonight," Uncle Paul went on. "It's bad enough having those invert decadent princes in your home being fawned over by fools without that. Your Great-Aunt Edwina never did have any sense."

Stung, Morgan straightened up. "She was trying to add a little interest to the group, I expect," he said, although secretly he agreed. "She probably thought it would be good for Gloria to meet some genuine aristocrats."

Uncle Paul laughed, but his eyes remained cold, like wet pebbles in a stream. "It is not a good idea to introduce people like that to anyone in this house," he said.

"Apparently, my father does not agree with you," Morgan said, shifting his weight to the other foot.

"Your father does not see the filth in our world."

"Perhaps he does not feel the need to go looking for it."

His uncle crossed his feet at the ankle and settled deeper in his chair. "You didn't know he was a member of the Committee of Fourteen?"

"*Was*, Uncle Paul. As I understand it, he did the job necessary for cleaning up those cesspools of disease called saloons for health reasons and then left the group."

"And you think the job is done? With someone like that perverted Nijinsky the idol of society and even your own family welcoming those two decadent nobles who live together unashamedly in the same hotel suite?"

Morgan stared at him. How did Uncle Paul know that? Why did he know that? And why was he telling him these admittedly disgusting details? He shifted his weight again and reached into the silver ice bucket for ice for his drink.

"Give me your report on the dancer," Uncle Paul said.

"My *report*?"

"That *is* why you've been with him so much, isn't it?" his uncle said mildly. "So you can tell me the details of his private life?"

"I'm sure you know more about Mr. Nijinsky's private life with his wife and daughter than I do," Morgan said. He felt his face flush as the alcohol rushed through him, making his heart beat faster. Anger quivered in the background. "And I gather the count has a wife back home in Russia, by the way."

Uncle Paul smirked. "Anyone can have a wife, even Oscar Wilde."

"You don't," said Morgan. A chill went through him. Had he gone too far?

There was silence in the room. For a moment, he heard his little sister's voice soaring into the closing phrases of the Handel aria. Applause broke out, and Morgan smiled in spite of the strained atmosphere in the library. She did well, he thought. Good.

"My life is beyond reproach," Uncle Paul said, his voice tight with anger, "which is more than can be said for your *friend*."

Morgan stood up and banged his empty glass down on the table. "Beyond reproach? *Your* life? I've seen the evidence of your beyond-reproach life! I've seen the pictures of you and your dancer-mistress. I saw you watch her die without the slightest trace of feeling. And I saw how she was living in the appalling dirt and squalor you say you are trying to clean up!"

"How dare you talk to your uncle like that?" His father had come in sometime during this last exchange and stood ramrod-straight and pale just inside the door.

"I speak only the truth," Morgan said. "He speaks in innuendo and—"

"Get back to our guests. At once."

Morgan raised his chin and stood still for a moment. The air crackled with anger...and something else. Fear? Morgan stared at his uncle, who refused to meet his eye.

"Hypocrite," he said softly. He turned away and stalked out of the dark brooding room, past his furious father into the brightness of the main hall.

Through the open doors to the back reception room, he saw Gloria standing in front of the piano, launching into her recitation of 'The Boy Stood on the Burning Deck', her face bright with enthusiasm, one arm raised in a grand gesture as she had been taught. To the left in the front row, he caught the sardonic expressions on the faces of the Russians as they exchanged glances. How dare they laugh at his sister! At that moment, he longed to take them both by the scruff of the neck and fling their aristocratic carcasses out the back door like the curs they undoubtedly were.

He took a deep breath and went into the room, stepping into Gloria's line of sight and smiling at her encouragingly. He wasn't even sure she saw him, she was so caught up in the recitation.

"The flames rolled on...he would not go
Without his father's word;
That father, faint in death below,
His voice no longer heard."

"Is she doing this on purpose to inflame anti-war sentiment," Langley whispered in Morgan's ear, "or has she given any thought to it at all, apart from the sentimentality?"

"Keep quiet," Morgan murmured.

"She looks like quite the Amazon," Rolly remarked admiringly, and then hiccupped loudly. Luckily, applause broke out at that moment, drowning him out.

"The boy stood on the burning deck, eating peanuts by the peck," murmured Langley.

Morgan stifled his laughter and quickly moved away from his irreverent friend, then past the Drexlers. Mrs. Drexler was dabbling at her eyes with a lace handkerchief. "So affecting," she said. "So very, very sad."

TWENTY-FOUR

"Our Buds Dazzle at the Vanheusen Musicale
While Russian Princes Look On"
— Angela Burke, *New York Bugle*

From the moment Andy arrived at the imposing front door of Gloria's house, he realized he had made a mistake. He almost turned back, but just then a group of guests arrived behind him, stepping out of their sleek chauffeured car, laughing together, smiling at him inquiringly. Did they think he should be at the tradesmen's entrance, he wondered, standing here gaping like a peasant? Morgan and Gloria had talked as if this was a casual gathering, but here were these society types, the women in feathers and flashing jewels and the men in formal wear, while here he stood, so proud of his high starched collar and borrowed dinner jacket. Love makes fools of us all, he thought, and followed the others inside.

"You're Andy Cass, Morgan's writer friend," Mrs. Vanheusen said, smiling graciously, holding his hand a few seconds longer as if trying to infuse him with the courage he would need.

He bowed and thanked her for the invitation and moved on.

Behind him, he heard a whisper in Russian and froze. "Do they think this sentimental garbage is true art, do you suppose, *mon cher*?"

"Darling, one would not expect to find Kazimir Malevitch on these middle-class walls," a deeper voice whispered back.

Andy looked in the mirror on one wall and caught the reflection of Prince Romanoff and his companion, Count Ostroffsky, champagne in hand, eyeing one of Mr. Vanheusen's paintings. He recognized the Russians from their pictures in the society pages.

"I do believe it is an original," said the prince in English, his tone admiring.

"My father is quite a collector." Morgan sounded proud of his art patron father, of his family, of this house. Andy wished *he* was home in his own humble rooms.

"You came." Gloria was suddenly beside him, glowing like one of the pretty paintings her father was apparently so fond of.

"How could I resist?" Andy knew he was grinning foolishly at her, but he couldn't stop. "But you should have warned me this wasn't just a small informal gathering."

"It was supposed to be, believe me. It just grew, like Topsy in *Uncle Tom's Cabin.*" Her eyes shone and the simple pearls around her neck only accentuated the graceful vulnerable line of her neck. He found he was staring at the hollow in her throat where he could sense her heart beating. His hand longed to reach out, to touch her skin, feel that pulse, feel the—

"Andy?"

"Forgive me. I'm quite…dazzled. You. This house." He smiled at her boldly. "You haven't been walking in the park for the last few days."

"This *little* event doesn't just happen, you know." She grimaced, but even with her mouth twisted up like this, she looked beautiful.

The party swirled around them, bits and pieces of conversation flowing by, forming a sort of disjointed quilt of words. He saw Morgan moving about, greeting everyone, waving at him from across the room. There was a pattern to the movement in the room, which had at first seemed haphazard: the older people moving about in their own orbit near the outside of the circle; the young men closer in; and the sparkling young debutantes at the center, those barely moving bright stars around whom everyone else wheeled and swung. Gloria was different here. It wasn't just the beautiful velvet gown with the embroidered placket down the front, a satin rose caught up at her waist. She seemed like a highly glazed figurine, protected by a hidden shield of wealth and social standing. She even seemed taller, and her voice was different, her gestures more studied, her speech quicker, almost brittle.

He looked down at his sturdy, worn shoes. What could he offer Gloria that would please her, keep her interest, when she had all this? He had come here with a plan, but now, looking around, he wondered how his plan could possibly succeed. While they were standing there, various young men had spoken to her, tried to insert themselves between him and her. They had been fended off politely by the lady with an expertise he could only admire, but he wouldn't have much more time before she would be forced by good manners to move on to someone else.

"Gloria, I was wondering…" He dropped his voice, forcing her to lean closer. "I mean, you said you were interested in the theater, what it's like backstage, what the costumes and backdrops are like, yes? I can show you these things."

"Really?" Her eyes shone. "You can take me backstage at the Met? Why didn't you say so before!"

"No. Not the Met. But I *can* take you backstage at another theater, one someone I know runs. It's not in use right now," he went on hurriedly, seeing one of the young man heading towards them again with a determined look in his eye. "But it's the same. I mean, it has what the Met has, on a smaller scale, of course, but all the costumes and backdrops and props. Would you enjoy that?"

"Oh, I would! Yes, I would indeed!" She turned as the young man joined them. "Nigel, would you be a dear and get me some champagne?" Nigel bowed and moved away. "When can we do this backstage visit?"

Andy leaned even closer. "Can you come to the park again on Saturday? At two o'clock? Like before?"

"Not this weekend, I'm afraid. We'll be in the country for Easter. What about next Saturday?"

"I'll be there," Andy said, almost breathless with relief.

Gloria turned as the young man emerged again from the crowd, champagne in hand. "Nigel, you are a dear. This is Andy Cass, a reporter."

"Oh, I see." Nigel looked relieved, his narrow pale face flushing as he smiled at Andy. "Your colleague, Miss Angela Burke, is also here. Do you know her?"

"I read her column all the time," Andy lied blithely. He did know the name, but she was the society reporter and they had never met.

"Shall we find our seats, Gloria? I think the Ogilvie twins are almost ready to dance."

"Certainly. They are quite talented, don't you think?" Gloria hooked her arm through Nigel's in a way that told Andy they had done this many times before. She waggled her fingers at him in a little wave as they turned and made their way back to a room with an ornate square grand piano,

This house goes on forever, he thought, following Gloria at a distance. Without her by his side, he felt more out of place than ever. He wondered if Gloria was going to sing or play the piano. Did she even do these things? He knew so little of her real life.

The young woman who sometimes came to the park with Gloria sat down at the piano and arranged her silk skirts. She wore a pair of spectacles now, through which she peered intently at the music.

I should go, Andy thought, hovering in between the rooms as the guests, champagne in hand, took their seats in front of him. Some of the young men stood about in groups, the hand not holding champagne behind their back, as if trained in the same school, which, now that he thought about it, they probably had been. It looked like a painting, he thought, and I do not belong in it.

He turned towards the great marble entrance hall, his footsteps echoing in the empty space. Through the open door across the expanse of checkerboard marble, he glimpsed the warmth of floor-to-ceiling books, the gold lettering on their spines beckoning him. He glanced around. No one was there. The door stood wide open. He slipped in and began to peruse the well-stocked shelves.

"Isadora Duncan has a lot to answer for," remarked Morgan under his breath.

Langley stifled a laugh.

The Ogilvie twins were taking a bow, their faces pink with their recent exertions, their bare feet and thick ankles gleaming pale and faintly obscene under the layers of tulle of their long flowing tunics. As they left, Mr. Vanheusen bent over the prince's shoulder and whispered in his ear.

Invitation to cigars, Morgan thought. Guess I won't be included this time around. He glanced about for Uncle Paul, but he was nowhere in sight. Muriel was talking intently to Clayton Roberts III, who was running for some office on the city council. Morgan supposed their discussion was something to do with conditions for women garment workers. He sighed. Even talking politics, Muriel's classic beauty and simple style stood out in the dazzling crowd.

"Your father is showing us his latest acquisition." The count paused and smiled at him, his blue eyes sparkling. He's almost pretty, Morgan thought. "Is big secret, he say. You see it yet? You give me clue?"

"Not yet," Morgan admitted, his curiosity aroused.

"We go. Show us where is library, yes?"

As they made their way to the door, Morgan noticed that Langley had won his bet. Amy had approached him and now they were talking animatedly, Amy making great use of her fan as they strolled towards the dining room.

He paused at the library door, but his father beckoned him in. "Come in, Morgan. Your friend Mr. Cass tells me he's a great reader."

Andy stood awkwardly in a corner of the room, a book in his hands. His face was flushed.

"You read all these books, sir?" the prince asked Mr. Vanheusen, waving at the floor-to-ceiling shelves all around them.

"I read many of them in my youth, Your Highness. I have little time to read these days, I fear. Put those on the table," he added as two of the servants came in bearing platters of sliced game and oysters, dishes piled high with fruit and sweetmeats. Champagne followed, carried by the young footman borrowed for the night from their neighbors.

"I read little, also," the prince went on. "Myself, there is much more of interest to do, is that not so, Fyodor?"

"Our Russian writers, they are so...*triste*, are they not?" The count made a face and reached for an oyster.

"My latest artistic acquisition is Russian, which is why I thought you might be interested," Mr. Vanheusen said. "And perhaps you would be good enough to give me a little reassurance about its authenticity," he added with a sideways dip of his head, a mannerism that had always annoyed Morgan as bordering on the obsequious. As his father was talking, he reached down behind his desk and produced a square flat bundle about a foot across, a little longer in length, covered in burlap.

Morgan turned as the library door opened and Uncle Paul came in with a few business friends of his father's.

"Just in time, gentlemen. Morgan, move the easel over here."

Morgan jumped to comply, the relief at being included, and therefore forgiven, making him almost giddy. He turned the easel so that it was facing the room, which was slowly filling with cigar smoke. He helped center the picture, noticing its weight and heft. It must be painted on wood, he thought, just as his father pulled off the burlap covering and turned to face his friends.

"Bravo!" exclaimed the prince. "*That* is art. Great Russian art," he added.

"Didn't know you were a religious man," boomed his father's partner from the back. "A bit papist, though, isn't it?"

"Looks Byzantine," said Uncle Paul. "Nothing to do with the papacy."

"It's supposed to be very old," Morgan's father said. "Is it genuine?"

Morgan was staring at the picture in shock. An icon. Just like the one stolen from Madame Ostroffsky. He recognized the same pose, the same expression, the same symbols, even the same strange misshapen finger in the hand raised in a blessing. The large dark eyes stared out at the room mournfully, the gold leaf of the halo a dull gleam in the dark room. It was exactly the same, but somehow more powerful than the copy he had seen.

The count moved closer and examined the painting through his monocle. "Without a doubt," he said. "I verified this very one for an art dealer recently. Did you acquire it though Green and Green?"

"Yes. And I didn't really think he had stiffed me, but one can't be too careful about these things, especially as this is a new field for me."

"He is, after all, a Jew," remarked Uncle Paul, leaning closer to peer at the painting.

"So you're branching out, as they say?" asked a voice.

"This one was special." Vanheusen smiled tenderly at the painting. "What do you think, Morgan?"

Morgan thrust his hands in his pockets and took a deep breath. "I think it may be stolen," he said.

"What? You accuse me—"

"No, no! Not you, Father. Of course not. But the dealer may not be as aboveboard as you thought."

"What gives you this bizarre notion?" exclaimed Uncle Paul. "And even if by some strange twist of fate, it is true," he rushed on, "your father is now the legal owner."

"Possession is nine tenths of the law, yes, I know that. But ethically—"

"I think we've heard enough from you tonight," his father said, his voice brittle with bitterness.

A shriek suddenly penetrated through the closed door, followed by a high voice calling some name.

"Now what?" muttered Vanheusen.

Morgan opened the door and the count came with him into the hall, which now echoed to the strained, unnaturally high voice of Aunt Hattie, who was tottering down the grand staircase, wearing a strange collection of clothing over her lace nightdress. She had evidently made an effort to put up her hair, but it was already tumbling down on one side, partially obscuring the bizarre effect of the makeup painted on with an unsteady hand. Bits of colored paper stuck out here and there from the tangles, and a long purple velvet shawl with a heavy beaded fringe trailed along behind her on the stairs. She was trying to hold up an old skirt she had fastened around her waist with a black sash, but her bandaged hands were making it difficult. At any minute, she threatened to slip on the hem of her tattered finery.

"William!" she called again. "Oh, Willie! Where are you?"

"Aunt Hattie!" Morgan ran over and tried to take her hand.

"You're not William," she shouted, pulling away and almost losing her balance. "I want my William."

"Morgan, go get your mother," Vanheusen ordered.

Morgan turned to obey but saw his mother and a group of other curious guests already coming through the open door of the music room, whispering among themselves.

"*Mon Dieu*," murmured the count. "Who is this William?"

"He went down on the Titanic," Morgan said shortly.

"And he wasn't *her* William at all," whispered one of the ladies. "It was after he married Lucy Bainter that Hattie went all peculiar."

"So sorry I am late," Aunt Hattie said, finding her balance and coming down the last few steps into the hall. "I don't want to miss the dancing."

"Madame, it is a delight to meet you," announced the count, clicking his heels and bowing in front of her. "May I have the pleasure of this dance?"

"There is no dancing tonight," said Uncle Paul.

"For this lady, I think is dancing," said the count.

Amazingly, Aunt Hattie allowed the Russian to take her filthy bandaged hand and lead her into the middle of the hall.

"I'll get Miss Green," said Vanheusen. He glared at his wife, then hurried away.

The prince began to sing softly in Russian, a swaying melody that soon had them all mesmerized. By now, all the guests were gathered around. They watched in absolute silence as the dapper blond count and his glassy-eyed, ragged partner began to move smoothly over the marble floor of the large hall, while Prince Dimitry sang a waltz-like melody, his mellow baritone voice never faltering.

TWENTY-FIVE

"Mounds of Shells Tell of German Confidence
As Guns Sing Their War Symphony."
— Special Cable to the *New York Times*

The parlor maid walked the length of the table, blowing out the candles. Food lay untouched, still piled in pyramids, arranged in circles and swoops of color, decorated with bits of wilted parsley and fern, aspic slowly melting onto the silver platters.

"Save what you can," Margaret said, supporting herself with one hand on the door frame. "What can't be stored in the ice box, divide up amongst yourselves."

"Thank you, madam." The maid curtsied and ran off to relay the good news.

Margaret Vanheusen straightened her shoulders and went back to the library where her husband had taken refuge after the last guest had finally left. Dr. Wilcox, who kept his medical bag always near, had given Hattie a strong sleeping powder. The poor woman was now dead to the world, tied into her bed with Miss Green watching her, red-eyed and sniveling.

The library air was still thick with cigar smoke from Augustus's friends, but at least Paul had finally gone home. Margaret knew Paul had too much to say about how things were run in her house, but every time she felt his sad eyes on her, she felt the guilt of her long-ago decision to marry Augustus instead of him. In some strange twisted way, this gave him power in her house: the knowledge that she had almost said yes to his importuning voice, his coaxing, desperate wooing. He was so attractive back then, with almost Byronic good looks, but something had held her back, some hint at the coldness that lay behind his eyes. She had made the right choice, but Paul had never forgiven her. Funny how he never seemed to blame his brother.

Augustus sat slumped behind his desk. "How could you let this happen?" he said as she came in.

"It appears Miss Green thought Hattie was sound asleep and couldn't resist a trip to the kitchen to have a little fun."

"She's fired. See how much fun she has then."

"Wait, Gus, let's not be too hasty. She's learned her lesson, and up till now, she's been the perfect companion."

"Listening to you is what got us into this fine mess to begin with," Augustus said, rearing up from the desk and beginning to pace. "You said she would be all right in town now. You said it would do her good to go out in society a little, attend the theater, be introduced around. And look what happened? She has disgraced us! Made us a laughing stock in front of our friends and society at large. And two reporters in the house! Everyone will hear about this. And what about Gloria? This was supposed to be about her, have you forgotten that? Because of you, her party was ruined!"

"How can you say such things, Gus," Margaret asked, sinking down into the wing chair. "I worked very hard for this soirée. You can't blame me for tonight's débacle."

"Why not? You're in charge of the servants!"

Margaret clasped her hands tightly in her lap. "This will never happen again, Gus. I'll speak to her. I'll be very firm."

"It will never happen again because I won't have Hattie in this house any longer. She's going back to the country right away until the doctor can get her into an asylum."

"But—"

"No buts. She's going." He poured himself more scotch and flung himself back into his chair. "Look, Margaret." He leaned forward, trying to force her to look at him. "I've been patient. I let you have your way, follow your new modern ideas, and I admit that for a while, it seemed to be working. But lately, things have been deteriorating and we didn't pay enough attention. Now it's gone beyond merely eccentric. It's time to send her away."

Margaret raised her head, looking away from her husband into the soulful eyes of the icon. "She's my sister."

"Your sister has dementia praecox. You cannot fix it."

There was a soft knock at the door and a tired Boothby appeared. "The Mercedes is waiting, sir," he said. "That young man, Fred, has agreed to go with the ladies and stay for as long as he is needed. He won't talk, sir; he needs the job."

"Good. Get some help and carry her down the backstairs now, Boothby. And thanks."

Margaret watched the butler go and then turned to her husband. "You had it all arranged."

"Yes," he said. "Someone had to take control and get things back to normal." He dusted his hands together briskly. "A nightcap, dear?"

She shook her head and walked out the door, closing it softly behind her.

The farther he went, the more Morgan regretted his impulsive decision to walk out into the night. Lights gleamed from the great houses along Fifth Avenue and the occasional motorcar driving by, ferrying its owners back from dinner parties or other social events. One Rolls Royce Silver Ghost slowed down as it passed him, the group inside laughing, lifting champagne glasses in a toast to the lone pedestrian on Fifth Avenue. He raised his hat to them, but he now felt ridiculous, walking along with nowhere to go. He wondered if Jinks was dancing tonight, if he would mind a visitor, but part of him knew the eccentric, unpredictable Russian was not what he needed now.

I shouldn't have left, he thought, slowing his steps, abandoning Mother like that, leaving Gloria to cope with the fallout of that mad scene, just as he had before when he drove Jinks home from the country, leaving his parents to cope with over two hundred guests. He turned around and began to walk back. In one way, Aunt Hattie's meltdown might put his own bad behavior in the shadows.

Aunt Hattie, in varying stages of eccentricity, had been living with them for over a year. He had never thought much about her real state of mind. At worst, she had been mildly annoying, causing the odd awkward moment; at best, she was a gentler, more amusing version of his mother. He wondered how long that image of her stumbling down the wide staircase in her assortment of haute couture rags would stay in his head.

But even Aunt Hattie couldn't displace the bitter taste of the earlier scene in the library: the unexpected burst of anger he had felt, the righteous indignation. Had Uncle Paul ever seen where that poor girl lived? Ever stopped to think that when he tired of her, she had nothing to return to? All the talk in his family about responsibility, yet his uncle could throw away a life with no thought at all. Were there no real morals in his family? No real ethical code? And if that were so, where did that leave him?

He had just reached his own gate when the big Mercedes town car rolled out of the driveway and turned up Fifth Avenue. For just a moment as the long car swung onto the road, he caught sight of his aunt's pale face, slack-jawed, spittle drooling from the corner of her mouth. Then the face vanished as the powerful car drove away up the deserted street.

Inside the house, the great chandelier had been turned off and the only light came from the fluted wall sconces around the hall. Morgan paused, seeing the library door ajar. The familiar smell of his father's favorite cigars hung in the air. Squaring his shoulders, he crossed the marble floor, knocked gently on the door, and pushed it open.

His father sat at his desk, leaning back in his chair, gazing at the glowing icon on the easel nearby.

"It has a rather haunted look, doesn't it?" he said, not looking at Morgan.

Morgan moved into the room and slid into one of the leather armchairs. "Yes, it does," he said. "I hadn't noticed before."

His father puffed at his cigar, his eyes still studying the painting. "At least, we know it's genuine," he said.

Morgan cleared his throat. "I shouldn't have spoken out in front of everyone the way I did, Father. I apologize."

"You should know better."

"I was startled. I'm sorry."

His father straightened in his chair and looked at Morgan for the first time. "What is unforgiveable is the way you spoke to your Uncle Paul," he said. "In this house, you respect your elders."

Morgan gripped the arms of his chair. "I can't condone what he did," he said. "You taught me to take responsibility for my actions, but he has done just the opposite."

"What he does or does not do is none of your business!"

"But Father—"

"Now you listen to me, young man! While you live in my house, you will respect your elders. You will not do or say anything to bring opprobrium on us in any way. You will not question my taste in art, or what I decide to acquire. Is that understood?"

"I never questioned your taste in art, sir," Morgan said, stung. "And I never meant to imply that you had stolen the icon, only that it had been stolen."

"How dare you say such a thing! Or even imply it! And in public, too!"

Morgan jumped to his feet. "I apologized for that when I came in, Father. I am heartily sorry—"

"You are spoiled, Morgan. Utterly spoiled. Uncle Paul is right to think you have had too much handed to you on a silver platter. For months, I have been waiting patiently for you to find your feet and settle somewhere. I have set up interviews for you, but all your energies are wasted on racing motorcars, something I was led to believe you had sensibly abandoned. Motor racing is a hobby for millionaires like Carlo Benedetti and Louis Chevrolet, young man. You need a serious occupation. You are exhausting my patience."

Stunned, Morgan could only stare at his father, who had never before spoken to him so bluntly. He had known that he was supposed to find something to do, but he hadn't realized there was a time limit to this quest. And before tonight, he suspected there hadn't been. Tonight, he had been an embarrassment to his father in front of Uncle Paul and all his father's guests, and that would not be tolerated.

"Cat got your tongue?"

I'm just trying to understand why Uncle Paul's opinion carries so much weight, Morgan thought. He slumped against the back of the chair, exhaustion making his thoughts fuzzy.

"Sir, I will never be like Chesleigh," he said, bitterness rising in his throat like bile. "My sainted brother would never have mentioned the provenance of an artwork in public. He would have found a job, although he didn't have to since one was handed to him. And I'm sure if he'd felt like it, he could have raced any number of motorcars without arousing your wrath. But I am just me, and I'm sorry I'm such a disappointment. The only thing I can do is get out of your sight, leave this house, and live elsewhere!"

"Don't be an ass!" thundered his father.

But Morgan was already out of the room, racing across the hall, taking the stairs two at a time.

TWENTY-SIX

Guess I'm not the only one writing puff pieces, Andy thought, glancing through the story in the *Times*. He liked the idea that the women writing to the lonely men in the trenches and hospitals of France were called godmothers. It made him smile.

He had just written up his story on the shipping news: who was arriving on what liner, what freighters had made it into the harbor in record time, who was ready to take on more freight, who would be delayed. He was getting good at dashing off the kind of assignments his editor, Drury, was still handing him. Judging by what he was reading in other papers about the German submarine campaign, he wondered why anyone would take a passenger ship across the ocean at this time and had suggested writing a piece on that topic, but Old Dreary was unimpressed by the idea. Some of their biggest advertising came from shipping companies.

Andy refused to relinquish all hope for a major byline and doggedly kept at the art fraud story he had been gathering information on for weeks. Now and then, some tidbit came his way, sometimes from one of the other papers, but even they had run out of leads and the story had disappeared. Andy was convinced, especially after that bizarre incident at the Vanheusens' soirée, that the art frauds were continuing.

As he made his way down the narrow hall of the police station, he hoped Sullivan was in and that he would talk to him this time.

Sullivan was a man of moods. Sometimes he was a regular fount of information; other times, he imitated the clam and refused to even see Andy.

As he paused to tap on Sullivan's door, it opened and Sergeant Riley came out. He looked at Andy, grimaced and stood aside, motioning him in. Andy hoped that this was a good omen.

"You're like a bad penny, you are," Sullivan said, looking up from his messy desk. "What is it this time? You got a tip for me?"

"More of a hunch," Andy said.

"I've got plenty of those meself. What's it about?"

"This art fraud you're working on, is there anything new? A new wrinkle? A different direction to it at all?"

"That's your hunch? A new direction?"

"Russian art. Anything turning up in that line?"

Sullivan pushed his bulk away from the desk, pulled out the bottom drawer, and put one foot up on it. He leaned back and clasped his hands across his paunch. "What do you know?"

"Honestly, Danny Boy, I don't have any facts. Just a hunch."

"Don't you 'Danny Boy' me, Cass." Sullivan snapped upright in his chair again and pulled a file out of the drawer. "There's a rumor." He paused. "A rumor involving a hitherto upright and respectable art dealer getting into a spot of the dirty."

"Green and Green?"

"You didn't hear that from me. Sit down."

Andy sank into the worn leather chair and waited.

"We've been watching them for a while, tipped off by one of the forgers we picked up recently. The way it usually works, like I explained before, is the paintings are taken away to be cleaned, then replaced by good fakes. Up till recently, they've stuck to second-level artists, no one too famous, you know what I mean. And the problem for us is that sometimes no one notices for a long time, if at all. Then there's the out-and-out thieves who steal on commission, as it were, and sell to collectors. Easier to catch them *if* we do it fast before they offload the merchandise."

Andy nodded. So far, nothing new. He pulled out his notebook just in case.

"What's new is two things: We caught one of the thieves redhanded with a Millet in his bag, and he said he did it for Mr. Green

Jr. We've suspected the young Mr. Green for a while, but we had no idea Green and Green was in this deep."

"Did you pull him in for questioning?"

"Not yet. The miscreant also told us a few more things may be coming up. Right now, there's probably nothing incriminating in the shop. We'd rather wait. So there you have it. And none of it is for publication," he added, scowling across the desk.

"Of course not." Andy snapped his notebook closed at once. "Not yet," he added.

"Right. Not yet. So what have you got for me?"

"What I have may fit in with this Green angle," Andy said, getting his feet. "I'll tell you when I have the facts."

"You'd better, you imp of Satan, or I'll haul your immigrant ass in faster than you can say Jack Robinson. Now get out of here. I have some real police work to do."

Andy ran down the stairs and out into the April sunshine. He wished he could have talked to Morgan last night after that remark about the icon being stolen, but once the poor mad woman appeared, Andy had thought it prudent to slip away as quickly as possible. He would have to talk to Morgan later.

Green and Green, dealers in fine art, had their elegant quarters on lower Fifth Avenue, not far from Washington Square. In the window sat a large oil painting of a woman dressed in early Victorian fashion, smiling complacently as two young boys in sailor suits played with a hoop beside her. Inside, one whole wall was filled with portraits, men and women from bygone eras staring stiffly from their ornate frames, frozen in time. Useful for people in search of respectable ancestors, no doubt. The interior of the store was bright with light from two crystal chandeliers. A white-haired man sat at a Louis XIV desk in the middle of the room, talking on the telephone. He smiled and nodded at Andy, pantomiming that he should take a seat. Then he wound up his conversation and hung up.

"These telephone contraptions do contribute to bad manners, do they not?" he said, standing up and coming around the desk to shake hands. He looked Andy up and down with not a flicker of assessment in his brown eyes, though Andy knew he must be wondering what a man dressed as shabbily as he was doing in his shop. "I'm Edwin Green."

"Andrew Cass."

They shook hands. Mr. Green remained stranding and smiling, waiting for Andy to explain his presence.

"Your name came up the other night at the Vanheusens," Andy said, watching the effect of his words. "We were given a peek at Mr. Vanheusen's latest acquisition, a beautiful example of Russian art."

"Ah, yes." Mr. Green returned to his seat and sat down. "We are seeing more of these pieces these days. One man's misfortune is another's windfall. Funny old world." He shook his head. "And Mr. Vanheusen is still pleased with it?"

"Oh yes. Everyone was very impressed, including Prince Romanoff."

"You have an interest in Russian art, Mr. Cass?"

"I guess you could say it's in my heritage. You see, when my family came here, the name was Kassevetsky." He paused, wondering how to play it from here.

Mr. Green was wondering, too, apparently. He was looking across the desk consideringly.

"Perhaps I could talk to your son," suggested Andy.

Mr. Green laughed. "You have it wrong, sir. The other Green is my brother, Theodore."

"Forgive me. I thought Mr. Vanheusen mentioned the young Mr. Green, so I naturally assumed…"

"Ah, yes. Our nephew, Marcus. We call him Junior. He's in the back room with a customer, I think. Would you care to wait?"

"Thank you. I'd like to look around, if I may?"

"Certainly." Mr. Green waved a hand around at the walls and various easels standing about. "It's a shop, Mr.…Cass. Now, if you will excuse me." He turned back to the papers on his desk.

Andy wandered about, amazed at the variety on the walls. The farther back he went in the long room, the more varied the paintings became—and the more valuable, according to the discreet tag tucked in the corner of each piece.

Near the back, he found a case where a Fabergé egg was on display. The price tag was staggering. Even a prince could live well on the income from this objet d'art for a while, assuming he could bring himself to give it up. As Andy stood gazing at it—the intricate work, the brilliant blues and golds, the tiny diamond chips and seed pearls—he heard the murmur of voices coming from behind him. He turned and saw that a panel in the wall was actually a door, and it was slightly ajar.

Up in the front of the shop, a man and woman had come in and were in earnest discussion with Mr. Green in front of one of the paintings near his desk. Andy moved closer to the panel door.

"I know what you sell these things for," a man's voice was saying, a vaguely familiar voice. "What you're offering is insulting."

"You can always go elsewhere." That must be Marcus Green.

"That's exactly what I will do!"

"Not so fast, Rudy."

Andy pushed the door wider. On an easel under a strong light was another icon in the same style as the one he had seen last night. Beside it stood a tense, dark-haired young man, his face flushed and angry, a burlap bag in his hands. As the door opened wider, emitting a sudden creak, Marcus turned around, startled. His high forehead gave him a look of intelligence in spite of the piggy eyes.

"This is not part of the shop," he said, reaching over to close the door.

Andy pushed his way into the small room. "I recognize that icon," he said. "It's one of a pair."

"I wouldn't know."

"Your uncle said you're the Russian art expert."

"Hardly. Now please go."

"It's not for sale," the man called Rudy said suddenly. "I've changed my mind." He grabbed the icon off the easel and thrust it into the bag.

"Hold on now!" Marcus turned away from Andy, obviously taken aback. "You can't do that."

"Can't I?" Rudy turned away and disappeared through another door Andy hadn't noticed.

Andy rushed after him.

"Now see here!" shouted Marcus, but Andy kept going through a short cluttered hallway and out into the alley behind the shop, following the vaguely familiar young man and his precious parcel.

Andy chased the young man across Broadway, all the way to Second Avenue, where the crowds slowed him down enough for Andy to catch up. He pushed the young man against a building while he got his breath back.

"For God's sake, man, I don't want to do you any harm!"

"You're a journalist! All you want is a story!"

Andy stared at the face. He had seen him before, at Galina's funeral...and before that..."Randy," he said. "Randy McKinnah."

"Who *are* you?"

"I'm Andy Cass from the old neighborhood. Remember? Three doors down and two floors up? Past the redoubtable Mrs. Putinoff?"

Randy slowly relaxed as recognition dawned. "Little Andy Kassevetsky?"

Andy nodded vigorously.

"Why didn't you say so?"

"I didn't recognize you at first. Even if I had, I couldn't get close enough. You're a veritable greyhound!"

The young man laughed. "It's Rudy now, by the way. I've got to sit down. Let's go to Tam's."

A few minutes later, they were drinking strong tea and nibbling at poppy seed cakes at Tamarov's.

"I'm sorry about your sister," Andy said. "I know you two were close."

Rudy turned away. He didn't say anything for a moment, then suddenly blurted out, "For a while, I thought I had killed her. I would have killed myself if it hadn't been for...someone I love. And then the child. I'm responsible for her now. Who else would pay for her keep?"

"Galina had a child?"

Rudy nodded.

"Why did you think you had killed Gail – Galina, I mean?"

"It's not a nice story, Andy. I'm not a nice person."

Andy sipped his tea, nibbled at his cake. Waited for Rudy's feeling of guilt to spill over.

"I do odd jobs for your Uncle George," Rudy began. "You know how he hates the Ballets Russes and especially Mr. Nijinsky."

Andy nodded. His tea was getting cold, but he sipped at it anyway, waiting to hear the worst.

"George had this crazy idea that if Nijinsky stumbled in his debut, Galina would see he wasn't such a god after all and come back to dance for George's company."

"But Rudy, Uncle George's company has disbanded."

"Not in his mind, it hasn't. And he's beginning to put it back together again. He's contacted some dancers and he's hired me to paint a new backdrop."

"So what happened with Mr. Nijinsky?"

Rudy sighed. "George paid me to slip a small vial of blue liquid he gave me into the flask that Nijinsky always has backstage with him. I didn't know Galina would drink from it! And anyway, George assured me it was harmless. It was just laudanum. It would only make him a little awkward. Would make him stumble, George said.

"Oh God, what have I done!" Rudy ran his hands through his hair.

"It was her heart condition, Rudy. You didn't kill her."

"But I keep thinking, if she hadn't drunk it, she would have been all right."

"She would have died anyway. That's what the coroner said."

Rudy took a deep breath. "I wish I could believe that."

Andy ordered more tea. When it came, he tipped a bit of gin into one cup from a small flask he carried with him. He pushed the cup across the table to Rudy. "Tell me where you got the icon?"

Rudy covered his face with his hands. "From Galina," he said. "Her little girl, Natasha, has a sickness in her lungs. She needs special care and medicine. Galina was desperate, Andy! She took the icons from the house of her mentor, Olga Ostroffsky, and I copied them. She returned the copies, and I sold the originals to Marcus Green, one by one. The last one is in this bag under the table. What'll I do?"

"Have you ever copied any other pictures? For someone other than Galina, I mean?"

"So far, I have done about half a dozen. Marcus wants more, but I've had enough. When I refused to do any more, he dropped the price for the last icon. He's trying to force my hand."

"That's fraud, what you're doing," Andy said.

"You think I don't know that? I'm not stupid, just desperate!"

"Do you know any of the others involved in this scheme?"

"Why?"

"If you do, there may be a way for you to get through this."

"I never saw you as a miracle worker, Andy, but so help me God, if you pull this off, I'll worship at your feet."

"Well, don't start yet," Andy said. "I have to go. You all right?"

"I'm fine," Rudy said, picking up his precious bag. "Thanks to you," he added.

"I'll keep in touch." Andy handed him his card, and the two young men parted.

All because of Morgan and his careless invitation, Andy thought, as he headed back to the office, I might have a story even Old Dreary will love!

TWENTY-SEVEN

"American Barber's Grim War Story:
Trench Horrors Graphically Portrayed by
Romeo Houle, Who Exchanged Hair Cutting for Fighting."
          —*New York Times*, 1916

Morgan missed Easter with his family. He missed the hour-and-a-half–long ride in their private rail coach manufactured in the Vanheusen factory in his great-grandfather's day. He missed its ornate ceiling, mahogany paneling, and brass lamps now fitted with electricity. And he missed the feeling of anticipation these trips still generated, the closeness of the family in these familiar surroundings. Vanheusens had been travelling like this to their old country place for many years. But now he had closed the door to all this by his impetuous behavior.

He suspected that an abject apology would probably rectify the situation, but he was too proud and too stubborn. Instead, he settled into a small hotel not far from the Astor. At first, he enjoyed the unusual freedom, and the only thing bothering him was that Muriel might not understand what had happened between him and his father. He wrote her a series of letters on hotel stationary, none of which really said much because he didn't know how to explain it in writing. He wanted desperately to see her, but she never responded.

It wasn't long before he began to see the unpleasant results of being on his own. First, it was a visit to his tailor's to pick up some new shirts and a morning coat he had ordered a few weeks earlier. The tailor hemmed and hawed, looking embarrassed and almost wringing his hands with concern. Finally, he whispered that he would like to know where to send the bill since Mr. Vanheusen

Senior had made it clear two days before that he was no longer paying for the young gentleman.

"Of course," said Morgan. "I was just about to give you my new address."

He told the man where he was staying and walked out into the street, back straight, cheeks flushed. He turned right and started to walk. For a few moments, he didn't see the people on the sidewalk, hear the shouts of the drayman urging his horses along. His father was teaching him a lesson and it hurt, but going back home now was out of the question. Getting a real job suddenly assumed a much more important role. In fact, he decided, it should become his main occupation. Back at his hotel he drew up a list of contacts whom he had not yet visited and began working through it methodically. Uncle Cedric was number three.

Cedric Fallin was not related to the Vanheusens by blood. He was an old friend of Morgan's father who had always been around. The two families visited each other in the summer, went to the same schools, studied music from the same teachers. Morgan's older brother, Chesleigh, had even married Cedric's daughter Leticia, a few years ago, which had made everyone very happy. That the younger sister, Betsy, had her heart set on Morgan was only one of the things that made him nervous around Uncle Cedric. Maybe it was the man's uncanny light eyes, which seemed to see so much more than surfaces. Even after all this time, Morgan still felt uncomfortable around him.

But what do *I* know about people, he thought in the gilded cage of the elevator smoothly rising to the fifty-second floor of the towering Woolworth Building. Although he had always been of the opinion that Uncle Paul took too much interest in their household and had far too much to say about how they were raised, it had never occurred to him that the man was a hypocrite. Morgan had assumed that because his uncle had no children of his own, he was using the Vanheusen siblings as his surrogate family. And his father had always indulged his younger brother.

But now that Morgan knew more about his uncle, his feelings had changed. How could the man have sat in their box at the Metropolitan Opera and watched his mistress die before his eyes and show no emotion at all? Not even a glimmer of interest.

And how could his father, who had always appeared to be a paragon of right thinking, refuse to see anything wrong with keeping stolen property? Still, it was his uncle he blamed for the fact he no longer lived at home.

Morgan shook his head and took a moment to brush lint off his lapels. Uncle Cedric insisted on being well groomed, probably believed that clothes do indeed make the man.

"Once more unto the breach," Morgan muttered and opened the outer door.

"Mr. Fallin is expecting you, sir." Miss Rozen stood and ushered him to the etched glass door of the inner office. As usual, she wore a crisp white blouse and long black skirt cinched in tight at the waist that rustled as she moved. Her hair was piled on top of her head, poofing out at the sides, giving her the look of a Gibson Girl, albeit an aging one, so fashionable a few years ago. He smiled at her and entered the office.

Here everything was polished wood floors covered with Turkey rugs, warmly gleaming brass lamps, and walls lined with books. He knew from earlier visits that most of the books were fake, but they looked good and gave the place an air of being in someone's study in spite of the lofty view outside the windows. There was even a Franklin stove in one corner. It wasn't lit today, of course, but it still contributed to the homey atmosphere.

"Come in, Morgan. So good to see you," boomed Uncle Cedric, rising from behind the huge walnut partners' desk to shake Morgan's hand.

Morgan smiled and prattled on nervously about the family, about their mutual friends, about how much he appreciated having this chance to talk to him. He carefully avoided any reference to the soirée that had ended so badly just last week. Thank God, Uncle Cedric had not been able to attend.

"Of course, I'm interested in helping you get started on your chosen career, Morgan," Cedric said at last. "I was disappointed your brother had his sights set on your father's operation rather than mine, but he is the eldest, after all. I guess that was to be expected. So you don't see yourself going into the family business? Since Harry's death—"

"No, sir, I don't have any interest in that direction. In fact, the only part of the business that might interest me is if they would convert some of it to producing motorcars."

"Really? Well, they are the coming thing. Going in that direction might be a wise move."

"What really interests me, though, is racing them, sir." The instant the words were out of his mouth, he regretted them.

"That, my boy, is a hobby, not a business," Cedric said crisply.

Morgan swallowed, silently calling himself every kind of idiot. Why should Uncle Cedric give him a position now? He had just admitted that all he really liked to do was drive fast cars. He could add listening to the new jass music from New Orleans and relaxing at Madame Hahn's, none of it exactly the sort of curriculum vitae points that would endear him to an employer, especially Uncle Cedric. He wasn't even sure what the man did in his fancy office, but he knew that others had described him as ruthless. He certainly looked the part with his cold stare and thin lips under a greying mustache.

Morgan shifted uncomfortably under the man's scrutiny.

"Young man, your father is worried about you, do you realize that? Why, at your age, he was already heading part of his father's company. You have a good head on your shoulders, I know that. You did fairly well in college; were on the sailing team, the tennis team, and even took part in the Gilbert and Sullivan productions they put on every year, as I recall. What are you doing now?"

"I'm trying to find a place for myself," Morgan began unsteadily. He hadn't been expecting this assault. One part of his mind wondered if this was some sort of shock tactic. Another part whispered that Uncle Cedric was annoyed because he was not shaping up as a suitable prospect for Betsy, and this secretly pleased him.

Or Uncle Cedric could have heard from his father—a frightening thought.

"The thing is," he went on, feeling his way, "I don't even know what you do here, sir."

"Basically, I buy failing companies and make them strong again. So if you work for me, you may be doing a lot of traveling, working in the field, as we say. Good work for a young man, not so good as one gets older." He smiled deprecatingly. "But what I need to know is, are you ready to work? Or are you still sowing your wild oats?"

"I think I'm just about finished, sir."

"When you know for sure, come back and talk to me." Cedric stood up abruptly, startling Morgan.

They shook hands and Morgan left, wondering what had actually happened. Had Cedric politely kicked him out of his office? Ask questions next time, he told himself. Be better prepared. Show some interest.

"Wild oats," he muttered, bouncing down the steps to the sidewalk. That's what I should be doing over in Europe. But immediately he felt guilty, thinking about what was happening over there now, remembering the graphic description of the horrors of life in the trenches as described by Romeo Houle in the *Times*, so different from the bombastic overblown descriptions coming from the journalists who watched from a safe distance. They made the whole sordid thing sound more like grand opera, with their talk of "the grandeur of the battle symphony", describing the firing of guns as "flashes of flame, like fireflies in the summer night." A summer night when fireflies killed.

He hailed a cab and gave the address of a well-known lunch spot popular with his set. He would soon have to forego these luxuries, he thought morosely, staring out at the passing crowds. He found several of his friends ensconced in the small upstairs dining room, finishing up a late lunch. Rolly greeted him like a long-lost brother, throwing his arms around him, breathing wine-soaked fumes in his face. Noah Bierman shook his hand formally. He was dressed soberly for his job in a law office. Langley Blackwell-Thomas nodded lazily and stretched out his long elegant frame, thumbs tucked in his waistcoat pockets.

"You dressed for a funeral, old chap?" he drawled.

"Yes. My own. I just had a job interview of sorts with Cedric Fallin."

"Ooooh, the Big Bad Wolf himself. Can't see you working for him, old chap."

"Neither can I." Morgan unbuttoned his jacket and ordered wine and a light lunch from the waiter hovering at his elbow.

"Did you hear about Sydney?" Noah asked. "He went to Canada and enlisted in their army."

"What! I knew he was talking about it," Morgan said, "but no one took it seriously."

"Guess we were wrong." Rolly belched and pulled out a pipe and tobacco pouch. "Poor stupid bugger."

"I think it's rather brave, actually," said Langley, pouring more wine.

"It's not our war, Langley. Let them take care of it themselves."

"It seems to be taking a rather long time," Langley said. "Perhaps they need help."

"We are a neutral country." Rolly was beginning to slur. "Like Shwitzerland. Not our job to help them."

"Not like Switzerland at all," Morgan said, cracking a roll and buttering it. "Switzerland doesn't have to worry about submarine torpedoes. Anyway, even our president has changed his tune about being neutral. Remember all those preparedness speeches he made? I wouldn't be surprised if we get into it eventually."

"Doesn't mean he's right," muttered Rolly.

"One of the men in my office did the same thing as Sydney," Noah said. "Just left his job, went to Canada, and enlisted. No one even talked about him. It was as if he had vanished. Then last week, we heard he was dead. Killed in England before he even got a chance to fight."

"Bad luck." Langley picked up a handful of grapes and began dropping them into his mouth, one after one.

"Sherves him right."

Everyone stared at Rolly, who looked back, his eyes slightly unfocussed.

"You're drunk," Morgan said.

"I have to get back to the office." Noah got up abruptly and left.

"I didn' mean to break up the party," said Rolly.

"Do shut up, old thing."

Morgan began to eat. He was hungry, having missed his usual lunchtime in his eagerness to be on time for Uncle Cedric. A few minutes later, he noticed that Rolly had fallen asleep.

"He can't seem to help himself, can he?" said Langley, taking the pipe out of Rolly's slack fingers.

"My father says that's what comes of coming into one's inheritance too soon."

"He may be right. I wouldn't know." Langley's father had invested all their money into a scheme that went belly-up a few years earlier, leaving the family in much reduced circumstances. The family fortunes depended on Langley making a good marriage, but he didn't seem to be having any better luck in that department than Morgan was having in the job market.

"Thank God for Sadie's!" Langley exclaimed now.

"You have any luck at the card tables last night?"

"Capital luck, sir! But you know what they say: Lucky in cards, unlucky in love."

"Claptrap," said Morgan.

Langley laughed and slid further down on his spine. "Have you given any more thought to my offer of sharing digs? You can't keep staying at that hotel if you're trying to save money. Or are you planning on crawling back home?"

Morgan shook his head. "Now that I'm out, I'm staying out. I checked with my bank yesterday. I have some money, just not a lot."

"You've got a trust fund, haven't you?"

"Eventually, yes, but how to survive till I get it?" He sighed. "We could try sharing for a month and see how that goes."

"Capital! Not quite your usual neighborhood, I know, but it's gone down in the world enough to be interesting but not enough to be questionable. Shall I help you move your things this afternoon?"

"I can get most of it in my car."

"Which reminds me, when are you driving in another motorcar race?"

"Look, I told you. I'm not driving for Chuffy Harris as long as that despicable Kit Caulder works for him."

"You didn't tell him why, did you?"

"Just because Caulder isn't a gentleman doesn't mean I am not one."

Langley shook his head. "You are not on the playing fields of the old alma mater, dear boy."

Morgan laughed, pushing back his chair. "I'll see you later today at your place. You can keep badgering me there."

"And I will," Langley said. He set off down the stairs, leaving Morgan to pay the bill for both of them.

When will I learn, Morgan thought, and decided to take the El back to his hotel.

TWENTY-EIGHT

"BUDS BLOOM IN THE PARK FOR RED CROSS WAR RELIEF"
—*New York Bugle*, late edition

Gloria smiled warmly at Nigel as they walked through Central Park towards the pergola where a cloud of flower-bedecked white hats bobbed and dipped in the sun-dappled afternoon. The debutantes were gathering to take part in an event in support of the Red Cross war effort abroad. Gloria usually enjoyed these fanciful occasions, but this was her first appearance since the fateful soirée a mere week ago. She felt almost grateful to Nigel for carrying on as if nothing untoward had happened, but for her, the pall of that night lingered on, hovering over the family's Easter spent in the country, with Aunt Hattie an unseen guest at every meal, every outing, even at church. No one spoke of the woman who lay somewhere in that sprawling country house in a twilight world between waking and sleep, awaiting her final journey to the asylum. The first ball of the spring season was scheduled for next week at the Ritz-Carlton, but still Gloria felt a heaviness weighing her down. She couldn't keep the image of poor Aunt Hattie's grotesque last dance out of her mind. Worst of all, she had no one to talk to about it. That would be disloyal.

She missed Morgan. Even with all the teasing he subjected her to, she wished he was still at home. She felt as if he had deserted her. What made it worse was that she had no clear idea why he had left so suddenly, leaving behind a strange unsettled atmosphere. It was as if the house was holding its breath, waiting, poised for something else to happen, some final outrage to end the almost operatic series of events. Her parents were behaving as if nothing had happened, as if Morgan had just gone back to college or out for a weekend of motorcar racing and Aunt Hattie would return any day after a few weeks in the country.

"A penny for your thoughts," Nigel said.

"They aren't worth that much," Gloria assured him, squeezing his arm gently and leaning closer for a brief moment of intimacy. "I'm sorry I'm not very entertaining today. Thank you for accompanying me in spite of my grumpiness."

"It is, as always, a pleasure." Nigel bowed, but his puckish smile dissolved the formal gesture into informality. "May I ask you one question?"

"I'm sure you may ask me many, Nigel, but whether or not I answer is quite another thing."

"Why did Morgan leave home?"

Startled that he should come so close to her thoughts, she almost stumbled on the grass. "You'll have to ask him," she said, turning away. But she had the feeling Nigel would not be the last one to ask that question under the cover of friendship. At least she knew no one would be so gauche as to ask about poor Aunt Hattie.

"There you are!" exclaimed one of the Ogilvie twins, reaching out to draw her into the frothy mass of debutantes milling around the pergola. "Did you know you're in the *New York Times* this morning?"

"I hope it's a good picture."

"No, no, not just a picture or society report! You've been voted the number three belle of the debutante season by the Third Division of the Eighth Brigade, Canadian Mounted Rifles." She said this last part all in one breath, as if she had memorized it. "Did you know? I said you didn't, but Gwen said you knew already and that's why you were late, so you could make a grand entrance. So which of us is right? Me? Gwen?"

"I have no idea what you're talking about," Gloria said, looking from one expectant twin to the other. "Muriel?" she called, catching sight of her friend in the throng. "Do you know about this *Times* article?"

Muriel led her to a long trestle table where mounds of flowers waited to be arranged for the tableaux and picked up a copy of the morning paper shoved carelessly in amongst the blooms. "Here's the article. Some Canadian soldiers at the front got hold of a copy of the *Times* with you in a group picture taken of most of us at some event, and they took a vote and named their top ten beauties. You made number three."

"Three? Who's number one?"

Muriel laughed. "Louise Shilling. Ann Thompson is number two. I didn't even make the list."

"They weren't voting on brains, dear," said Mrs. Whittaker, one of the organizers, as she tied a Red Cross armband on Gloria. "Imagine those poor men sitting over there in a muddy, smelly trench, gazing at a picture of all that American youth and beauty! I think it's sweet of them to let us know, don't you?"

"It feels a bit peculiar, actually." Gloria gazed at the picture of the regiment, which covered the entire width of the *Times*, thinking of the long journey the paper had taken: a couple of weeks on a ship, most likely, then on a train, then a boat crossing the Channel, then transferring to a horse-drawn cart out to the trenches in France somewhere. All those miles. Her face. Her friends' faces. By this time, some of the men she was looking at might very well be dead.

"Are you cold, dear?" asked Mrs. Whittaker solicitously.

"I'm fine, thank you." Gloria moved away to let another girl take her place.

"How does it feel to be a beauty queen?" Morgan whispered. He had made his way into the throng of debs, one finger on his lips, and Gloria's jump of surprise was very gratifying.

"Morgan! What are you doing here?"

"I freely admit this event wasn't high on my list of what to do this morning, but after reading the paper, I had to come."

"So I am the reason for you putting in a rare appearance?"

"One of them." He winked and looked over her shoulder to where Muriel was standing, sorting ribbons.

"How nice to see you," Muriel said quietly. "I got your letters. I now think you should go into politics, as you are a master at using many words to say very little."

"Can you leave your ribbons to fend for themselves for a few minutes?" he asked. "I couldn't really explain in a letter. I don't know if I can explain at all, but I'd like to try."

"You don't owe me any explanation for what you choose to do,

Morgan," she said, dropping her spectacles into her beaded reticule, "but I'm quite ready to leave all this for a stroll in the park any time. It's my second season, you know, and I sincerely hope Mother will be satisfied after this and let me alone for a while."

"I thought you went to Barnard last year?"

"I wanted to. I was even accepted, but Mother thought coming out was more important." She made a face and pushed the box of ribbons into the arms of another girl. "Take care of this for me, will you, Sophie?"

The girl nodded, looking up at Morgan under long pale lashes.

Muriel took Morgan's arm as they turned along the nearest path. "I'm sorry your musical soirée ended so unfortunately," she said. "Your poor mother must have been quite upset. Your aunt is her sister, isn't she?"

Morgan nodded. "We thought she was cured."

"Some things one doesn't recover from."

"Muriel, William Forrester was never her fiancé. He barely knew her. Besides, he was married to someone else by the time he went down on the Titanic."

"Clearly not in her mind," Muriel said.

Morgan shook his head, wondering how to get off the topic of poor Aunt Hattie's delusions and back to his problems with his father and why he had moved out.

Muriel paused by a bench, then sat down, smoothing her skirt over her knees. Her hands in their white lace gloves looked like large exotic butterflies.

Morgan reached over and caught one. "I'm in a quite untenable situation," he said. She looked into his eyes, waiting. He took courage from the fact that she didn't pull her hand away. It lay warm and alive in his, and he felt its warmth seep slowly into him. "I have always admired my father," he went on, measuring his words one by one, trying to present his case fairly. "I always thought he was a man of strict principle, even though I know that in his eyes, I can never measure up to my brother."

Muriel made a soft noise, but he shushed her with a wave of his hand.

"We are totally different, Chesleigh and I, and I thought my father had come to terms with that. Chesleigh would sooner die than be seen on the ground with grease on his hands, delving into the innards of a motorcar. My father seemed to be giving me time to settle in after college, especially after I missed out on my shot at the European experience I had been looking forward to, thanks to this war, but now—"

"The war is more than an inconvenience to your travel plans, Morgan." Muriel pulled her hand away. "Haven't you read the reports in the *Times* from Romeo Houle, the young barber who enlisted in Montreal with the French-Canadian regiment?"

Morgan flushed. "I didn't mean to belittle what their soldiers are going through!"

"Mr. Houle is an American."

"I know. I'm just trying to explain the background for this row with my father."

Muriel looked over her shoulder to where the cloud of debs was beginning to form itself into a tableau beside a group of musicians who were settling into chairs to one side.

"You don't have to go yet, do you?" Morgan asked anxiously.

"I'm in 'Autumn'," she said. "Appropriate, don't you think?"

"Oh, *The Four Seasons.*"

"Vivaldi," she said.

"I see."

They were silent for a few moments while Morgan tried to gather the threads of his story, but the more he tried, the more scattered everything was and the more nervous he became that Muriel would get up and leave. He wanted her approval. He could hold his head high if she was on his side. But what was his side? And how could he accuse his father of theft when he was pretty sure his father had no idea that what he was buying was stolen? It had all seemed so clear when he had stormed out of the house, but now it just seemed petty and rather childish. And the Uncle Paul thing… well, he couldn't talk about that to a young lady.

Around them, a breeze carried waves of music in their direction over the heads of the crowd gathered around the shifting *tableau vivant*.

At last, he forced himself to speak, pushing out the words quickly before he lost her, trying to explain about the icon and how he knew it was stolen.

Muriel was silent for a moment when he finished. "How much do you know about Russian icons?" she asked.

"I remember what I saw in that old lady's parlor," he said. "It's Nijinsky who's the expert. And the count," he added.

"But the count wouldn't know the old lady," she said.

"Jinks says she was a famous dancer back in Russia. Her husband was some sort of relative of the count's."

"Many years ago. The count is quite young. Your friend would have recognized her because he grew up where she was revered, surrounded by paintings of famous dancers, I expect."

He nodded. "But I know what I saw," he said stubbornly.

"And I admire your principles," she said, standing up. She turned and smiled at him. "Really I do," she went on, "but you must learn to choose your battles. Besides, you don't have to prove your principles to me. I am fond of you, my dear, just as Gloria is fond of you, and I will always be your friend, no matter what you do. Now I really must get back."

He rose and watched her go, her slim figure upright and graceful. He couldn't say what if it was about this woman that he found so seductive. There were many faces more beautiful, other figures more voluptuous and alluring. But intelligence shone from her eyes. Compassion was in her expression whenever she heard stories of cruelty or oppression. It was this, he knew, that drove her to suffragette meetings, and it was this compassion and integrity that made her visit women in prison, and send baskets home to the family of their ailing kitchen boy until her mother stopped her. Morgan wanted her approval, and the sense that she knew this took away from his own feeling of worth now that he had it. He felt deflated as her parting words echoed in his mind: 'I am fond of you, just as Gloria is fond is you.'

My life is getting much too complicated, he thought, slumping back against the bench. Things used to be so simple, so clear. He glanced at a young man leaning against a nearby tree watching the tableau. His bright head of red curls looked familiar.

"Andy Cass?" he called.

The young man turned towards him, startled.

"I'm surprised the *Bugle* is covering this event," Morgan said.

"We have a photographer here, but I'm just hanging around

hoping to talk to your sister. I didn't get a chance to say goodbye the other night."

"What a shambles! Honestly, Andy, it's not always like that at our house."

Andy waved his hand in dismissal and glanced at the tableau again. "I wonder if it has occurred to any of those young ladies that if they donated the money it cost for the flowers and the musicians, not to mention the decorations, they would have much more money for the Red Cross effort in Europe."

Morgan laughed. "I doubt it," he said. With the possible exception of Muriel, he added to himself.

Andy crossed the path and sat down beside him, pulling out a battered cigarette case and a pack of lucifers. He flipped open the case and offered it to Morgan. After the ritual of lighting and dragging in their first deep breath was over, they both leaned back and relaxed. After a moment, Morgan coughed and picked a bit of rough tobacco from his lower lip.

"Not what you're used to, I'm sure," Andy remarked, "but they're cheap."

"Cheap has a lot to recommend it," Morgan said, with a new appreciation of this fact. "I can get used to them."

Andy looked at him curiously.

"My ill-considered comment about the icon escalated into a full-blown row with my father after everyone had gone, with me taking the impossibly high ground and then stomping out the door. I'm sharing digs with a friend for a while in Greenwich village."

"Interesting place."

"A little too interesting sometimes," Morgan said, remembering the previous night and being wakened up at four in the morning by a shouting match between his artist neighbors: two women who seemed to save up their recriminations until they exploded at an impossibly high volume very early in the morning.

Andy nodded.

"'Interesting' is fun to visit, but living there is another story."

"Exactly why I live in Brooklyn."

They smoked for a while in silence, Morgan sunk in gloom, Andy obviously mulling something over.

"I've been researching a story on art fraud," Andy said at last, leaning forward, his elbows on his knees. "You mentioned the dealer, Green and Green, and I went there to nose around. I found something interesting." He dropped the cigarette and ground it under his heel.

Morgan straightened up and turned to face him. "My father had no idea—"

"I know, I know. I'm just investigating a story. Your father is not involved."

Morgan relaxed. "What did you find out?"

"Green's nephew's the dodgy one. I walked in on him doing a deal with an artist I used to know over a Russian icon that looked about the same age and style as your father's. The artist calls himself Rudy these days, and he's Gail's—I mean Galina Petrovna's brother. The problem is I don't know how to find him. I went to his old address, but the people there say they haven't seen him for a long time."

"I think I saw him that time Nijinsky and I went to Galina's room, trying to find out something about her."

"We might find an address at the theater, I suppose."

"The Met?"

"He's good friends with one of the Ballets Russes dancers." Andy took out his cheap pocket watch and checked the time. "They'll still be at rehearsal."

"Let's go." Morgan got to his feet.

"Are you sure you want to be involved?"

"I got myself thrown out of the house for this," Morgan said, tossing away his cigarette. "I want to get to the bottom of it."

TWENTY-NINE

"RUSSIAN ART FLOODS MARKET: IS IT ALL GENUINE?"
—*New York Bugle,* late edition

The Metropolitan Opera House dominated the corner of 39th and Broadway, stretching for almost an entire block. Andy went to the stage door and tried to talk his way inside using a combination of charm, apparently fluent Russian, and a flash of his press credentials. But the old man guarding the entrance shook his head and began to close the door.

"It is imperative that I see my friend, Mr. Nijinsky," Morgan said, stepping forward.

The old man looked at him closely, his rheumy eyes lingering on the well-cut clothes, the expensive gloves, the highly polished leather shoes.

"My name should be on the guest list," Morgan added, hoping Jinks had remembered to do what he had promised. He spelled his name and waited.

The old man pulled out a heavy ledger and carefully ran a gnarled finger down the list of names. Finally he nodded, grunted, and held the door open for the two men.

"Impressive," murmured Andy.

"It was just so I could get in easily to pick him up from time to time after the show. He likes my car."

"I don't blame him."

The old man pointed towards the second story and Andy took the lead.

"You sure you know where you're going?" Morgan asked. "You've been here before?"

"Once," Andy said, making his way through the maze of narrow passages and up several flights of stairs. "The rehearsal hall must be this way." He pushed through a thick door into a wide corridor.

"There seem to be several," Morgan said, pointing to the sign painted on the wall.

Andy paused, considering. "I read that Nijinsky is working on a new ballet. He'll probably want the whole company, so it'll be the main space, I'd say."

"You're well informed," Morgan remarked.

"I follow dance news pretty closely. Let's try down here."

When they arrived at the rehearsal hall, Morgan paused to look in the round window of the dark oak double doors. He drew back abruptly as shouting erupted and something hit the wall close to his head. A wailing scream rose and rose, ending in an anguished shriek. Cautiously, Morgan inched the door open and peered in. At the far corner of the room, a group of dancers huddled together, their eyes wide with shock as they watched Nijinsky shredding the material of somebody's costume with his hands, tossing the ragged scraps over his shoulder as he ranted. Then he suddenly lunged forward and grabbed one of the men, spinning him about, forcing one of his arms above his head in an ungainly pose, his head pushed down at an unnatural angle.

"Is for new ballet," a voice whispered in his ear.

Morgan jumped back into the hall, letting the door swing closed. A slender young man with great dark eyes was standing beside him, a towel around his neck. Judging by his clothes, he was coming from another rehearsal. He looked familiar.

"Léonide Massine," the young man said, holding out his hand. "Vaslav is great dancer, genius with choreography, but he cannot explain well his ideas. Lately, he is often…"

"Frustrated?" suggested Morgan."

"Yes, exactly."

A scream erupted from inside the closed room.

"All will be well soon," Massine said, nodding his head as if trying to reassure himself. "Diaghilev give him this job for *Till Eulenspiegel*. He knows him better than anyone. All will be well when everyone get used to this different way to move."

"I hope so." Morgan took another quick peek inside the room, just in time to see Nijinsky fling himself at the opposite wall in a rage. The dancers drew away from him, watching wide-eyed as he slid down the wall and sat there, pale and glassy-eyed.

"Is he all right?" Morgan asked, one hand on the door, ready to go inside if needed. "Maybe I should get help? Or you go. That would be better."

"No, no! Me, I am last person he want to see." Massine laid a hand on his arm. "Best leave him now," he said.

Morgan nodded, shaken.

"He not remember this later, but others will. Be good friend to him," Massine went on softly. "He not have many here now."

Morgan was about to say he understood why when he heard Andy's voice calling his name. He turned away, relieved to distance himself from the madness. Massine was already disappearing down a flight of steps.

Half an hour later, Morgan, Andy, the dancer Pavel Lermentov, and Rudy gathered around the small round table in the window of Bennino's, a tiny restaurant not far from the Met. It was clear that both Pavel and Rudy were known here, and their favorite drinks and antipasto were brought to the table right away. Rudy had a leather rucksack stuffed under the table and he seemed very nervous. Pavel kept trying to reassure him.

Andy was doing most of the talking, but Rudy kept interrupting.

"And how is it going to help me to confess to a crime I haven't committed?" Rudy said angrily, draining his glass of Hamm's beer. "What did you see at Green and Green's anyway? How do you know that what I was selling was not a copy? Or the real thing given to me by a client to sell?"

"That's the point," Andy said patiently. "I need to know the details to be able to help you. Look, the police are far more interested in Green Jr. and his clients than they are in you, can't you see that?"

Rudy ran both hands through his already-tousled black hair and shook his head.

"I've been working on a news story about art fraud for weeks now," Andy went on. "This is the first break I've had and I told my source at the police department about it. I can practically guarantee they'll drop all charges against you for solid information that will help close the case and put some people behind bars where they belong much more than you do."

"What is practically?" Pavel asked, his blue eyes drilling into Andy.

"It's as close to a guarantee as you're liable to get from the police, that's what it is."

"Is easy for you," Pavel shouted suddenly. "You not the one maybe end in jail. Why you not leave him alone?"

"And he was doing so well before I came along?" Andy asked sarcastically.

Pavel dropped his eyes.

"I've known you a long time," Andy went on, leaning across the table and looking at Rudy earnestly. "I thought you were going to be a real artist."

"You haven't been in touch with either me or Galina for years," Rudy said bitterly. "What do you know about our lives? I see you working where you want to work, your name in the paper, interviewing Nijinsky even. You are successful. You can feed yourself, your family. But me, I scramble hard to get food on the table and shelter over my head. I sell everything, even myself, you understand? Right now, if it wasn't for Pavel, I would be on the street."

"Shhhh," murmured the dancer.

"You're right," Andy said. "I've lost touch with most of the old neighborhood friends. The last I heard, you were doing all right, though, painting sets for theaters, doing murals, things like that."

"Eventually, it wasn't enough." Rudy hung his head and ran his finger around the rim of his empty glass.

Morgan ordered another round. He could feel Andy's tension magnifying his own. What if this exploration of Rudy's art frauds led to his father? What if his father really had known the icon was stolen? Would Morgan discover that more pieces hanging on the walls of his parents' home were also stolen? Or were they mere copies that his father had been duped into paying full price for? He remembered Prince Romanoff and the count looking at the paintings and laughing together behind their hands. Did they know? He felt his face flush hot with shame.

"Rudy, my name is Morgan Vanheusen," he began leaning over

the table in his intensity. "Could you tell me—"

"You!" Rudy reared back and spat at him. "You're the one!"

"What one?" asked Andy, looking back and forth between them.

Pavel handed over his handkerchief to Morgan to wipe off the spittle while the horrified waiter looked on.

"I'm not the one," Morgan said, drawing back, "but I don't blame you for spitting when you heard the surname. It was my uncle who dishonored your sister."

"Your uncle?" Andy said.

"Paul Vanheusen."

"Member of the Committee of Fourteen?" Andy grinned, obviously appreciating the irony, but he quickly wiped the smile off his face when he looked at Rudy's stricken expression.

"Nothing I say can undo the wrong," Morgan said. "I'm sorry."

Rudy wiped foam from the beer off his mouth with the back of his hand. "He said he loved her. Then when she told him about the baby coming, he said he never wanted to see her again. She was heartbroken."

"Baby?" Morgan stared at the man.

Rudy wiped his eyes angrily. "I was forced to do some things I'm not proud of to help out, but as my old Russian neighbor used to say, 'Ah, you can even get used to Hell'."

The four men were silent, each sipping wine or nibbling at the olives. Morgan kept seeing Uncle Paul's face in his mind, red with indignation. You bloody hypocrite, he thought.

"She couldn't dance for a long time," Rudy went on quietly. "Then she finally got a job with the Ballets Russes. She was so happy, but they don't pay anyone well. Except your friend Nijinsky," he added bitterly, glancing at Morgan.

"Didn't Uncle Paul give her some money at least?" Morgan asked tentatively.

"Oh yes, thirty pieces of silver for breaking her heart." Rudy almost snarled across the table. "She thought it was a small fortune, but it wasn't. Not really. The money soon ran out after a few months, before the baby even came. Galina did not do well before the birth. And then the baby got sick. She needs medicine and special treatments."

"And you were forced into a life of crime," Andy prompted.

Morgan could practically see him slanting the story he was writing in his head.

"After the baby was born, Galina was desperate. She finally had a chance to dance with a great company, but that meant she had no time for any other job. She began to steal small things from her mentor's house. The poor old woman could barely see, she said. She hoped they wouldn't be missed."

"Annya missed them," Morgan said.

"You know Annya?"

Morgan told them about going to Madame Ostroffsky's house with Nijinsky, about the Russian recognizing that the icons were fake, about talking to Annya who was so bitter about Galina and her stealing. "She didn't tell the old woman because she couldn't bear to hurt her any more," he finished.

"Galina thought she knew," Rudy said.

"So that's when you started making copies and selling the originals to Marcus Green," Andy prompted.

Rudy shifted in his seat, glanced at Pavel, took a nibble of bread.

"Tell all," whispered Pavel. "I not care what you do."

Morgan looked at Pavel, noted the expression of utter devotion on his face. He cleared his throat. "Might as well be hung for a sheep as for a lamb, Rudy," he said.

Rudy drained his glass. "I had already done a little copying for some people I know. It started innocently enough. I did a copy of an Old Master for a friend as a gift. Art students do it all the time as a way to learn different styles. He showed it to everyone and eventually I had a visit from a man who wanted me to copy another painting, for a good price. I thought, why not? I needed money, Galina needed money, and the man said he wanted it for his own house, just like my friend, so it seemed innocent enough. It never occurred to me that what I was doing was fraud. But then he wanted more copies of other paintings he brought over to my studio and I finally realized what was going on, but it was too late. They blackmailed me into the fraud business. When Galina brought me the icons, I was already in over my head. I copied them and sold the originals one by one to Green Jr."

Andy was making notes now. "How did you meet Green?" he asked, looking up.

"He's the man who commissioned the forgeries."

There was silence at the table. In the kitchen, someone was whistling 'A Bicycle Built for Two.' Andy's pencil whispered across the paper of his dog-eared notebook.

"I wanted to stop," Rudy said softly. "I had a big fight with Galina a short time before she…died. She wanted me to sell the last icon right away, but I knew Green would give me a better price later on when there were would be fewer Russian items on the market. But now I need money for Natasha. What am I going to do?"

Morgan stared at him, wondering if any of his father's precious collection were actually painted by Rudy. "When did you start doing this copying?" he asked.

Rudy shrugged. "About two years ago. Just before Natasha was born. Galina needed doctors, food, rent. She couldn't dance, couldn't do anything. There were complications."

When Galina disappeared from the old woman's world for a while, only to appear again as a thief.

"This is a real breakthrough," Andy said, putting his notebook away. "Detective Sullivan's going to welcome you with open arms! Let's go."

"To the police station?" Rudy said, alarmed.

"Why not? He promised me he'd go easy on you if I brought you in."

"But this is not certain," Pavel said.

Rudy pushed his rucksack into Morgan's hands. "Keep this for me," he said. "It's all I have in the world."

Morgan watched them go, stunned. When he pulled out the contents of the satchel, the dull golds of a painting glimmered in the sunshine. He pushed Olga's fourth icon back inside the rucksack and shivered.

"How much is it worth?" asked Langley, eyeing the icon lying on the table between them in their loft back in Greenwich Village.

"I have no idea," Morgan said, "but probably a lot more than Green would give Rudy for it."

Langley lay back among the cushions of the tattered divan and drew lazily on his pipe. "You could probably buy your own racing car with the money, if you sell it."

"And to whom would I sell it?"

"Your father."

Morgan stared at him, his mouth slightly open. "Are you mad? I couldn't do that!"

"You say you'd like to own a racing car, right?"

"My own motor is modified to race pretty well, you know."

"Come on, you want your own car, you know you do. Isn't that what you've been maundering on about every night since you moved in?"

"Not every night," Morgan objected. "Mostly I just want to race someone else's motorcar."

"All right, then, every night you're not raving on about the glories of Sapphire, the quadroon from New Orleans, who, I admit, is a pretty fine specimen of pulchritude."

Morgan sighed. "I can't afford to go to Sadie Hahn's place anymore," he said.

"You could if you sold that thing." Langley pointed a long finger at the icon glowing dully from the muddled mess on the table. "By the way, what happened to the thief?" he asked, putting his feet up on the table.

"The thief is dead, and her brother, the artist, is off offering 'to help the police with their enquiries', with Andy urging him on."

"Cass wants a story. Does the artist know where you live?"

"I didn't tell him. I didn't get the chance."

Langley stretched, his long hands clasped above his head. "I have been invited to Miss Amy's for tea," he said and made a face.

"Langley, I wish you'd leave that poor thing alone."

"She is pining for me," said Langley. "It would be cruel to deprive her of my presence. May I borrow your diamond cufflinks?"

"I need them back!" Morgan said sharply. "They're my graduation present."

"Yes, yes, I shall return them forthwith, old thing. By the way, is there a reward for the return of that *objet*?"

"The owner doesn't know it's gone, remember?"

"Oh. Silly me. About the race thing, though. Some people get paid to drive, you know. Think about that, will you?" He turned and fixed Morgan with a piercing stare.

"I am a gentleman."

"But not a millionaire like your pal Carlo Benedetti. And incidentally, I'm willing to bet *he* gets paid for driving in a race."

"You'll bet on anything!"

Langley grinned, then inspected himself in the small looking glass balanced on the dresser. "Oh, but I am a handsome dog, am I not, sir?"

"You are, sir. And an unmitigated bounder, to boot."

"Ah, boots! Must buy new boots. Oxblood is all the rage these days. Tra la." He bowed and swept out the door, slamming it behind him.

Morgan sighed and shook his head. He couldn't help enjoying Langley, but at times, the man seemed practically amoral. The best thing to do was probably to take the icon to the police station. It was evidence, after all. But he heard again Rudy's tearful voice: 'It's all I have.'

He stuffed the icon out of sight in Rudy's leather satchel and pushed it under the daybed in the corner.

THIRTY

"VICE DECLINES HERE, SOCIAL BUREAU SAYS;
Institution founded by John D. Rockefeller, Jr., Reports on its
Work..."

—*New York Times*, 1916

Detective Sullivan glowered across his desk at Rudy. "Remember, you're not off the hook yet. I'll have my eye on you, my young buck, and if you so much as drop garbage out a window, I'll haul you in, and Bob's your uncle, you're back in the hoosegow. And this time, you stay there. Understand?"

"Yes, sir." Rudy nodded, his pale face bathed in sweat.

"We make a great team, eh, Sullivan?" Andy said, getting to his feet.

"That's Detective Sullivan to you, boyo, and don't you forget it. Now get out of here, the both of youse. Out of my sight!"

Andy and his charge turned tail and almost ran out of the musty office.

Sullivan grinned. That Cass had a good head on his shoulders and he went after the facts like a bulldog. But Rudy, or Randolph as was written on his certificate of birth, was sly. He had insisted on holding back the names of most of the artists who had participated in the fraud. They had all been duped, too, he argued, and although Sullivan doubted that they were all as naive as Rudy claimed to be, he gave in. For now. He really only wanted Green Jr. and a few of the people he had sold to, and these he now had. It was an impressive list: leaders of industry, bankers, society doyennes. He just hoped Green Jr. kept as good records as Rudy.

Sullivan leaned back, put his feet up on the desk, and twiddled

his thumbs for a moment. One new name that had emerged interested him: Olga Ostroffsky. Her name had come up in the Ballets
Russes dancer's death investigation—or non-investigation, to be
more exact. So the dancer had stolen from this Olga person, who
was unaware of it, thanks to the talents of Rudy. Or was she? Did
she know something Rudy didn't? The odds of two such different
investigations inadvertently crossing into each other intrigued him.
Rudy was the link; Olga, the Russian connection.

He hauled himself to his feet and shouted out to his sergeant
that he would be out for a few hours. Checking his notes, he then
pushed the notebook back into his pocket and set out for Olga's
house.

This neighborhood was a step up from Galina's. Olga Ostroffsky's
tall narrow house looked neat and tidy. No garbage littered the steps
or lay rotting in the basement area. Repairs were needed, though.
Paint was peeling from the door and the surrounding woodwork.
The bricks needed pointing. As he went down the cement steps to
the basement entrance, he almost tripped at the bottom where a
chunk of concrete had crumbled away. If this woman was actively
involved in art fraud, she wasn't doing very well at it.

He rang the bell and waited. He was just turning to leave when
the door slowly opened, revealing an old lady, her white hair piled
on top of her head in an elaborate style that even Sullivan knew had
gone out of fashion years ago. Her dress was also elaborate and old,
the once-vibrant blue silk faded, like her eyes.

"Mrs. Ostroffsky?" he said, "I'm Detective Sullivan from the
police."

"Really!" she exclaimed, apparently delighted to see him. "Do
come in. You're just in time for tea."

The detective, not used to being welcomed so effusively, smiled
and followed her down the narrow, damp hall into a crowded parlor. He saw the fake icons at once, their jewel colors glowing against
the dark wall. Rudy was very good.

"My maid is out, I'm afraid, but she has already prepared the
tea, and I have some biscuits in the pantry." She paused, one thin
age-spotted hand on the top of a carved chair. She seemed to move
at ease among the labyrinth of tables and footstools and chairs,
the lamps with their beaded shades, and a whatnot where china

figurines and family photos jostled each other for space.

Sullivan sat on the chair by the tall, lace-curtained window and watched her still-erect, willowy figure move to the Russian samovar bubbling on a table in a corner. Her hands hovered over the glasses there, her fingers seeming to sense when the glass was full, where the edge of the small tray was. "I'll just get the biscuits," she said, moving to the tiny kitchen just out of sight.

She kept talking as she rattled the crockery. "I grew up in a bakery, you know. Until I went to the ballet school in St. Petersburg, I helped my parents with the bread and sweet biscuits. Sometimes I cook just to get that rush of nostalgia that comes with the smell of baking."

Sullivan stood as she came back in, then helped her steady the tray, which almost missed the table beside him. She didn't seem to notice.

"So good of you to visit," she said, sitting down gracefully in the high-backed chair and putting her tiny feet on the embroidered footstool. "Mr. Nijinsky came by to pay his respects a while ago. So thoughtful of him." She smiled and took a sip of tea from the tall glass. "It's wonderful to know some people still remember me. Do you know Mr. Nijinsky?"

"I've met him, yes." Sullivan raised his glass, but the tea tasted too strong for him and he put it down again. "You don't get much company?" he said, trying to keep her talking.

"Not any more," she said. "I used to have students, and even after I stopped teaching, some of them kept dropping in to tell me their troubles and their triumphs."

"Was Galina Petrovna one of your students?"

"Oh, yes. She was very talented. How did you know she took lessons from me? Did she mention me?"

"Yes, indeed she did," Sullivan said, picking up a biscuit. "Did you know her brother, too?" The old lady shrugged her thin shoulders and glanced out the window. Her face had gone vague, as if she were falling asleep or had suddenly forgotten he was there.

"He's an artist, too," Sullivan went on, but he felt as if he was losing her.

"Odd how people change," she said, "and how quickly they forget, how they sometimes even betray those who love them. But in the end, it doesn't matter, does it?"

"Everyone gets older," Sullivan said. He took a nibble of the biscuit. It tasted stale, the strong almond flavor almost overpowering. He wondered how old it was.

A clatter at the door brought the color back to the old lady's face. "My, what an eventful day," she exclaimed, clapping her hands together.

Sullivan got to his feet as a poorly dressed woman struggled in with a heavy string bag. "I've just been around to Omar's and got some leftover—" She stopped, staring at Sullivan. "I'm so sorry, madame, I should have come around the back way."

"Oh, Annya, you don't have to use the back way." Madame Ostroffsky turned to Sullivan, her face all smiles. "Annya is really more my friend than my maid these days," she said. "She came with us from Russia after I married my dear husband. She knows me better than anyone and is as faithful as the day is long, aren't you, my dear?"

"Of course, I am," Annya said, looking from her mistress to Sullivan, who stood with the biscuit in his hand. "No, no," she went on, suddenly grabbing the biscuit from him and scooping up the plate on her way to the kitchen. "These are too old," she called back over her shoulder. "I bring new ones."

"Not for me, thanks," Sullivan said, following her to the kitchen. "I wonder if I could talk to you alone a moment," he said quietly. "I'm Detective Sullivan from the police and I have a few questions about Galina and your mistress's religious paintings."

Annya's haggard eyes stared at him as she stood there frozen, the tin of biscuits in her hands. All the desperation of her hard life was in that look, and Sullivan almost stepped back from the force of it. "She know who you are?"

"Yes, but she never asked why I was here," he said.

"Galina was snake," Annya hissed. "You go. We talk around corner at Ivan's in a few minutes."

Sullivan nodded. Returning to the parlor, he picked up his hat from a table and was about to say goodbye to Madame Ostroffsky when he realized she had fallen asleep. Her 'eventful day' had worn her out.

Ivan's turned out to be a small, dingy tea room with three tables and a large samovar bubbling on the counter. A few minutes later, Annya joined him and said a few words in Russian to the sullen man behind the counter.

"Vodka," she told Sullivan as two glasses and a bottle appeared at their table. "Sometimes better than tea."

"I'm with you there," he agreed, grateful he didn't have to drink any more of the concoction from a samovar. He took a sip and his eyes watered. "Powerful stuff," he muttered. "So tell me, why is Galina a snake?"

"She steal. And Madame Olga, she think of her like daughter. This is after she left and ignore my poor lady for more than a year!"

"She was in the family way," Sullivan said, blushing.

"She have baby?" Annya looked bewildered.

"Yes. And the baby is sick and needs medicine. Galina was betrayed herself, Annya."

"Why she not tell? Why she not ask for help? Stupid, stupid girl! She could be alive now!"

Tears rolled down her cheeks as she wrung her hands. "So much ruined because she not tell us. Foolish, foolish pride!" She shook her head and wiped her eyes. Then she finished off the vodka and reached into her capacious bag. "Take these," she said, thrusting the biscuit box at Sullivan across the tiny table. "Take and test for poison."

"What?"

"I not know for certain sure, but I think…I think maybe Madame Olga know about fake paintings. I see her one day holding icon in her hands and the look on her face was so…so like she lost her one dear child. She didn't know I was there and she talk to herself like she does sometimes. She say, 'No, no, is too light.' I think she could tell because fake painting is on wood that is different kind. So is not so heavy like real ones."

"And she didn't say anything to you?"

"Nothing. Never." Annya was crying again. "Galina take only thing she has left from husband. Thing her husband value most. My poor lady could not stand this. I think she do something to Galina."

"What did she do?"

"I not know! But she bake these! She save only for when Galina visit. Then one day when I clean up, one fall on floor and cat eat.

Later, I find him stiff and dead. I thought he eat rat poison from trap or something. Lots around here. But I begin to wonder. She never give almond biscuits to anyone else until today. I think she know who you are, why you come!" She thrust the box at Sullivan, grabbed her bag, and rushed out the door, weeping loudly.

"Jesus, Mary, and Joseph," muttered Sullivan, looking at the dented tin that held the biscuits Madame Ostroffsky had served him: biscuits smelling strongly of almonds. Like arsenic.

"Mary, Mother of God." He crossed himself.

He found Dr. Webber stretched out on a dilapidated old sofa he had pushed into the dank stairwell outside the back door of his cave. The sun barely penetrated here, but the good doctor was lying with his face to the sky, smoking a stinky cigar. From time to time, he would take a sip from his leather flask.

"Do ya ever do any work at all, you old souse?" Sullivan called cheerily.

"Bring me your corpses, your bloodied stiffs, your mangled masses."

"How about some poison cakes?"

"Gave them up for Lent," the doctor said, slowly righting himself and peering into the dim interior of his cave where Sullivan stood holding a tin box.

"You're in luck then. Lent's over, haven't you heard, ya heathen? He is risen."

"Not in my morgue."

"Lucky for us Catholics He never made it to your morgue then, isn't it?"

Webber took out his cigar cutter, nipped off the glowing end of the stogie, and slipped the truncated cigar into his vest pocket. "Waste not, want not," he murmured. "So, what have you got for me?"

"Galina, the dancer. You said you found traces of arsenic in her hair. I was just at her old mentor's house and she had these in her kitchen. Tried to feed them to me, she did. The maid said the old girl baked them herself. Can you test them? Find out if there's arsenic in 'em?"

Webber opened the tin and sniffed the contents several times.

"You didn't notice anything about the taste?"

"I just thought the biscuit was stale, sort of like everything else in the place. Then the maid came in and grabbed it away from me."

"Good thing, that," said Dr. Webber. "I don't have to test to know there's arsenic in them, but I will to find out how much. Not a big dose, I expect, since the dancer girl's hair showed she had been exposed for a while. Do you know how long she'd been feeding her these lovelies?"

"Apparently ever since she found out the girl had stolen her treasures," Sullivan said. "Probably weeks, I'd say, possibly a month."

"She was a tough gal," Webber said, putting on his spectacles and making his way back towards his lair, where vials of strangely colored liquid gleamed and glass jars, some filled with pickled human organs, lined shelf after shelf.

"You know, Doc, it looks a bit like a still back there," Sullivan remarked, following him. "You wouldn't be breaking the law and brewing moonshine by any chance now, would you?"

Webber turned around, slipped his glasses down his nose, and glared at Sullivan.

The detective shrugged his big shoulders. "Just thought I'd ask, seein' as how it's part of my job and all." He grinned.

When Webber didn't return the grin, Sullivan turned away, clamped his hat on his head, and walked off, whistling 'Danny Boy.'

THIRTY-ONE

"MOTOR CYCLIST KILLED.
Bitale's Machine Hits Hole in Road and Bounds to Tree.
—Special to the *New York Times*

For the first time in his life, Morgan had not looked forward to his usual visit with Great-Aunt Edwina. She was too perceptive and if she had even a whiff of his need for money, she would offer to give it to him and he couldn't bear that.

But today, Gaddie was tired. She lay on her chaise longue surrounded by dogs, a compress on her forehead.

"A woman of my advanced age can be forgiven for suffering from the vapors from time to time," she announced.

Morgan had not stayed long. As he drove out from under the archway of the Dakota onto Central Park West, he turned downtown towards the Checkered Flag. Something Langley had said the other day kept playing through his mind: 'Drivers get paid for racing. Why can't you?' He had had an offer of regular employment just yesterday, but he was not inspired by the thought of working in a musty old law office, doing research. His one year of law in college had convinced him this was not for him, but desperation had driven him to seek out this interview with the father of an old school friend. He had a few days to think about it before deciding, but his bank account was dwindling fast. Between asking Great-Aunt Edwina for money and taking the job, the job would win, but it was far from what he wanted.

It was early for most of the crowd that frequented the Checkered Flag, but one man was hunched over at the corner table, a ledger open before him as he sipped a martini. Another man lounged with a friend at the next table, smoking a cigar and gesturing widely as he talked. A young man Morgan recognized as a pumper for Stubby Galino sat at the bar talking to Kit Caulder. Kit's back was to Morgan, and for a moment, Morgan thought of turning around and leaving. But almost at once, anger stiffened his spine. He caught the bartender's eye and sat down at the last table by the window.

"So now I find myself with an extra motorcar as a possible entry in the Trophy race and no driver," the man at the next table was saying. "It's feast or famine."

"Ain't that the truth," muttered his companion.

Morgan accepted his favorite cocktail and took a closer look at his neighbors. Blaze Remington, he thought. An owner in need of a driver.

On impulse, he leaned forward and tapped the man on the shoulder. "Excuse me," he said, "but I couldn't help overhearing. Are you looking for a driver?"

Remington twisted around and looked at him over his half-moon glasses. "Do I know you, sir?"

"I'm Morgan Vanheusen." He paused. Remington continued to stare at him. "I used to test drive for Heinrich Hochman."

"That was a while ago, wasn't it?" Remington said.

"More recently, I've been—"

"Wait a minute. You're the young man who almost beat me in your stripped Prince Henry. I remember you now. Come, join us." Remington puffed on his cigar as Morgan pulled his chair over to their table.

"I'm Frankie McComber," the other man said. His teeth were rotting in his head, but in spite of that, he had an infectious grin that lit up his sunburned wrinkled face. "I saw you race that special at Chuffy's the other day," he went on. "What happened, anyways?"

Morgan paused. "Bad luck," he said after a moment.

"Hah. Luck had nothing to do with it." Kit Caulder stood beside him, grinning. "He's lost it, Mr. Remington. All washed up."

"I heard he did pretty well," Remington said, taking another puff on his cigar.

"Didn't win, though, did he?"

"It was a trial run. It wasn't about winning."

"It's always about winning, sir." Kit raised his hat, turned on his heel, and walked away without a word to Morgan.

"He's right about one thing," Frankie said. "Luck had nothing to do with it."

Morgan caught the bartender's attention and ordered another cocktail. Damn Kit. He looked across the table at Remington, trying to gauge his reaction. The big man was slouched back in his chair, his eyes half closed, puffing at his cigar.

"Caulder is an ass, sir," Frankie said to the air in front of him.

"Good driver, though," Remington said. "Too bad he's not available."

"You don't want the likes of him, sir," Frankie said.

"He wins," Remington said. "What about you, Vanheusen? Can you win?"

"With a good motorcar, yes," Morgan said recklessly. "But I need practice. At Harris's, I had never been in that special before. I'd never even seen it."

"Hmm." Remington suddenly opened his eyes and stared at Morgan fixedly. "What about a Stutz Bearcat?"

Morgan felt a rush close to a sexual thrill run through him. "Oh, yes," he said. "Yes, I'm familiar with the Stutz."

Remington took a drink of his martini, still studying Morgan's face. "I don't want dilettantes, Vanheusen. No one who's driving just for a lark, you understand? I want professionals. And I pay them. No amateurs need apply."

"That's the way I feel about it, too," Morgan said. "I wasn't ready to commit before, but I am now."

"What I want is someone to test the Stutz against my other cars—some specials, some not. The top four cars will be entered in the trials for the Metropolitan Trophy Cup at Sheepshead Bay in a week. Not a lot of time, but enough to see if the machine is up to it. Interested?"

"Am I? Yes, sir."

"Another thing. The testing is at my track up in Newtonville. If I take you on, you'll stay there until we bring the motorcars down by train a day before the race. City boy like you all right with that?"

"I'll do whatever it takes, sir."

"We'll see," said Remington. "We're testing a few other hopefuls tomorrow. Why don't you come up and give it a try?"

Remington slid his card across the table, stubbed out his cigar, and shook hands. "Frankie will give you the details," he said. He waved and lumbered off to the door.

Frankie watched him leave. "His bark is worse than his bite, sir," he said, grinning. "I've worked for him for years. And he knows all about you, don't be fooled. We'd even talked about you as a possibility before you arrived, but he thought you wouldn't be interested."

"I'm interested, all right," Morgan said.

"Those other lads he's got coming, they're a common lot. You'll be a standout, no contest. And I told him what Caulder did, sir. I seen it. Harris is blind, I guess. If it was me, I'd blackball the bastard."

Morgan laughed. He felt lighter than he had in a long time. Just hearing someone else express his feelings about Caulder was a relief. "It takes all kinds, I guess," he said.

"We could all do without his kind, sir," Frankie said darkly. "Mark my words, he's going to get someone in a real peck of trouble one of these days."

"Let's hope that someone is Kit," Morgan said. He raised his glass to Frankie and they clinked in a silent toast.

Frankie was right. About everything. The minute Morgan took to the track out at Remington's country estate in the bright blue Stutz Bearcat, he knew he would win a spot on the team. The days flew by as he immersed himself in the familiar yet brand-new world of racing, intoxicated with the bone-rattling speed, the reckless freedom it inspired, the joy of controlling all that power. Remington was always there, Frankie by his side. Remington didn't say much, just leaned on the rail, chomping on his cigar, but Morgan soon learned to pick up the signals that showed his pleasure, his annoyance, his disgust. And he learned a great deal from listening to the other drivers, most of whom had been in the game for years.

Friday came all too soon, and the cars were loaded on the train bound for the Cherry Street Motorworks in the city. Saturday morning, they would be driven to the speedway to be ready for the trials in the afternoon. Morgan travelled on the same train, finding the trip back into his old life strange. Even the city looked different to him now, the familiar streets bathed in a different sort of light. Sitting in the Checkered Flag where he had first connected with

Remington, he felt as if he had been away for a long time. By the time he climbed the stairs to the loft he shared with Langley, he was staggering with exhaustion. Glad not to find his friend there, he fell into bed, finally overcome by fatigue. He was asleep almost at once.

He awoke with a start. Disoriented, he looked around, rubbing his face with one hand. The sun shone into the dust-filled loft with an annoying optimism, gilding the battered divan and bringing out the once-brilliant threads of gold in the screen in front of Langley's narrow bed. Uncharacteristically, his friend was fully dressed and shaving in front of a bit of mirror balanced on the shelf by the window. The sunlight accentuated the lines and shadows in his gaunt, handsome face.

"What time is it?" Morgan asked, stretching. "I want to get to Sheepshead Bay early."

"Plenty of time, old sport." Langley gave a last swipe of the razor over his chin and wiped the foam away with a bit of toweling, throwing it down on a pile of clothes when he was finished.

"You are a pig." Morgan got up and stretched again.

"Grouchy, aren't we?" Langley folded the razor and slipped it into its leather case. "Neatness counts now, does it?"

Morgan sighed. "I like neatness," he said, "but living with you, that's just a hopeless dream."

"Confess it, my boy. We were doomed to end up in digs together. Two black sheep. Baaa."

"Oink." Morgan filled a basin with water and splashed his face. Nothing was going to spoil his first day as a professional racing driver. Of course, it might also be his last, he reminded himself, if he didn't make the cut. Or if Caulder pulled one of his tricks. He dried his face vigorously and pulled a clean shirt out of his drawer. "You're up early."

"Haven't gone to bed. Lady Luck did not smile on me last night," he added, his voice a tired drawl. "So I'm counting on your performance today to save my fortunes."

"What are you babbling about?" Morgan stood still as the church bells chimed the hour outside the expanse of windows. "Eleven o'clock! For God's sake, Langley, why didn't you wake me? I have to get the motor to Sheepshead Bay!"

"I told you, I just got in. And anyway, you have oodles of time. You said you start at four p.m. Oodles of time."

"You nincompoop! I wanted to leave by ten at the latest. I have to be there early enough to run mechanical checks on the engine and get gassed up. Any number of things can happen!" Morgan rushed across the room, tripped over a footstool, cursed, and pulled a jacket out of the wardrobe, sending the wooden hangar clattering to the floor.

"Messy, messy," chided Langley, smiling. "Pull yourself together, old chap, and have some cold pheasant." He reached into his leather bag and pulled out the remains of a bird, loosely wrapped in a linen serviette with the Ritz Hotel logo in one corner.

Morgan stopped and sat down to eat. He had to admit that rushing off to the garage on an empty stomach was not a good idea. It wouldn't take that long to drive to the speedway.

He smiled as he chewed, thinking of the Bearcat he had come to know as intimately as a lover. After one week, he was now attuned to its every growl and shudder, the way the gears shifted, the feel of his heel sunken into the floor in the metal heel cup, the feel of the leather seat wrapped around him like an armchair. They had taken off the monocle windshield, so the rush of the wind on his face at high speeds made goggles mandatory and gave his cheeks a perpetual windburn. It was a great machine, even faster than the Bearcat that had won the race last year.

This was his chance! He couldn't have a better motorcar for his debut as a professional driver. And now he was off to a hurried start, thanks to Langley. At least, he had provided breakfast.

"I'll walk you to Cherry Street," Langley said, opening the door for him. *"Après vous."*

"Go to bed," Morgan said, dropping his watch into his vest pocket. "I can manage three blocks on my own."

"Not to worry, old chap. I have to meet my esteemed *pater* at noon anyway."

On the way, Langley regaled Morgan with stories of his degenerate gambling friends, including the Russian prince and his friend, the count, who had been at the Vanheusens' soirée. But Morgan was barely listening. He was running down the checklist in his mind of things to do, planning the route he would take to get to the speedway, trying to remember the spots the article in the *Times* had warned about yesterday: construction, heavy traffic areas on Saturday, narrow roads, sharp turns, and detours.

As they rounded the corner onto Cherry Street, he noticed the garage door at Remington's end of the converted stable building was partly open. Was Remington here? Had he sent one of the other drivers to take Morgan's place because he was late?

Morgan pushed the door open. "Holy jumping Jehosophat!" he yelled.

"What language!" Langley commented, strolling up behind him.

Morgan stared at a scene of destruction, one hand covering his nose. This could not have been done by burglars. Nothing was missing, except the tires. Everything remained in place on the garage walls, every implement hanging within its own outline. And the beautiful Bearcat was covered in mounds of horse manure.

"Someone doesn't want you to get anywhere in this thing today," Langley remarked, looking around.

"Kit Caulder," Morgan said. "The bloody little rat!"

"He the one you told me about from Hochman's place?"

"The bastard! If he thinks he can stop me by doing this, he's in for a shock. Come on, Langley, help me!"

Langley made a moue of distaste as he looked at the spilled oil making the floor slippery, the horse dung piled in the seats, the nuts and bolts scattered about in the slimy mess. He sighed. "If I didn't have a lot of money riding on this, I'd decline and gracefully withdraw," he said, taking off his jacket. "Where do we begin?"

"Get that mop. We need the floor cleared up first. And watch out for any hardware mixed with the oil."

"Perhaps I should trot over to the Checkered Flag to get help," Langley suggested, half out of his jacket. "It's practically around the corner."

"Go. Hurry! But I expect most will be at the speedway by now."

Morgan picked up the mop and began to swab the floor, but only managed to spread the oil more evenly.

"Sawdust," a voice said from the door.

"Frankie! Why aren't you at the track?"

"I was. Now I'm back. I knew he'd try something." Frankie

dumped a pail of sawdust on the floor and began to spread it around, letting the oil soak into it. "We can get this done fast, sir."

"My friend went to get help."

As he spoke, three men Morgan had seen around the Checkered Flag spilled through the door, rolling up their sleeves. Langley followed behind.

"We can give you an hour, hour and a half tops, but then we gotta go, sir," the first one said. "We all know what slimy fellow did this."

"We'll need tires," Morgan pointed out as he began to shovel manure out of the Bearcat.

"Let me do that, sir," another of the men said, taking the shovel out of his hands. "You and your friend go down the way to Stanton's, you know them? He'll fit you up with new tires that'll do for the Bearcat real good."

"Good enough for a race?"

"Good enough to get you to the speedway. They'll have spares there."

Morgan grabbed Langley and rushed out the door.

THIRTY-TWO

"Nijinsky Works on New Ballet for Fall Season of Ballets Russes."
—New York Dance News

Andy couldn't believe his luck! But he was wary. He felt as if this dream-come-true was so fragile, it might shatter around him if he let too much happiness out. He couldn't help smiling, though, as he gazed at Gloria across the tiny table in Zoltan's, drinking in her vibrant beauty, her perfume, her elegance, the sound of her voice. He had been saving his money since that disastrous Vanheusen party where he had issued his invitation in hopes that he might finally get to step out with Gloria like a real suitor, not just a saunter in the park as if they met by chance, with someone always lingering in the background. Of course, he knew that girls of Gloria's class always had a chaperone, but just once he wanted to be to be alone with her, to hear her talk without the sort of desperate gaiety he had witnessed in all the girls at her party. She wasn't like that. He had seen the real Gloria in their dappled sunshine walks in Central Park. And now he had her to himself all afternoon to show her something of his world, to watch her open curiosity and quick mind blossom in new ways. She loved the theater. He could show her what one was really like backstage behind all the glitter and colored lights. With Uncle George safely gone to Brighton Beach to visit old friends, as he always did on Saturdays, they would have the place to themselves.

"Are they real gypsies?" Gloria whispered, leaning across the small table as the violins wailed and a colorfully dressed girl with long black hair and gold bangles sang smoky laments on the tiny stage. There were a few other couples in the room, but Gloria drew all eyes with her fair beauty and her fashionable, and obviously expensive, blue serge suit with its short, loose jacket trimmed with braid and stitching.

"I don't know for sure," Andy said, motioning to their waiter, "but they probably are."

"I've never heard music like that," Gloria said, pulling on her gloves as Andy paid the bill for their tea and honey cakes. "It's so achingly sad."

Outside, the street was teaming with shop girls and matrons, barrow men shouting out their wares, and carts hauling produce to the nearby market. As they emerged from Zoltan's, Gloria was an instant target for a swarm of street urchins, who suddenly converged on them like locusts, clamoring for pennies, holding out their grimy claws as they whined and wailed, importuning Gloria to take pity on their hunger, buy their plaster trinkets, listen to their songs.

Gloria spun about, helpless under the assault as Andy shouted and pushed them away roughly. He grabbed her arm to keep her moving and flagged down a cab, deciding in that instant that it would be worth spending some of his remaining money to get Gloria safely to the theater.

"Whew!" she said, collapsing back against the worn upholstery of the motorcab. "The poor little things! I wish you'd let me give them something."

"No! They would have mobbed you."

Gloria looked at him, startled by his vehemence.

"Forgive me. I didn't mean to snap at you, but these children are professional beggars, Gloria. They all have a specialty, and while you were digging about in your bag, they'd be robbing you, their grimy little hands picking your pockets clean, sliding off your bracelets, unclipping your broach. Believe me, you can't ever give them anything."

"But surely that's only charity," Gloria said. "And don't they go to school? Some of them look very young."

"It's Saturday. Besides, they have to work for a living." Andy tried to think of how to distract her from the wretched beggars.

"But you went to school," she continued. "Your family was very poor, you told me."

"I *had* a family," Andy said, sudden anger hardening his voice. "We stuck together. My older brother put me through school, and when my turn came, I put my younger brother through and so on. We had pride, and we had parents who loved us."

Gloria was silent and Andy cursed himself for his lack of tact. She had no idea of his world. He shouldn't be angry because she had leapt to the wrong conclusions.

"We're not far from the theater now," he said, looking out the window. "It's not the Met, you know," he added, smiling at her tentatively.

"I thought that was the point," Gloria said.

But Andy was suddenly besieged by doubts, seeing his wonderful idea crumbling before him, trying to imagine his uncle's old wreck of a theater through Gloria's eyes. "Perhaps this isn't such a good idea," he said uncertainly.

"Why ever not?" she said. "You did promise me a theater, Andy. Surely you didn't lure me out here on false pretenses?" She arched her eyebrows inquiringly and put her head on one side, smiling in a way that made him feel weak.

"I just don't want you to be disappointed. It's old and falling apart, I suppose by most standards, but everything's still there. It used to be great. My uncle could put on great shows in his day. I'd heard about him all my life, even before I met him: about his travels around Europe, staging dance programs everywhere. Ballet and Russian folk dancing mostly, some Russian comedians and clowns at times, whatever he thought people wanted. He loved only ballet, but the Ballets Russes began to steal his audience everywhere he went. Bad timing, I guess, but he got bitter about it. Then he tried to do something else. He even had a dancing bear here a while ago, but it died, poor thing."

"Oh dear." Gloria looked horrified.

"It was old," Andy said hastily.

The cab stopped at a dilapidated building, and Andy paid him quickly, climbed out, and helped Gloria down. He had been here earlier in the day and picked up the key from old Josef next door, whom he had known for years. The old man had peered at him closely. "Don't burn the place down," he said in his cracking voice, handing over the key. Andy laughed. The old place had been electrified years ago. No need to have fears about fire from flaring gas jets for many years now.

He steered Gloria across the street past the one-legged man with the purple bulbous excrescence hanging from his cheek, who sold plaster saints nearby. He felt Gloria catch her breath and turn away, pressing closer to him. Quickly he pulled out the key, opened the side door, and ushered her into the lobby.

"It needs a good cleaning," he said as she stopped and looked around in the dusty half-light coming in through the dirty windows. Most of the glass doors across the front had been boarded up to stop neighborhood hooligans from breaking them, so what light there was came from the narrow windows high above. Before them was his uncle's pride and joy: a large picture in stained glass that would be lit from behind when all the lights were on. It was a representation of Sleeping Beauty, made by Russian artisans many years ago and given to George as a thank you for all he had done for the community.

George had been a real philanthropist in his day, Andy thought, helping many families come to America, his included, and he wanted to tell Gloria this so she would understand and not judge him by this moldy place only. But the story was too long, too far removed from her world, which was free of pogroms and starvation and despotic tyrants who could take one's land and life at a moment's notice, merely on a whim. He thought of the story of George's sister, his Aunt Irena, snatched by soldiers and never seen again. No one to turn to. No justice. No retribution. "He was an officer of the czar," Uncle George had explained with a shrug. And that was that.

Andy found the main switch and turned on all the lights.

"Just like the toy theater my brother Chesleigh had years ago," Gloria said. "I always wanted it, but he wouldn't give it to me. Wouldn't even let me play with it. Harry and Morgan used to steal it when he was away and bring it to the old nursery for me to play with. They got into trouble every time, but it never stopped them."

"You have three brothers?"

She shook her head. "Two. Harry passed away two years ago."

"I'm so sorry," he murmured.

She reached out to touch the worn red velvet curtains leading to the inner lobby, their voluminous folds looped back by heavy gold braid. Dusty chandeliers, half their bulbs gone, softened the light, casting a kindly dusk on the yellowed programs framed on the walls, on the fly-specked pictures of performers who had once been stars here long before George arrived, on the faded rug and peeling paint, on the gilded banister of the stairway leading to the upper boxes.

Andy took her hand and led her out of the lobby and down the aisle of the theater proper. The curtain was raised, showing ghostly objects placed here and there: one suggesting a house with a balcony; another, a huge window, a sort of abstract set in sepia that the audience would have to fill in themselves.

"Oh," said Gloria, obviously intrigued. "May I go on the stage?"

"Of course! Just wait here a moment while I turn on some stage lights." He bounded away from her and leapt up on stage, turning to his left where he remembered the lighting board was. About six years ago, he had been a sort of volunteer stagehand for his uncle for two months, learning how to fly scenery, run the lights, even build sets. And best of all, he helped to run one show! He would forever more have a special soft spot for *Giselle*.

"Let there be light!" He pulled the lever and the stage came out of the shadows.

It looked as if a new set was being assembled, what for he couldn't guess. A new backdrop featuring wild bright colors in the style favored by the Ballets Russes designers hung at the back, with room for at least two others in front of it. Was Uncle George actually staging a new show? Had he found backers after all? Hired new dancers? He thought of poor Galina who had danced on this stage in one of the last shows put on here. *Giselle*, as it happened.

"There are steps at the other side," he called down to Gloria.

He held out his hand and helped her up beside him. She turned around slowly, taking it all in.

"Wonderful," she said. "Thank you for bringing me here, Andy. I can feel the energy of all these dancers who have performed here. Amazing." She smiled dreamily and raised her arms, pointed her slim foot in its buttoned shoe, her ankle alluring and slim, and turned slowly full circle.

Andy applauded. "Why not try that in a costume?" he suggested, and then wondered if they could find anything that wouldn't fall apart with old age. But when he led her to the costume room, he was surprised to see that someone had been at work here, too, cleaning, mending, making new costumes, or at least he didn't recognize them. Maybe George had borrowed them from another company? But who would trust him anymore, not since he sold tickets to a show that never happened and then disappeared for three months after Galina deserted to the Ballets Russes. But his uncle was full of mysteries, and he had performed miracles before.

Gloria was delighted with the bright colors, the sparkle and unexpected detail of the costumes. She held one after the other in front of her, dancing about the crowded space in delight.

"I haven't had so much fun in ages!" she exclaimed, and Andy thought of the stilted, ritualized parties she attended so often, her spontaneity stifled under ceremony.

"Did I ever tell you about the Ballet Charlotte Russe we put on at the Ritz in February? There was a big headline in the *Times*: 'Debutantes Caper in Leap-Year Dance at the Ritz.' It was in aid of the Stony Wold Sanitarium. I danced as a fantasy ballerina. Mr. Challit, the dancing master, helped us with the whole thing. It was great fun."

"I remember reading about it," Andy said. "Some of the debutantes dressed up as cigarette vendors."

"That's right. But this is real. Much better."

Andy breathed a sigh of relief. "Why not try on one of the costumes and come out on stage. Get a feel for the whole real theater experience."

"Would that be all right, do you think?"

"Who will know? I'll show you to a dressing room. Just this way. I'll wait onstage."

Andy was starting to get concerned when Gloria finally reappeared, walking slowly on stage in her stockinged feet. She wore a waltz-length tulle dress that showed an alluring glimpse of her embroidered silk hose, with Giselle's blue apron and long chiffon sleeves. Incongruously, she had put on a short red cape, the hood pulled up over her head so that she resembled Little Red Riding Hood more than Giselle. It occurred to him that she was used to having a maid dress her, so doing this herself would have been difficult, especially since the dress was done up the back. She had cleverly gotten around that with the cape.

"You look wonderful!" Andy cried as she slowly turned, center stage, a wide smile on her lovely face, her golden skin soaking up the lights as if born to be there. Yet in spite of the costume, she looked more debutante than ballerina, he thought fondly.

"Brava!" called a voice from the boxes.

Andy froze.

Gloria almost lost her balance, but she caught herself and put her hand to her eyes, peering into the darkened theater. "Hello," she called. "Hello, out there."

Andy swung around, his eyes probing the shadows gathered in the theater behind him. In one of the boxes, he saw a figure leaning over the balcony rail. Although he couldn't make out the face, the large stooped shape was familiar, as was the deep rumble of his voice.

"Uncle George," he called. "It's me. Andy."

"Thank you for bringing her, boy," George called down. "But get the poor girl some shoes, will you? Can't dance without shoes! Go! Go!" He made shoving motions with both hands, urging Andy off to do his bidding.

Andy laughed with relief and hurried off to get shoes he hoped would fit Gloria well enough to satisfy the old man's instinct for a certain theatrical authenticity.

When he got back with several pairs of toe shoes he had grabbed from the costume room, he found the stage lights had been subtly changed. Gloria stood still, her hands clasped in front of her, her feet together, one slightly ahead of the other, as she had been taught. Her face was flushed.

"I'm so glad you came back!" George shouted from somewhere in the wings. "Put the shoes on! Come, come! Time moves on."

Andy knelt down in front of Gloria and started to ease on the left shoe. Holding her small warm foot made his heart race. He turned his face away from this intimate touch as he eased her foot into first one pink slipper, then the other. Luckily, they fit well enough.

"Do you want me to get your photography equipment?" he called.

"No, no, is gone, all. Is sold to buy more costumes, paint for scenery. So all is good now that you are back."

"I didn't go anywhere, Uncle George," Andy said, puzzled. He watched the old man emerge into the light, carrying what looked like two pistols and some candlesticks. "Uncle, I'd like to introduce my friend, Miss Gloria Vanheusen."

"Not now! Not now!" George swatted him away as he would an annoying insect. "We have work to do, haven't we, my pet." He leered at Gloria, who looked at Andy, a small frown of confusion creasing her forehead.

"Perhaps we should come back another time, if you're busy," Andy said, reaching for Gloria's hand. "We'll just—"

"Go away, boy. Go work lights. You remember how?"

Andy hesitated, looking from Gloria to his uncle. She looked poised, but a little bewildered by the old man in the big moth-eaten coat that made him resemble the bear who used to shuffle and turn on this very stage. George was blinking in the bright lights, his face red and sweating, his eyes burning with an unsettling light. The pockets of his coat bulged with things, props he had picked up backstage perhaps, or brought down from his chaotic little office upstairs.

"Could I get you a cool drink before we leave?" Andy suggested, thinking of the calming blue liquid he sometimes used to ease his uncle's anxieties.

"Get away!" shouted George, turning on him. "I ask you one thing! One thing only! Do lights. If you not do that, leave now."

"Not without Gloria."

"I not know this Gloria," George said.

"I've been trying to introduce her to you, George." He stepped forward beside Gloria and bowed slightly. "Uncle, may I present Miss Gloria Vanheusen. She was interested in seeing a real theater backstage."

George started putting candles into a candelabrum on the table onstage. A worn piece of gold velvet served as a sort of tablecloth, puddling on the floor at one end.

"Uncle George?"

"I talk with you later, boy. Galina and I must work now."

"Galina?"

"You bring her to me." George spun around and clasped him

by the shoulders, his big hands surprisingly strong. "Kassevetsky thanks you," he said. "My dream now close."

"Uncle," Andy said gently. "This is my friend, Miss Vanheusen. Galina is…has passed on."

There was no indication that his uncle had even heard the words. "We have now new season to plan. She dance with Nijinsky again, but here, right here in Kassevetsky Theater! Bravo! All the people come back to me!" He spun away from Andy.

"But I thought you hated Nijinsky," Andy said.

"No, no! Is Sergei Diaghilev I hate for what he do to me. Nijinsky dance with my Galina once. He do it again, only here on my stage! Go to lights!"

Andy stepped around his uncle to face him again. "Uncle, Miss Vanheusen and I have to go now. I'll see you tomorrow." He held out his hand to Gloria and began to walk with her, arm in arm, toward the wings.

"Stop!" George's bellow almost stopped them both. Andy felt a tremor in Gloria's arm tucked into his, but he kept going, winding his fingers in hers.

"Andy, away from my girl! Now!"

"She's not your girl," Andy said.

A sudden explosion of sound made them duck. Gloria pulled her hand away and covered her ears. Andy swung around in fury.

"What the…" His voice trailed off as he saw George holding a smoking pistol in one hand, its mate in the other. "I thought they were props," he breathed.

But now that he saw them in the bright stage lighting, he remembered the dueling pistols that had always been kicking around his uncle's office. He remembered the stories about George's proficiency with them, too. But how many bullets did they hold? He thought perhaps only one shot, but did he want to risk Gloria's life or his own on this vague memory? Even if that memory was accurate, it meant there was one shot left.

"Mr. Kassevetsky," Gloria said, her voice clear and firm, "I'm afraid you're confusing me with someone else. My name is—"

"No, no, little one. Hush now and let me feast my eyes on you. Pirouette, please."

"I have taken lessons from Mr. Challit but only for the ballroom:

the waltz, quadrille, that sort of thing. Oh, and there was the silly little thing I did for the Charlotte Russe Ballet, so I'm afraid you will be sadly disappointed."

"I am never disappointed in you, my sweet. Let me see you dance." George waved the gun around in a circular motion.

Andy broke out in a sweat. "Dance," he whispered. Perhaps seeing her inexpert movement would bring him out of this trance. But to his surprise, Gloria moved very well, sliding into a graceful waltz with more arm movements than one would see in a ballroom. She actually seemed to be enjoying it.

As he watched, Andy wondered if he could make it upstairs to the telephone, but that would leave Gloria alone with this madman.

"You are out of practice, little one," George said. "Andrei, get lights. Change to soft spot. And call Nijinsky. We need him now so we can rehearse *pas de deux*."

"Uncle George, I can't call Nijinsky. Listen, Galina is dead. This is my friend—"

"How dare you say these things!" shouted George, lunging so close that Andy could smell the teeth rotting in his head. He reached out for the pistol, but George leapt back, suddenly as quick on his feet as a dancer. "You do as I tell you, Andrei Mikailovitch!" then added in Russian, "You impertinent piece of dung."

Gloria pulled off her hood. "Mr. Kassevetsky, please look at me. You can plainly see—"

"You poor child. You forget so soon your old friend George? No Mister here, my dear. Now we dance. You!" He whirled on Andy. "Send message to bring Nijinsky."

"George, he won't come for me! I'm only a journalist, not a friend. I did one interview with him."

"He. Must. Come." George glared at him, his eyes shiny like glass, the passion usually there now turned to madness.

"Morgan is a friend of Mr. Nijinsky." Gloria's voice was trembling now that she obviously had finally realized the danger they were in. "I think he might be able to…maybe…"

"I can telephone him and ask," Andy said, moving towards the wings and the spiral staircase that led to the telephone and the police.

"But he's not home today and there's no telephone in the garage where he is," Gloria said innocently. "You can send a message, can't you?"

"*Da*. Is good." George went into the wings and pulled the speaking tube used to communicate with other parts of the theater close to his mouth. "Petro!" he bellowed. "Get on stage now!"

Andy watched his uncle intently, but the man never took his eyes off him. He might be mad but he wasn't stupid. "Where's this garage?" he asked Gloria. She was now very pale and leaned against the table for support.

"Cherry Street Motorworks. It's in Greenwich Village somewhere, I think. Morgan told me he's driving for Mr. Remington today, but he didn't say when."

"You're sure he'll be there?"

She bit her lip. "No," she said in a small voice. "And I have no idea where Mr. Nijinsky might be."

"At the Met," George said, striding back to the stage. "He is choreographing new ballet. He work all the time there. But today, he come here instead. He rehearse with my little one."

"Oh, dear God," murmured Andy.

"He dance *Spectre de la Rose* with you, my dear. Perfect role for young girl, yes? Young girl, full of dreams."

Gloria looked close to tears. At least, she has seen the ballet, Andy thought miserably.

The boy Petro arrived, scrawny and dirty, his dark hair tumbling over his eyes.

"He doesn't have his shoes on," Gloria said.

"Don't need none, miss," the boy said, moving forward on the balls of his feet, as if he was trying to make himself taller or perhaps just because he was nervous around the irascible Russian.

George thrust some paper at the boy who passed it on to Andy along with a fountain pen George had produced from a pocket somewhere in the depths of his coat.

"Write we need Nijinsky to come now. Dance *Spectre*. Write that."

Andy went to the table beside Gloria and frowned in concentration, trying to think of what he could write that could possibly lure Morgan away from the race of his life…or at least get him to send the police. But he knew his uncle would insist on seeing the message.

"Hurry!" shouted George, waving the pistol in the air.

"This isn't going to work!" Andy shouted back.

Another deafening roar from the pistol made Gloria cry out and drop to the floor. The boy swore. He ducked back, away from George.

Andy bent over the table again. *Morgan, Gloria says please get Mr. Nijinsky, who is at the Met, and bring him to the Kassevetsky Theater, where your sister and I are waiting* in extremis.

He glanced over his shoulder and saw George reloading the pistol. Quickly he scribbled: *HELP! My uncle has gone mad!* on the bottom of the paper. He tore this part off and slipped it to the boy, who promptly shoved it in his pocket.

Gloria took the pen and wrote: *Remember that night with the electric car? Your turn! Do likewise!!!*

"Tell the boy where to take note," George said.

While the old man peered at the scrawled message, Gloria told Petro what she knew about the place.

"Car racing garage?" the boy exclaimed, obviously excited. "Swell! I know where that is. My brother works for Stubby Galino. He sometimes has cars there. But they're running elimination trials at the speedway today, you know," Petro went on, bouncing up and down on the balls of his feet. "If he's a racing pilot, he might be there already."

"Where is it?"

"Brooklyn. Sheepshead Bay."

"We could telephone there and find out," Andy said.

"No telephone," George said. "They take away last week."

Andy's heart sank. He had been counting on getting to that telephone. Beside him, Gloria was trying not to cry. All he had to count on was a boy excited about motorcars, and Morgan whose heart was set on racing today. Would the boy have enough sense to call the police?

THIRTY-THREE

"First Race of the Year in East at Sheepshead Bay
To Take Place May 13th.
Numbers at Trials Listed for Today High."
— *New York Racing News*, May 1916

Morgan and Langley were alone with the Bearcat, now with cherry-red wheels that clashed with the electric-blue body. The seats were still faintly redolent of manure even after two hours of frenzied activity.

"I couldn't have done it without their help," Morgan said, polishing his goggles with a handkerchief. "I don't know how I can ever repay them."

"Don't let that bastard win." Langley leaned back against the wall of the garage and blew a perfect smoke ring into the air that was already heavy with the smell of oil and gas and the cleaning agent Morgan was using on the engine, now revealed in all its coils and plugs and mystery under the folded-back hood.

"I have to get there first," Morgan said grimly.

"You are good at this, aren't you?" Langley went on, the drawl suddenly gone from his voice. "How fast can that blue thing go?"

"A car very much like this one won the American racing championships last year. I got her up over a hundred and twenty at Remington's, but none of that matters if I can't get the damn thing there in time for the trials! I'll kill that Caulder!" He slammed his hand down on the fender.

"You're sure he's the one who did it?"

"Of course, I'm sure! Even the men who helped us knew who'd done it. No one else cares if I make it or not. I'm no real threat to anyone but Kit, or that's what he thinks."

"Why?"

"Who the hell knows? He thinks I just swanned in and took his place at Hochman's, thinks I'm just a spoiled rich boy. He had just been promoted when I arrived and was promptly demoted to pumper again for a while, or at least that's the way he saw it. Damn! Look at the time!"

"You can still make it. And you replaced everything he fooled around with?"

"I think so, including the fuel. Now would you please leave and let me get on with it!" Morgan climbed into the Bearcat and began checking the gears.

"Behold, an urchin approaches, stage right," Langley said, pushing himself away from the wall as a ragged barefoot boy ran into the garage.

"Message for Mr. Morgan Vanheusen," the boy said, looking from one to the other.

"I'm Vanheusen."

"A *billet doux*?" Langley asked. He peered at the grimy note the boy pulled out of his pocket and shuddered. "I think not. Some mechanic, perhaps, with an idea to shine up the valve thingamabobs. Toodle-oo. I'll see you there. And *bonne chance, mon ami*. Remember, my fortune, such as it is, rides with you."

"No one bets on a trial, you idiot!" Morgan shouted at his friend's retreating back. He jumped down and reached for the note.

"Lots of people do, sir," the boy said. He was walking around the car, his eyes drinking in every detail. "A Stutz Bearcat!" he murmured reverently and leaned in to take a closer look at the engine. "Smells like a horse's ass in here."

"Don't I know it."

"You got the four-cylinder bi-block, huh? How much horsepower?"

"Sixty. You know cars?" Morgan smiled, watching the pleasure on the boy's face as he made a slow circuit of the motorcar, now restored to its gleaming blue beauty.

"My brother works for Stubby Galino. He's at the Sheepshead Bay qualifiers today, driving a Duesenberg."

"Good car. What fuel mix is he using?" Morgan asked.

"Half and half. He says it's still best."

Morgan nodded. "Who gave you this note?" He glanced down at the crumpled thing in his hand. He could barely read it, the ink was so blotched and the paper so grimy.

"The loony I work for sometimes. I move stuff, run errands, shovel coal and stuff like that. But I'm going to be in the racing car business soon," he added.

Morgan nodded absently. He moved into the light to see the note better. "Are you supposed to wait for an answer?"

"He never said. But I can show you where the theater is, if you like."

Morgan was frowning. "What the hell? Andy Cass wants me to come there *now*? And Gloria… Are they mad?"

"No, sir. I don't think so. But the old coot sure is."

"What old coot?"

"Kassevetsky. He's waving pistols around and that."

"*What?*" Morgan stared at the boy who repeated the part about the pistols. Morgan read the note again while the kid leaned over the engine, making appreciative noises. At least, he wasn't touching anything.

'*In extremis.*' That was not a phrase that sounded like Andy Cass. And it *was* Gloria's handwriting in the last part, at least what he could make out. Something about the electric car… And Nijinsky.

"Look, I don't have time for this," Morgan said as the church bells chimed the half hour. "Why do they need me?"

"I told you, sir. The old coot's lost it entirely. He's waving pistols around, but all he wants is this Nudgesky character to come. Then it'll be okay. He calms down real fast when he gets what he wants."

"But I have to get to Sheepshead Bay," Morgan said. "I'm really late already. I'll get someone else to go pick them up."

"It ain't a taxicab they need, sir," the boy said, turning away from the car. "The girl, she's real scared. She said only you could get the Nudgekey character." He suddenly dug into his pocket again and pulled out another piece of grimy paper. "Here. There's this, too."

Morgan read Andy's desperate message and shook his head, incredulous. "He must be joking."

"This ain't no joke, sir. Come on! We gotta go. Now."

"Damnation! I can't!" Morgan ran his hands through his hair. He took another look at the cryptic note. Yes, she had helped him with Nijinsky that time, but she hadn't thrown her whole career out the window by doing so!

"Christ almighty!" He looked distractedly at the clock on the wall. "Where is this place?"

"Not far." The boy gave him the address and a few shortcuts he knew to get there.

"But my motorcar is still in the country," Morgan said, pacing around the garage, putting back a few things Langley had taken off the shelves. His hands were shaking. "We'll have to try and find a taxicar."

"We could take her, sir." The boy pointed to the gleaming racer.

"Are you mad?" shouted Morgan. "That belongs to Blaze Remington!" For an instant, it occurred to him that Stubby Galino could have set this whole thing up to take out the competition. Or was Kit Caulder behind this, too? Although he didn't know Andy's handwriting, the postscript was definitely Gloria's, and she never played practical jokes. "How bad is this old character who's waving the guns? Think carefully. Is he just being histrionic or is my sister in real danger?"

"I don't know about the history stuff, sir, but that old Russian is mad as a hatter. He thinks the lady is that dead dancer girl, Galina something. He wants to see her dance again with that big-name Russky dancer."

"Oh my God." Morgan turned away, tears of frustration, fear, and rage threatening to spill over. Surreptitiously, he wiped his eyes with the heel of his hand and cleared his throat. There was no way out. "How would I know where Nijinsky might be on a Saturday afternoon?"

"Old coot says he's at the opera house, sir. Something about rehearsing."

"And how does the old coot know?"

The boy shrugged. "He knows about dance stuff."

"Damnation!" Who needs a career, Morgan thought, slamming the hood cover back into place. "Crank 'er up, kid."

Morgan slid behind the wheel, and after a few energetic cranks, the engine caught. All four cylinders roared into life. The kid jumped in beside him. It wouldn't be easy handling this nervous bundle of power through the crowded streets, holding down the speed without stalling.

"After I pick up Jinks—if he'll come, that is—you'll have to ride on the running board or sit on the toolbox somehow," he shouted. "Can you do that?"

"Sure. Easy peasy."

Out on the street, the car caused quite a stir. It wasn't built for city driving and the noise of the powerful engine was horrific. Morgan was used to it. He raced the engine when stuck behind dawdlers, nosed ahead whenever the slightest space opened up, forced pedestrians to jump out of his way. The last time he had seen the Russian, the God of the Dance appeared to be suffering some sort of breakdown, shouting, practically foaming at the mouth, then staring ahead as if in a trance. What if he was like this now? How could he possibly even get through to the man, let alone convince him to come to an old theater to save his sister from a madman?

The traffic got worse the closer they got to the Metropolitan Opera House. He used his horn frequently, which only seemed to make things more chaotic, causing more than one horse to rear. Morgan pulled out his watch and swore. "I'll never make it in time!"

"The qualifiers don't start for another two hours," the kid said. "You can make it easy if you keep driving like this."

Morgan steered up onto the sidewalk to get around a stalled van, earning loud curses from the group of men standing there waiting to cross.

"Awright!" said the kid. "Now cut down that alley, turn left, and you should be right behind that opera place."

"Are you sure?"

"Positive. I've delivered messages for the old coot there lots of times."

Morgan was out of the car almost before it stopped. "Stay there and don't let anyone touch her," he shouted, running up and pounding on the stage door.

It seemed to take forever before the door opened and the ancient he had met before peered out at him, blinking as if the light of day was something he rarely saw.

"Remember me? I need to see Mr. Nijinsky."

The man looked him up and down, taking in his stained cover-all, his disheveled hair, the oily rag hanging at his belt.

"Oh yes, I know, I look a wreck. I've been working on my motor-car, see?" He pointed to the Bearcat, already surrounded by gawk-ing young men and boys. "I promised I'd show him but I don't have much time. I'm in a race today. At Sheepshead Bay," he added.

"I see, I see," the man murmured, nodding his head over and over as if on a spring. "There's no performance here today, you know."

"But he said…I mean, I thought he was here. He has to be here!"

The man backed away, still hanging onto the door as if he wasn't sure whether he should let this man in or not. Morgan pushed by and made for the stairs he remembered from before.

"Now see here!" shouted the doorman.

Morgan paused on the second floor and looked through the first rehearsal hall window, where he had last seen Nijinsky. No one was there. He listened. No sound gave him a clue. Then he heard crash-ing chords of discordant music coming from farther down the cor-ridor. Rushing to the door, he flung it open on a scene of pandemo-nium. A group of dancers in rehearsal clothes lurched about, their bodies stretched at odd angles, while Nijinsky leapt from one to the other, shouting at them in Russian. Morgan couldn't tell if he was pleased or furious.

He shifted from foot to foot for a moment, then started across the room, determined to get Nijinsky's attention. The others had seen him, but they kept moving, one eye always on Nijinsky. But the dancer sensed something was wrong and turned, staring at Morgan as if he had never seen him before. The piano faltered, then stopped.

"I'm sorry to interrupt," Morgan began uneasily. The others shuffled their feet. The accompanist got up and began putting away his music.

"Is all right. Ve need break," the pianist said, but before snap-ping his music case closed, he eyed Nijinsky warily. "Ve go?" he asked. "Is time for break way past, yes?"

Nijinsky reached for a towel and mopped his sweaty face. He was wearing a loose-fitting white blouse, open at the throat, and trousers gathered in close to the leg from his knees down. On his feet were soft leather sandals. He must have been working hard for a long time. The others looked exhausted, too, and were slipping out of the room as quickly as they could.

"I didn't mean to break up your work, Jinks," Morgan said.

The Russian threw the towel down on the barre that ran around two sides of the room. "Is time," he said. "When I work, I not notice, but now is time."

"Oh, good!" Morgan clasped his hands together and tried to look eager. "I wanted to take you out in my Stutz Bearcat racing car."

"No, no. Now I go home."

"Jinks, I need to take you somewhere. It's very important to my sister that you come with me."

"I need rest now," Nijinsky said.

"But I have a Stutz Bearcat waiting," Morgan went on desperately. "A real racing motorcar."

The doors slammed open and the tall imposing figure of the impresario Diaghilev breezed in. "Vashti! You forget already our little meeting? You promise to show me about this *Till Eulenspiegel* ballet."

"I show already," Nijinsky said, biting his thumbnail.

"And who is this? You have mechanic? You buy car?"

Morgan bristled but kept quiet. They were speaking English for his benefit. He wasn't going to react until he knew what Nijinsky was going to do.

"Is American friend. Morgan," Nijinsky said, shrugging into the jacket he had picked up from a chair. "We just now leave." He grabbed Morgan's arm and pulled him towards the door.

"But Vashti!"

"Ve go!" shouted Nijinsky, pulling Morgan through the door and down the corridor. For a small man, he was very strong, Morgan noted, almost falling in his efforts to keep up with the dancer who had an iron grip on his arm.

"Where is car?"

"Outside the stage door. You can let go now," he added.

Nijinsky released him. "Sergei think he snap fingers and I am there like little dog. Is not so."

"Good. And then—"

"I go for ride. Then I go home."

"Sure. After we visit Gloria."

"Maybe I drive," Nijinsky suggested.

"Well," Morgan said. Maybe when hell freezes over, he thought. As Nijinsky hopped into the car, it occurred to Morgan that he could just as easily hop out again if he decided to go home. There was no way to stop him, unless they were going very fast, which was impossible in downtown New York.

Nijinsky ran a hand admiringly over the walnut dash, as the kid turned the crank. "I buy car soon," he announced, "but bigger."

"I need your help," Morgan said desperately. "Remember when I helped you out at Sadie Hahn's?" But his words were lost in the roar of the engine as the sporty car swept down the street, almost jerking out of his control.

"Where is this place?" he shouted at the kid, who now crouched on the running board, clutching the door at his side.

The kid's words were lost in the noise, but his waving arm pointed out the way. Maybe we can get there before Nijinsky changes his mind, Morgan thought, just as the car plowed into the back wheel of a horse-drawn wagon, which had suddenly lurched to a stop in front of them.

"Nincompoop!" shouted the driver, turning on his seat and shaking a fist at Morgan. "Why for you drive fancy car like that in street? Have you no care to us regular peoples? *Ay dios mio!*" He leapt down to tend to his horse.

Traffic had ground to a halt all around, and Morgan swore under his breath.

"If you go up on the sidewalk, you can get to an alley halfway down the block," the kid shouted in his ear.

Morgan looked behind him to judge if he had any room to back up, and found himself staring right into the red face of a policeman.

"Uh oh!" The kid slid off the running board and disappeared into the crowd.

THIRTY-FOUR

"SENATE TALK ON COOKING.
Smoot Wants All Girls Taught How to Manage a Home."
— *New York Times*

"High! Higher!" shouted George from the center of the stage, waving his arms at Andy on his perch in the shadows above the stage.

Gloria cringed. The crashing noise of the heavy canvas backdrops thumping to the stage, the raised voices, the madness swirling in the air made her hands shake so much she kept pricking her fingers with the needle as she tried to sew a flounce on the bottom of her costume. From where she was crouching in the front row, she could barely see Andy on the catwalk up above, hauling on the ropes that controlled the scenery. It looked like hard work for only one person, but Andy was putting everything into doing the job. Even from where she sat, she could see his shirt was drenched with sweat.

For what seemed like hours, the madman had kept Andy busy, moving furniture around, climbing up to change light gels, lugging huge canvas backdrops farther back on the stage. They were getting everything ready for Mr. Nijinsky. And if the great man didn't come? Gloria wished she had her jeweled watch, but it was pinned to her jacket back in the dressing room. Surely the boy had left an hour ago at least. Had Morgan already left for the speedway? She wished she had paid more attention when he had told her the details about the event in his last letter.

Gloria crouched further down in her seat. Her hands were cold and her feet in the stiff unfamiliar shoes did not feel like part of her at all. It was hard to sew with the full wide skirt still on her, but ever since she had been caught trying to sneak back to the dressing room to get changed into her own clothes, George had managed to keep an eye on her at all times. She kept working. Apparently, she was taller than Galina and the difference was bothering George, but not enough to make him see reality. Nothing a flounce couldn't fix, apparently. Gloria wiped her eyes surreptitiously, but the tears slid down her cheeks in spite of all her efforts at control. From time to time, she pricked her finger and droplets of blood oozed over the white net of the costume. She was not used to sewing without a thimble, not used to sewing in general, for that matter. If he had wanted some embroidery, that she could have accomplished very well.

A coil of rope crashed onto the stage very close to where George was standing. Gloria cried out and jumped to her feet. George shouted out a string of Russian, waving his pistol at Andy. The gun went off, causing a shower of dust and plaster to fall around them.

Gloria threw down the flounce and tried to run up the aisle to the door, but her outfit and the shoes betrayed her. Tangled in the long flounce, she fell heavily, knocking the wind out of herself.

"Careful, my pet," George called from the stage, kicking some debris out of the way. "Come up here now. We rehearse. Everything must be perfect when the great man arrive, no?"

"George, you can't rehearse without the second row of lights. Half the bulbs are missing. I have to replace them."

"No matter, no matter." George waved the pistol above his head, dismissing Andy's desperate effort to stall.

"But Mr. Nijinsky is used to the best."

"Is rehearsal only, fool! You come here now and sweep this up. Is your fault!"

"I need to finish the sewing," Gloria whispered, holding the rest of the flounce in her hands.

"Speak up, pet." George leapt down nimbly, put one arm around her shoulder and led her back to the stage.

"I haven't finished sewing this on," Gloria said louder.

"No, no. Is fine without." He grabbed the material out of her hands and flung it from the stage. Seeing that it still hung from the costume, he ripped off the rest of the flounce she had just sewn on, taking a piece of the skirt with it and threw it into the wings. "There. A little short is good." He stepped back and looked at her, his bushy eyebrows almost meeting as he scowled. "What is wrong now? That costume not fit right? Turn around."

"Sir, may I please just go home now? I can't dance the way—"

"Turn!" George thundered.

"Do what he asks," Andy called from above. The sounds of rattling metal followed his progress down the ladder to the stage.

Gloria whirled around to face her tormentor "I can't!" she shouted at the top of her lungs. "I don't know how. And there's no reason to keep up this charade. Morgan will be here soon and he'll bring the police."

"Why?" asked Andy, suddenly beside her. "Why would he think to do that?"

Gloria started to cry. "I said 'your turn' in my note," she sobbed. "He should understand!"

"Why you cry, petkins?" George flung a huge arm around her and folded her into his pungent chest. The smell from his old coat made her gag and she almost threw up. "Ah, Galinochka, darling, you are nervous about dancing with the great man, no? But you did it once already. Is easy, no?"

"No!" she shouted into the coat. "No! No!"

A strong hand gripped her shoulder and shook her. "Enough hysteria!" George pushed her away so hard she would have fallen, had Andy not been there to catch her. "Tighten the back of that dress," George told Andy. "Now! We waste time with nonsense."

"It's fine the way it is," Andy said.

"Do it or I will."

"I'm sorry," Andy whispered as his hands reached under the cloak and found the hooks, most of which were open.

Gloria took a deep breath as she felt the stays tighten against her ribs. Galina must have been small.

"It's too tight," she whispered.

"I'll leave a few open," Andy whispered back. "It won't be long now."

"He's not coming," Gloria whimpered. But crying took too much effort, and she had to concentrate just on breathing.

"There isn't enough light here to dance, George," Andy said, doing up the last hook.

"No matter. We use candles, like in old days." George pulled out matches from his pocket and lit the candles in the candelabrum on the long table. "And take off silly cloak!"

"I'm so sorry," Andy murmured, easing the cloak off her shoulders.

George whirled around and stared at Gloria. "Why you change hair color?" he shouted. His face was getting redder as he glared at her strawberry-blond hair.

"This is my natural hair color. I didn't change anything, Mr. Kassevetsky. I tell you—"

"No matter. Silly girls, they change hair color, hair style, as easy as changing hats to them. We change back later. Now dance." He reached over and cranked up the Victrola, which sat on one end of the table. "*Spectre de la Rose*. Remember?"

Gloria sat down in the armchair, which was close to the table. Too close, if she remembered the ballet clearly enough. But never mind. She didn't know the choreography anyway, and even if she did, she certainly couldn't dance it. But sitting in the chair she could manage. Perhaps that would mollify him until they could escape. She laid her head to one side, stretched her legs out in front of her, toes pointed, folded her hands in her lap, and closed her eyes.

"Perfect," said George. "But that's for the second part. Now up and dance your solo."

Gloria looked at Andy, tears streaming down her face.

"Uncle George, stop." Andy stepped between them. "Please listen to me. Galina is dead. This is my friend, Miss Gloria Vanheusen, and she has to go home now." He turned and reached out to take Gloria's hand.

Moving so quickly neither of them saw it coming, the old man grabbed a candlestick from the table and hit Andy hard on the back of the head. Andy sank to the floor without a sound.

"What have you done, you mad person!" Gloria shouted, dropping to her knees.

"Oh, he has hard head like Cossack," said George casually. "Is good as new again soon. Now you dance."

Gloria, beyond words, just stared at him.

"I not know you have sweet spot for Andrushka." The old man leered. "Now, if you want him to be all right and not shot dead, you dance. Now!" he thundered.

She scrambled to her feet and looked around desperately for a way out. But what would this madman do to Andy if she ran? And how could she run in these damnable shoes anyway? Blinded by tears, she raised her arms and cautiously began to turn around and around in the middle of the stage as the music began pouring out, scratchy and uneven from the old Victrola.

Charlotte Russe, she thought desperately. Remember the Charlotte Russe.

THIRTY-FIVE

"Nijinsky to Buy Peerless Motorcar"

—*New York Bugle*

"Officer, I must get Mr. Nijinsky to the Kassevetsky Theater," Morgan shouted above the growl of the Bearcat's engine, gesturing to the dancer who seemed to have drifted off inside his own world again.

The policeman scratched his head. He obviously recognized the Russian's name and probably his face from the numerous pictures in the newspapers, but the driver of the wagon was complaining bitterly about the damage, waving his arms and crowding into the officer, demanding justice.

"Look, I'll pay for repairs," Morgan said. "Here's my card." He reached inside his coveralls to his trouser pocket and pulled out his card.

"You pay now. *Ahora mismo!*" shouted the wagon driver.

"I don't have any money with me, but I give you my word as a gentleman, I will pay. Just give me your card: name, address, that sort of thing. Please! We need to go!"

"I have to report the accident," the policeman said. "You'd better come with me."

"Sir, we're going to the Kassevetsky Theater!" shouted Morgan. He threw the car into gear.

Everyone jumped back as the powerful machine roared up onto the sidewalk and down the alley the kid had pointed out earlier. With any luck, Morgan thought, the police will follow us to the place and deal with that damn fool Kassevetsky. So far today, however, luck did not seem to be with him.

"*Ochen horoshoe!*" shouted Nijinsky, suddenly coming alive again. "Make the blood to dance, no?"

Morgan was using all his strength to steer the recalcitrant Bearcat around the sharp corner into the street with one hand while gearing down at the same time with the other. It was less crowded here, and at once, he saw the kid waiting for them outside an old building with boarded-up windows.

"Over here!" the boy shouted.

Morgan narrowly avoided a man pushing a barrow and pulled up in front of the dilapidated theater. At this rate, he would be too exhausted to drive in the race. Even if I could get there in time, he thought, jumping down. "My sister's in there? Why?"

"What is this?" asked Nijinsky, jumping down beside him.

"Kassevetsky's theater," the kid said. "It's falling apart, but the old coot thinks it's still up and running. Mad as a hatter, I tell you."

"And my sister's in there?" Morgan repeated, staring bewildered at a row of boarded up doors.

"Come on. I'll show you." The kid pushed open the last door in the row and slipped inside.

Morgan had a sudden impulse to jump in the car and take off for Brooklyn, but instead he locked the crank inside the car's tool box and he and Nijinsky followed the boy. They could hear music out in the dusty lobby. Nijinsky parted the curtains and listened, his head tilted slightly. Morgan looked over the dancer's shoulder. Gloria was turning around and around on the stage, dressed in some weird costume, her cheeks wet with tears.

"Damnation!" he said, trying to push past Nijinsky.

"He is mad?" Nijinsky said softly to the boy.

"Completely," the kid said, joining them. "And he has pistols."

"What he want?"

"You," said the kid. "He wants you to dance with her."

Nijinsky nodded and started down the long aisle towards the stage.

"Can he handle it?" said the kid.

"God, I hope so," Morgan said. "I don't know about Gloria, though."

The kid crossed himself and kissed his thumb. Together, he and Morgan followed Nijinsky to the front of the theater.

Nijinsky was almost to the stage when George spotted him and burst into applause.

Morgan wished he was close enough to grab the pistols George had put down on the table when he started clapping.

"You want I dance, I dance," Nijinsky said. "I love dance. Then I take lady home."

"Certainly, certainly. Galina need rest then."

"Who is this and why he on stage?" Nijinsky pointed to a hunched man lying motionless on one side of the stage.

"Oh, that Andrei. He need rest, too."

"Not on stage." Nijinsky motioned Morgan and the kid over to move the inert Andy into the wings. George had the pistols back in his belt by the time they were finished.

Morgan poked Andy. "*You* are why my sister is in this mess!"

Andy's eyes flickered but didn't open. Morgan kicked him

"Leave stage!" shouted George, pulling one of the pistols out of his belt.

"Do it," hissed the kid. "He knows how to use that thing."

As if to demonstrate, George aimed the gun at the gold cherub on the closest private box and shot its head off. Gloria screamed and covered her head with her arms.

Nijinsky looked at George. "If you wish us to dance, you do not shoot. We need quiet to hear music. Now I look at stage." He began to pace around the stage, as if measuring it in his mind, moving back the chair and the stool, walking around the center area several times, studying the floor. Looking for rough spots, Morgan wondered.The dancer even disappeared into the wings for a minute or two and then returned.

"I dance. Then you come up and we talk about girl."

"You dance with girl like before?"

"Before?"

"You danced with Galina before," Morgan said. "That's what he means."

"Yes, but this time you dance *Spectre*," George said. "Is better for young girl. And I not have music for other thing."

Nijinsky nodded. "Music."

George motioned to the kid to crank up the Victrola, and Nijinsky raised his arms.

The transformation, even without costumes, proper lighting, or the right set, was amazing. Nijinsky became someone else as the first notes of the music floated onto the stage. Gloria sank down in the chair and closed her eyes, her pose almost exactly right, as the great dancer leapt about her, gliding and moving sinuously with the music. Then he reached down and took Gloria's hand.

Startled, she looked up at him, fear in her eyes.

"We dance, mademoiselle," he said softly. "We dance, like in ballroom. You can do that?" She nodded, lifted her arms, and let him sweep her across the stage. It was an odd dance, but somehow he made it look as if it was supposed to be that way. Morgan glanced at George, but the old man was smiling. As the dance went on, a frown appeared, but he said nothing until the music stopped and Nijinsky folded Gloria back into her chair.

"As you see, I change choreography," he said. "Come here, please. We talk."

George responded in Russian as he lumbered up on the stage.

"We speak English," Nijinsky said. "I love Russian language, Russian dance. But now we speak English so my friend understand."

"Yes, yes, if you wish."

"Stand here," Nijinsky said and waited until George was center stage with him.

"Why you change choreography?"

"I have rehearsal all day for new ballet. I am tired. The girl is also tired. We need only to get the feel of the dance today, you agree?"

The old man nodded, smiling beatifically.

Nijinsky began to pace around the old man as he talked. When George tried to follow him, he told him to stay put. "I need move. You need stay. Now we make agreement."

George nodded enthusiastically.

"I hear about your company. I love dance like you, but you not like the Ballets Russes."

"I do, I do. Is Diaghilev I not like," George said. "I not want to hurt you when I get Rudy to put potion in your flask. No, no. It just make you stumble little bit so then maybe he fire you and you come to me. So now you here is all right, no?"

Nijinsky stopped and stared at him, his slanted dark eyes almost hypnotic. Then he shrugged and moved off stage right as if looking for something.

Suddenly, George screamed and reached out for the table as the floor gave way beneath his feet. His desperate fingers clutched at the velvet cloth pooling on the ground, pulling it down with him along with the burning candles and the phonograph. George's screams increased in volume as flames leapt up through the trap door, reaching long yellow and red fingers for something else to devour.

"Get out!" Morgan shouted, rushing over to Gloria. He grabbed her hand, yanking her out of her chair.

Gloria screamed as the fire caught the filmy curtains of the set, reached for her hair, and roared up the wall. She clamped one hand to her head and stumbled after her brother.

"What's down there?" Morgan shouted to the kid.

"Paint for the backdrops, turpentine. Canvas."

Shots exploded from the trap door as the bullets in George's pocket exploded.

"Run for it!" shouted Morgan.

"I can't run in these shoes!" Gloria cried.

"I take." Nijinsky grabbed the terrified girl in his strong arms and rushed up the aisle.

"Andy!" shouted Gloria, pointing over Nijinsky's shoulder. "Morgan, get Andy!"

Morgan hesitated only a moment before kneeling beside Andy and pulling him up and over his shoulder. The man grunted, obviously beginning to come around.

"Wha..?" he mumbled.

"Shut up or I leave you," Morgan shouted, starting up the sloping aisle, followed by the agonized shrieks of the poor mad Russian as fire raged and crackled around him.

Policemen were running down the aisle by now.

"There's a man under the stage," Morgan called to them. "Save him!"

He staggered outside and dumped Andy unceremoniously on the sidewalk. "I have to get Gloria home." He paused for a moment to catch his breath, then unlocked the toolbox of the car.

Nijinsky had already placed Gloria in the passenger seat. "You go. I get taxicar."

Morgan pulled the crank out of the box, slid it into place, and pulled. As he swung into he driver's seat, a fire engine pulled up, its bells clanging.

"I'm so glad you came!" Gloria sobbed. "Please take me home."

"What the Sam Hill were you thinking?" Morgan yanked the wheel to the left, narrowly missing a fireman, and careened down the alley.

Gloria bent down and began to undo the ribbons of the toe shoes. "Not now!" She threw the shoes out of the car. One hit the wall and bounced back, hitting the rear wheel. "How's Andy?"

"I don't give a damn!" Morgan said viciously.

"Take me home please." Gloria was trembling and her teeth chattering.

"I'm going as fast as I can," Morgan shouted, skidding around a corner. Without the boy to guide him, he had no idea of any short-cuts he could take to get to Fifth Avenue. As it was, he had to ask the way several times, and all the while, Gloria sat beside him, straight-backed and silent. Staring ahead. He could feel how taut her body was, and he began to worry when she refused to say another word, even after he apologized.

What had happened to his glorious day? First, sabotage to the car, now this. No race. No money. Remington would fine him and probably fire him, maybe even blackball him, too, so no career. And his father would have his worst prognostications confirmed.

He was relieved to turn up Fifth Avenue at last and see home up ahead.

"We're almost there," he said, glancing at Gloria.

She only blinked and seemed to catch her breath a little, as if finally able to relax, as he drove up the driveway and swung around under the porte-cochère to the front door.

Morgan pulled on the brake, leapt out, and ran around to help Gloria down. Boothby was already coming down the steps, and out of the corner of his eye, Morgan saw his father striding down behind him.

"She's all right," Morgan said, turning to face him.

"Get that thing out of my driveway," his father said, pointing at the garishly painted blue and red Bearcat.

Morgan turned on his heel and walked back to the driver's side.

By now, his mother was in the doorway, one hand to her mouth. "My poor child," she cried, opening her arms to the girl. "What are you wearing? Where are your shoes?"

His sister bent her head and melted into her mother's arms, shaking with sobs.

"What have you done?" thundered his father.

"Saved her life!" Morgan shouted as the car roared down the driveway. And much thanks I'll get for it, he added under his breath.

The cathedral bells were chiming the half hour as he passed St. James. Perhaps there was still time to get to Sheepshead Bay. He had meant to telephone Remington from his parents' house, but his father had effectively put a stop to that idea. Was there still time? He took out the notebook where he had copied down the directions printed in the yesterday's paper. Remington had confirmed this was the best and fastest way to get to the track because it avoided the most populated parts of Brooklyn. Morgan had driven to Sheepshead Bay last year for the inaugural race, but never under stress. Apparently, there were several detours now, involving a couple of dangerous turns as noted in the newspaper, the whole trip taking just over half an hour. This was Saturday, which might make a difference. It was three thirty. The race started at four. Could he make it?

Certainly not by going south on Fifth Avenue, he decided, and swung the car into a sudden wild U turn. Heading north, he revved the engine and was soon humming along at fifty miles an hour, passing everyone else on the broad avenue. Luckily there were no horses about, and he could keep up a steady speed until 59th Street where he headed east to the Queensboro Bridge.

Once in Brooklyn, his spirits rose. He might make it after all! Weekend traffic on this route was light, and although he managed to frighten two horses pulling a produce wagon, for the most part he kept a steady pace, at last swinging down Eastern Parkway and onto the last stretch, Ocean Parkway. Nearly there. He could almost smell the place: the heady scents of speed and machines, the hum and roar of highly tuned engines.

Two more quick turns.

He took the first turn a little fast and the car swung out dangerously, then righted itself. Catching his breath, he pulled on the brake and steered into the second hairpin turn more slowly. But he was still going too fast, and the Bearcat skidded off the road. Hitting a lamp post, the car spun out of control and crashed into the fence. He was thrown onto the grass on the other side and lay there stunned, listening to the roar of the other racers revving up at the starting line without him.

The next thing he knew, Remington was standing over him shouting, while a scrawny doctor with thick spectacles perched on his beak of a nose was feeling him all over.

"No broken bones," he announced.

"There will be when I get through with him!" shouted Remington. "You moron! I trusted you! Look what you've done to my machine! You broke a damn axel! You're finished, Vanheusen!"

"He needs to be checked out at the hospital," the doctor said, "just to be sure."

Morgan closed his eyes against the pain in his battered body as they lifted him onto a stretcher. The last thing he saw were the gates to the Sheepshead Bay Speedway disappearing in the distance.

THIRTY-SIX

"Nijinsky gives performance of his career to private audience. Racing pilot for Remington team wins in race to help dancer save lives but crashes outside speedway."
— *New York Bugle*, Sunday edition

Gloria sat at the breakfast table, absently moving a piece of fish around her plate. When she caught her mother's anxious glance, she raised the fork to her mouth and took a bite, chewing the tasteless salty lump with a smile, determined to behave as normally as possible. But she didn't feel normal. She couldn't quite remember what that felt like. She touched her hair, the part that had been singed, even though it had been trimmed and her hair done up so that nothing unusual was visible. And she could still smell the smoke, hear the screams, shrink with terror at the remembered sound of a bullet whizzing over her head.

"Try the apricot jam, dear," her mother said, handing her the silver dish with its blue insert.

Gloria nodded, smiled, then took a generous helping. As she spread a little on her toast, she looked around the table, so different from the Sundays, which now seemed so long ago, when Morgan sat opposite her and they exchanged sly winks; when Aunt Hattie sat beside her, nodding and humming contentedly to herself. It was frightening how quickly the familiar could slide away underfoot, like standing on melting ice.

"If your father doesn't come soon, we'll be late for church," her mother remarked. "I can't imagine what's keeping him."

Mr. Vanheusen strode up to the breakfast table at that moment, as if he had been waiting for his cue. Shaking a newspaper at his family, he shouted at Gloria, "Why does your brother insist on dragging our name through the mud?"

Gloria felt the tears well up and blinked. "That's not what he was doing yesterday," she said and was disgusted to hear the quaver in her voice

"Really, Gus," said her mother. "What newspaper is that? I put the *Times* right there by your plate."

"Boothby brought this to my attention. The servants read the *Bugle*, I gather." He threw the paper on the table and sat down at his place. "I fail to understand what that boy is trying to do to us."

Her mother glanced at the article. "It's by that journalist friend of his," she remarked, passing it to Gloria.

"At least, he had the decency to leave Gloria's name out of it," her father said. "Why does Morgan have to have friends in low places?"

Gloria didn't hear her mother's response. She was reading Andy's article:

"In a scene that could be from one of the ballets he loves, Vaslav Nijinsky stepped on stage yesterday to dance for one of his long-time worshipers, Russian philanthropist and impresario George Sergeivitch Kassevetsky, who brought Russian dancing to New York long before the Ballets Russes arrived earlier this year. Mr. Nijinsky, fresh from rehearsing his new ballet Till Eulenspiegel *and still dressed in his rehearsal clothes, answered the urgent plea from his countryman, knowing that someone was in danger in that theater and would come to harm if he did not respond.*

Arriving at the nearly deserted theater, he found the old man dangerously delusional, waving loaded pistols about and insisting that the terrified young girl on stage was the dead dancer Galina Petrovna. Nijinsky stepped into this chaos with grace and poise. He calmed the old man with his superb dancing, even eliciting smooth and graceful movements from the young lady, who had not been trained as a dancer. Nevertheless, she lived out many a ballerina's dream as she danced with Mr. Nijinsky to the music of Spectre de la Rose. *Charmed by the scene, Mr. Kassevetsky rushed on stage to compliment Mr. Nijinsky, and at that moment, a rotting trapdoor on the stage gave way and the old man crashed to his death, taking a lighted candelabra with him. The old place burned to the ground, but not before everyone there except Mr. Kassevetsky was saved.*

Alerted to the serious situation by a message delivered by a young boy who worked at the theater, racing pilot Morgan Vanheusen abandoned his

dream of driving in the Metropolitan Trophy Cup trials at Sheepshead Bay yesterday to drive Mr. Nijinsky in the new Stutz Bearcat, the only vehicle available to him at the time. The car belongs to Mr. Blaze Remington, and it was responsible for saving several lives, a far, far better thing than winning any race."

Her mother had been reading over her shoulder. "I think it makes Morgan sound rather like Sir Galahad," she said now.

"Poppycock!" said her father, attacking his eggs.

"It wasn't quite like that," Gloria said. "The trapdoor wasn't rotten, for one thing. Mr. Nijinsky pulled the lever that opened it. I saw him."

"Oh, my dear." Her mother patted her shoulder.

"Mr. Cass is a journalist," her father answered dismissively. "He's not interested in the truth. He just wants to make a good story and show Nijinsky in a good light."

Gloria sat all through the church service staring ahead of her, hardly aware of the familiar stained glass windows, the soaring nave above her head, the restlessness of the five Smithers children in their family pew in front of her. The glorious music was soothing to her seared soul and she tried to sink into it, have it obliterate the strains of *Le Spectre de la Rose* that thrummed like a nightmare just beneath the real world. She wondered if she could find one of the powders Aunt Hattie used to take for sleeping and just slip into velvet darkness for the next few days, avoiding all the fear and uncertainty that had seeped into her world as a result of yesterday's horror.

During the sermon, she sank back into the pew as much as she could against the unyielding polished oak, bending her head and fixing her eyes on the kneeling cushion. It was red plush with braid along the edges, curved in the middle from the weight of her knees all these years. Contrite, she thought, perhaps I should be contrite for leading Andy on, for accepting an invitation I knew my parents would not approve of. And I am. I'm heartily sorry! Across the aisle, Nigel Morse smiled at her and she felt ridiculously grateful.

As they stood up for the hymn, she sensed eyes on her, people watching her, singling her out. Who had read Andy's piece in the paper? What other servants had seen fit to show their employers that article? And who had figured out that the damsel in distress was Gloria Isabelle Vanheusen.

My father is right, she thought in panic. It's as bad as if I were in disgrace now. I must do everything I can to regain my good name. For a moment, an endless series of lunches in swank hotels, formal dinners, and stilted conversations with young men, most of whom she had known all her life, flashed through her mind; balls and banquets, musical evenings, and silly plays put on by the debutantes for their amusement and that of their suitors. She had enjoyed it all, but her hunger for something new had led her down a dangerous path. I was bored, she thought. Now the certainty and calm of her old world seemed like a relief, a shelter from the nightmare she had experienced in the Kassevetsky Theater.

When the congregation sank to their knees for the General Confession, she murmured along as usual, but for the first time she could remember, she really meant every word.

That afternoon, Muriel dropped by for a visit. She had driven herself, and her cheeks were bright with color from the wind and sun, her hair escaping from the confines of her hat carelessly perched on the back of her head.

"Let Maggie fix your hair," Gloria said, rising from her chair in the conservatory.

"Tish tosh," said Muriel, tossing her hat onto the divan. "Maybe later on," she added, apparently seeing Gloria's shocked expression. "Don't worry. I won't look like the wreck of the Hesperus when I leave." She smiled reassuringly at her friend.

Gloria smiled back woodenly. "I have no fear of you ever looking that bad."

Muriel pushed back the stray hair and shoved some hairpins into place. "There," she said, "that should hold it for a while." She sat on the divan opposite Gloria. "What's the matter?"

"Whatever do you mean?"

"You look pale and there are dark circles under your eyes."

"You haven't heard any gossip?"

"I don't listen to gossip."

"Of course not." Gloria sighed and handed over the copy of the *Bugle* she had managed to purloin from the library.

Muriel was a fast reader. She looked up a few times from the article and scowled, then read on. "Andy Cass," she said at last.

"He shouldn't have written this piece," Gloria said heatedly, close to tears again.

"Ah. You're the damsel."

Gloria nodded miserably. "I went without a chaperone."

"Well, no use crying over spilt milk," Muriel said briskly. "No one reads this rag but servants anyway. How did you even see it?"

"Our thoughtful butler." Gloria began to shred a bit of lace on the edge of her handkerchief.

"You had a real adventure, more than any of the others in our circle ever had, but now it's over. You can concentrate on something else."

"An adventure!" Gloria sputtered. "Is that how you see it? I could have been killed!"

"I'm sorry, dear. That was thoughtless of me. You know I didn't mean it the way it came out. I'm afraid that I'm so bound up in my own view of things, I sometimes trample on other people's feelings. But I do think it would do you good to get on with things now—important things. For example, I'm going to a suffragette meeting tonight with Alice. Will you join us?"

"You and your maid?"

"Alice is an intelligent woman. We have a lot in common. Will you join us?"

Shocked at the suggestion, Gloria drew back, trying to physically distance herself from the very idea. "Certainly not!" she said. "At any rate, I'm otherwise engaged this evening."

"Surely you're not going to Elsie Hollander's dinner at the Ritz?"

"And why not?" Gloria said, bridling. "Elsie is a friend of mine. This dinner is in her honor and I'm a deb. It's my duty to go."

Muriel sighed. "Perhaps it's too soon after your little adventure to expect you to join the cause."

"I am not like you, Muriel," Gloria said heatedly. "I like parties and balls. I enjoy the excitement and fun of being a debutante. And yes, I appreciate what you are doing and wish you all the best with women's suffrage, but I cannot and will not join you."

Muriel gave her a long look. "You are not like your brother," she said.

"No, I'm not. For one thing, he's a man, and why he worships you is quite beyond me."

"On that, at least, we agree," Muriel said, laughing. "I have no intention of ever marrying. I have told him this repeatedly, but he will not hear me."

"But you're a debutante, too," Gloria said.

"Only to appease my mother, you know that. In return for doing this season, she will allow me to go to Barnard in the fall. If I don't get engaged first, of course." She smiled at the amusing suggestion.

"I don't understand you," Gloria said.

"No, my dear, you don't." She picked up her hat and plunked it on her head, fastening it in place with a hatpin. "I'll see myself out."

Gloria watched her go, feeling frozen in place. She understood wanting to know what was going on in the world. Since meeting Andy, she had begun reading the *Times* with more attention, but lately the grueling war stories from the front written by Romeo Houle were giving her nightmares. One did not need all the shocking details to understand what was going on in the world, just enough to throw in an intelligent word or two on the subject. Muriel was going too far.

Besides, Gloria thought in horror, why would anyone *not* want to get married? Well, being a bluestocking would almost guarantee that Muriel would get her wish to be 'a spinster of this parish' forever.

THIRTY-SEVEN

"J.J. Rachetti to replace injured rookie race pilot Morgan Vanheusen in the Metropolitan Cup next week at Sheepshead Bay."
—*New York Bugle*

Morgan limped out of the Brooklyn Hospital on Monday morning and stood in the watery sunshine waiting for Rolly Danvers. He hadn't wanted to stay that long, but the medical authorities insisted. Something to do with insurance and a suspected concussion, but details were a little muzzy. Apart from his leg, which was painful but not broken, some bruised ribs, and a dislocated shoulder, he was in good health. 'Better than you deserve,' as Blaze Remington had remarked.

"You're finished, Vanheusen!" Remington had thundered, looming over the prone Morgan, blocking out the sun. "Finished!" He had probably had a lot more to say, but at that moment, Morgan had passed out from the pain of his shoulder. Remington had not followed him to the hospital. I expect he went with the Bearcat, Morgan thought, and he had to admit that if he were the owner, he would be with the car, too, assessing the damage, hovering over the mechanics, worried that his beloved motorcar might not get a chance to compete in the opening of the eastern racing season.

"Damnation!" Morgan said out loud.

The blare of a horn announced Rolly in his green Pierce-Arrow as he skidded to a stop in a spray of gravel. "Aren't you a sorry sight!" he shouted, jumping out and coming around to help Morgan into the passenger seat.

Morgan gritted his teeth and settled himself gingerly into the car, arranging his leg in the most comfortable position.

Rolly stood back and looked at him consideringly. "You do look a bit of a wreck."

Morgan thought of the many times he had dragged Rolly home after a night of carousing, pushing him into the arms of his valet and driving away. Rolly had tried everything, from the opium dens of Chinatown to the underground sex clubs like the Libera Club that Morgan had first glimpsed that night with Rolly and the Russian aristocrats. But he seemed shocked by the physical signs of Morgan's accident: the bruised cheek, the bandaged forehead, the pronounced limp, and the obvious pain when he had climbed into the motorcar.

As Rolly continued to stare, Morgan punched him playfully on the arm. "I'll be fine," he said. "Start the engine, man, so I can get home."

"What happened?" Rolly asked, steering the car with exaggerated care into the street. "You were supposed to win!"

"If you mean qualify, yes. And I tried," he said wearily, "but fate intervened."

"But how did you manage to crash *outside* the track?" Rolly insisted. "And I know about it because it's in *Motor Racing Today*."

"Damnation," muttered Morgan. "Now I really am finished."

"You thought they wouldn't notice?" Rolly laughed. "So tell me what happened, since I came all the way out here to get you. Did you sleep in?"

"You're close," Morgan said. He rearranged his sore leg, wincing as they hit a rough spot on the road, and wondered how he could satisfy Rolly's curiosity without involving Gloria. Rolly was a notorious gossip, especially after a few drinks, and he always had more than a few drinks.

"This is just between us," he began, leaning closer to his friend to give weight to his words.

"Of course! What do you take me for?" exclaimed Rolly, outraged. "I am a gentleman, sir."

"Of course, how gauche of me. But this involves Mr. Nijinsky."

"I knew it!"

"Rolly!"

"Excuse me. Please continue."

The story Morgan told involved Nijinsky needing a ride. As he talked, any number of holes in the story seemed obvious to him, but Rolly ate it up. Of course, a celebrity like Nijinsky would ask a favor that couldn't be denied, couldn't even be questioned.

"And not a word of this. To anyone!" he cautioned Rolly again.

"It was a woman, wasn't it?" Rolly whispered as the Queensboro Bridge came into sight.

"I beg your pardon?"

"Come on, there's always a woman involved in these things. He has one, doesn't he? Other than his wife, I mean."

"No, he does not!" Morgan realized as the words left his mouth that he was being too vehement.

"Come on, we all know the ladies are swooning over him everywhere he goes," Rolly went on. "They throw themselves at him. Though why, I have no idea," he added, perplexed. "He doesn't look like much to me."

Morgan laughed, reassured to see Rolly galloping off in that direction. Out of nowhere, he had a sharp picture of Jinks dancing with the Negro boy at Sadie Hahn's. "Certainly not," he repeated softly.

By now, they were in Manhattan. "Don't go near Fifth Avenue," Morgan said suddenly. "I don't want to run into my family."

Rolly nodded and made an abrupt turn south on Madison.

All the rest of the way, Rolly prattled on about the new chorine at the Tootsie Club, about the showgirl he had been with last night, about the beautiful debutante he met at his cousin's country house the previous week.

"Thank you for picking me up," Morgan said, climbing down carefully when they arrived at his lodgings. "I appreciate it, but right now, I have to lie down and rest. Doctor's orders."

Rolly settled back in his seat, obviously disappointed. "Do you need any help getting up the stairs?"

"No, thank you. I'll take my time." He waved, one hand on the doorknob, waiting for Rolly to leave. Now he would have to deal with Langley, who was not as easy to hoodwink. He might actually have to tell him the truth.

The loft was strangely quiet, a relief after Rolly's constant chatter. Morgan hobbled to the divan and stretched out his leg. I'm finished in the racing game, he thought bitterly. His father was right.

It was not his world, after all. He would have to find a real job, perhaps crawl back to Uncle Cedric and just race his own car for fun, although the thrill of that had passed for him ever since he had had his hands on motorcars with real power. No, he admitted to himself, now that he had had a taste of the real thing again, he couldn't settle for less. For two years, he had let misplaced guilt over his brother's death deprive him of his passion. Great-Aunt Edwina was right: Harry's fatal accident was not his fault.

He fell asleep, the image of the open gates of the Sheepshead Bay Speedway, so close but so unattainable, sharp in his mind.

He awoke with a start. His mouth was dry, and for a moment, he didn't know where he was. Sunshine poured into the room through the slanted windows, showing up the dust in the corners and on the bookcase and table. The place needed a good cleaning, but neither he nor Langley could afford any help. For a fleeting moment, he thought of his airy rooms at home, the ordered neatness of everything, the wonderful meals served on time, the care taken of his clothes without him having to lift a finger. He sighed. Lost to him. Like everything else in his life.

He sat up painfully, got to his feet, and hobbled over to the basin to throw some water on his face. Where was Langley? Monday morning was invariably his time to sleep in after a busy weekend fleecing the card players in various clubs or dancing till dawn with the chorines on 42nd Street after decorously paying court at some debutante function earlier in the evening. "Have to clear the lungs, don'cha know, old chap," he would say with a wink.

In the act of throwing more cold water on his face, Morgan stopped. Another thing Langley had said recently came to him with sudden clarity: 'My fortune, such as it is, rides with you, old chap.' You can't really bet on a qualifying trial, can you? But that messenger boy whose brother was in the business had agreed it was done, and in his heart, Morgan knew some people could find a way to bet on how fast someone could cross the street. And Langley knew a lot of bookmakers.

Hobbling to the telephone, he put in a call to the Checkered Flag and asked to speak to Langley's bartender/bookmaker friend, Sam. After a few moments, it was clear that yes, indeed, Langley had placed a considerable amount of money on Morgan qualifying and making the team. And had lost everything.

Morgan hung up the telephone and looked around the loft with new eyes. The disarray in the place now had a different look to him. For one thing, everything he saw belonged to him. There were none of Langley's clothes in sight. No books lay carelessly open on the table, no boots or shoes lay strewn about, no riding crop, no clean boiled shirts from the laundry down the street hanging by the window, no cigar box…

Panic hit him in the gut. His breath came in short gasps as he hobbled over to the wardrobe. Everything belonging to Langley was gone, and so was Morgan's Gladstone bag.

"You bastard!" Morgan yelled. He stood still for a moment as a sudden cold premonition shot through him. The icon! Awkwardly, he bent down and reached under the divan. His cold fingers felt around, reaching right to the wall. Nothing but dust.

"How could you?" he shouted to the empty room. After a moment, he began a methodical search of the premises. What else could Langley have taken? He soon discovered his antique studs and diamond cufflinks among the missing items and felt absolute fury against his erstwhile friend. His father had given them to him at his graduation. They had belonged to his paternal grandfather. No one outside the family should have them!

In the top drawer of the old desk they shared, he found a note:

> *Sorry about the cufflinks, but after your ignominious accident, outside the damn track, no less, I figured you owed me. I bet everything on you. Failing your win, I had no options left, except to propose to Amy, and frankly, old thing, I couldn't do that to either one of us. As for the icon, it was stolen. It wasn't yours anyway.*
>
> *So long. Next time make it inside the track*
> *Langley*

Morgan sat at the desk for a long time, his head in his hands. You utter bastard, Langley, he thought. How could you? But he knew the man. He had known him to do worse things. Now he just shook his head sadly, seeing his life stretch out ahead of him: no racing career, no Langley, no Muriel, no diamond cufflinks, no family, and no icon to give back to Rudy.

A knock at the door brought him out of his stupor. "Come in," he called, struggling to his feet and reaching for his walking stick.

Andy Cass stepped into the room.

"You are not welcome here," Morgan said at once.

Andy raised his hands in front of him in an imploring gesture. "Please, Morgan, I know you must hate me, but please just tell me one thing. Is Gloria all right?"

"And how in hell would I know?" Morgan asked, sinking back onto the divan. "I just got out of the hospital. No one will talk to me at home, I can almost guarantee that."

"I went there to find out," Andy said miserably. "I even went to the tradesmen's entrance. I just wanted someone to tell me how she was."

"Boothby threw you out."

Andy nodded. "He did say he was sorry to have to do it, but he had his orders."

Morgan laughed bitterly. "Ever the gentleman's gentleman, our Boothby." He inspected Andy, who looked almost as bad as he did himself, minus the bruises. "Sit down. You look terrible."

"I haven't had much sleep." Andy sank into the dilapidated armchair, which smelled faintly of wet dog, and ran a hand over his haggard face. "George Kassevetsky was my uncle, you know," he said quietly.

"Oh, I'm sorry. I had no idea."

"Why would you? He was very good to a lot of people in our community over the years. Many will mourn him in spite of his madness and obsession with his rotting old theater."

Morgan laid his head back on the divan and said nothing. Who was he to pontificate on mad relatives?

"Believe me when I tell you, Morgan, I thought he was out at Brighton Beach visiting old friends. That's been his Saturday routine forever. I wouldn't have taken Gloria to the theater if I had known he'd be there."

"You shouldn't have been with her unchaperoned in the first place," Morgan said. "But it's partly my fault, too, I suppose. I should have sent you on your way the day I found out about your rendezvous in the park with my sister. Life would be a lot better now if I had."

"But I would not have those lovely memories," Andy said, his voice choking.

"But you'd have your uncle, and I would have my racing career."

"You might still have that," Andy said after a pause. "Did you see my article in the *Bugle*?"

Morgan grunted. "I read it in the hospital. One of the nurses brought it to me. At least, you didn't mention Gloria by name. And I would have been happier if you'd left my name out, too."

"I put it in on purpose, don't you see?" Andy leaned forward, gesturing with his hands. "I thought it would explain why you were late."

"Remington doesn't give a tinker's damn why I was late!" Morgan said, his voice rising. "But I appreciate the thought," he added, seeing Andy slump back, deflated.

"I had another idea," Andy began tentatively. "Of course, you might not be interested in this, and there isn't a lot of money involved, not that that matters to you."

"Look around at my palatial surroundings and tell me money doesn't matter to me. If I had it, would I be living here? And I might not be for long," he went on morosely, "seeing as how my wonderful former friend and roommate ran off in the middle of the night, taking my valuable diamond cufflinks with him. And the icon as well, by the way. I don't see how I can swing the rent alone for even this fleabag."

Andy sat up. "He took the icon? Oh my God! When did he leave?"

"I just got here this morning. He was gone. That's all I know. And I refuse to turn him in to the police, if that's what's you're thinking."

"How chivalrous," Andy sneered. "Rudy was counting on that icon to give him money for the little girl. Now what's he going to do? This will be the second time a Vanheusen has betrayed his family."

"Oh, for God's sake, Cass, I didn't do it on purpose!"

"The result is the same."

"Telling the police wouldn't help Rudy, anyway. The damn icon was stolen property, remember? Finding it would put the noose around his neck."

Andy sighed. "You're right. What a mess!"

"What was that idea you were going to tell me about?"

"I thought you might write up the Metropolitan Cup race next week for the *Bugle*. My editor, Old Dreary, says if he likes it, you're hired as race reporter. Personally, I think he's impressed that you're a friend of Mr. Nijinsky."

Morgan shook his head. Was this how he would be known forever? A friend of Mr. Nijinsky. Am I really his friend, he wondered. "Look, Andy, I never was much good at writing. I don't think this is for me, but thank you for thinking of it."

Morgan stood, grabbed his cane, and saw Andy to the door. He was just making his way back to the divan when the jangle of the telephone startled him. He would have to disconnect it now that he had so little money, he thought, reaching for the receiver.

The voice of Blaze Remington thundered down the wire. "You up and about now?"

"Yes, sir."

"Good. Come and see me at my club tomorrow at noon. We need to talk."

"The Oaks, sir?"

"Yes, and don't be late this time!" He banged down the receiver.

Damnation, muttered Morgan. He reminded himself that even when happy, Remington had a tendency to shout. Somehow, this wasn't reassuring.

THIRTY-EIGHT

"New York City crime soars as wiretapping debate rages on."
—New York Bugle

Detective Sullivan patted himself down, checking for note-book, pen, cigarette case, keys, and wallet. All was in place. But before he closed the art fraud case, he had to decide what to do with this young lad, Rudy, sitting across the desk from him. He stared at the pale young man who looked as if he hadn't eaten a good meal in a very long time. Artists. They were their own worst enemy. Why couldn't this young man have decided to be a stone-mason, for instance, like his uncle Patrick? Steady work, some art-istry involved, and enough money to keep the belly full.

He sighed. "Well, thanks to you, we have Green Jr. behind bars. Are you getting all this, sergeant?"

"Yes, sir."

"At this very minute, he is spouting off about all his buddies, trying to get a good deal for himself. We don't really care about a small fish like you, but you did break the law, didn't you?"

"Yes, sir." Rudy's voice was soft, barely audible.

"So if I let you go, what will you do?"

"Be eternally grateful, sir."

"Yes, yes, but apart from that?"

"I need to find some way to take care of my niece, sir, now that Galina's gone."

"Yes, well… What I want from you, boyo, is to hear of any rum-blings you might get wind of. Anyone approaches you for a little painting job featuring someone else's work, I want to know. Anyone approaches you with money and a list of paintings he wants copied,

I want to know. Someone will try to take up where Green Jr. left off, and I want to know who, you hear?"

Rudy swallowed, his Adam's apple bobbing. "I doubt that anyone will come near me now, sir. It's all ruint, isn't it?"

"I sincerely hope so." Sullivan leaned back in his chair, which creaked under the strain. "You know, I hear Our Lady of Miracles Church is looking for an artist to repair their altar screen. It has water damage because of a leaky roof or some such. Tell Father O'Shaughnessy I sent you."

"Thank you, sir!"

"Now go! Get out of my hair. And remember, if you get in trouble again, all this is still on your record!"

"I understand. Thank you, sir."

The boy almost kissed Sullivan's hand and then fled down the narrow dusty corridor.

"Give me your notebook, sergeant."

The surprised policeman handed it over and watched with round eyes as his superior ripped out the pages to do with Rudy's latest interrogation.

"I'm going out," Sullivan said, handing back the notebook.

There was just one more thing nagging at Sullivan: Olga Ostroffsky, the sweet little old lady who had served him a tea biscuit laced with arsenic, who had systematically tried to kill the dancer Galina Petrovna. How could he just leave her on the loose? At the very least, she needed to be somewhere where she could be looked after, where she couldn't harm anyone else, including herself. Ordinarily, he would have shouted at his sergeant to make this call, but Olga was not an official case. This was on his own time. He pulled the tall black telephone towards him with one hand and picked the receiver up off the cradle.

"Hello, Central? I need the number for Dr. Lemieux at Belleview."

Twenty minutes later, having secured a place for Olga in the locked ward at the hospital, he set off on his own to her narrow little house. Once out of sight of the police station, he hopped into a hackney and gave the address to the driver. Unlike many of his ilk, this cabbie was a taciturn sort who resisted all the detective's efforts at chatting about the neighborhood and they drove in complete silence.

No one answered Sullivan's repeated knocks at the door. It hadn't occurred to him that the old lady might be out, though he supposed she must go out sometimes. He peered through the window at the dusky interior. But how often did an old lady like that go out? He rattled the door handle in frustration. The door creaked open under his hand.

A sweet, acrid smell met his nostrils and he knew what he would find.

"Mother of God," he murmured

He pulled out his handkerchief and put it to his nose as he made his way through the crowded rooms. The kitchen was shining clean, everything put away neatly. A small sitting room, obviously Anna's, was also tidy and clean, the floor gleaming with wax on the worn wood. The last room must be Olga's. Sullivan paused, knowing what he would find on the other side of the door. He squared his shoulders and opened it.

The smell hit him like a fist in the gut, so strong his eyes watered. Olga and her maid Annya lay peacefully side by side on the bed, their thin bodies barely wrinkling the crocheted bedspread under them. They were both dressed in their best, right down to their shoes, the worn soles betraying the age of Olga's once-fashionable footwear. Annya clasped Olga's hand in hers.

Murder? Suicide?

Sullivan closed the door and walked out of the house. Perhaps it's better this way, he thought. Better for Olga, anyway. He wondered if she had left the door unlocked on purpose, just for someone like him. He wondered if there was a note. He hadn't seen one. Somehow he doubted they would find anything but papers concerning their funerals.

A few hours later, Sullivan was sitting in the coroner's office. "What do you have to tell me?" he asked, looking across the desk at the bleary-eyed Dr. Webber.

"Right now, I can't tell you anything you don't already know. The old girls died of poison, obviously a suicide pact, or possibly a murder-suicide, as you suggested. In either eventuality, they are beyond the law of man now. You can close the case on this one."

Sullivan sighed. "It was hardly a case at all."

"Still, I know you like to cross the 't's and dot the 'i's. Care for a tipple?" He handed a glass to the detective.

"I should probably bust you right now for making this rotgut," rumbled Sullivan, but he took a careful sip. His eyebrows went up. "Well, we can have a wee wake for the girls," he said, and took another drink.

"To Olga, one of the greatest dancers in the world," Webber said.

"You knew she was a dancer?"

"I saw her once in London. She was way past her prime and dancing with a man young enough to be her grandson, but she was sublime."

Sullivan handed his glass over to be refilled. "I think you should sell this stuff to the drivers for the Indy 500 Mile Race for fuel," he said, laughing. "You'd make a fortune."

Sergeant Riley stood in the doorway and coughed. "The chief wants to know the verdict, sir."

Sullivan opened his mouth to respond, but Webber beat him to it. "Death by misadventure," he said firmly.

"But sir, I thought—"

"Don't think. Listen," snapped Webber.

"You heard the man, boyo," added Sullivan. "Now be off with you and tell the chief. The case is closed."

The two men drank in silence for a few moments after the sergeant had gone.

"The funeral," Sullivan said at last, holding out his class for a refill. "I'm right, aren't I? It's because of the funeral."

"I don't know what you're talking about, you barking mad Irishman."

"A pox on your Protestant soul," Sullivan said cheerfully.

"At least, you now admit I have one," Webber remarked, "which is progress."

THIRTY-NINE

"ARMORED CARS FOR ARMY.
100 Machines Ordered from the Locomobile Company."
—Special to the *New York Times*

Blaze Remington was eating lobster, a large white serviette tucked under his chin like a bib. "Can't go wrong with lobster," he said, rubbing the dripping butter off his chin with another serviette. "Sit, sit. You're making me nervous. What would you like to eat?"

"I'm not hungry, thank you, sir."

"Nonsense. Bring him some crab cakes. Young men always like crab cakes." He waved his hand dismissively at the servant. "Now let me look at you." He leaned forward across the table, peering into Morgan's face, disconcertingly close. "Looks as if you were lucky," he pronounced, settling back again. "Could have killed yourself, pulling a stunt like that, and I don't want any more Barney Oldfields on my team." He forked some more lobster into his mouth, all the while scowling at Morgan.

"Barney Oldfield's on your team?" Morgan said, surprised by the famous name.

"Just an expression. The race is next week, as you know. My question to you is, will you be well enough to participate?"

"*Me*, sir?" His voice squeaked in astonishment.

"It seems your dashing ways have earned you a lot of support. All the papers are picking up on that story by your pal Andy Cass, making you out to be some sort of a hero, putting a lady's safety and good name above your career. What tommyrot! But if I fire you now, it makes me look bad."

Morgan cleared his throat. He could hardly breathe. "I'll be fine, sir," he said. "Just a few bruises. Nothing's broken."

"Good. The Bearcat needs a paint job, a new fender, a new axel, and new wheels, but other than that, it's fine, too. We'll talk remuneration later. I want you out there on Thursday to take her around the track a few times, get used to letting it out. But not too much, understand? We don't want to tip our hand too early on how fast that baby can go. So let her out cautiously on the far stretch, away from the railbirds. The track is built for speeds of a hundred forty miles per hour, remember, but all you have to achieve to qualify is ninety. Can you do that?"

"Yes, sir! Thank you, sir! I really appreciate this chance—"

"Eat, eat! Your crab cakes are getting cold."

Morgan began to shovel in the seafood, but he couldn't taste a thing. He was on the team! He would be paid! He was no longer an amateur!

An hour and a half later, he was in the Checkered Flag in a mood to celebrate. Everyone had cheered when he hobbled in, and so far, he hadn't paid for a thing.

"Of course, he had to take you back, Mr. Vanheusen," said Sam. "He said so himself. You're the underdog now, and everyone loves an underdog."

"Woof." Morgan grinned. "It's all a lot to process. And please, no one is allowed to bet on me to finish."

"Of course not," Sam said, giving the bar an extra polish. "We'll bet on whether or not you make it inside the track!" Sam paused to answer the telephone. "I think it's you he wants, sir. He's hard to understand."

Morgan leaned over the counter and put the receiver to his ear.

"Morgan, I need see Miss Gloria, see she is all good now after… fire."

"Jinks! How did you get this number?"

"You tell once where you go talk motorcar things. Yuri find for me. I send flowers to Gloria, but…*il faut que je la visite après le catastrophe.*"

Morgan laboriously translated the French. "You need to visit her. Yes, of course." He slid back onto the stool, pulling the telephone with him. "It's Tuesday," he said. "Mother has her at-home this afternoon and Gloria is always there. They would love to meet you. I can drive us. My car is back now."

"I take taxi car to you at three o'clock. Is good?"

"Perfect." Morgan gave him the address and hung up.

Nijinsky's phone call opened a door he hadn't been able to figure out how to crack himself: a way to go home again, to talk to his mother, to his father, to get a chance to explain. Even apologize. He grimaced. Driving his own car shouldn't be too hard, even in his present state. And at last, his family would get the chance he had deprived them of: a chance to meet the Russian dancer who was still the toast of the town.

Aware at last of the chatter around him, he joined in for a while, then excused himself and hobbled home. He took a long soak in the tin tub with the wooden rim that stood in a corner of the loft behind the screen Langley had painted. Then he dressed carefully for this first visit home since that fateful soirée before Easter. Now it was May, he was on his own, and he had a job, although whether his father would consider it a real job remained to be seen—if his father was even home this afternoon.

Looking for a clean shirt in the top drawer of the bureau, he thought of the icon again. How could he ever make its loss up to Rudy? How could he redeem the Vanheusen family name in the eyes of the young man left with a sick niece to care for?

When Nijinsky arrived, Morgan was waiting in his motorcar. The Russian hopped in and settled down beside him.

"Not exciting car like Bearcat," Nijinsky said, obviously disappointed.

"It's quite exciting enough for me now, thank you very much."

Nijinsky nodded.

"I can't thank you enough for what you did on Saturday," Morgan said, driving sedately out of the lane. "I don't know what I would have done if you hadn't helped."

"That man, he try to hurt me. I know this. I tell you before, I tell policemans. No one believe me. But is true. He say himself." He was leaning forward, talking fast, spittle flying from his lips. "I even see him in hotel bar one time I wait for you."

"I'm sorry no one realized what was happening with the old man," Morgan said, turning north, "but I guess no one could put the pieces together then."

"*I* know." Nijinsky nodded sharply. For emphasis, he hit the parcel tied with a large lilac ribbon that he was carrying on his lap.

"What's that?" Morgan asked, nodding at the package.

"For Miss Gloria. I buy from Paderewski toy shop on Broadway. I go there often to talk to his wife in Polish and get things for Kyra."

Morgan was having a little trouble handling the steering. Turning the wheel sharply hurt his ribs, and he didn't notice when Nijinsky stopped talking. Although he would never admit it, he was also a little nervous about the kind of welcome he would receive. He hadn't spoken to his parents in three weeks. Of course, his mother would be glad to see him, he was sure of that. He winced as he turned the wheel to go north on Fifth Avenue. It was all straight ahead now, a little more than halfway to the park, then a left turn into their circular driveway.

There were several motorcars parked there, and a taxi car was just leaving as they pulled off the street. Morgan parked and followed Nijinsky up the front steps.

For the first time Morgan could remember, Boothby looked taken aback when he answered the door.

"Mr. Nijinsky to see my mother and Miss Gloria," Morgan said, trying not to grin.

"Certainly, sir. May I take your hats, gentlemen?"

Morgan followed the sound of laughter, women's voices, and a man's voice that was familiar but not immediately placeable. The salon was abloom with flowered hats, with the odd bird sporting extravagant plumage nestled among the petals. A man's broad shoulders and blond head were facing away from him as he entered. Morgan watched with a melting pleasure as his mother's face broke into a broad smile of welcome.

"Why, Morgan, aren't you a sight for sore eyes! It's so good to see you! I was imagining all sorts of dreadful horrors, from open wounds to broken bones."

"Exaggerations all, Mother," he replied, bending to kiss her cheek. Then straightening up, he made the introductions. "Mother, may I present Mr. Vaslav Nijinsky. Vaslav, my mother."

Nijinsky bent over her hand. "A honor, madame," he said.

Morgan could hear the intake of breath as the ladies craned

forward to see the great dancer, to drink him in, to take note of everything about him: his gold tie pin, his large flashing ruby ring, his chiseled cheekbones and slanted black eyes, his very foreignness here amongst the lace and flowers of this New York salon.

Gloria looked pale, but otherwise seemed her old self. She opened the gift and took out a large Russian doll.

"Is *matrushka* doll," Nijinsky explained, and he took the doll from her hands and unscrewed it, to show a smaller doll inside. "Has many dolls inside, down to very tiny. *Un petit bebe dans le fond.*"

"*Que c'est mignon! Merci beaucoup, monsieur.*"

A Russian doll, Morgan thought, concealing more and more secrets within. He smiled and glanced around at the others in the room and saw his brother.

"Well, you old speed devil, you," Chesleigh said in a hearty manner Morgan had not heard from him before. "You make great dinner conversation. Don't know what I would have done without you lately. My own life is so boring as to be quite devoid of interest."

"You are a respectable married man. You're supposed to be boring," said Morgan, shaking his hand. He looked into Chesleigh's eyes, those flat grey eyes he had never been able to read. "What are you doing here?"

"Business. I needed to see Father about a few details. And I like coming home now and then."

"Is Leticia with you?"

"Not this time." He lowered his voice. "She is…*enceinte*, you know."

"Congratulations."

"We don't want this public knowledge yet. Bad luck, you know. She won't even let me get the nursery ready."

Remembering how their own mother had lost three children before Harry was born, Morgan nodded. "Better to err on the side of caution."

His mother gestured him to her side. "Thank you for dropping in to reassure me you're all right. And for bringing Mr. Nijinsky. Meeting him at last is wonderful. And the ladies are beside themselves. They'll dine out on this for days." She smiled. "Your father is in the library. He was closeted with Chesleigh all day, and I know he would love to see you. Go. Make your peace. We are fine here."

She squeezed his hand and let go, giving him a little push.

Morgan made his way into the hall and looked across the black and white marble floor to the partially open library door. He was not really prepared for his father, but perhaps it was better this way. He took a big breath, grasped his walking stick firmly, walked to the door, and knocked.

"Enter."

All I need now, thought Morgan, is for Uncle Paul to be in there with him. He pushed the door open.

His father was alone, perusing a pile of papers on his desk, checking them against the ledger open beside him.

"Hello, Father."

"Morgan. Did you come to see Chesleigh?"

"No, I brought Mr. Nijinsky to visit."

"I see. Well, it's about time, isn't it?" His father smiled—a thin smile, Morgan thought, one not quite lighting his eyes.

"I didn't know Chesleigh was here."

"He's down for the week, ironing out a few business difficulties."

"Yes, so he was telling me just now."

"He's got a great idea for streamlining production of rail carriages."

"Have you ever thought of switching over to motorcar production?" Morgan suggested. "Or perhaps something like the armed cars Locomobile in Connecticut is making for the army."

"If you recall, we did our patriotic bit supplying railcars to transport the Expeditionary Forces against Pancho Villa. Thank God they have that mess mopped up, thanks to Colonel Dodd."

"I read in the *Times* that when they read the telegram of victory in the House, some of the southern Democrats raised the rebel yell."

"At least, the Senate was more restrained." Mr. Vanheusen took another sip of cognac. "I think our factories will stick with what we know, Morgan. Unless you'd like to come into the firm and head up a new division." He smiled, obviously thinking this a huge joke.

"It's tempting, Father, but I already have a job."

"Splendid. I hope it's a good one."

"If it's good enough for Louis Chevrolet, it's good enough for me," Morgan said.

"Mr. Chevrolet is a millionaire in his own right and has been driving for several years. Until you get to his level of expertise—and I understand from what I hear, you are determined to persevere in this direction—you'll need backing. But we'll talk about that later. Take a seat." His father motioned to the wing chair. "That leg must hurt."

"Bruises, mostly," Morgan said, settling into the chair cautiously.

"Cognac or sherry?"

"Cognac, thanks."

"Well, I'm waiting to hear an explanation of how Gloria was put at such risk that she needed to be rescued in such a public and bizarre manner. I'm sure that little adventure has made you the toast of some, but not in my books."

"I blame myself, sir. I knew about her friendship with Andy Cass, but I had no idea they had anything like this planned. I should have been more attentive."

"You are her big brother, Morgan. Chesleigh isn't here, and he has other responsibilities. By default, you are your sister's defender."

"I did get her out of there in one piece," Morgan pointed out.

"She should never have been there in the first place."

There was no response to that. They both sipped their cognac in silence. The ticking of the grandfather clock in the corner was suddenly very loud.

Mr. Vanheusen shifted in his chair. "Given that she got herself into that difficulty," he said quietly, "there is no way your brother would have been able to extricate her himself. Certainly not with such panache."

Morgan stared at him, amazed. This was the closest his father had ever come to praise.

"Did she tell you her news? Nigel Morse has asked for her hand in marriage."

"But she turned him down at New Year's."

"The young man is nothing if not persistent, and last night, she said yes. The official announcement will be in the *Times* tomorrow, and we'll be hosting an engagement dinner at Sherry's or the Ritz sometime next week. Your mother will let you know the details."

"Well, that's...a surprise."

"Nigel is from a very good family," said his father, and now the smile in his eyes was genuine.

All Morgan could see was Gloria, white with fear, dancing stiffly with Nijinsky in that wreck of a theater, tears streaming down her cheeks.

His father took the stopper out of the decanter and offered more cognac to Morgan. He refilled his own glass and sat looking into its golden depths for so long, Morgan wondered if he had forgotten he was there.

"When I was not much older than you," his father began, "I fell in love with your mother. We met at a cotillion. Paul was there, too, of course, and he danced with her nearly all night long as I watched in a turmoil of jealousy. I was weak with love. Have you ever felt that way about a girl?"

"Muriel Standish, but she doesn't seem very interested in me."

His father gave a short harsh laugh. "The only marriage that one is interested in is a Boston marriage, my boy. Move on. Anyway, as I was saying, I arrived early at the next ball and asked your mother for a dance. I watched in mounting excitement as she wrote my name over and over with the little gold pencil dangling from her wrist, nearly filling her dance card. When Paul got there, he was angry with me for stealing 'his girl', as he put it. To make a long story short, we were both madly in love with Margaret and she chose me. It broke your uncle's heart."

"And that's why he never married?" Morgan asked.

"So he says. I happen to know he has many an *affaire de coeur*, but never with anyone he could remotely consider as a wife, so your accusation about the little dancer you mentioned the other day was nothing unusual."

Morgan took a sip of his cognac. "I don't see how this excuses his behavior," he said quietly.

"He is not unique, as you should know. You claim to be a man of the world, do you not?"

"Perhaps my world is different."

"Men are men," his father said dismissively, "as anyone who frequents Madame Hahn's should know. I'm sure everyone who goes there is not young and unattached." His eyes suddenly sought Morgan's, boring into him.

Morgan nodded. "But they don't preach and pretend to be better than everyone else. They don't belong to the Committee of Fourteen or ask me to spy on a friend because they do not approve of his behavior."

"Paul does take things to extremes," his father admitted, "and that's one reason I left the committee. As for your Russian friend, scandal follows him wherever he goes. We are not as accepting of some things as are the Europeans. Perhaps Paul was right to keep an eye on things."

Morgan didn't answer. Through the open door, he heard his sister's laughter.

"There's one more thing I'd like to talk to you about, if I may," his father said after a moment's silence. "It's about the icon." He glanced at the one still on the easel near the desk. "Beautiful, isn't it? When I bought it, Green said there might be another on the market soon."

"There were four in all," Morgan said. "You bought number three, and I had the last one in my apartment until it was stolen a few days ago."

"What?" His father half raised himself from his armchair, his very mustache bristling. "Explain yourself."

"My friend and roommate lost a lot of money betting on me to qualify for the race last weekend, and while I was in the hospital, he absconded with everything of value in our loft, including the icon."

"Good God, Morgan, what kind of people have you been consorting with lately?"

"My old school friend Langley Blackwell-Thomas, actually. It occurs to me he may have run off to Canada to enlist. Lately, he's been more and more for us entering the European conflict."

"What twaddle! We should stay out of it. But even if he does want to enlist, why steal?"

"He would need money for his officer's kit, I imagine: uniform, horse, his commission."

His father sighed. "Oh well, water under the bridge, I suppose. Perhaps Green will have another of the group of icons coming in. You said there were four?"

"Marcus Green has been arrested. It appears he was at the heart of an art fraud ring." Morgan began telling his father about Rudy and about Galina's sick little girl and how Rudy had depended on selling the icon to pay for her care. "And now it's gone. It must seem to him that once again, a Vanheusen has betrayed his family."

"Morgan, you are naïve." His father smoothed his mustache with one finger. "Obviously, the girl tricked your uncle, thinking he would marry her if she was in the family way. Why, the baby may not even be Paul's, if indeed there is one," he added.

"But Father—"

"Think, Morgan. She was a dancer who no doubt performed for private parties when not on stage. She would know how to tease and manipulate men. And such women know how to prevent these things from happening. She thought she could arrange it so that a wealthy man would support her for the rest of her life."

Morgan stared at the remaining liquid in his glass. He had never questioned the story Rudy told, hearing only the tears in his voice. "Still, the baby is innocent of any wrongdoing, surely," he said uncertainly.

"Who told you this baby story? An artist of questionable repute, who claims to be the mother's brother." His father shook his head and smiled, as if talking to a child.

"But Father—"

"Don't be ruled entirely by your heart, young man."

Morgan set his glass down abruptly, almost missing the edge of the desk. For a moment, he felt as if he was in one of his beloved motorcars, balanced precariously on two wheels on a hairpin turn. He saw it all so clearly. Two things could happen: He could hold true to the straightaway of unpaved road that he knew was there and probably crash, never seeing his family again, or he could ease around this unexpected bend and follow the course as laid out by his father. 'Choose your battles, dear,' his Great-Aunt Edwina had said.

He cleared this throat. "I hadn't thought of it like that."

His father closed the ledger, screwed the top back on his fountain pen, and pushed himself away from the desk. "I thought not," he said.

He came around the desk and put his arm around his son's shoulders. "Come. It's time for me to meet your friend."

Morgan swallowed hard and nodded. As they crossed the broad marble hall together, he thought of the large Russian doll Nijinsky had given Gloria, hiding secret after secret within its brightly colored depths.

AUTHOR'S NOTE

Off and on, it has taken more than fifteen years to write this book. In researching the period, the Ballets Russes, and Nijinsky, I read widely (in fact, far more books then is reasonable to mention here), from *The Queer History of the Ballet*, by Peter Stoneley, and *The History of Gay New York: 1890-1940*, by Roger Chauncey, to *The Historical Atlas of New York*, by Erick Homberger & Alice Hudson, and *Treasury of Russian Poems, Quotations and Proverbs, in Russian and English* by Victoria Andreyeva. I haunted second-hand bookstores and on-line rare book dealers. I even sought out and read several novels published in 1916 to get a better feel for the period.

Much of the information on debutantes, the war, fashion, and reactions to Nijinsky comes from newspapers of the time. I couldn't have written with such authority on the period without the archives of the *New York Times* and *newspaperarchives.com*, an amazing online resource. As for Nijinsky himself, I based my portrayal on many books, including the definitive Richard Buckle work on the dancer, as well as the first Russian biography of the man (in translation) by Vera Krasovskaya. And of course I read *Nijinsky*, by his wife Romola Nijinsky, *Nijinsky, God of the Dance*, by Derek Parker, and both versions (expurgated and later unexpurgated) of the dancer's amazing and unsettling diary. And in the mix there were, of course, books on the Ballet Russes and Diaghileff, such as *Diaghileff, His Artistic and Private Life*, by Arnold Haskell. But enough about research!

My heartfelt thanks as always to Cheryl Freedman, who commented with her usual perspicacity on the manuscript over the years and generously gave it the much-needed copy edit! My thanks, also, to Istvan Kadar for his design help with my idea for the cover, to David Dodd for his font expertise, and to the Toronto Reference Library, whose ephemera collection contains some wonderful Ballets Russes programs from the very performances my characters so enjoyed.

—*Caro Soles*

ABOUT THE AUTHOR

CARO SOLES's novels include mysteries, erotica, gay lit, the occasional bit of dark fantasy, and science fiction. She received the Derrick Murdoch Award from the Crime Writers of Canada for her work in the mystery field, was short listed for the Lambda Literary Award and the Stoker Award. Caro lives in Toronto, loves dachshunds, books, opera, and ballet, not necessarily in that order.

Curious about other Crossroad Press books?
Stop by our site:
http://store.crossroadpress.com
We offer quality writing
in digital, audio, and print formats.

Enter the code FIRSTBOOK
to get 20% off your first order from our store!
Stop by today!

CPSIA information can be obtained
at www.ICGtesting.com
Printed in the USA
LVOW13s1433100717

540844LV00002B/207/P